Too Much the Lion

A Novel of the Battle of Franklin

By Preston Lewis

Bariso Press ★ San Angelo, Texas

San Angelo, Texas
www.barisopress.com

ISBN: 978-1-964830-08-7

Cover design by: Preston Lewis
Edited by: Harriet Kocher Lewis

Library of Congress Control Number: 2025900206
Printed in the United States of America

**In Memory
of
Michael Shaara**

Author
of
The Killer Angels,
the Classic Novel
of
the American Civil War

Bariso Press
Harriet Kocher Lewis, Editor & Publisher

Contents

Maps

Photographs

Foreword

Too *Much the Lion* is the story of the Battle of Franklin and the five days leading up to the disastrous conflict as lived by select generals, infantrymen, and civilians in the waning weeks of the Confederacy. In a war filled with tragic encounters, this was one of the most heartrending, yet least remembered battles of the Civil War, largely because it occurred in the Western Theater, far removed from the aura of Robert E. Lee and the Army of Northern Virginia.

The Confederate Army of Tennessee produced no Robert E. Lee, but instead fought under a succession of mediocre commanders whose battlefield triumphs were limited to a single decisive but bloody victory at Chickamauga. The army's commanders had little else to show for the sacrifice of Rebel men and boys. Though the overall leadership lacked the tactical flair of a Lee or a Stonewall Jackson, the Army of Tennessee possessed some superb generals such as cavalryman Nathan Bedford Forrest and division commander Patrick Ronayne Cleburne, who both appear in this account, though the focus is on the lesser-known Cleburne and his division.

With more than 8,500 combined casualties, the Battle of Franklin does not make the top twenty list of Civil War battles with the most losses. Even so, Union and Confederate forces endured five of the most ferocious hours of combat during the War Between the States. Besides the hubris of Army of Tennessee commander John Bell Hood, the events of the preceding night at Spring Hill contributed to the next day's ill-fated attack—dubbed "the Pickett's Charge of the West"—at Franklin.

In one of the greatest blunders of the Civil War, the Union army slipped past the Army of Tennessee during the night at Spring Hill, Tennessee, and escaped the trap Lieutenant General Hood had set but failed to execute. Charges and countercharges about who was at fault echoed through the years, and historians remain conflicted about who forfeited one of the South's last opportunities for a victory over Union forces. The interpretations of the events at Spring Hill in *Too Much the Lion* are entirely those of the author after considerable research and head-scratching.

In addition to the many generals mentioned in this historical novel, two Confederate infantrymen who left accounts for posterity provide perspective from the viewpoint of the foot soldier. While novels about war rightfully focus on soldiers, battle takes its toll on civilians as well, so two Franklin families—the Carters and the Figuers—provide perceptions beyond those of the troops. Two slaves serving Confederate officers as manservants—one elderly and one in his teens—also enter the narrative.

Except for two characters, all the names listed are those taken from historical accounts. The name of a Franklin doctor was fictionalized, and the last name of the slave named "Henry" was added since the historical account only listed his first name. Otherwise, the names are actual, including the lists of casualties and the causes of their deaths. The interpretation of each character is that of the author, based on his research.

Too Much the Lion is told entirely from the Confederate viewpoint, both soldier and civilian. It is important to remember that by late 1864, both Southern combatants and noncombatants had endured three years of death and deprivation. Both citizens and warriors alike were tired of war, its hardships, and the uncertainty it created for their futures.

For those unfamiliar with the organization of a Confederate army, the Army of Tennessee operated under Lieutenant General John Bell Hood in overall command of three infantry corps and a cavalry corps under the direction of Major General Nathan Bedford Forrest. This account focuses on the corps under the command of Major General Benjamin Franklin Cheatham of Tennessee. His three division commanders included Major General Patrick Ronayne Cleburne of Arkansas and Major General John C. Brown of Tennessee, who are pivotal in this account. Major General William B. Bate of Tennessee also served as a division commander under Cheatham, but he played a lesser role in the events as depicted in *Too Much the Lion*.

Three brigades under the commands of brigadier generals Hiram B. Granbury of Texas, Daniel C. Govan of Arkansas, and Mark P. Lowery of Mississippi reported to Cleburne, their division commander. Between seven and ten regiments designated by number and state served under these three brigadier generals.

Two of the four brigades in Brown's division appear in this account. Commanders of those brigades were brigadier generals States Rights Gist of South Carolina and Otho F. Strahl of Ohio. While other generals and combatants show up in this account, their roles are nominal in this telling of the story of the Battle of Franklin.

In compiling this narrative, the author has attempted to stay within the historical framework of the events leading up to and culminating in the Battle of Franklin and its aftermath. Occasionally, time elements may have been compressed or slightly altered for the sake of the overlapping narratives from the different viewpoints.

If nothing else, perhaps *Too Much the Lion* will drive readers to the historical accounts of the Battle of Franklin to make their own assessments and draw their own conclusions of the tragic encounter in the waning months of the Civil War. If *Too Much the Lion* accomplishes anything, perhaps it will give Patrick Ronayne Cleburne his due as one of the noble generals of the Civil War, much like *The Killer Angels* elevated Joshua Lawrence Chamberlain into the public consciousness.

Too Much the Lion is a novel of war, and war is the failure of man to live up to the "better angels of our nature" as President Abraham Lincoln first used the term in his 1861 inaugural address before the start of the conflict that killed more Americans than any other in our nation's history.

By its very nature, however, any novel of war is also an anti-war novel, for it shows the dire consequences on individuals of political and military deceit and hubris. Perhaps *Too Much the Lion* offers lessons for today if we are honest and humble enough to accept them.

Too Much
the Lion

Saturday Morning,

November 26, 1864

Patrick Ronayne Cleburne

Chapter One

Patrick Ronayne Cleburne
Turnpike South of Columbia, Tennessee

Like the unceasing tears of the dying Confederacy, the November raindrops fell cold and bitter against his cheeks. His gray kepi with its short bill allowed the precipitation to trickle down his face and cling to the neatly trimmed goatee concealing the scar from a Yankee bullet to his jaw. As occasional slivers of sleet pecked at his cheeks, he scratched at his beard to soothe the interminable itch that lingered long after the wound he sustained outside Kingston, Kentucky, had healed. A Yankee bullet had entered his open mouth while he was shouting commands and shattered two molars before exiting his left cheek. His jaw and cheek mended, but the infernal irritation and a ragged pockmark he tried to hide with his whiskers remained. Flecks of ice flew from his goatee as he brushed his gloved hand against the beard. The frigid, early-morning air slapped his face, numbing all feeling above his neck except for that damnable itch.

Riding astride his bay mount Red Pepper through the frigid precipitation, Major General Patrick Ronayne Cleburne advanced through the hills of middle Tennessee, more exhausted than frozen. Fatigue weighed down his slender frame, as if he bore the burden of a legion of corpses lost from Shiloh to Chickamauga, from Missionary Ridge to Ringgold Gap. He twisted in his McClellan saddle to view his division as his men trudged north toward Nashville. The sight reminded him not of the cocky boys who had marched off to war three years earlier, but rather of a legion of ragged scarecrows no longer struggling to save the Confederacy as much as to stay on their freezing feet, often shoeless. Exhaustion etched his men's faces with wrinkles of worry about the inevitable. Hunger left their eyes as empty as their stomachs and the barren fields they passed. His soldiers could no longer grit their teeth against the hardships because their sparse diet left their molars as loose as the rags that served as uniforms on their shoulders. Never had he felt more helpless to do anything about their plight. Cleburne could not produce the food to fill their bellies. He could not cobble the shoes to cover their feet. Nor could he supply all the ammunition they needed to end this conflict and return to their homes. Neither could he change the leadership that was marching them toward destruction.

Four months earlier, John Bell Hood became the latest in a line of commanders who had failed the Army of Tennessee. By their blood and sacrifice, the troops had earned better than Hood. Though a courageous combat leader at the brigade level, no doubt, Hood lacked the strategic and logistical skills necessary to lead the Army of Tennessee. In July, Confederate President Jefferson Davis relieved Joseph E. Johnston and elevated Hood, at thirty-three, to command the army during the battles for Atlanta, which subsequently fell, largely due to Hood's defects as a strategist and his profligate use of his troops. Johnston, for all his shortcomings, never squandered men as Hood had in offensive attacks meant to bludgeon the entrenched Union army. The Confederacy no longer had the manpower for such extravagant assaults. Though Hood never recognized that numerical fact, his soldiers did, and Hood's appointment cast a gloom over the entire Army of Tennessee.

Cleburne still fumed that Hood had received the appointment rather than his friend and corps commander William J. Hardee, who Hood still blamed for his own failures in holding Atlanta. Hardee could stomach Hood for barely two months before requesting a transfer that granted him command of the Department of South Carolina and Florida. Cleburne considered resigning his commission as a major general to join Hardee as a mere staff officer, but decided against it. He could not abandon the men of his division—considered the best fighting unit in the Army of Tennessee—to the vagaries of Hood's delusional leadership. Further, he had held some hope that he might succeed Hardee as corps commander. No division commander in the Western Theater had compiled a better battlefield record than Cleburne, but politics trumped merit. Tennessean Benjamin F. Cheatham earned the appointment, and now Cleburne reported to him. Cleburne suspected Hood bypassed him for a promotion because of his friendship with Hardee. Moreover, Cleburne recognized that President Jefferson Davis would never grant him another promotion, despite his well-established battlefield successes.

The vindictive Davis still carried a grudge against Cleburne for his audacious proposal of the previous winter to augment Confederate manpower. Whenever a Union soldier was lost, a replacement was found. Whenever a Confederate soldier was lost, a replacement was nowhere to be found. The Confederacy had drained the South of all but the youngest boys and the oldest men. The Southern cause was bleeding to death one casualty at a time by Northern numbers and iron. Back in December, Cleburne understood that fact and gathered his regimental commanders to outline a solution: free any slave who would fight for the South. Most of his subordinates, who had come to respect the Irish general for his battlefield skill and tenacity as well as his compassion for his fighting men, endorsed his recommendation, though a handful of other officers outside his division were adamant against it, including Major General W.H.T. Walker, a Georgia slave-owner. Requesting a copy of Cleburne's recommendation, Walker forwarded it to Jefferson Davis as evidence of treason.

Joseph E. Johnston, once he learned of Cleburne's proposal, squelched discussion of the document within the Army of Tennessee, but not before the proposition had reached Richmond, courtesy of Walker. Jeff Davis reprimanded Cleburne, who twice previously had earned commendations from the Confederate Congress for his battlefield devotion to the cause. However, Cleburne saw the cause as sullied because the South's political leadership preferred to risk their nation's nascent independence rather than abandon slavery. As Cleburne described the option in his manifesto, "as between the loss of independence and the loss of slavery, we assume that every patriot will freely give up the latter—give up the Negro slave rather than be a slave himself." The realization that he had miscalculated came as a punch in the gut to Cleburne. Davis and the other politicians, most of them wealthy slave owners themselves, preferred to bury their fathers, brothers, cousins, nephews, and even their own sons before freeing a single Negro.

Following the presidential reprimand, so much had transpired— including the death of Walker in the fighting around Atlanta—that Cleburne could no longer disentangle the political intrigue from the legitimate decisions of army command. Politics and battlefield blame always seemed to triumph over common sense and wartime wisdom, so much so that Cleburne just wished the hostilities to end, regardless of the outcome, so he could get on with his life and marry Susan Tarleton of Mobile, Alabama. As he rode toward Columbia, Tennessee, he gave Red Pepper free rein to find his path along the saturated Tennessee road traveled by his soldiers, and he thought of her constantly. He had met Susan at General Hardee's January wedding, when Cleburne took his first leave since hostilities began. Cleburne stood as Hardee's best man while Sue Tarleton served as maid of honor. Both her beauty and her shyness, which matched his own, entranced Cleburne. At twenty-four, she was a dozen years his junior, but so enchanting that he fell in love with her at first sight. Before his fourteen-day leave ended, he asked her to marry him. At first she hesitated, but agreed to accept his letters if he wrote. He had written to her almost daily since.

In March, he took his second furlough to visit Susan and once again asked for her hand in marriage. This time, she consented, and he returned to war an engaged man. Cleburne would have been married by now had Hood in a face-to-face meeting approved his request for a third furlough in late September. The disappointed general answered his commander's denial with a smart salute that hid his bitterness. He rushed back to his tent to write his sweetheart with the bad news. Susan responded with her disappointment and one of her embroidered and perfumed handkerchiefs, which he carried in his coat pocket. Sometimes, as he rode, he fondled the fabric's softness to remind him of her. At other times, he retrieved the cloth and held it to his nose to inhale the aroma of her perfume, but never on a rainy day like this one, for he dared not risk the precipitation washing away her fragrance.

Cleburne reined his mount off the road and turned to watch his threadbare soldiers pass. He grimaced at their ragged uniforms and the tattered oilcloths they used for cover against the rain and sleet. More than anything, his men needed shoes. They could scavenge grub, meager though it might be, but not footwear. Some men tied rags around their feet while others trod barefoot down the pike. After Hood assumed command of the Army of Tennessee, the primary source of shoes had become the footwear taken from battlefield dead, friend and foe alike. In the aftermath of battle, nearly everything was stripped from the deceased, including their dignity, as soldiers swarmed like locusts over the carcasses to supply what Hood and his quartermasters could not. Hood made certain that powder and ammunition reached his troops, but gave scant consideration to the food that fueled them or the accoutrements, like shoes, that brought some comfort to their dreary infantry existence.

"Things will get better," Cleburne said to a passing string of his soldiers, though he—and they—understood the unlikelihood because thousands of Yankees awaited them just over the horizon. Further, a hard winter was fast approaching.

"We trust you, General," replied one soldier, "just not the horrible Hood. He spills his bravado and our blood."

Cleburne stifled an agreeing nod, knowing it was inappropriate to confirm any criticism of their commander.

"We know you can't answer," the fellow continued, "but you've always looked out for us, never asked us to do something you wouldn't do yourself. Not Hood! He looks after himself and his reputation."

"That's the truth, ain't it, boys?" another private blurted out.

"Yeah," a chorus of infantrymen answered as they marched by.

Cleburne sat stone-faced in the saddle, determined that his expression not confirm his men's assessment. Relieved when the soldiers moved past him, he turned his bay steed to the north and put him in a trot far enough from the road so not to fling mud on his men as he passed the Polk family plantations on the route to Columbia.

At times, the rolling landscape reminded him of home in County Cork, Ireland. Though never as wealthy as Tennessee's plantation owners like the extended Polk family, Cleburne's physician father was prosperous enough by Ireland's standards. Cleburne had planned to follow his father's career path until Trinity College of Medicine in Dublin denied him admission, primarily because of his difficulty with Latin and Greek. Humiliated by that failure, he joined the British Army, serving three years in the Forty-first Regiment of Foot, spending much of his enlistment at Fort Westmorland, an island fortress used to imprison Irish debtor families unable to feed themselves, much less pay their rents to landowners after the potato famine took its toll. Repulsed by how the impoverished Irish Catholics were treated, both in prison and out, the protestant Cleburne bought his release from the British Army with the meager inheritance from his father's estate, then emigrated to the United States with two brothers and his sister. His siblings settled up north, but Cleburne moved to Helena, Arkansas, working first as a druggist and then studying law and beginning practice in his new home on the banks of the Mississippi River. His British Army experience and his local popularity made him the perfect candidate to command the first company of volunteers Helena sent to defend the Confederacy. He despised slavery as much as he did the de facto serfdom of his Irish brethren, but he could not take up arms against the very people who had so warmly welcomed him to their community.

Just off the road ahead, Cleburne saw through the precipitation the ghostly form of a petite, redbrick gothic church nestled in a grove of towering magnolias. The structure's angled roof pointed toward the heavens, and fingers of ivy reached from the walls toward paradise. In an instant, the building brought back memories of Ireland when he lost his father. As he neared this place of worship, he studied the church graveyard, which reminded him of the Athnowen churchyard where he had buried his father twenty-one years earlier. Having lost his mother before he was two, Cleburne at fifteen was an orphan on the verge of manhood. His father's modest bequest plus Cleburne's frugal nature and medical ambitions kept him going until Trinity College dashed his career hopes and propelled him to the army. Those reminiscences flooded his mind as he directed his horse toward the graveyard. He dismounted, dropped Red Pepper's reins so the gelding might graze as Cleburne ambled among the tombstones. By the inscriptions on the grave markers, he realized many from the Polk family rested beneath his boots.

As he looked around, he glimpsed his aide-de-camp waiting a respectful distance away near the road. Cleburne removed his kepi despite the rain and meandered among the dozens of stones of the deceased. These departed would never know how lucky they were to have a marker engraved with their names for posterity. Over the last three years, Cleburne had seen too many unmarked graves, their occupants unknown except to God. He had witnessed hundreds of bodies shoved into pits that became mass graves without a marker or a shred of dignity. Such a waste of youth he hoped never to see again, but he knew he was dreaming. After all, John Bell Hood remained in command.

After circling the graves, Cleburne made his way back to Red Pepper, tugging his kepi atop his head, picking up the reins and leading his bay toward Lieutenant Leonard H. Mangum, his former Helena law partner who now served as his aide-de-camp. Mangum acknowledged him with a crisp salute. Cleburne returned the salute, then waved his arm toward the pastoral graveyard.

"It would not be hard to die," he said, "if one could be buried in such a beautiful spot as this."

Mangum nodded as Cleburne mounted Red Pepper and continued toward Columbia.

Hiram B. Granbury
Columbia Pike

The men he led to battle remained the focus that sustained Brigadier General Hiram B. Granbury as commander of eight Texas regiments, plus a Tennessee and a Louisiana regiment. The fine home he had built for Fannie at the corner of Third and Clay Street still stood in Waco, Texas, which had endured the conflict unstained by the trod of Yankee boots, but the house would be empty and cold without her. Granbury had seen so many die by bullet and shrapnel during battles at Raymond, Jackson, Chickamauga, Missionary Ridge, Dug Gap, Resaca, Pickett's Mill, and Jonesborough. Those deaths, he understood. It was war. But Fannie was just twenty-five, passing away in Mobile, Alabama, where she had gone for surgery. She died not from a Minié ball but from an ovarian tumor that had made her last days painful and lonely while Hiram fought for the Confederacy.

Six hundred and seventeen days had passed since her death, a third of the number they had spent as man and wife. As her condition worsened, Granbury had taken leave from the army and journeyed five hundred miles from Port Hudson through the tattered Confederacy to Mobile, where he saw her admitted to Providence Infirmary, a hospital operated by the Daughters of Charity. He sat by her bed daily, holding her hand and watching life seep from her petite, pain-racked body. Comforted by his presence, she had smiled through her discomfort. Both prayed for naught that she would make it to their next wedding anniversary. Eleven days before they were to celebrate their fifth year together, Fannie Sims Granbury took her last breath in her hospital bed. "Don't forget our love, Hiram," she whispered through the pain, then closed her eyes a final time. Her breathing slowed, then stopped. The grieving husband kissed her forehead, his tears falling on her cheeks. At least she no longer felt cancer's sting, and Granbury thought her cold lips had the wisp of a smile at the corners as the discomfort had evaporated with her life. He stayed in Mobile through the following afternoon for the funeral and burial at Magnolia Cemetery. Though he had enough money on him to pay for the service, the plot, and the burial, Granbury lacked the funds to purchase the headstone she deserved to memorialize their love. When this infernal war ended, the grieving husband vowed to return to the grave and to place a granite marker at her head or, better yet, have her delicate remains disinterred and carried to Waco where he would one day lie beside her. On that day when Granbury bought the tombstone, he would have her name—and his—engraved in the stone to honor their childless marriage.

Following her death, Granbury returned to the army by circuitous train routes that took him through Mississippi where he had been born. As he traveled, Granbury wondered why the people close to him died so early. His father Norvell had been a God-fearing Baptist minister, who had taken the call to preach at twelve. He delivered the Word on horseback to rural Mississippi congregations, carrying a Bible in one hand and a hymnal in the other with a change of clothes in his saddlebags. Reverend Granbury baptized over a thousand converts in Mississippi streams and rivers during his ministry, and everyone adored him except the American Home Mission Society, which voted to expel all slave-holding pastors. The elder Granbury next joined the recently formed Southern Baptist Association and continued his service to God and man. Reverend Granbury's wife, Nancy McLaurin of South Carolina, was a supportive spouse and a nurturing mother for Hiram and his five siblings. But despite his parents' devotion to God and each other, they died of consumption five months apart while Hiram was in his final year at Oakland College, a prestigious Presbyterian institution, near home. The six siblings divided his mother's and father's estate equally, with Hiram getting eighty dollars, a horse, a saddle, a bed, and an eight-year-old slave named Oliver, who he subsequently sold.

A year later, Hiram graduated from college after developing what he thought would be a lifelong friendship with Dr. Richard Chamberlain, the college's founder and president. Barely twelve months after settling in Seguin, Texas, Granbury received news that Chamberlain had been murdered, stabbed by a hot-headed secessionist in the volatile debate over the course Mississippi should take in dealing with the federal government over States' Rights and slavery. Two years later Granbury moved to Waco to read law and establish a permanent residence. There he met and married Fannie while establishing a law practice successful enough to build the fine home that his young wife deserved. But national politics had intervened as Texas debated the growing calls for secession. Governor Sam Houston himself had visited Waco to plead for secessionist passions to cool rather than boil over from the fires of disunion rage.

"Secession or revolution," cried the hero of San Jacinto, "will not be justified until legal and constitutional means of redress have been tried, and I cannot believe that the time will ever come when these will prove inadequate. These are not new sentiments to me. I uttered them in the American Senate in 1856. I utter them now."

Granbury remembered Houston talking of his children and their peers as the aging leader stood on the threshold of his own grave.

"My sands of life are fast running out. As the glass becomes exhausted, if I can feel that I leave my country prosperous and united, I shall die content. To leave men with whom I have mingled in troublous times, and whom I have learned to love as brothers; to leave the children of those whom I have seen pass away, after lives of devotion to the Union; to leave the people who have borne me up and sustained me; to leave my country and not feel that the liberty and happiness I have enjoyed would still be theirs, would be the worst pang of death. I am to leave children among you to share the fate of your children. Think you I feel no interest in the future for their sakes? We are passing away. They must encounter the evils that are to come. In the far distant future, the generations that spring from our loins are to venture in the path of glory and honor. If untrammeled, who can tell the mighty progress they will make? If cast adrift and the calamitous curse of disunion is inflicted upon them, who can picture their misfortunes and shame?"

Though Houston's words had lingered in Granbury's mind, the man who had won Texas its independence and later its statehood did not linger in Waco. Two thousand spectators simmered at his words, turning surly as the speech ended and forcing his party to hasten the aging soldier and statesman to his carriage and out of town.

When it came time to vote, the men of Waco and McLennan County rejected Houston's admonitions, voting to secede, 586-191, in line with seventy-seven percent of other statewide voters who preferred to abandon the Union for the Confederacy, making Texas the seventh state to do so.

Houston's words rang true in Granbury's mind as he rode north with the Army of Tennessee through the rain and pelting sleet. He had endured the loss of his parents, his mentor Richard Chamberlain, and the hundreds of boys that had left McLennan County with him to fight the invading Yankee horde descending upon the South like a plague. He accepted those losses as the reality of life and war, but he could never shoulder the passing of his beautiful Fannie, nor the realization that he, unlike Governor Houston, would never have a son or daughter to carry on his name or even his memory. His eyes watered at the thought as his mount walked beside the Texans, trudging toward Columbia. Lost in his memories, Granbury missed the first call to him.

"General, are you okay?"

Granbury shook his head and looked to his side where Captain Samuel T. Foster, himself a lawyer and now in charge of the Twenty-fourth Texas Cavalry-dismounted, offered a casual salute. "Just thinking about Fannie," he said, returning the acknowledgment and offering silent thanks that the precipitation disguised his tears.

"Such a terrible loss in a time of so many terrible losses."

"Thank you, Sam. Her death devastated me, but hers was just one among many."

"I fear even more deaths under General Hood's command. Some days, the pages of my diary fairly burn with rage at what has happened in the months since General Johnston was kicked aside." He hesitated before continuing. "I heard one Georgian describe General Hood as a man with the heart of a lion and the head of a cigar store Indian."

Granbury remained silent as his gray eyes beneath his tall forehead looked west. The slouch hat that covered a thick growth of unruly black hair added another three or four inches to the general's height. His well-formed face featured a tightly manicured mustache that contrasted with the disheveled mop atop his head.

"I heard how his appointment sapped the brigade's spirit when it was announced."

Foster nodded. "Many of my men knew they had died that day without a bullet hitting them. Though they still walked, Hood had killed them, certain as a Yankee sniper with a wagonload of ammunition. It was just a matter of time. A few talked of desertion and mutiny. Some soldiers refused guard or fatigue duty, and it wasn't just Texans complaining."

"I wish I had been with the troops that July day rather than in the hospital."

"How's your wound healing, General? Chickamauga, wasn't it? All the battles run together."

Granbury nodded. "Chickamauga. I was lucky for a gut shot, so the doctors told me."

"Chickamauga was the devil's dance, for sure. With someone other than General Braxton Bragg holding our dance card, we might've wiped out Rosecrans' army and ended this war. Had General Cleburne been in charge, he would've destroyed the Yankees. Fact is, most soldiers thought Cleburne should've been named commander of the Army of Tennessee, not Hood."

Granbury nodded. "It's an honor to serve under General Cleburne, but he's got one fault that's hindered his promotions."

"What could that be?"

"He's too honest. He tells the truth, not what his superiors and the politicians like Jefferson Davis want to hear. I'm sure you heard he proposed to free any slaves that fought for the Confederacy, didn't you?"

Foster stared at his commander. "I'd heard such rumblings, but figured they were false."

Granbury shook his head. "To the contrary. General Cleburne knows the South is doomed because the Yankees outnumber us. He proposed granting freedom to any slave that would take up arms against our invaders. Word got to Jeff Davis, and the president ordered him never to mention it again. To my knowledge, he never has. That's the difference between Cleburne and Hood. Cleburne never brought it up after that, but Hood would've kept stirring the pot, talking poorly of the president. Not Pat Cleburne. I've never heard him speak poorly of Jefferson Davis, despite how the president humiliated him."

"It's a shame," the captain grimaced, "when flattery outranks competence."

The sleet intensified, and the two officers rode silently forward as their men trudged along beside them. When the icy pelting slackened to a light rain, they resumed their conversation, talking about the rich land carpeted in grass, the good timber with little brush, the plentiful water.

"It never gets this green in Live Oak County, even in the spring," Foster observed.

"That's what I've heard about south Texas," Granbury acknowledged.

Halfway between Mount Pleasant and Columbia they came to Ashwood Hall, the plantation home built for Lieutenant General Leonidas Polk, himself a fatality of the war five months earlier at Pine Mountain outside Atlanta. An artillery shell sliced General Polk in half before felling a nearby tree. A West Point graduate and a founder of both the Protestant Episcopal Church in the Confederate States of America and the University of the South, which he envisioned as a world-class institution for the Confederacy, Polk was reputed to have baptized more Southern soldiers than any other man of the cloth.

The two officers directed their horses off the road and stared at the Corinthian architecture of a massive two-story mansion with manicured grounds.

"How does a fellow manage a home that big?" Foster asked.

"I hear he had four hundred slaves before the war," Granbury replied.

"I heard tales that General Polk baptized John Bell Hood. Any truth in that?"

Granbury nodded. "It's a shame the bishop was Presbyterian rather than Baptist."

"How's that? I'm Baptist."

"My father was a Baptist preacher. We baptize by immersion, Episcopalians by aspersion, sprinkling water over the head."

Foster shrugged. "So?"

"A Baptist preacher might have drowned General Hood."

Both laughed, then rode on, stopping on the road near a chapel in the woods. They paused, spotting Lieutenant Mangum sitting on his mount between the pike and a churchyard cemetery. They observed in silence as their beloved Patrick Cleburne strolled among the tombstones, holding his kepi in his hand despite the intermittent rains. Granbury noticed a sadness in Cleburne's posture as his shoulders slumped, his chin rested almost on his chest, and his arms hung weakly at his side while he wandered around the stone monuments to lives long gone. The sight of his commander strolling among the headstones saddened Granbury, too, for it reminded him of all the boys he had lost since leaving Waco, and how few of them had markers to memorialize their brief lives. Too, he thought of Fannie and the headstone he owed her.

"Come on, Captain," Granbury said, "let's give General Cleburne his privacy." Both men continued toward the fates that awaited them up the road in Tennessee.

Mary Alice Carter McPhail
Carter Home, Franklin, Tennessee

At times Mary Alice Carter McPhail wondered if she should have stayed in Texas rather than returning to Tennessee. Once the hostilities began and it became certain her husband Daniel would be dragged into the fighting, she had acquiesced to her father's pleas to return to Franklin for the safety of herself and her children. Fountain Branch Carter had worried that hostile Comanche would plague his daughter and grandchildren in Texas, but Washington-on-the-Brazos, where Texas had declared its independence from Mexico, was far to the southeast of the Indian frontier. Fount Carter, though, fretted that if the Indians didn't threaten his daughter's family, then the Yankees would, even though her home sat near the Brazos River a hundred and twenty miles northwest of Galveston, the primary target of Northern efforts to conquer Texas. From the limited correspondence with her Texas friends, Mary Alice knew that Washington County remained untrammeled and unsoiled by the boots of Yankee soldiers. The best she could discern from the few letters reaching her, not a single skirmish had occurred back home, as Yankee attacks focused on the Texas Coast.

Meanwhile, around Franklin, Mary Alice had lost count of the skirmishes and minor encounters that had stained the soil of Williamson County with foreign and local blood. She figured the total approached fifty, at least, and feared more would come, as the Carter farm—split in half by the macadamized Columbia Pike that ran north to Nashville—stood on the south side of the Harpeth River Valley town. The weathered and eroding trenches of the largest of those clashes still scarred Fount Carter's property just fifty yards south of her home's covered back porch where Mary Alice had played as a child. On this morning, she stood bundled and drinking a cup of coffee—if the parched-grain substitute for coffee beans could be called that—as the late November rains pummeled her father's land.

When she left the Lone Star State, she had feared she might never see her husband again, as he was heading off to war with the Eighth Texas Cavalry or Terry's Texas Rangers, as the unit became known. Though she lived daily with the worry of a widow-in-waiting, Mary Alice had never expected to lose a child. After returning to Franklin, she had buried little Frances McPhail in the town cemetery's Carter family plot, her four-year-old daughter a victim of disease. Her grief had been deep for her lost girl, but so many had died since Fort Sumter that her tears were but a drop in the flood of sorrow that had washed across the Confederacy. After losing Frances, Mary Alice protected her surviving children—Adelaide and Marcus—as only a mother could, but she stood powerless to shield her husband from danger, wherever he was. The last she heard, Terry's Texas Rangers were chasing General Sherman through Georgia, but no one knew for certain, as only sporadic reports came from Georgia, often with conflicting information, as if Sherman and his few pursuers had dropped off the face of the earth. Mary Alice wondered if she would ever see Daniel again, but thanked God for the one brief but fruitful visit they had managed since the start of hostilities.

Despite the piercing dampness of the morning chill, Mary Alice enjoyed the quietude of her first cup of coffee before the nine children living in their grandfather's home awoke for another day. Once they arose, the noise and havoc of playful kids—all under thirteen years of age—echoed through the house. With the frigid rains, the youngsters would remain housebound for the day, their restless energy and noise trying the patience of the adults, even in their spacious dwelling. Fount Carter over the years had built an ell-shaped, two-story brick dwelling with a wide basement. The place was better than most homes in town, but not as luxurious as the region's plantation mansions such as Rippavilla near Spring Hill, the Polk plantations around Columbia, Beechwood Hall with its curved staircase, Harrison House with its pillared entry and balcony, and Carnton, the showplace of the McGavock family just a mile and a half southeast of the Carter home.

Fount Carter had done well for himself by hard work and determination, but he was sixty-seven now and showing his age and the strain of the war. He and his late wife Mary had brought a dozen children into the world, losing to disease and illness five of them, the first four as infants or young children and the latest being James Fountain Carter, deceased in 1859 at twenty-eight. James's widow Sallie Carter, twenty-eight, with her son Fountain, eleven, and her daughter Ruth, six, now lived in the Carter home. Moscow, a widower and Mary Alice's oldest brother, shared the quarters with his four children, Lena, eleven; Walter, ten; Annie, six; and Hugh, four. Mary Alice's sisters Frances Carter, twenty; Sara Carter, twenty-seven, and Annie Carter McKinney, a childless twenty-eight-year-old widow, also stayed with their father.

Though the Carter patriarch had prospered before the war, the conflict had taken its toll on him and his prosperity. The year before the war started, Fount owned more than twenty slaves, but now that number had dwindled to a trio—adults Jack and Calfurnia or "Callie" and little three-year-old Oscar, who spent most of his time playing with the Carter and McPhail children. Other than a pair of slaves who returned occasionally to work for food, the rest had disappeared after Yankee victories at Fort Donelson and Fort Henry and the ensuing occupation of Nashville in 1862. Ever since Nashville fell, Franklin's citizens had lived under de facto Yankee occupation, whether or not the blue-bellies were even in town.

Mary Alice recalled the first day the Northern soldiers entered Franklin on a brisk February Sunday morning in 1862. Though Rebel units had retreated down the Columbia Pike the previous day, the withdrawal remained orderly. That Sunday things changed. The entire Carter family had attended Sunday school that morning when the sound of galloping horses, rumbling wagons, and trotting gray-clad soldiers interrupted their lessons. Worshippers glancing out the windows saw panic in the retreating Confederates as they charged along Main Street toward its intersection with Fifth Avenue, which converged with the Columbia Pike. The First Presbyterian Church stood at the southeast corner of that intersection with a straight view down Main to the courthouse square. Church elders and curious men stepped outside to investigate.

"The Yankees are coming," shouted a mounted Confederate captain to the parishioners as he urged his men to move faster to avoid capture or worse.

Spinning around, the churchmen rushed into the sanctuary, gathering their wives and children, then racing back to their horses, buggies, and wagons to rush home. No sermon followed that morning, as who needed an oration on the devil when his minions would shortly march down the town's streets? Mary Alice and her sisters carried or herded all the Carter and McPhail children to the wagon, where Fount Carter helped them and the adult women climb aboard. After both he and Mary Alice did a count confirming they had as many as they came with, Fount jumped in the driver's seat, grabbed the reins, released the brake, and squeezed the wagon in line with the escaping Confederates. Mary Alice remembered the terrified youngsters, screaming, and grabbing at the adults.

Her niece Lena pointed to the courthouse. "Look, Auntie," she cried.

Mary Alice twisted toward the town square, gasping at the sight. There on the streets of Franklin trod a blue tide of soldiers, as if the distant Atlantic had flung across the Confederacy an unstoppable wave of destruction. With their officers on horseback waving swords in the church's direction, Mary Alice sat transfixed at the enemy—dozens, hundreds, thousands of them—all marching straight for her. Unlike the Confederate stragglers running in a panic south along the Columbia Pike, these troops marched with the precision of a parade drill, unflappable and unstoppable.

"Hurry, Father," called Mary Alice. "There's so many of them."

Until that moment, the war had seemed so distant, a conflict that Tennessee women sent their men to fight and hoped they returned from distant places, but never a struggle that they expected to wrap itself around their town, their homes, and their families. It all changed that sermon-less Sunday for Franklin folks and the Carters, as Fount slowly guided the wagon team through the retreating Confederates, who scurried ahead with drooping chins and grim determination. In her heart, Mary Alice wanted her butternut protectors to turn around, make a stand, and drive the invading horde back to their Yankee quarters, but in her mind she knew the scattered and bewildered Confederates offered no threat to the multitude in blue flowing along the streets. It took thirty minutes to cover the half-mile route between the church and home because Fount yielded to every army wagon, horse, or soldier trying to distance himself from the enemy.

When the family reached home, Fount let the women and children out at the house, then guided his wagon to the outbuildings, where he unhitched the team and hid them in the thicket of locust trees behind the slave quarters. Returning to the house, Fount changed from his Sunday best into everyday work clothes and scurried to the toolshed, grabbed a shovel and a pick, and rushed into the basement. While the women calmed the children, Fount started digging a hole in the dirt floor of the northernmost cubicle in the three-room basement.

After the women settled the children of their initial fear, the young ones clumped around the windows, parting the curtains just enough to watch the last of the Rebels scamper by in their noisy rush for safety. The younger kids soon grew bored and left the window, but the older ones watched for a half hour until the leading Yankee troops approached.

"Do they have horns?" eight-year-old Fountain asked.

"Sure they do," his older sister Lena replied. "They're Yankees, ain't they?"

As troops marched by the front of the Carter home, nine-year-old McKinley scratched his head. "I don't see any horns, Lena."

"They hide them with their hats and caps," she answered, then thought for a moment. "Or maybe our Southern boys cut them off."

Mary Alice and the other women snickered at the children's conversations, but they had heard so many stories about the rapacious invaders they worried they might be violated or driven from their home. Having not seen her father since returning from church, Mary Alice slipped from the parlor out the back door onto the covered porch. Hearing noises in the basement, she opened the southernmost entry on the veranda and descended the stairway. The glow of a lantern and the sound of tools striking earth led her to the far room. There she saw Fount Carter excavating the dirt floor.

"Pray tell, Father, what are you doing?"

"What's it look like, Mary Alice? I'm digging a hole."

"But why?"

"So we won't starve."

She gasped. "You think they'll take our food?"

"Not if they can't find it," he replied, never looking up from burrowing into the hard-packed, earthen floor.

For the following month, Fount worked on the hiding place, keeping it a secret from all outside the family. Fount carried buckets full of dirt out to the garden at night to scatter the loads of soil, then brought in pork from the smokehouse and stacked it on the table in the front room until the cache was ready for filling. Then they wrapped the meat in burlap bags and stacked them on the wooden floor he had placed at the bottom of the four-foot-deep pit. Next, he hid vegetables the women had canned, sacks of potatoes they had grown, as well as sacks of flour and cornmeal they had purchased. After loading the pit with supplies, the Carter patriarch purchased one-by-twelve planks to cover the entire backroom floor, then moved the table from the front room to the back room. That is where the clan would take meals in the future instead of the entry room. The provender would be difficult to get to when the family needed it, but not as hard as finding other food if the Yankees confiscated what was theirs.

That Sunday seemed so long ago. Many hardships had since ensued, but Fountain Branch Carter would not let three generations of his family starve, even if they were forced to drink parched-grain coffee as Mary Alice did this rainy Saturday morning on the Carter back porch.

Hearing the soft creak of the deck, Mary Alice turned to see her oldest brother approaching. At thirty-nine Moscow Branch Carter was a decade her senior and a veteran of the Mexican War as well as the War of Northern Aggression, serving in the Twentieth Tennessee Infantry as a lieutenant colonel until his capture and later parole on the condition he not take up arms again against the Union. He had returned home months ago. Having another man around the house was reassuring, but it also brought worries. If Moscow picked up a gun to defend family or home, he would violate the terms of his release and be subject to imprisonment or to execution, if identified as a guerilla.

Moscow slipped beside Mary Alice and put his arm around her shoulders. "I'm surprised to find you out here in the cold."

"I needed my coffee, if you can call it that, before the children wake up."

"I figured you'd take it in the basement where it's warmer."

"There's something peaceful about a rain, almost calming."

"If you've got a roof over your head, that's true, Mary Alice, but a downpour is pure misery for a soldier. I worry about our brother. Rumors say Hood is south of Columbia and headed for Nashville. If that's true, Tod'll pass near here."

Mary Alice smiled. "Some of my favorite times growing up were playing with little Tod in the locust grove. I wish these times were as innocent as those, and this war was settled."

Moscow patted her shoulder. "The war won't settle anything without creating a new set of problems, Mary Alice."

"Says the man who's fought in two wars for two different countries."

Her brother hesitated before responding. "The music of the fife and drum can inspire a soldier, but shot and shell inspire nothing but death."

"But I thought you men risked war for glory. Is that not true, Moscow?"

"That claptrap called glory doesn't put bread and butter on the table or support a family. That's what's important. We're lucky we still have our father. He's focused on providing for his family as he always has. Glory comes from digging a hole in your cellar to cache food for your children and grandchildren. Men like our father are the real heroes of this war."

Lt. Gen. John Bell Hood
Ashwood Hall Plantation

His friends called him "Sam," a name John Bell Hood had acquired during his time at West Point, but no one in the Army of Tennessee used that appellation. He knew the soldiers referred to him as "Old Pegleg," which was tolerable, and his officers pinned him with unbecoming epithets, which bordered on treasonous. Such name-calling was to be expected as he whipped the Army of Tennessee into fighting shape. Since becoming commander of the motley army, Hood had seen his men and officers disappoint him time and time again in the battles around Atlanta.

On the portico of Ashwood Hall, Hood stood alone on his crutch, his right pants leg empty, save for the stub of a thigh that ached from the abrasion of the wooden leg he had removed inside the mansion. He watched his troops trudging toward Columbia in the sleet and rain. They had marched almost two hundred miles since the losses at Atlanta, often in unseasonably cold and wet weather. Hood realized the fate of the Confederacy rested on his shoulders because Robert E. Lee was pinned down in the trenches around Petersburg and Union General William Tecumseh Sherman was scorching his way across Georgia. As army commander, Hood questioned whether his men had the mettle to match his vision for saving their infant nation.

Frustrations plagued him that he must not only fight General John Schofield's army just a few miles away in Columbia and later General George H. Thomas's forces in Nashville, but also his own officers, who had been infected with the malady of General Joseph E. Johnston, a reluctance to attack entrenchments. Victories came from attack, not from defense. Hood understood this from experience under Robert E. Lee, starting at the Battle of Gaines' Mill when he led his Texas brigade in an assault that broke the Union line and opened the way for a Southern victory. Hood had saved Gaines' Mill, and Gaines' Mill had saved Richmond, ultimately convincing Union commander George McClellan to abandon his peninsula campaign. In Virginia, Hood's Texas brigade had turned the Yankee lines with shot and the cold steel of Confederate bayonets, which dripped Yankee blood in the aftermath.

At Gettysburg he had fought at Devil's Den and Little Round Top until an artillery shell exploded overhead, sending shrapnel through his left arm, from his hand to his biceps. Had he been a Confederate private, his arm would've been amputated, but as a general he received special care. Though his limb survived, its usefulness did not. His left arm hung limply at his side, its only military function being to fill the sleeve with the braided Austrian knot designating his rank as lieutenant general.

After recovering from his Gettysburg wounds, Hood served under James Longstreet's Corps with the Army of Tennessee to stem the Federal advance into Georgia. Even with his useless arm, Hood led the headlong charge that again turned the Union line, providing the pivotal moment in the Battle of Chickamauga. While he rallied his troops, Hood tumbled from his horse after a Minié ball shattered the bone of his right thigh. As his aides carried him from the field for the amputation that saved his life, his troops again put Yankees to the blade and routed them toward Chattanooga. In the checkered history of the Army of Tennessee, Chickamauga remained the only clear victory, and Hood understood why. Aggressive attacks carried the day, even against entrenched forces. This army feared making a frontal assault with a timidity that bordered on cowardice. Sam Hood planned to change that, recapturing Tennessee and saving the Confederacy, even if he had to be lifted into the saddle and strapped to his horse every day before leading his army to victory. He vowed never to let his men down, and he prayed they showed the same devotion to him that he showed to their joint cause.

Watching his haggard troops straggle down the road, Hood wondered if they were courageous enough to pay the same—or an even greater cost—as he had. A life lost in the defense of your country is never a life lost unless the country itself perishes, he believed. Hood pledged to himself that no matter how many of his men fell into their graves, their loss would not be in vain because he would save the Confederacy. He would whip the Yankees before him at Columbia and then at Nashville. After those victories, he would invade Kentucky all the way to the Ohio River, forcing Abraham Lincoln to reconsider the Union's war aims.

Behind him, the grand double doors of Ashwood Hall opened, and Isham G. Harris, the former governor of Tennessee, stepped onto the portico, followed by six of Hood's staff. Harris had led the state into secession, refusing in the wake of Fort Sumter President Lincoln's call for 50,000 Tennesseans to join the army and smother the blooming rebellion. Harris vowed to supply not a single Tennessean to the Union cause, saying he would rather cut off his right arm than use that hand to sign such an order. When Union armies took over Nashville in 1862, Lincoln effectively chopped off Harris's right arm by appointing Andrew Johnson as military governor of Tennessee. Since then, Harris had been governor-in-exile, bouncing around the Confederacy as an assistant to various Southern generals, including Hood at this time.

Harris sidled up to Hood. "It swells my chest with pride," he said, pointing to the passing troops, "to see Tennessee boys back here with their Southern compatriots. They shall drive the infernal Yankees from our homes and from our minds."

"Indeed, Governor," Hood responded, "that is my plan, if I can get the boys to fight my way."

"Under your leadership, General, the Army of Tennessee is certain to carry the day for the South."

"With God's willing hand upon my shoulder, I shall bring about that victory."

Harris placed his palm upon Hood's coat sleeve above his useless left arm. "I am confident of that. Might I suggest in the interim that we visit Hamilton Place and pay our respects to Lucius Junius Polk, brother of our late lamented General Leonidas Polk. As you know, the Polks are an influential family. I'll need their support to govern Tennessee when victory vindicates our cause."

"Ah, yes, politics, the keystone to success."

The governor snickered, patting Hood on the back. "All of us know of your sway with Jefferson Davis. You play the game well."

"Then let us visit the Polks at Hamilton Place this afternoon."

Rev. Charles T. Quintard
Hamilton Place

Dr. Charles Todd Quintard awoke rested on the featherbed mattress beneath the roof of Hamilton Place, the plantation home of Lucius Junius Polk, former state senator and adjutant general of Tennessee. The Episcopal Reverend Quintard began this day as he had ended the previous with a prayer for God's mercy. On this morning, he kneeled beside his bed on the carpeted floor and beseeched the Almighty to recognize the justice of the cause and to end the bloodshed so that two nations might emerge from this conflict and follow their own vision for the future of their divided peoples. He prayed for the Confederate soldiers marching on the Columbia Turnpike toward Nashville and, with God's blessing, for the independence of the Southern states. He beseeched the Almighty for the rain and sleet to abate and lessen the misery of the troops. Quintard asked for adequate rations to provide the needed nourishment for the marches and battles ahead. Finally, he submitted his wish that those fated to die would first find salvation in the arms of Jesus Christ, the Savior of mankind from all its inherent iniquities.

As he arose from his morning prayer, Quintard stepped to the window and parted the drapes, shaking his head at the continuing precipitation. Not only must his boys contend with the Yankees but also with the rain, the cold, and the mud. Winter had struck early this year, and it would bring sickness and disease, further depleting the strength of the Confederacy and weakening its chances of independence. Quintard's conscience flooded with guilt that he had rested warm and dry for the night while the boys that did the fighting shivered beneath primitive shelter, if any at all, to ward off the chill and the precipitation. Still, the troops kept marching and fighting, forever hoping and praying that this horrible conflict might end so that they, too, could sleep peacefully at night in soft beds in their own homes.

Thirty-nine years after his Connecticut birth, Quintard could never have foreseen during his northeastern childhood that he would one day join in a war of rebellion against the United States. Nor had that thought entered his mind when he graduated from University Medical College in New York City in 1847. After a year's practice in New York, he moved to Athens, Georgia, and married a local, his beloved Eliza Catherine Hand. A year later, they went to Memphis, where he taught at the Medical College of Memphis. There he met the most important man in his life, James Hervey Otey, the Episcopal bishop of Tennessee. With his unmatched devotion to God and Jesus Christ, Otey inspired Quintard to realize it was more rewarding to both the physician and his patients to save their immortal souls rather than just prolong their earthly lives.

Under Otey's tutelage, Quintard changed the direction of his life and the eternal destination of his congregations. When war came, Quintard joined the First Tennessee Infantry Regiment as chaplain and physician. He had traveled with those Tennessee boys to Virginia and back, but so few of them remained. Most of the original volunteers were either dead or crippled for the rest of their lives. Among the survivors, Sam Watkins came to mind, and Quintard took special satisfaction in his survival as he had put in a special word for young Watkins after he had deserted for three days earlier in the war to visit his sweetheart in Columbia, Tennessee. Through God's grace, Watkins had avoided the severest punishment and continued to fight for the Confederacy.

As for himself, through luck and devotion to God and cause, Quintard had risen above other ministers to become the de facto chaplain of the Army of Tennessee. In that capacity, he had walked not only with the common foot soldiers like Watkins but also conversed with and advised the likes of Jefferson Davis, Robert E. Lee and the successive commanders of the Army of Tennessee from Braxton Bragg to Joseph E. Johnston to John Bell Hood. Saddest of all, he had admired Leonidas Polk, known by all as "the Fighting Bishop." Until his cannonball evisceration, Polk was bishop of the Episcopal Diocese of Louisiana and founder of the south's Protestant Episcopal Church, when it separated from the national Episcopal Church. Beyond that, the late general was the brother of Lucius Junius Polk, whose hospitality and bedroom Quintard now enjoyed.

The reverend stepped away from the window and moved to the writing desk where he sat and reviewed the previous day's entry in his diary, wondering what events and people this new day would bring. He planned to remain at the plantation overnight before rejoining the army as it headed northward. The next day being Advent Sunday, Quintard hoped to deliver God's gospel to the Polk family, their guests, and visitors. He decided to focus on the Psalms for his message. Just as Lucius Polk had provided refuge for him for the night, God is a shelter for all who are afraid. Scribbling sermon notes on a piece of stationery, he heard a rap on the door.

"Massa Revrund, you be ups and abouts?"

It was Henry, the fifteen-year-old slave he had purchased for a thousand dollars eight months earlier in Georgia.

"Yes, Henry. I'm awake. Please come in."

The door swung open and Henry entered, carrying Quintard's boots. "De's boots been shined, Massa Revrund."

"Thank you, Henry. Place them at the foot of the bed. Have you had breakfast?"

"I's done eaten with de servants. Wants me to saddles yo'r horse?"

"No thank you, Henry. I'll be staying in the house for the day. Should I need you, I will send for you."

Quintard recalled the day outside Atlanta when he had purchased the boy. Henry's owner had demanded five thousand dollars, but Quintard bargained the cash-strapped planter down to a fifth of that because the boy seemed abused, never looking Quintard in the face as the reverend and his owner haggled over his fate. When they agreed upon the price, Quintard borrowed money from his wife's Georgia relatives to make the purchase in what they thought was a fine investment. Quintard intended to use Henry as his attendant. After the papers were signed and the money exchanged, the reverend mounted his horse, pulled Henry up behind him and rode away.

"You'll be my manservant, Henry," Quintard informed him, "help me prepare for each day, but henceforth I want you to look me in the eye when I speak."

"Yas, sah," Henry replied, "buts I's don't rightly knows what dat job means."

"You'll do tasks for me each day, like saddling my horse, delivering messages for me, keeping my boots shined, things of that nature, nothing strenuous."

"What's dat stren-u-cuss mean?"

"It's stren-u-ous. It means tiring, exhausting, leaving you tuckered out."

"What's should I's done be callin' youse?"

"Reverend is fine."

"Yes, Massa Revrund."

"What's your last name, Henry?"

"Can't says I's rightly knows, Massa Revrund. Don't remembers me ma or me pa, so I don't knows I's ever heard it be said."

"Most slave's take their first master's name."

"Nots me. He done been too mean. Don't cares for dat name to falls on dese ears again."

"If you could choose your last name, Henry, what would it be?"

"Lets me ponder dat question."

They rode in silence for two miles before Henry spoke again.

"Iffen I's tells youse, wills youse not be mad?"

"Of course not, Henry. Few people ever have the opportunity to select their surname. Make the best of it."

"Well, Massa Revrund, I's likes me last name to be 'Free.' Yas, sah, dat I's would. Henry be Free."

For a moment, Quintard sat stunned, disbelieving the young slave dared to address his emancipation, even subtly, with his new owner. He hesitated too long.

"Mass Revrund, youse be mad?"

"No, Henry. You just surprised me, a boy your age and limited learning, being so perceptive. It's a fine name, Henry B. Free. That's what I'll call you from now on. Praise the Lord."

"Praise de Lord," Henry echoed.

Henry had been a dependable servant since that day, and Quintard had treated him with dignity and respect, knowing that if he abused him, it would set a poor example for others and undermine his teachings of God and His kingdom. After Henry slipped out of the room and shut the door, Quintard resumed writing notes and studying his Bible for his sermon the next day, though somehow the topic failed to inspire him. After thirty minutes of Biblical reflection, he arose and changed from his nightclothes into his uniform. He exited the room and walked down the stairs, admiring the fine carpets and polished woodwork. The house floor plan was modeled after the White House, where Lucius and his bride, a grandniece of President Andrew Jackson's wife, had been married. With Abraham Lincoln in the executive mansion, Quintard understood this would be as close as he ever got to the residence of the U.S. commander-in-chief.

He descended the steps and headed to the dining room where his host, Lucius Polk, awaited.

"I hope you slept well, Reverend."

"Indeed I did. Finest night's sleep I've had in months. Don't remember a feather mattress so soft."

"Can we do anything else to add to your comfort? We'll do what we can, though the war has limited our resources, as you would expect from being under the boot heel of an invader."

"Might I ask a favor of you? If you don't object, I would like to deliver a sermon tomorrow. It has been weeks since I've taken the word of God to planter folks. As tomorrow is Advent Sunday, I feel God is calling me to speak."

Polk strode over and threw his arm over Quintard's shoulder. "Of course, Reverend. It would be our honor. Might I ask that you baptize my infant niece and my new grandson?"

Quintard smiled. "I'd be honored to baptize the newest members of the Polk family."

"We'll set up the parlor for your sermon and invite what family as can make it, assuming the Yankees don't disrupt our plans."

Their conversation trailed off into reminiscences of Polk's brother Leonidas before others gathered for breakfast. Quintard smiled at the positive reaction of the diners when Polk announced the reverend would deliver a sermon in the Hamilton Place parlor Sunday morning.

Saturday Afternoon,

November 26, 1864

Rev. Charles T. Quintard

Chapter Two

Rev. Charles T. Quintard
Hamilton Place

After a modest lunch, Lucius Junius Polk and Reverend Quintard retired to the study where they visited in private, sharing their fears over the dwindling prospects for the Confederate States of America. Tennessee had faced difficult times since the Union army occupied Nashville with the prospect of even more grueling challenges ahead, should the Confederacy fail. Barely an hour into their discussion, a servant knocked on the parlor door and announced that Lieutenant General John Bell Hood and Governor Isham Harris desired to visit with Polk.

"What an unexpected surprise," Polk said to Quintard, then turned to his servant. "Please see them in. As the attendant pushed open the double doors, the lanky Hood hobbled in on his crutch, his elongated, bearded face sagging with the worries of the Army of Tennessee. Polk and Quintard stepped to assist, but his two aides waved them away as the general made it to a divan and collapsed on the seat. One aide grabbed his crutch, and the other took a cushion from the couch and tucked it behind Hood's back. The general's artificial leg protruded from the couch like a misplaced tollgate. Once seated, Hood appeared less sorrowful and more optimistic.

Harris settled on the opposite end of the divan from Hood and greeted Polk warmly, then nodded at Quintard. Harris's mustache drooped down either side of his mouth, accentuating a perpetual frown, and his receding hairline had abandoned the crown of his head. He sat nervously wiggling his fingers.

"I'm sure the three of you have important matters to discuss," Quintard announced. "If you will excuse me, I shall return to my room to work on the sermon our gracious host has permitted me to deliver in his parlor tomorrow morning."

"Absolutely not, Reverend," said Hood. "Please stay as your spiritual guidance is important in these trying times."

"I shall help any way I can." Quintard settled back in his seat.

Hood nodded, then turned to Polk. "Thank you, Lucius, for your hospitality. We will need your political skills once I drive the enemy from Tennessee and reclaim this state for its rightful and elected governor. Tennessee belongs to its citizens, not these Yankee invaders."

Polk placed his right hand over his heart. "General, I am always available to serve the citizens of Tennessee."

"I intend to retake Nashville and chase the enemy all the way to the Ohio River," Hood reiterated. "Then the Union will be forced to turn their attention to me or lose the war."

The governor-in-exile nodded his agreement. "As we move deeper into Tennessee, more young men will rise up to join our cause. When we enter Kentucky, even more volunteers sympathetic to the Confederacy will enlist. With their help and God's, we cannot fail."

"Surely, Providence is on our side," Quintard responded, "but our setbacks are God's warnings for the Confederacy and its people to purge themselves of sin. Only after we triumph over the sin in our hearts can we defeat the Yankees and save our foundling nation."

"Amen," answered Hood. "The sin of my army remains a fear of attacking entrenchments. My predecessor instilled such cowardice in them. Under me, they will overcome that fear or die trying."

Quintard grimaced. He knew Johnston was popular among the soldiers because he had never wasted men in attacks on impenetrable breastworks and fortifications. Military dogma suggested it took a force at least three times that of the entrenched troops to have a sliver of hope for success. The Confederacy lacked such numbers. By Quintard's estimations, Hood's obsession with assaults had produced no better results than Johnston's defensive strategy, though the casualties had been greater, much greater. Hood had lost Atlanta, not Johnston. The hopes of the Confederacy now rested on a crippled general to relieve Grant's pressure on Lee's Army of Northern Virginia and perhaps even divert Sherman, wherever he was in Georgia, to chase after Hood's army instead of marching to the sea. Quintard studied the crippled commander. A man of thirty-three, he looked twice as old and always appeared exhausted, as surely he must be from having but one leg and a single functioning arm. To walk, he required a crutch. To ride, he had to be strapped in the saddle by others. Rumors floated of him falling from his horse on several occasions. Despite the general's physical limitations, Quintard saw in him a sincerity of purpose and a Christian's commitment to the task before him, no matter how overwhelming.

Lucius Polk thanked Hood for returning the Army of Tennessee to the state of its name and wished him every success in driving the Yankee invaders from Nashville and the rest of the state. Polk and Harris spoke both of joint acquaintances, many of whom the war had taken, and of the challenges Tennessee would face once the hostilities ceased. Years would pass before life returned to normal after a conflict so costly in men and resources. As Hood and Harris announced their pending departure, Quintard spoke a prayer beseeching the Almighty to provide General Hood with wisdom in choosing his battles, with compassion in preparing his soldiers for what they must endure, and with the stamina to see the war to a successful end.

After finishing his prayer, the reverend walked to Hood, clasped his good hand and wished him every success. Polk and Harris arose from their seats, shook hands as Hood's aides retrieved his crutch and lifted him up from the divan, sliding the crutch under his functional arm. Hood hobbled toward the study door with his retinue behind him. Quintard and Polk watched them exit, then studied one another, each waiting for the other to say something.

Finally, Polk spoke. "Are we so short of officers that our hopes for independence rest upon John Bell Hood's wrecked body?"

"General Hood needs an angel looking over his shoulder," Quintard answered, then grinned as he realized he had stumbled on a stronger topic for his Advent sermon. He would preach from Psalms 91:1-6.

"By your smile, Reverend, you seem to find more faith in General Hood than I do."

"My faith's in God, Lucius, not man, but through you, He showed me the scripture for tomorrow's sermon."

Sumner Cunningham
Columbia Pike

One foot in front of the other time after time after time in the wintry afternoon drizzle. That had been Sergeant Major Sumner A. Cunningham's day. He marched on the shoulder of the Columbia Pike trod by thousands of Confederates, most as tired as he was, but none as scared. Cunningham concentrated on his stride, but the specter of death kept interrupting his thoughts. The muddy soil tugged at his feet, as if trying to pull him into the grave he knew awaited him. No soldier in the Forty-first Tennessee Infantry—a regiment known more for its timidity than its bravery—trembled more than Cunningham, for he acknowledged himself to be the biggest coward in a regiment of weaklings. Though others might think he shook from the cold or from the malaria that struck him periodically, Cunningham knew better. The shakes came from bald, naked fright. Each day on the march, he lived in total terror. Cunningham had achieved the highest rank a non-commissioned officer could attain, not because of his battlefield prowess, but mostly because he was better educated than his fellow soldiers. Besides managing the recordkeeping and logistics for his regiment, Cunningham excelled at anticipating battle and placing himself on the sick roll in time to avoid the carnage. That remained his greatest skill as a soldier. If he did not fear hanging or a firing squad more than a combat demise, he would have deserted long ago.

Death had called upon the star-crossed Forty-first Tennessee in many guises. Cunningham wondered where and how it would find him. Minié balls, canister, and grapeshot killed dozens, like George W. Parsons, Tommy Russell, William Marsh, J.W. Downing, Ephraim Bradford, George Alexander, Tommy Bonner, John W. Oliver, W.C. Myers, Jimmy Greer, Willy McClure, J.A. Hill, George W. Mann, J.W. Bryant, R.F. Trillman, and George T. Wiseman, all at Chickamauga. G.W. Buntley, Barbe Collins, Erwin Jett, Willie Myers, and C.M. Carter perished in the recent battles for Atlanta. Before that, Robert Ewing took a bullet to the head on Missionary Ridge, and Johnny Thomas grapeshot to the chest at Murfreesboro. J.K. Wiley died at Fort Donelson while William Phagan, Jackson Cox, and W.W. Conaway met their ends from shrapnel at Port Hudson. The fatality list totaled so many he could no longer remember all their names. Cunningham, however, would never forget the very first, Captain Thomas N. McNaughton at Fort Donelson.

A native of Bedford County, Tennessee, Cunningham, at eighteen, joined the Confederate army in the months following Fort Sumter. Swept up in the secessionist oratory by men too old to fight themselves, he eventually joined the Forty-first Tennessee, an infantry regiment destined for mediocrity. Only once in the entire war had the unit been feared, and then only because the detachment was quarantined with smallpox. So poor was its fighting record that commanders held the Forty-first in reserve during most battles, praying the outfit would never be needed for anything beyond retrieving the wounded or burying the dead on the battlefield.

The regiment's timid reputation started at Fort Donelson when the Forty-first became the last outfit to reinforce the doomed post on the Cumberland River, and one of the first to hand over its arms to Union soldiers. Cunningham spent most of the battle hiding in a trench, terrified by the shelling of Union gunboats and the memory, scorched in his mind, of Captain McNaughton, who had rushed to the initial sound of fighting. Minutes later, Cunningham passed the meaty pulp that had been his captain. A gunboat's exploding shell had eviscerated McNaughton. Cunningham had lived in terror every day since. Bravery came easier when hot oratory rather than sizzling iron filled the air. Cunningham survived Fort Donelson through surrender.

After a spell in a Union prison in Indianapolis, he was exchanged for a Yankee captive and resumed his army enlistment, avoiding major battles at Vicksburg, Port Hudson and then bloody Chickamauga, where his regiment attacked Snodgrass Hill without him. He missed the conflicts at Lookout Mountain and Missionary Ridge. Even though absent from the large battles, Cunningham could not escape brushes with death. At the skirmish at Raymond, he had been close enough to hear the whizzing Minié balls as they flew around him. On another occasion, as he lounged in camp with messmates listening to Sergeant John T. Patrick read from a contraband Yankee newspaper, a sharpshooter's bullet cracked Patrick's skull open like a watermelon. Perplexed why his friend died instead of him, Cunningham gave up his blanket to wrap around his pal for burial. Fear remained Cunningham's constant companion. Later, he avoided the fighting at Kennesaw Mountain against Sherman's army and the ensuing encounters around Atlanta.

Beyond the battlefields, less glorious killers—diseases with names that Cunningham could not spell—terrified him as well. Diarrhea killed Manson Albright and Alfred Bradford. Jason Kelly and Danny Beasley fell to smallpox. William Hooper succumbed to dysentery. J.D. Chesser and Billy Allsbrook died of typhoid. Willie James suffered from fatal rheumatism, and Henry Sanders expired from a fever the doctors could never identify. John W. Hicks coughed up his lungs with consumption. Accidents claimed other men. Charles Hide ate too many oranges at Bowling Green, then passed. James H. Wade was crushed between two railroad cars outside Atlanta. Just days earlier, a pair of soldiers had died chopping trees to corduroy the muddy road when a falling tree split their skulls. Cunningham never asked their names. He no longer cared. He just wanted to survive this infernal war and go home.

As Cunningham marched toward Nashville, he feared the next battle would be different. Deep within his terrified soul, he expected that either he or his fear would die wherever the generals moved the next chess piece of war. Walking toward Columbia, Cunningham shivered as he looked to the murky sky, spitting rain and sleet upon his cheeks. The night would bring fitful rest, which he craved, as well as the frigid cold, which would torment his sleep. On such icy nights, he regretted giving his blanket as a burial shroud for his late sergeant friend because John T. Patrick no longer felt the cold. His lost woolen cover would have provided Cunningham more of the warmth he needed.

Even though he marched among thousands of men, he walked alone, two paces to the left of the last company of the regiment. That was the accustomed place for the sergeant major in marches. Even if he was a terrible soldier, Cunningham considered himself an exceptional sergeant major. He could attend the details of guard and fatigue, could make the assignments and could verify the roll numbers. He could maintain the rosters and manage his superior's needs. He made certain the buglers and drummers sounded the right calls at the right time. He kept the regimental books and records and saw that the wagons were ready to roll each day. Cunningham could do everything but fight, and he knew a fight was coming. God help him!

Ahead he spotted a country church through the trees and the veil of drizzle. Maybe he should say a prayer or a verse. He had memorized the Twenty-third Psalm as a child. He started the verse in his mind, but the words came out wrong.

> *General Hood is my shepherd; I shall not die.*
> *He maketh me to march through Tennessee; he leadeth me toward the great battle.*
> *He restoreth my courage; he leadeth me in the paths of danger for the Confederacy's sake.*
> *Yea, though I walk through the valley of the shadow of death, I will fear no evil, for General Hood is with me; his rifles and his cannons comfort me.*
> *Thou preparest a grave before me in the presence of mine enemies; thou anointest my Enfield with oil; my haversack runneth over;*

*Surely fear and death shall follow me all the
days of my life; and I will dwell in the
grave of the South forever.*

Even God's word mocked his fear. In frustration, he tightened his grip around the Enfield rifle he carried and gritted his teeth. Cunningham cursed himself, blasphemed his fear, swore at the Confederacy and, most of all, cursed the Yankees, who sought to murder him. Hearing a murmur among the troops, he saw soldiers ahead of him straightening their shoulders and their rifles. Cunningham feared the enemy awaited ahead, but he detected neither nervousness nor fright in the men of the Forty-first Tennessee. He heard the whispered word "Forrest" and shook his head. Were his men losing their sanity? They had been trudging among trees for days.

Up ahead on his side of the road, Cunningham saw a clump of soldiers surrounding a single officer astride a magnificent gelding. Beyond them, other officers sat on their mounts amused by the show, as if they were watching a circus parade. "Forrest," came the word again. Then Cunningham sensed the excitement. The officer had to be Nathan Bedford Forrest, known to the Yankees as "the Devil Forrest" and to his allies as "the wizard of the saddle." Cunningham felt at once comforted and nervous in the presence of the lieutenant general, comforted that Forrest would be with the Army of Tennessee on this campaign, nervous that he must pass within sight of such a legendary fighter. He stared at a commander who wore his uniform as if he had been born in it. In Forrest's chiseled face with its hollowed cheeks and its determined black eyes, Cunningham saw an unmatched invincibility. With leaders like Forrest, how could the Confederacy ever lose the war? With soldiers like himself, Cunningham asked, how could the South ever win?

Cunningham straightened his shoulders and stiffened his muscles to disguise the tremors rippling through his body. Even if he wasn't a fighting soldier, he could march like one in front of this ferocious combatant. Within thirty yards of the belligerent general, he called upon his last reserve of energy to lift and lower his feet with parade-ground precision. Coming within twenty yards of Forrest, he lifted his chin and tightened his lips in a show of the determination he could manage on a march but never on a battlefield. At ten yards from the determined cavalry officer, Cunningham stared at Forrest, whose burning eyes locked on his own for a moment. Then Forrest acknowledged his stare with a slight, almost imperceptible nod.

Cunningham caught his breath. What was the proper thing to do? Should he lift his rifle in a present arms salute? Or, should he just keep marching? Drawing even with Forrest, Cunningham raised his Enfield from his shoulder, then stumbled on the slick, dimpled path. He lurched forward in the mud, dropping his rifle as the thin-soled shoe of his leading foot stepped on a fresh, slippery horse turd. Cunningham tumbled into the cold, wet muck, his chest landing in another pile of horse droppings.

The laughter of Forrest and his officers rang in Cunningham's ears as he scrambled to arise, grab his weapon, and brush the muck and manure from his army blouse. His face burned hot with embarrassment. As much as he feared death, Cunningham would have accepted it gladly at that moment, just to deafen the humiliating hoots that trailed him down the road toward his fate.

Sam Watkins
Nearing Columbia, Tennessee

As he tramped along the edge of the macadamized pike, fearing with his every step that his ragged shoes might finally disintegrate around his sore feet, Corporal Sam R. Watkins of the First Tennessee Infantry blamed Tom Tuck's damned chicken for the cold, spitting weather and the bad luck that had engulfed the Army of Tennessee since July. Good fortune never accompanied the Army of Tennessee for long, as Watkins had witnessed from the very beginning, but it had disappeared since John Bell Hood replaced Joe Johnston as commander.

Watkins cursed the rooster for bringing even worse luck. Tom Tuck had carried the fighting cock with him ever since joining the First Tennessee, keeping the fowl in his knapsack with his neck and head sticking out everywhere they marched. When Tuck first skirmished against the Yankees, he left his rooster behind with the unneeded gear, but as rations diminished and hunger increased among his men, he even carried the cock into battle for fear someone would chop off the fowl's head, pluck, and fry him for supper. Tuck first named the bird "Southern Confederacy," but that was a mouthful, eventually shortening it to "Confed" and finally to "Fed." With Fed in camp, the First Tennessee never needed a bugler, as the rooster alerted the entire regiment of dawn's arrival. At first, Tuck's fighting mates resented the chicken for disturbing their sleep, but as combat and exhaustion conditioned them to slumber through anything, they tolerated Fed's clucking and crowing. Too, the other privates realized that Fed would not live forever and, when he died, they hoped to be among the friends Tuck would endow with a piece of chicken, whether fried, boiled, roasted, or raw.

Thus, Fed became the regiment's mascot. As for food, Fed fared better than the men, always finding plenty of bugs, vermin, and litter around the camp to scrounge up a decent meal. Pampered as he was, Fed maintained his fighting mettle everywhere he accompanied Tuck, who was always looking for a cockpit where he could match the cock against a local favorite. Tuck was so confident of Fed's fighting prowess, he never clipped the bird's comb or the waddle beneath its beak as some sporting men did to reduce fighting targets and injury possibilities.

Recalling Fed's final fight helped keep Watkins's thoughts off the piercing cold and the pricking sleet that tormented each step as he neared his home in Columbia. Outside Atlanta, when the regiment camped on the southern bank of the Chattahoochee River, a hulking man who spoke in a slow drawl that reflected poor intelligence and even poorer common sense walked into camp with a fighting rooster under his arm. He declined several offers to sell the bird for supper, inquiring if it were true that one of the men had a gamecock because he sought to match his fowl against the Tennessee bird. The men directed him to Tom Tuck, who studied the scrawny bird tucked beneath the behemoth's arm and nodded. He was game, if the man had money to wager. The intruder said he had ten dollars in Confederate money and twelve more in Yankee greenbacks to bet against anyone with cash.

Soldiers gathered around the two sporting men, murmuring they would take some of the fellow's money as the only entertainment they had had the last few weeks was dodging Yankee bullets and harvesting lice from their dirty bodies. After placing their wagers and designating Watkins to hold the money, Tuck and his opponent prepared their cocks, hooking sharp blades or "gaffs," as the sporting men called them, over the birds' leg spurs. Then the two men entered the human ring, holding the birds at their chests and letting them eye their feathery foe.

"This here's Fed," Tuck told his opponent. "Does your cock carry a name?"

"He does! Goes by 'John Hell,' he does."

"Odd name," Tuck answered.

"He gives 'em hell, he does."

The men circled, thrusting their roosters at one another, the angry birds squawking and flapping their wings. When Tuck and his new

Georgia pal nodded, each threw his rooster at the other. The fowls flailed their wings, landing on their toes, then lunging at each other with their gaffs as the spectators roared their support for Fed. In an instant, John Hell's steel pierced Fed's head and neck. The First Tennessee's fighting cock tumbled over dead as the soldiers stood in stunned silence. Watkins distributed all the winnings to the gloating Georgia fellow.

"Told you boys he gives 'em hell," the victor said, stuffing his money in his pants pocket, then grabbing his rooster and removing the gaffs. "There ain't a meaner cock in all of Georgia, than John Hell," he boasted as he tucked his rooster back under his arm, split the crowd, and disappeared into the trees from wherever he had come.

Tom Tuck stooped and picked up the feathery carcass, looking at the bird with moistening eyes. "Alas, my beloved Southern Confederacy has fallen on the field of battle, but our departed warrior left no will and no instructions for his funeral, so I will pluck him, gut him, and fry him, then sop my biscuits in his gravy as I chew on his defeat."

Striding toward Columbia, Watkins smiled at the memory as he had been one of the six soldiers Tuck selected as honor guards for the deceased bird. As Tuck dressed the carcass, the pallbearers built a fire beneath the tripod where they would hang their boiling pot. They dumped a wad of bacon grease in the kettle and suspended it on the tripod hook over the growing fire. After the lard melted and bubbled, Tuck reverently dropped pieces of Fed into the cooking oil. The aroma wafted across the camp and soldiers relished the fragrance, even if they were not among the select few who would enjoy the taste of the late, lamented Southern Confederacy, the greatest Tennessee fighting cock ever to take up the South's righteous cause against the evil northern flock.

Just as the bird finished cooking, however, the gods of war frowned on the First Tennessee again. Six Yankee cavalrymen, waving their sabers and screaming like Comanche warriors, galloped through the camp, scattering the Tennessee boys as they lunged for their weapons. Riding by the cook fire, one cavalryman leaned low to the side of his saddle, thrust his sword under the pot handle and yanked it from the fire, knocking over the tripod and escaping with the kettle and the treasured remains of the First Tennessee's brave bird. By the time Watkins and his allies grabbed their rifles, the thieving Yankees had disappeared into the woods before a single shot could be fired in their wake. Tuck and the honor guard blasphemed the treacherous blue-bellies, calling their raid one of the most despicable acts of the war and wondering if the fellow with the victorious cock had been a Union spy, since he carried Union greenbacks.

Fed's death became an omen of what was to follow as the next day on picket duty on the south bank of the Chattahoochee River, Watkins first heard the news from a Yankee sentry across the water.

"Hey, Johnny Rebs, are you listening?" came a fast-talking voice.

"Leave us alone," answered Joe Sanders. "We don't care to talk, not after your cavalry stole our chicken."

"Don't know nothing about no chicken, but I do know Joe Johnston's been replaced in command."

The other Rebel sentries on picket duty eyed one another, shaking their heads in disbelief. Only Sanders responded.

"You're a damned liar, you are, Billy Yank!"

"I'd never lie to you, Johnny Reb. I'd shoot you, but I wouldn't lie to you. My momma taught me better than that. Fact is, Joe Johnston's been relieved, and General Hood's taken his place."

Sam, like the rest of the boys, figured the enemy sentry was yanking their tails just to hear them squawk.

Sanders answered, "Even Jeff Davis wouldn't name that crippled fool to command the Army of Tennessee. Now I know you're not just a liar, but a damned liar instead!"

"I'll tolerate no man calling me a liar, Johnny Reb. If you'll come out and show yourself while the rest of you Secesh stand down, I'll do the same. Then we'll settle our differences with a duel. Either show your manhood or prove you're a coward."

"I'm game," Sanders said, emerging from the cover and standing boldly on the bank.

Moments later, his lying Yankee tormentor appeared. "My rifle's loaded."

"As is mine," Sanders yelled back.

The Yankee stooped and picked up a stone. "Keep your weapon at your side, Secesh, like me. I'll throw this rock in the air. When it splashes in the water, lift your rifle and fire away."

Sanders nodded. "Let's settle this."

Watkins and other pickets on both sides of the river emerged from their cover to watch the exchange.

Billy Yank tossed the stone toward the sky. It seemed to hang for a moment before falling back to earth and splashing in the Chattahoochee. Both men raised their rifles and fired. Both missed. They dropped the butts of their weapons to the soft river bank, pulled a cartridge from their belt boxes, bit off the end, dumped the powder in the barrel, pushed the padding and Minié ball down the shaft, yanked their ramrods, shoving the load in the barrel, then cocking the hammer and placing a percussion cap on the nipple. As soon as they reloaded their rifles, both aimed at the other and shot again, missing each other in their haste. They repeated the process until Sanders fell dead on the fifth volley.

"Sorry, Secesh, but you never should've called me a damned liar." The Yankee retreated into the woods.

Watkins and three others propped their weapons against trees and walked to Sanders sprawled dead upon the bank. Watkins picked up the dead man's rifle, shoved the ramrod back in its sheath, then grabbed Sander's right arm as his helpers grabbed his remaining limbs. They toted him back to cover, grabbing their rifles as they slipped into the woods to await their relief. Then they carried the body to camp.

In their bivouac late that afternoon after they had buried Sanders, the bugle blew assembly. Once the troops gathered, the colonel read the formal order directly from Jefferson Davis himself that he was appointing John Bell Hood to head the Army of Tennessee. Men wept throughout the ranks, and Watkins blasphemed the Yankee pickets who knew more about what was happening with the Army of Tennessee than did the soldiers who fought its battles. Five infantrymen shook their heads and shouted profanities, then dropped their rifles, cartridge boxes, canteens, and haversacks on the ground, emptied their pockets, and sprinted toward the river, which they swam to the other side, preferring Union imprisonment to service under John Bell Hood.

The shock of the command change lingered for days, leading some to speculate about Fed's death from John Hell, which rhymed with John Bell as in Hood, and may have been a portent of what was to come, the end of the Southern Confederacy for which the deceased rooster had been named.

Those thoughts plagued Sam Watkins as he marched in the cold toward Columbia, passing the landmarks of his youth along the way. He walked on the road's shoulder so he could make a dash to the next Tennessee walnut tree he sighted. The walnuts were ripe, having shed their husks, with many falling to the ground while others still clung to the overhead branches. Toward sundown, Watkins spotted a tall walnut tree about fifty yards from the road. He stepped out of line and edged that way, like he was going to relieve himself, but others watched suspiciously and saw beyond him the tree with its promise of nourishment. Two dozen other soldiers fell in behind him, then dashed for their supper, sprinting as fast as their weak legs would carry them. Seeing them sprinting forward, Watkins raced ahead, wondering if his shoes would withstand the strain.

Beneath the tree he fell to his knees on the carpet of leaves and placed his rifle at his side as he grabbed nuts and shoved them in his haversack while other soldiers dropped beside him, gathering what would become their next meal. Watkins flung leaves aside, searching for walnuts hidden under them, partially covering his own rifle as around him other men scrambled for their own nourishing nuggets. Two soldiers climbed the tree and stood on branches, jumping up and down to shake loose other walnuts. A shower of the brown orbs fell upon the gray-clad gatherers. By the time he finished, Watkins had enough walnuts to last him for two days. He picked up his rifle, brushed leaves from his tattered uniform and started back for the column, which kept marching north.

When they stopped for the night, the regiment camped five miles south of Columbia where Watkins had grown up and where his beloved sweetheart Virginia Jane Mayes, or "Jennie" as he called her, awaited his return for their wedding day. If it weren't for Jefferson Davis and the Confederate Congress, Sam would already have been married. He had enlisted in the First Tennessee for a year, but the politicians in 1862 had passed a conscription law mandating three-year enlistments for men eighteen to thirty-five. Just as his enlistment was to end, the new law went into effect. Six months later, another conscription law extended the age limit to forty-five. Then in February of this year, the legislators had broadened the age range from seventeen to fifty. By the end of 1865, Watkins figured they'd be calling on the blind, the deaf, and the dumb to serve, then reconsidered, deciding the dumb were already serving in the Confederate Congress in Richmond. Watkins enlisted in the war believing in the doctrine of States' Rights while the Yankees had fought for the concept of centralization. In its various conscription acts, the Confederate government had imposed upon its men the same centralized power it professed to be fighting against. Next to the Yankees and General Hood, Watkins loathed Davis and the politicians the most.

As the men partnered to put up their pup tents for what shelter they could make against the rain, if not the cold, Sam thought of Jennie. He reached in his haversack and from among the walnuts pulled out his pocket Bible, where he kept a lock of her hair and a letter he called a talisman against the charms of other beautiful and interesting women. Sam opened the Bible, lifted the clip of her brown hair to his nostrils and smelled her fragrance before replacing it in the Bible and unfolding the letter. He read the first lines of the correspondence. Wrote Jennie, "I write to tell you that I love you yet, and you alone and day by day I love you more and I pray every night and morning for your safe return home again." Sam smiled as he enjoyed the rest of the letter. He had read it so many times he could recite it without even looking, but he enjoyed seeing the words written in her delicate hand. Sam gently returned the letter to the Bible and the Good Book to his haversack. He pulled out a handful of walnuts and cracked them beneath the small tarp that provided cover for him and his friend Billy Carr. As Sam consumed the meaty nuts, he heard the noise of walnut shells cracking throughout the camp. The racket serenaded him to sleep.

States Rights Gist
Encampment near Columbia

Where was Uncle Wiley? Brigadier General States Rights Gist slapped his thigh in frustration as he rode among the troops of his encamped brigade, three regiments of Georgia boys and two of his fellow South Carolinians. The day had been long, the march exhausting, wet, and cold. The enveloping sky hung overhead as gray as his frock coat. Without his overcoat, he occasionally brushed the sheen of frigid mist from his frayed uniform. Despite the precipitation that slipped past the bent brim of his hat and kissed his neck, he advanced with his collar turned down to hide his rank in case enemy snipers hid in the trees outside Columbia, Tennessee. Before the war, Gist had been so proud of his selection as a brigadier general in the South Carolina militia that he could never have imagined hiding the insignia of his rank. He was even prouder when the Confederate Congress designated him a brigadier general for the Confederacy. He never imagined that three years later he would camp with his men near Columbia, Tennessee, instead of his beloved Columbia, South Carolina.

Gist twisted in his saddle, looking for Uncle Wiley. Where was his manservant? Around him, his men made camp, trying and failing to start small fires with wet wood. Their efforts smoldered rather than flamed, adding to the day's many frustrations. As Gist meandered among his troops, he overheard talk of taking Columbia and stealing any stores of food the town possessed.

Every mention of Columbia took his memory back to another Columbia, the capital of South Carolina, in the days before Fort

Sumter, when he and the entire South had been cocksure of victory. His confidence had waned, if not his belief in the cause and its right to self-destiny. In the dwindling light of day, he feared the Army of Tennessee was on a fool's mission because its commander, John Bell Hood, was himself a fool. Why should the army attack this worthless Tennessee community, when it should be defending South Carolina's capital against William Tecumseh Sherman? Once the merciless Sherman finished with Georgia, he would turn north toward Gist's home state, where there would be hell to pay for firing upon Fort Sumter and starting a conflagration now more than three years long.

As the summer battles for Atlanta had raged, Hood time and again had thrown his men against entrenched forces, bleeding the Confederacy of critical manpower. Failing at victory, Hood headed north, intent on disrupting General Sherman's supply lines. The unpredictable Sherman merely shrugged, deciding he and his army would live off the fruits of Georgia. He turned east from Atlanta for a march to the sea, stealing provender from Georgia folks and leaving a swath of looted and blackened homes in the wake of his two-legged locusts. Rather than defend Georgia and its people, Hood moved northwest, convincing President Jefferson Davis that he alone could save the South by reclaiming Tennessee and taking the war through Kentucky to the very banks of the Ohio River.

While the papers—both northern and southern—speculated upon Sherman's progress, no one beyond his own army knew for certain his location because when he left his supply lines, he had also abandoned the telegraph connections that would carry news of his victories or failures to Washington and General Ulysses S. Grant. Unless Sherman's men starved to death—an unlikely possibility considering the fertility of Georgia's cropland—they would turn north toward South Carolina once they reached the Atlantic.

Gist worried not just for South Carolina but also for his wife Janie. They had married on May sixth the previous year, just four days after Robert E. Lee's victory at Chancellorsville. Prospects for the South had never looked better, nor for him on his wedding day at her palatial Live Oak Plantation. He wished circumstances had allowed the traditional rounds of parties among South Carolina's aristocracy or that Janie, ten years his junior, had had the opportunity for the finest dressmakers and milliners in Charleston to sew her a magnificent trousseau of dresses and hats for her wedding celebration. Like many things, the war had intervened, accelerating the timetable for the ceremony such that Janie's sister Mary did not have time to journey from Edgefield for the nuptials. Fewer than forty-eight hours after they exchanged their vows and shared their wedding bed, Gist rode away with his troops for Mississippi. He had visited with her a few days at Christmas, and later she had called on him at Dalton, Georgia, in May to celebrate their first anniversary. He honored his wife with a dress parade of his regiment. Then he said goodbye to Janie as his men marched off to slow General Sherman. He still treasured the memory of the soft touch of her hand, the reassurance of her smile, and the comfort of her embrace. By his count, they had been married four hundred and seventy days and together less than one in twenty of those days. He wondered if he would live to celebrate another anniversary or, even worse, if she would, since General Sherman would certainly turn upon South Carolina with a vengeance after he devastated Georgia.

A son of Southern privilege, Gist was educated as well as any man in the Army of Tennessee, having attended private schools as a youth and then South Carolina College, learning Greek and Latin, logic and rhetoric, calculus and trigonometry, moral and political philosophy, composition and elocution, civil engineering and agricultural chemistry, among other subjects. After graduation, he had spent a year behind the four Ionic columns of the Harvard Law School, but the frigid climate and the cold hearts of abolitionist Senator Charles Sumner's adherents had driven him back to South Carolina's warmer climate and more comforting political embrace. After Sumner had called plantation owners bigoted, narrow, provincial, and selfish in his anti-slavery bombast, Gist had reveled in the caning that Congressman and fellow South Carolinian Preston Brooks had administered to the Massachusetts senator with his walking stick on the floor of the U.S. Senate in 1856.

From his time in Massachusetts, Gist came to agree with Alexis de Tocqueville's observation that prejudice against the Negro race remained stronger in states that had abolished slavery than in those where it still existed. Up north, Gist had seen no white carpenters, bricklayers, or painters working beside blacks, though it remained a common sight in South Carolina. In his reading of *Democracy in America*, Gist had underlined de Tocqueville's words, "I am obliged to confess that I do not regard abolishing slavery as a means of warding off the struggle of the two races in the Southern states. The Negroes may long remain slaves without complaining; but if they are once raised to the level of freemen, they will soon revolt at being deprived of almost all their civil rights; and as they cannot become the equals of the whites, they will speedily show themselves as enemies." That, Gist believed, stood as the greatest fear of the South and—if they would ever admit it—of the North as well.

Returning from Cambridge to the Palmetto State, Gist had read law and been admitted to the bar, establishing in 1853 his first law office in the ironically named Unionville. He suggested the locals rename the town "Seccessionville." That same year, he joined the local militia at the rank of captain. His family's political connections started a meteoric military rise, especially for a man with no formal martial training. The following year Governor James H. Adams, the father of Gist's future bride, appointed him as his aide-de-camp at the rank of lieutenant colonel. Two years later, he advanced to brigadier general.

When his cousin William Henry Gist attained the governor's mansion in 1858, secession talk grew hotter as the 1860 presidential election loomed. Nominee Abraham Lincoln enthralled the new Republican Party and terrified true Southerners everywhere. South Carolina's new chief executive named States Rights Gist his special envoy and sent his young cousin on a secret mission to the governors of other Southern states. Talk of nullification and secession had always burned hottest in South Carolina, home of the late Senator John C. Calhoun, whose theories of nullification still shaped Palmetto State politics. South Carolina had always preached secession the loudest, and the fire-eaters stood ready to abandon the Union, but no one knew with certainty if any other states would follow. Governor Gist sought answers and support, but the question was too inflammatory, considering the growing vindictiveness of the national debate over slavery, to send by mail, which could be stolen or surreptitiously read. Nor was the telegraph safe, as messages passed through so many hands, and the click-clack was decipherable by so many ears. Instead, the younger Gist hand-carried letters of inquiry to other Southern chief executives.

The providentially named States Rights Gist became the harbinger of Southern secession, delivering letters to the governors of North Carolina, Georgia, Florida, Alabama, Mississippi, and Louisiana on a four-week circle of the deep south by train and stage. Though North Carolina and Louisiana's governors failed to commit to secession, the chief executives of Alabama, Georgia, Mississippi, and Florida offered support, as long as one or two other states seceded first. Gist conveyed the messages to his governor.

By December of 1860, when Gist's two-year term as governor expired, Lincoln had been elected president to await a March inauguration. Francis Wilkinson Pickens followed William Henry

Gist as governor of South Carolina and orchestrated the firing on Fort Sumter, once Lincoln assumed the presidency. The new governor in January appointed States Rights Gist as South Carolina's adjutant and inspector general to organize the state's militia for war. That April Gist witnessed the bombarding of Fort Sumter, proud that South Carolina had finally stood up for States' Rights and self-government closer to the people. For an officer with no formal military training, Gist prided himself on his ability to shape a company or a regiment or a brigade into fighters. He had acquitted himself well at First Manassas, in Mississippi on the outskirts of Vicksburg, at Chickamauga and Chattanooga, and then in the Atlanta campaign.

As Gist wandered among his troops this rainy evening, he looked for Uncle Wiley and wondered what lay ahead for himself, for South Carolina, and for the Confederacy. Everything had soured after the calendar had turned to 1864 with battlefield losses, changes in command, and the mutinous proposal by General Cleburne to free slaves who took up arms in defense of the South. Had Cleburne never heard of Nat Turner and his short-lived but fatal 1831 armed uprising? Though he had little faith in General John Brown, who had been appointed division commander instead of himself when Frank Cheatham was elevated to command his corps, Gist preferred to serve under him rather than under the traitorous Cleburne.

Of all the calamities the Army of Tennessee had faced during the year, none surpassed President Davis in removing General Joseph Johnston from command and replacing him with John Bell Hood. Perhaps Hood was West Point-educated unlike himself, but Gist had never wasted men's lives as remorselessly or attended so little to their need for sustenance as Hood had since taking command. After entering Tennessee, Gist's men had scrounged for food or managed on a single ear of corn or a solitary biscuit if Hood's quartermasters provided the flour. Mostly, the supply officers failed to provide rations. For that reason, Gist sent his trusted manservant Wiley Howard in search of a decent meal, loaning his own gray overcoat to him. Not only did he send Uncle Wiley in search of food with his only overcoat, he also mounted him on the gelding he had named "Joe Johnston" in honor of the Army of Tennessee's previous commander. Gist would never name a steed for John Bell Hood, unless it was the rear quarter of the horse.

In the cold, intermittent rain, his men made their camp and coffee two miles outside of Columbia. Gist rode among their tents on his second horse, "Kitty," a lesser equine in strength, endurance, and spirit, but one less likely to panic at the sound of gunfire. Soldiers of the Forty-sixth and Sixty-fifth Georgia saluted as he passed. He greeted them, but he didn't know them as he did the boys of the Sixteenth and Twenty-fourth South Carolina regiments, having known many of their parents or their pastors. It calmed him seeing the troops because it took his mind off Wiley Howard and his favored gelding. Returning to his small tent, he dismounted, gave Kitty to an orderly to attend, and retired for the night, hoping Uncle Wiley would be waiting for him in the morning.

Sunday Morning,

November 27, 1864

Kitchen Building and Back Porch
Fountain Carter Home

Chapter Three

Hardin P. Figuers
Figuers Home, Franklin

On some days Hardin P. Figuers cursed the year of his birth, but not on this frigid, sleeting Sunday morning. Had he been born two years earlier, he would have turned of age to fight for the Confederacy and drive the Yankee invaders from Tennessee, the land he loved because he knew no other. As a soldier, though, he would be enduring this horrid weather with little to shelter himself from the piercing cold and the soaking precipitation. While he stared through the frosty parlor window of his home on the southwest side of Franklin, he shivered at the thought of what soldiers in the Army of Tennessee must be facing as they returned to free their homes, families, and state from their oppressors.

Dreary Sundays like this one saddened his mother, who sat darning socks by the fireplace, her rocking chair squeaking as it swayed back and forth on the parlor's Brussels carpet. The last Sunday in February had dawned with similar weather and on that day, after a brief illness, Hardin's little sister Harriet Agnes Figuers had departed this world, taking with her a bit of her mother's heart and most of her spirit. Not once since they buried Agnes in the local cemetery did Hardin remember seeing his mother smile. Death had been a constant companion in Tennessee since the war began, but Agnes's demise had been so sudden and so unexpected. One day she stood healthy and vibrant, and then twenty-four hours later she lay fevered and still. Three days later, she passed away, barely eleven years old. The deaths of men and boys had become so commonplace since Fort Sumter as to be expected, but not a young girl, not his kid sister, not his mother's little girl, not Agnes with her self-righteous confidence.

Much as she had annoyed Hardin for always tattling on him to their momma, he missed the guidance that only a snitch of a sister could provide. During the first Christmas after Fort Sumter, their widowed mother had explained to the children they would not be getting any toys for the holiday because of the war and the resulting hard times. Their younger sister, Mary Louisa, had taken it the hardest, sniffling over the unfortunate turn of events. Seeking to ease Mary Louisa's fears, Hardin had taken her aside and informed her Santa Claus would not be coming that December because the Yankees had shot him. Mary Louisa bawled and blubbered even more until her mother came to check on her. Hardin had merely shrugged ignorance at the cause of Mary Louisa's grief until the eavesdropping Agnes enlightened their mother.

"Hardin told her the Yankees shot Santa Claus, and he wouldn't be coming ever again."

"Goodness, Hardin, where do you come up with such outlandish tales?" his mother asked, then turned to Mary Louisa. "Not even Yankees would shoot Santa Claus, Mary Louisa. Hardin told you a big old fib."

"If they shoot at Tennessee folks, they'll shoot at Santa Claus," Hardin shouted back as he glared at Agnes.

"Don't believe him, Mary Louisa." Agnes crossed her arms across her chest and raised her defiant chin at her brother. "Yankees can't shoot well enough to hit Santa Claus. That's a fact."

Hardin knew Agnes had just lied because too many Franklin and Williamson County boys would not be returning home when the war ended, all victims of Yankee aim. "Momma, Agnes told a fib, too."

"Hush, both of you," commanded their mother, staring at Hardin.

Standing behind her mother, Agnes stuck her tongue out at him. Hardin answered in kind, drawing a swat across the cheek from his mother and a smirk from his sister. "Don't stick your tongue out in this house, Hardin."

"But Agnes—"

Before Hardin could finish, Bethenia grabbed and twisted his ear. "Enough said, Hardin Perkins Figuers. Drop it."

"Then let go of my ear," he protested.

When his mother released her grip, Hardin quickly rubbed his lobe to confirm it remained intact. Agnes strode around him, as innocent as an angel listening to a church sermon. Oh, how he missed her, even if she got him in trouble more times than he could remember. As he looked outside at the white veil of snow and sleet, he wished she were still here so he could ambush her with a snowball. Certainly, she would have tattled to momma, but that was the fun of having a know-it-all sister. Agnes was now with their father, who had died when Hardin was five years old. Unlike other boys his age, Hardin never worried about losing his dad to a Yankee bullet or a camp disease. His father had already passed by the war's start, and Hardin had little recollection of him. Though engulfed by war, the Figuers family endured losses from disease rather than battle.

As he stared out the window through the gap in the damask curtains, he studied Carter's Creek Pike just south of his home, and wished for a break in the weather. The street remained as empty as the smokehouses around Franklin, their meats taken mostly by Yankees as much for mischief as hunger and occasionally by Confederates, whose rations never seemed to match those that the Union army wasted. Hardin wearied of his imprisonment in the house with his mother and Mary Louisa, who was struggling under her momma's watchful gaze to knit a pair of mittens for the frigid months ahead. His older brother Tom sat on the sofa reading a volume of *The History of the Anglo Saxons*, one book his lawyer father had added to their modest library before he died.

Though Tom was of an age to shoulder arms for the Confederacy, their mother Bethenia had fudged on his years, saying he was twelve months younger than he actually was. She did not care to lose a son to a cause whose outcome she doubted since the fall of Atlanta. Of course, Tom was not as adventuresome as Hardin, preferring the solitary companionship of a book to the comradery of fighting men. Rather than read, Hardin wished he could go hunting with his slingshot. Once the war started, he had put plenty of meat—squirrel, rabbit, quail, and dove—on the family table with his stone shooter. Hardin had even sent a squad of Yankee infantry scurrying with his slingshot. His mother, though, berated him for his valor, fearing the Yankees might shoot him if they realized Hardin had shot down the hornet's nest that put the skedaddle in them near the locust grove where the foot soldiers had bivouacked.

Hardin turned from the window and sighed. When would it end, the weather, the war, the deprivation? He asked himself those questions, hoping only that the fighting lasted long enough for him to taste battle firsthand. Tough and sorrowful as times were, he knew his widowed mother had managed better than many, scrimping by on the modest estate left by her husband and eliminating frills like Christmas gifts, especially when they were scarce in number or exorbitant in price. "Christmas is four weeks from today," Hardin announced out of boredom.

"So it is," answered his mother. "Another slim one it will be, children. Maybe some rock candy, but nothing else."

Mary Louisa dropped her knitting in her lap. "Did the Yankees shoot Santa Claus again?" she asked, staring at her youngest brother. "I can't believe you told me that, Hardin. Only time I cried more was when Agnes died." Her eyes welled with tears.

Hardin thought he saw a glint in his mother's eyes as well, but she looked toward the fireplace and continued darning the sock. "Yankees were shooting everybody else, Mary Louisa, so why not Santa Claus?"

"Because he's imaginary, Hardin."

"So the Yankees couldn't have killed him anyway."

Mary Louisa sighed as her shoulders drooped. "I didn't know that then, Hardin."

"I can't help what you don't know, Mary Louisa."

Bethenia clucked her throat. "No more arguing, you two. There's enough fighting in this world as it is without us adding to the conflict."

Mary Louisa jutted out her chin. "I wish Agnes was here to side with me. I miss her."

"We all do," Bethenia answered. "Let's talk about something else, or not talk at all."

Hardin strode past his mother, backing up to the fireplace to warm himself after standing near the cold window. "Do you think it's true what the grapevine telegraph is saying? Do you believe General Hood will march our boys through Franklin on the way to Nashville?"

"Likely, just gossip," she replied. "General Hood couldn't hold Atlanta, so why should we think he can take Nashville?"

"Why not, Momma? Isn't God on our side or is He just as imaginary as Santa Claus?"

"Hardin Perkins Figuers, don't say such things, not under this roof, nor under the sky that God has provided us." Bethenia shook her darning egg at her son. "Never again do I want to hear such blasphemous talk in this house."

From his sofa seat, Tom lowered the top of his book and frowned at Hardin, as if to say don't rile mother, but Hardin couldn't take advice from a sibling old enough to enlist on his own without his mother's permission, yet stayed home to avoid the danger.

"Whose side is God on, Momma?" Hardin crossed his arms over his chest, stepping from the hearth.

Bethenia exhaled a frustrated breath.

"Whose side?" Hardin awaited her answer with his chin jutted forward.

"The side of the righteous."

"Then He's on our side!" Hardin stamped his shoe on the carpet in triumph.

"Only God knows who is truly righteous. To question Him is blasphemous."

"When I am of age, I'll fight, regardless of what God thinks or what you think, Momma. I don't want to hide my head behind a book and pretend I'm still too young to wear a uniform and carry a gun." Hardin stared at Tom, waiting for the shame to wash across his face and flush his cheeks, but Tom just kept reading.

Bethenia returned her gaze to the sock, darning egg, and darning needle, then resumed her handiwork.

"I don't care to become an old man who didn't do what he could for the cause. I want to see battle, Momma."

Tom slammed his book shut and glared at Hardin. When he spoke, his words carried menace. "If the gossip is true, you may see battle yet. Both armies must pass through Franklin on the way to Nashville. Attack my courage all you want, Hardin, but many courageous boys I once knew are now dead, twenty-seven by my last count. Whether the Confederacy wins or loses, Tennessee will need whole men to rebuild it."

Bethenia turned to her elder son. "Do you think the Union army will pass through Franklin, Tom?"

"Highly likely, I'd say."

The matriarch looked at Hardin.

"If the Yankees return, I don't want any mischief from you," she scolded. "Times are dangerous. Do you understand?"

"Yes, ma'am."

"I don't want you shooting down any hornet's nests with your slingshot."

Hardin laughed. "You should've seen them run, Momma. They high-tailed it out of their camp like a blue-bellied stampede."

"I said don't shoot any more hornet's nests around them, Hardin Perkins Figuers."

Hardin grimaced. "Momma, it's winter. The hornets have disappeared for the season. They won't return until spring."

"It's the mischief I don't want you involved in. I can't think of all the things you can do with your slingshot. Promise me you won't do anything foolish, like shooting a horse on the rump or stinging a cavalryman with a stone shot."

Grinning, Hardin shook his head. "That's a great idea, Momma. Thanks for passing it along."

"You know what I mean, Hardin Perkins Figuers. No mischief, and that's final."

Hardin knew he was licked. "Yes, ma'am. No mischief, not until I can enlist on my own, at least."

Patrick Cleburne
Camp near Columbia

Major General Patrick Cleburne awoke to the splatter of raindrops pelting the canvas of his tent and to the annoyance of the interminable itch in his cheek. A dose of melancholy dulled his spirit more than the infernal weather. Two months earlier to the day on September twenty-seventh, Cleburne had reported to John Bell Hood's headquarters with a simple request. After a hundred and twenty straight days of maneuver and combat against William Tecumseh Sherman's armies, the opposing forces had separated to pursue new strategies, Sherman marching through Georgia and Hood starting for Tennessee with the goal of taking Nashville, conquering Kentucky, and challenging Ohio itself. Hood expected his victories and his threat to Ohio would force Abraham Lincoln to recognize the Confederacy and end the war.

Except for desultory raids meant to harass Sherman's rear guard and supply lines, major combat had stopped in the aftermath of the Southern losses around Atlanta as Hood developed his strategy to save the South and elevate his reputation for battlefield mastery to the heights earned by Robert E. Lee. With the armies moving in different directions with dissimilar goals, Cleburne on that autumn afternoon requested Hood's approval of a two-week furlough.

Cleburne had marriage on his mind. His commander had victory in his head. Patrick Ronayne Cleburne desired to wed Susan Tarleton in Mobile. John Bell Hood vowed to imbue the Army of Tennessee with his fighting spirit and lead the men to triumph, himself to glory, and the South to independence. Cleburne had requested and received only two leaves since the war began, the first to serve as best man in General Hardee's wedding, where he had first met Susan Tarleton, and the second to ask for her hand in matrimony. She had agreed, and that September day with hostilities unlikely for weeks, if not longer, Cleburne had visited his commander to make his entreaty for his third leave. Wearing his laundered and pressed uniform, he stood smartly at his commander's desk.

"General, I've come to ask for a two-week furlough for the purpose of marriage."

Still smarting from his losses around Atlanta, Hood scowled. "I need you here, ready to battle," Hood informed him.

"Union forces are days away from us, heading in the opposite direction, and we will be going into winter camp soon. Please reconsider, sir."

"Some commanders might use winter as an excuse not to fight, but not me," Hood answered. "We'll catch the Yankees sleeping."

"Ammunition and provisions will be harder to supply in cold weather," Cleburne responded. "The quartermaster has a tough enough job keeping us supplied as is."

Hood slammed his good right fist on the desk. "Once I can get my soldiers to fight like men, we will win Southern independence."

"Our men have comported themselves admirably in battle, sir, especially given the overwhelming numbers they've faced."

"Balderdash, General Cleburne. They need more grit in their craw. Beyond that, I can't spare you for two weeks."

"I'll modify my request to ten days, sir, and leave tomorrow. No encounter of significance will occur in that short of a time, not with Sherman heading toward the Atlantic and us moving toward Nashville."

"The answer is no," Hood said curtly, again pounding the desk with his hand, then waving it at the door. "You're dismissed!"

For an instant, Cleburne considered offering his resignation. He would rather serve as a foot soldier under Hardee than a general under Hood, but Cleburne could not abandon the troops who had been so loyal to him. After his moment of doubt, Cleburne offered his commander a crisp salute, turned, and exited the headquarters.

Cleburne's face simmered with anger. His troops had saved the Army of Tennessee multiple times, and while he was proud to command the best division in the Western Theater, all soldiers, regardless of their units, deserved the respect of their leader. Cleburne's resentment turned to rage when a fellow Arkansan on Hood's staff accompanied him outside to his horse and handed him a penciled copy of the telegram the commander had sent to Jefferson Davis after Atlanta fell. "Had the officers and men of the army done what was expected of them, I would've saved Atlanta," the missive stated, among other excuses.

The general thanked his acquaintance for sharing the message, mounted his horse, and rode back to his division. As he retreated to his troops, Cleburne wondered if the rumors were true that Hood took laudanum to deal with the pain of his injuries. He considered the gossip, then dismissed it. The opiate would surely have improved

Hood's judgment of his men and his own capabilities as a commander. When the Georgia pines screened his view from Hood's headquarters, he wadded up the paper and tossed it away. He returned to his tent and wrote his betrothed of the discouraging news, seeking her patience and understanding of military matters.

That was sixty-one days ago, Cleburne recalled, and not a single skirmish of note had occurred in the interim. He could've enjoyed a two-month furlough and an extended honeymoon with Susan Tarleton during that span with no damage to the Confederacy. To ease his gloom from the loneliness and the continuing rain, he arose from his cot and moved to his uniform, extracting Susan's handkerchief and inhaling her sweet perfume. Returning the frail cloth to his suit, he dressed, then sat at his field desk and wrote a short note to Susan, telling her he loved her more than ever and longed for the day they could march down the aisle as man and wife, then stroll hand-in-hand toward their future. Though he was tired of war and its cruelties, he avoided revealing his weariness, preferring to sound uplifting without adding to Susan's worries about what lay ahead for the South. He read his letter again, relieved he had not added to his fiancée's concerns, but disappointed he failed to convey his feelings more eloquently to his dear one.

Accepting that he could not pen a more expressive note, he put down his pen, blotted the paper, then folded it. As he inserted it into the envelope, he heard the voice of his aide-de-camp.

"Morning, General," Lieutenant Leonard H. Mangum said, opening the tent flap and poking his head inside. "Writing orders, I see."

Cleburne felt his cheeks flush. Mangum knew he always wrote Susan at the start of each day, but offered such folderol just to see him blush, though never in the presence of others when it might embarrass him.

Mangum reached for the letter. "Should I read your directive of the day to the men, General?"

Cleburne yanked the envelope to his chest. "You know better than that, Leonard."

The lieutenant answered with a smile and a quip, "Matters of the heart rather than matters of the army."

"You well know what it is."

"And I'd be honored to send it on its way to the lovely Miss Tarleton, though I suspect you'd prefer to deliver it in person."

Cleburne sighed. "Two months ago today, General Hood denied my request for a leave to marry her, saying battle was forthcoming.

Nothing's happened since then other than talk and tarry by General Hood." Cleburne placed the envelope on the writing desk and picked up the candle, angling it over the flap for the dripping wax to seal the letter. Replacing the taper in the holder, he blew on the wax until it congealed. He offered the correspondence to his aide. "Please post this letter."

The lieutenant took it and tucked it inside his blouse. "I'll keep it dry. Wouldn't want the ink to get wet and run, or Miss Tarleton might think it's from your tears."

Cleburne felt his face flush again, but he disguised his embarrassment by scratching the itch around the purple scar on his left cheek. "The rain'll stop one day, though the tears will continue for years after this war ends. Too many lost for too little gain."

Mangum nodded.

"Will you affix a stamp to the letter, Leonard?"

"I always do, sir, because I understand why you don't keep stamps."

"Thank you." As the postage of the Confederacy was printed with a lithograph of Jefferson Davis, Cleburne cringed at the image of the man who had reprimanded him for merely suggesting slaves be freed to fight for the Confederacy. Had Davis explored that option earlier in the year, its implementation might have delivered some victories that would have demoralized the Yankee populace and perhaps changed the outcome of the November election. But the voters preferred Lincoln and more death, giving the president over two hundred electoral votes—more than he received in 1860—and a second term to continue his policy of Southern destruction. Four years earlier, Lincoln had received just under two million votes, less than forty percent of the national total. Earlier this month, he had claimed fifty-five percent of the ballots and over two million votes. It seemed as if the Yankee military dead had returned from the grave to vote him back into office.

Unlike Lincoln, Jefferson Davis had not been elected by Southern voters. Instead, delegates to the Confederacy's constitutional convention had unanimously voted him the provisional president of the new nation. Cleburne wondered how many votes Davis might garner in an election on this rainy day. The slave owners would all cast ballots for him, most certainly, but the men who did the fighting would not. And, if women could vote, Cleburne knew not a mother one would support him. The mothers had lost too many husbands and sons.

"After you post the letter for me, Leonard, please return. I want you to inform my brigade commanders to meet with me in my tent at three o'clock this afternoon, once I have an idea of what our objectives will be in the coming days."

"Yes, sir."

"Now, please attend to my correspondence before the rain gets any worse."

"Will do, sir." Mangum slipped outside the tent and scurried off in the downpour.

For several minutes, Cleburne sat on his camp stool, wondering what fate had in store for him and his men today other than another soaking. After a burst of rainfall peppered his tent, Cleburne arose to step to the entrance of his canvas shelter. He brushed the canvas flap aside and looked across the bivouac where his men protected themselves as best they could from the downpour.

Cleburne studied the low clouds spilling the tears of the Confederacy on Tennessee and wondered if the sun would ever again shine on the South. And, on him and Susan!

Mary Alice Carter McPhail
Carter Home

Missing church bothered Mary Alice McPhail, especially when so many prayers were needed to revive the Confederacy. Since July of 1863, it seemed God had answered no prayer for the South. In the intervening months, countless Southern women had dyed their dresses black in mourning for a lost husband or sweetheart. In the ensuing sixteen months after the fall of Gettysburg and Vicksburg that July, spirits had sagged across the South with little to lift the hopes of soldier and citizen. This very month had started with the great optimism among Southerners, who prayed that Abraham Lincoln would lose his re-election bid to Democrat George B. McClellan, a former Union general who understood the price of battle unlike Lincoln, who had never led troops in this war nor experienced its battlefield devastation. But yet again, God had failed to answer the South's fervent prayers as McClellan won only Kentucky, Delaware, and his home state of New Jersey. Fifty-five percent of Northern voters cast their ballots for more war, when all the South wanted was for the Yankee troops to go back to their own homes and leave Southern people alone. Even the vote in Union-occupied portions of Louisiana, which had shed blood for the Confederacy from the beginning, went to Old Abe, though it was certainly a crooked ballot count. Mary Alice knew so many prayers must be answered soon or the final sands would fall through the hourglass of the Confederacy.

This last Sunday in November, the Confederacy needed prayers now more than ever for Hood's and Robert E. Lee's armies, but the weather lingered cold, wet, and blustery. Getting the Carter family dressed and to the church dry was an impossible task, much like sorting out the rumors drifting north from Columbia about Hood's and Schofield's armies. Too, the Carters now possessed only two remaining draft horses for plowing and transportation, the rest being impressed by the Union army. Those two draft horses were all that remained of Fountain Carter's working stock. They would be necessary to plow the fields come spring or the family might starve next fall and winter.

After breakfast, Mary Alice herded the children up from the basement into the parlor and conducted an impromptu Sunday school lesson, talking about the miracle of David against Goliath. Then she taught them a new song she had learned from Winnie Nichols, who was a legend around town for her answer to a Northern officer that Sunday morning when Yankees first stained Franklin's streets. As she stood on the steps of her venerable Main Street home, a Union captain drew up in front of the women, tipped his hat, and inquired of the Harpeth River, "Ladies, what beautiful stream is that?"

"That, sir," replied Winnie, "is second Bull Run, and you are on your way to second Manassas."

Enraged by the smirk of an answer referring to the most recent Union defeat back east, the officer plopped his hat back on his head and pulled his sword, waving it at Winnie, who jutted her chin forward in a silent dare for him to strike her. Nearby officers heard the remark and laughed, shaming the swordsman for his poor sense of humor. He sheathed his saber and rode past Winnie's defiant and smirking gaze.

Winnie had learned of a new hymn called "Jesus Loves Me" and sung it for Mary Alice, who caught on to the tune and wrote down the words to share with the children. After relating how David smote Goliath with a stone in his slingshot, Mary Alice took the sheet with the song lyrics from the sitting table at her side and hummed the melody for the kids, then provided them with the lyrics a line at a time. The little ones liked the song and picked it up quickly. They sang joyously and enthusiastically. After the song, Mary Alice said a closing prayer asking for blessings upon the South and special protection for her husband and her brother. As soon as she finished the prayer, the kids jumped up and scurried about the house, Mary Alice smiling as she heard Lena and Adelaide singing the new song.

After the Bible lesson, Mary Alice sat in the front room, thinking back to Winnie Nichols' victory over the invading officer. It was memorable because there had been so few such victories since. After that Sunday morning arrival of the Union army, Yankee soldiers had passed through town frequently, sometimes camping around the city and harassing citizens with their drunkenness, their foul language, and their unending arrogance in searching houses and taking what they wanted, but they never found the basement cache at the Carter residence.

That fall of 1862 after the Yankees had departed Franklin for a spell, a detachment of Rebel cavalry six hundred strong rode through town. Though it was evening, Franklin folks showed little emotion for fear Northern sympathizers among them might identify them to Union officials intent on crushing the spirit and soul of the rebellion. By that time, Mary Alice had tired of watching the ever-changing string of soldiers—friend or foe—passing on Columbia Pike outside their front door. She was reading her Bible that night in her room when her sister Fanny came to tell her a cavalryman had asked for her by name. Bewildered and frightened the soldier might bring bad news about her husband, Mary Alice bolted up, dropped her Bible in the chair, and scurried with her sibling to the front door where the fellow awaited.

Mary Alice glanced at Fanny. "Are you sure he wanted to see *me*?"

She nodded. "That's what he said, Mrs. Mary Alice Carter McPhail."

Fear surged even stronger through her body that this messenger carried word that her husband had been wounded or killed. Her hand trembling, Mary Alice opened the door and saw a slender man in a dirty Confederate uniform, his head lowered so the broad brim of his hat hid his face.

"Yes," she said, "I'm Mrs. Mary Alice Carter McPhail."

Slowly, the man lifted his chin. "I'm your husband."

Mary Alice screamed and flung herself into his arms, smothering his whiskered cheeks and lips with kisses. Daniel carried her inside, closing the door behind him with his boot as other family members rushed to see what raised the commotion. Fount Carter came into the parlor with a pistol at his side, ready to protect his daughter.

"It's Daniel," Mary Alice cried. "Children, your father's here."

Adelaide and Marcus, both under seven at the time, approached their dad, who released Mary Alice and squatted down to greet and hug them. The two children flew into his arms, returning his affection. Releasing them, he stood up, kissing Mary Alice on her cheek.

"I can't stay long, maybe an hour, no more than an hour and a half," he said.

"Would you like something to eat, Daniel?" Mary Alice asked.

"If you can spare it, but what I'd really like is a bath and a shave if it wouldn't be too much trouble," he replied, releasing his wife and removing his hat.

"And your uniform needs a washing," Mary Alice observed.

"Don't have time for that."

"I'll get started," Mary Alice answered and turned to leave, but Fanny grabbed her arm.

"You stay with Daniel," she said. "We'll tend to food, laundry, and your children."

Mary Alice motioned for Daniel to be seated in the parlor, but he declined. "I'm too dirty, and I've been sitting in the saddle all day."

Save for their son and daughter, the rest of the family left the parlor to make hurried preparations for their special visitor. Within twenty minutes, Fanny returned and invited Daniel to step to the basement for a quick supper of pan-fried ham, cold potatoes, pickles, and bread.

"It was the best Callie could do on short notice," Fanny announced as she herded the couple and their children toward the basement table.

Daniel sat on a bench seat, lowered his head in prayer, then lifted his chin, and took a bite. "Tell Callie thank you," he said to Fanny.

"You tell her, Daniel. She's heating water for your bath. Father's stropping his razor for you as well. When you're done, run to the cookhouse."

Mary Alice studied her husband, then sat beside him. "You've lost weight."

"All of us have."

His son and daughter moved to the table, stood on the bench seat opposite him and leaned over the table to watch their father devour everything in front of him. As soon as he was finished, he and Mary Alice stood up, leaving the basement and heading to the cookhouse. "Adelaide and Marcus, you follow your Aunt Fanny upstairs and do what she says." Mary Alice paused, then turned to her sister. "Keep the children out of my room until Daniel leaves."

"For goodness sakes, why?" Fanny winked and left, herding Marcus and Adelaide up the steps.

At the cooking shed, Daniel thanked Callie for fixing the quick meal. "It's the best I've had in months." He pointed to the tin tub. "And thank you for heating me bathwater."

"Yes, suh, my honor to helps a fightin' man," Callie answered, then left the couple alone.

Mary Alice helped her husband undress and bathe. He shaved in the tub, then she assisted him in drying him off with a pair of towels Callie had left.

"Get dressed and we can spend some time in my room, Daniel."

Daniel shook his head. "No."

Mary Alice drooped in disappointment until he explained.

"I don't want to put those dirty things back on until we've visited. I'll run to the house with the towels. You bring my drawers, pants, and boots. I'll return for the rest later."

Together they bolted to the dwelling, slipping inside Mary Alice's room, opening onto the porch beside the room her father and Moscow shared. Alone for a brief spell, they shared intimate moments together.

They lay silently beside each other until Daniel finally spoke. "I don't want to go, but I must." Arising, he pulled on his underwear and pants, then fished his socks out of his boots and slid them on before jerking his boots over his feet.

Mary Alice dressed as Daniel ran to the cookhouse and put on his shirt, hat, gun belt, and revolver. They met on the back porch, kissed passionately, then slipped inside, offering hurried goodbyes to everyone. Holding his son's and daughter's hands, Daniel walked to the front door. There, he gave Adelaide and Marcus a hug and a kiss, telling them to be good and to mind their mother. Then he wrapped his arms around Mary Alice and planted a hard kiss on her lips.

"I'm Kentucky-bound, so let that last until this war is over," he said. "I love you, sweet Mary Alice."

She waved as he bounded down the steps, untied his horse, mounted, and galloped into the darkness. Mary Alice had not seen him since, nor had he seen his young son who arrived nine months later. The arrival of little Orlando or "Lannie," as the children dubbed him, caused considerable gossip among the community's nosey women, but Mary Alice ignored the talk, for she knew she had committed no sin against God nor against her marriage vows. Further, she had brought into the world a new baby that offered a little joy to the family in a time of so much sorrow.

After Daniel's departure, periodic Confederate incursions blessed Franklin as Southern troops headed elsewhere, but mostly Yankees tormented the town with scouting missions, passing troops, supply trains, and occasional occupations. One Yankee commander, fearing an attack by bushwhackers on his way to Nashville, had rounded up a dozen Franklin men and marched them as human shields in front of his unit halfway to Nashville before releasing them in Brentwood. Then the turnpike bridge over the Harpeth was burned, some said by Rebel cavalry, others blaming Union arsonists.

During the ensuing winter while Confederate troops gathered at Murfreesboro, nine thousand Yankee soldiers occupied Franklin, building an earthen fortress on a bluff across the Harpeth River and moving in artillery to command the valley. Thirty-five cannons in Fort Granger, as it was dubbed in honor of the Union Commander Major General Gordon Granger, menaced Franklin and the surrounding valley. That April Union troops from Fort Granger fought General Nathan Bedford Forrest's cavalry south of town. Few if any bullets struck the Carter home, but just south of the residence Yankee soldiers dug modest trenches on both sides of the Columbia Pike to fend off the Confederates if they came closer. A handful of men had died or been wounded in or around those trenches, but nothing on the scale of Shiloh or Chickamauga. Those eroded trenches nineteen months later still scarred the Carter farmland.

That skirmish brought hope that the Confederates would soon reclaim Franklin, but it was not to be, as the Yankees still controlled the town and issued military justice. The ensuing June the Yankees hanged two Rebel spies from a wild cherry tree near Franklin's railroad depot. Rather than execute them on the grounds of Fort Granger, the Yankees made a public spectacle of the lynching to send a message to the town's citizens. With hundreds of Yankees in parade formation to watch the condemned men die, the invaders loaded them into the back of a wagon under the tree, placed nooses around their necks, secured the ropes over a sturdy limb, and drove the wagon out from under their feet. The strangling spies thrashed at the end of the swaying rope before falling still. The officers let the men hang for more than half an hour before cutting them down and dropping them into their coffins, which they loaded into the same dray from which the deceased had stepped into eternity. Sympathetic citizens followed the wagon to the cemetery to pay their respects, much to the disgust of the Union soldiers. Oddly, the two executed spies were lucky, for they were buried in wooden coffins, when so many others who had died since Fort Sumter were merely thrown in the ground in what they wore, assuming scavengers hadn't stripped them naked.

By the summer of 1863 when the hanging occurred and Mary Alice's Lannie was born, Williamson County showed the ghostly scars of war with homes ransacked, fences destroyed, horses stolen, cattle butchered for beef, provisions stolen from houses, and citizens living in fear of what might happen next. On some farms, the blue-bellies had chopped up wagons—sometimes for firewood but often for spite—or broken hoes, rakes, and shovels, or cut harnesses into useless pieces of leather, or battered plows into unsalvageable fragments of wood and iron. On other occasions, the Yankees even destroyed the crops in family fields. Mary Alice thanked God that her father managed to hide their two draft horses and plow from marauding Yankees so they could grow a large garden that kept his family fed and assisted several neighbors.

Just six months earlier, as their 1864 garden was filling out with spring growth, a detachment of Union cavalry rode down the Columbia Pike from town. Seeing them, Fount Carter had dashed to the toolshed, grabbed a pitchfork, and rushed into the garden as a dozen men and their captain peeled off from the southbound troops and started toward the vegetable patch. Fearing for her father, Mary Alice raced after him and watched the encounter.

"Get off my property," Carter yelled, waving the pitchfork at the trespassers, "and leave my garden alone."

The captain scowled, turning to his men and issuing his order. "Soldiers, prepare to trample this Secesh garden."

"I can't let you do it," Carter announced. "I'll die before I let you take food from the mouths of my family."

All the soldiers laughed.

"A pitchfork against sabers, pistols, and carbines, old man?" responded the captain.

"I'm doing you Yankees a favor," Carter shouted back.

"How's that?" asked the perplexed officer.

"If I let you fellows trample my garden, there won't be anything for you to steal come harvesting time."

The officer's stern gaze cracked with a smile. He turned to his soldiers. "Let's move on and leave his garden alone. Spread the word that no one is to touch it." Then he saluted Fount Carter. "We'll see you for supper this fall, old man." He yanked the reins on his horse and rejoined the devil's detachment on its march south.

As Mary Alice recalled the encounter, she realized her brother Moscow's wisdom in identifying the genuine heroes of this war as the men who protected their homes and families. While soldiers fought over politics, her father had made a stand over family. She felt safer with him around, even if he was old. She took her Bible to the front window and looked outside. The rain seemed to be slowing. Perhaps sunshine would brighten their Monday, and the weather would clear so the next Sunday they could return to church. Mary Alice knew the Confederacy needed prayer.

Rev. Charles T. Quintard
Hamilton Place

Reverend Quintard smiled at the gathering in Lucius Polk's parlor. Guests occupied every chair or stood around the walls, awaiting his sermon. Even General John Bell Hood, who had visited with Lucius Polk the previous afternoon, returned and sat in a seat by the door so he would not cause a disturbance if he departed to attend to army matters. This would be Quintard's first full sermon since returning to Tennessee. Somehow, it all seemed appropriate that it should come on Advent Sunday, the opening day of the liturgical year, and with General Hood in attendance.

With 1865 just a little over a month away, Quintard thought Hood's presence might be a sign of renewed hope for the Confederacy and its independence. Once the people of the South renounced their sins, perhaps then they could claim the victories that might be theirs in the next year. Quintard smiled when he saw his manservant Henry standing with two of the house servants in the parlor entry near Hood. The reverend had requested permission from Lucius Polk for Henry to attend and listen. Polk had agreed, provided two of his house slaves could stand with him in case his manners needed correcting, as the host hoped to avoid an embarrassing moment in his home from a darkie unrefined in the ways of house servants. Quintard knew Henry's attendance might be a risk, but he sought to provide for the youth's salvation, and build a moral foundation for his future in this world and the world beyond.

After Lucius Polk looked around the room and confirmed that all his family and friends were present, he nodded to the reverend. Quintard smiled and stepped before the gathering, offering a prayer and then inviting the worshippers to join him in singing "Amazing Grace." At first, he planned to ask the celebrants to stand, then realized the difficulty it would be for Hood to arise, so he let them sing in their seats. When they finished the final stanza, Quintard started with the baptisms.

"As today is Advent Sunday," he began, "this is a special occasion for our worship as we anticipate the coming of Christmas to rejoice the birth of our Lord and Savior. Over the next four Sundays, men of the cloth of all Christian denominations will consider the virtues of love, joy, hope, and peace. Today we will celebrate all four as the esteemed Lucius Polk has asked that I baptize the newest members of his family, both his niece and his grandson. With their parents' permission, I am honored to conduct the sacrament of baptism for babies Caroline and Henry."

Quintard thought it providential that the baby boy shared the same given name as his manservant, who stood on his tiptoes in the doorway watching as Caroline's parents carried forward their daughter in her white christening gown.

"In this infant, we find the love of her family and the joy of her smile. She offers the hope of a new and innocent generation to move us past our present difficulties. And, her innocence reminds us of the peace that must surely arrive in the coming year." Quintard next blessed the child, sprinkling her forehead with water in the name of the Father, the Son, and the Holy Ghost. The reverend said a prayer for Caroline's future well-being as a devotee of Jesus Christ.

After her parents took Caroline to their seats, baby Henry came to the front in the arms of his mother. The infant squawked, drawing frowns from his parents, but a gentle smile from Quintard. "So much for peace from this young one," he said, "but we will settle for love, joy, and hope in his life, as those virtues will ultimately bring peace for young Henry and for us as well." After blessing the little boy, Quintard sprinkled him with water and said a prayer for his future. As Henry's family returned to their places, Quintard asked the worshippers to join him in the first two verses of "Holy, Holy, Holy!"

After the hymn, Quintard opened his Bible, announcing he would preach from Psalms 91:1-13. He read the verses to the believers.

> *He that dwelleth in the secret place of the Most High Shall abide under the shadow of the Almighty.*
>
> *I will say of the Lord, He is my refuge and my fortress: My God; in him will I trust.*
>
> *Surely he shall deliver thee from the snare of the fowler, and from the noisome pestilence.*

*He shall cover thee with his feathers,
and under his wings shalt thou trust: His
truth shall be thy shield and buckler.*

*Thou shalt not be afraid for the terror
by night; nor for the arrow that flieth by
day;*

*Nor for the pestilence that walketh in
darkness; nor for the destruction that
wasteth at noonday.*

*A thousand shall fall at thy side, and ten
thousand at thy right hand; but it shall not
come nigh thee.*

*Only with thine eyes shalt thou behold
and see the reward of the wicked.*

*Because thou hast made the Lord, which
is my refuge, even the most High, thy
habitation;*

*There shall no evil befall thee, neither
shall any plague come nigh thy dwelling.*

*For he shall give his angels charge over
thee, to keep thee in all thy ways.*

*They shall bear thee up in their hands,
lest thou dash thy foot against a stone.*

*Thou shalt tread upon the lion and
adder: The young lion and the dragon
shalt thou trample under feet.*

Quintard finished the scripture and gently closed the Bible, smiling at those assembled before him. "God is our refuge in times of fear, and He will carry us through all the hazards surrounding us. By believing in Him, all of us will see our fears lifted by His firm hand. Trust in God will deliver us from all threats upon us as individuals and against us as a young nation. Through our faith, we shall entrust ourselves to His protection. Through our devotion to Him, we shall remain safe and we shall remain free to worship as we please and to govern as we must for the survival of our cause."

The reverend spent ten minutes elaborating on the need for repentance and faithfulness to earn God's protection and then turned to verse eleven, which promised God would give his angels charge over any person of such faith. Quintard thought it a bad omen when two soldiers came into the parlor, whispered something in Hood's ear, then helped their commander up from his seat and out of the parlor.

Once Hood departed, Quintard didn't know whether to be pleased or embarrassed that Henry had climbed onto Hood's empty chair and stood on the seat to see better.

"We have had setbacks as a young nation," the reverend continued. "No one among us has not felt the loss of a loved one, a friend, or a neighbor. And yet, we must trudge forward through the difficulties ahead. Though I fear more men must die until we achieve independence, I truly believe God recognizes our repentance and stands to provide the divine protection that will be our salvation as a nation. As we march forward, I have faith that God will provide an angel to watch over our shoulders and direct us to the victory that is surely the reward of a cause as righteous as ours."

"Amen," called Lucius Polk, others among his family echoing his word.

The words of affirmation touched Quintard, and he bowed his head, saying a silent prayer to God, offering his thanks for the opportunity to again preach, especially to an audience that counted women and children among its worshippers. So much of his preaching over the last few years had been to men only, often grim-faced soldiers on the precipice of their own mortality. It invigorated him to see women of all ages and their antsy children sitting before him and listening to the Word of God. Quintard hoped his sermon conveyed optimism about the days of battle ahead and the ultimate triumph of righteousness over wickedness.

"Now," he said, "would you please stand and bow your heads for our benediction?"

Waiting until all stood and lowered their chins, Quintard prayed, "Dear God, we come humbly to You on this Advent Sunday, glorifying your name and that of your Holy Son. We beseech You for the strength to do Thy will in the days ahead, the wisdom to always take the righteous path in securing our independence, and the courage to stand up against wickedness in all its manifestations. Provide our political leaders, our generals, and our soldiers with guardian angels to watch over them in the weeks ahead. Bless them all with your protection and grant the same security to all those gathered here today to hear the glory of your Holy Word. Amen."

Polk rushed up and grabbed Quintard's hand to congratulate him on an uplifting sermon. "You've given this old man hope, Reverend."

"And your family has invigorated me with your hospitality and the baptism of the two young ones. Tennessee has a glorious future once we get past our current difficulty. And, thank you for allowing my boy Henry to listen to the sermon, even if he did stand on your chair to see. I want him to follow in the ways of the Lord."

"Despite soiling the chair seat, your Henry was muted and respectful, especially for a darkie his age. After we have Sunday dinner, you're welcome to stay the night with us again, Reverend."

"I am tempted, I admit, but I cannot impose any more upon your hospitality than I already have. I must re-join the army and fulfill my duties to the soldiers, but before I do, I need to enter the names of your grandson and niece in the baptismal registry of your church."

"St. John's is nearby, just off the pike. I can have one of my servants accompany you."

"Completely unnecessary, General. I know the place and the way. I buried a wonderful friend there a few months back. I will have my Henry pack my things and saddle our mount. We will depart after Sunday dinner."

Quintard and his host exited the parlor behind the crowd. Henry waited outside the door. The reverend handed him his Bible. "Please, Henry, put this in my canvas bag and pack my things in the room. We'll be leaving after we eat."

"Yas, suh," he replied. "So's I needs to saddles de horse."

"That's good, Henry, thinking ahead like that."

"I's obliged for de fine words, Massa Revrund."

"Run along, Henry, and I'll join you in the barn after dinner."

Quintard eased his way to the dining room, accepting the handshakes and best wishes of the worshippers thanking him for his message of hope. With so many family members attending the sermon, the visitors ate in shifts. In the first group, Quintard seated himself and blessed the food at Polk's request. The food was abundant, especially for three years into the war, but Quintard took small portions from the platters of fried chicken and bowls of succotash and stewed carrots, so plenty would remain for those to follow. He took an extra chicken wing and a biscuit, which he sat on the side of his plate, telling his host he would take it for supper, if he did not object.

"How could I deny such a trivial matter to a man of God who baptized my grandson and niece?"

As soon as the first shift finished the meal, Quintard arose from the table, slipping the chicken wing and the biscuit in his pants pocket. He exited the dining room as house servants cleared the dirty dishes and replaced them with clean ones for the next shift. Quintard said his goodbyes, then dashed upstairs and checked that Henry had taken his belongings. Grabbing his coat and hat, he slipped downstairs, through the kitchen and out the door, scurrying through the icy rain toward the stables, where Henry stood in the doorway, holding the reins to their mount.

"Have you had any Sunday dinner, Henry?"

"A few walnuts, Massa Revrund. Dat's all. White folks gots de good stuff."

Entering the structure, Quintard reached into his pocket and pulled out the biscuit and chicken wing. "Here's something for you. Maybe we'll do better for supper."

Henry grabbed the offering. "I's be grateful, yas suh, I's do." Handing the reins to Quintard, the boy wolfed down the grub.

"You shouldn't gobble down your food, Henry. It's not acceptable manners."

Henry chomped on his meal and gulped it down anyway. "Yas, suh, Massa Revrund," he said, gasping for breath, "buts manners be of no account when I's hungry."

Quintard tousled Henry's nappy hair. "You have a way, Henry B. Free, of putting things in perspective for me."

"Glad to, long as youse puts grub in me belly."

"Where's your gum blanket, Henry? You'll need it in this weather."

Henry darted to a stall in the stable and yanked it off a nail, spinning about and returning to the reverend, who checked that his carpetbag and bedroll had been secured to the saddle.

"Good job, Henry," Quintard said as he stuck his left foot in the stirrup and pulled himself into the saddle. He leaned over and offered Henry his hand.

The slave grabbed it and jumped as the reverend yanked him onto the gelding's rump. Henry settled in behind the preacher, who waited for him to wrap the gum blanket around his back and over his head. Henry slipped his arms around Quintard, who nudged the animal into the rain and tugged the reins toward the church. In ten minutes they arrived at the house of worship, Henry slipping off the back of the horse, taking the reins, and tying them to a hitching post as the reverend dismounted.

"Wait with my horse for a moment, Henry. I must visit someone." Quintard jogged around the side of the stone church with its tall square bell tower toward the marker of James H. Otey, the bishop who had convinced him the ministry was ultimately more rewarding to himself and to mankind than medicine.

He spoke to the gravestone. "How are you, old friend? The war still rages, and we need decent men of God like you. What's it been, nineteen, twenty months since you received your heavenly reward in the arms of God? We've lost so many, but you know that because they've joined you. I've been blessed far beyond my worth, old friend, and your friendship was the greatest gift God ever bestowed on me. Thank you, Bishop Otey, for steering me in the path of God."

Quintard turned and scurried to the sanctuary door. At first, he missed Henry, then he saw him standing by the gelding's chest, screening himself from the precipitation that fell in sporadic fits. "Come inside, Henry."

"Youse sure dat's alright with everybodies? I's ain't been in no church before, Massa Revrund. Didn'ts know dat be okay."

The reverend opened the heavy door, and Henry slid inside in front of him, surprising the local pastor, who was sweeping up the floor from the mud that had been tracked in during the morning service.

"We don't allow—," the pastor started until he saw Quintard. "Reverend Quintard, welcome. I didn't realize you had returned to Tennessee. It's an honor to see you."

"I spent last night at Lucius Polk's home and conducted an Advent sermon this morning."

The young clergyman nodded with sad eyes. "That explains the small turnout today, that and the weather."

Quintard pointed to the broom. "Less mud to sweep up." He bobbed his head toward the youth. "This is Henry, my manservant. He's never been in a church before."

"Welcome, Henry," the pastor responded, pointing the broom handle to the balcony over the entrance. "That's where the servants sit for worship."

The reverend patted Henry on the shoulder and pointed to the stairs. "Run up there, Henry, and take a seat while we attend our business." As the slave scurried away, his master turned to the clergyman. I baptized Lucius Polk's niece and grandson this morning and wanted to enter their names in the parish registry."

"Certainly," replied the host. "Follow me." He led Quintard to the back into a small office, where he pointed to a desk with the leather-bound book atop it. "We've been out of ink for months, so enter the names in pencil. When this war is over and we can afford ink, I'll trace over their names to give them permanency."

"God's given them permanency in His heavenly kingdom now." Quintard smiled as he stepped to the desk, seating himself and meticulously adding the names of the baptized Caroline and Henry to the register. As he made the entries, he thanked the clergyman for his time and said he must catch up with the army.

"I'm told," said the youthful pastor, "that General Hood is accepting the hospitality of Amos and Cornelia Warfield at their Beechlawn Plantation on the Pulaski Turnpike this evening."

"General Hood stayed for part of my sermon this morning before being called away."

The young pastor chuckled, perplexing Quintard.

"I fail to see the humor in Hood's worshipping with me."

"It's not that," the young man responded. "Two nights ago, Yankee commander Schofield slept in the same bed Hood will sleep in tonight. The Warfields are blessed that Schofield's gone, and our commander has taken his place before sending all the Yankees to hell."

"Reverend, is that appropriate?"

"No, sir, but I am tired of this war and its destruction."

"Have faith, my son, that God will send the Yankees where they belong, and do not let your parishioners see your doubts. You must exemplify strength and integrity in difficult times."

"Yes, Reverend."

Quintard finished his record-keeping, arose from the desk, stepped to the clergyman, and hugged him. "Be strong, my son. We will get through this and be stronger for it." Releasing his counterpart, the reverend returned to the sanctuary, shaking his head when he glanced up at the narrow balcony and saw Henry leaning back in the front pew with his feet resting atop the railing. "That's not proper posture in the house of the Lord, Henry."

The slave yanked his feet from the barrier, arose, and wiped the dark wood with the sleeve of his coat to clean away the smudge of mud from his shoes. He rushed down the stairs, dragging his gum blanket, and met Quintard at the exit.

Before emerging into the rain, Henry turned to Quintard. "Can I's asks youse a question?"

"Go ahead, Henry."

"Why's darkies gotta stays up there and nots down here?"

"Tradition, Henry."

The youth scratched his chin and cocked his head at his master, then pointed to the balcony. "Do it means us darkies be closer to God dan youse white folks?"

Confound Henry B. Free, Quintard thought, for always coming up with questions that pricked his conscience.

Sunday Afternoon,

November 27, 1864

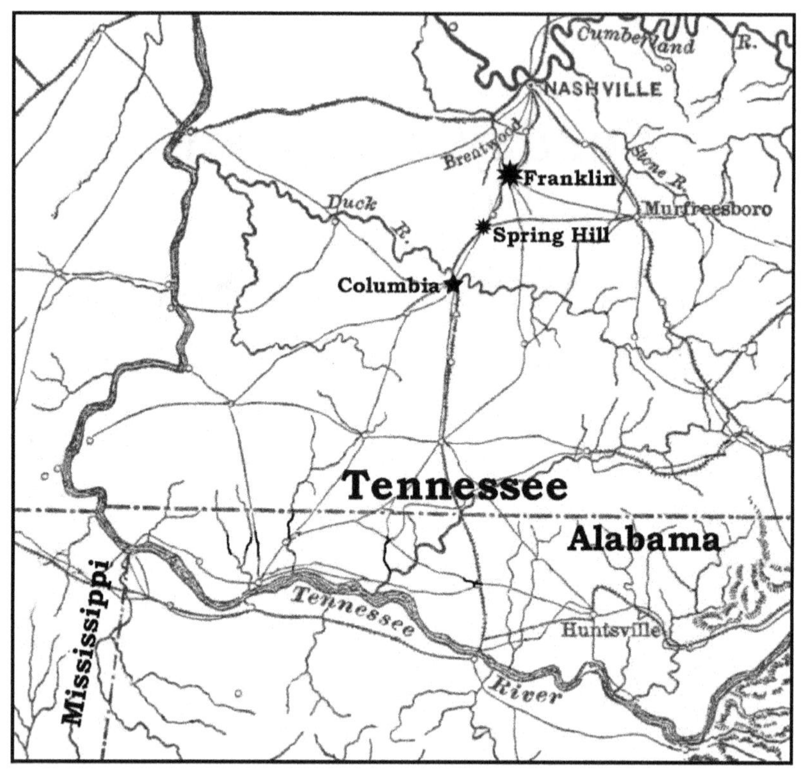

Middle Tennessee, 1864

Chapter Four

Sumner Cunningham
Approaching Columbia

Still, the rains came, but no matter how much precipitation fell upon his tattered uniform, the water could not wash away the humiliation of his tumble in front of General Nathan Bedford Forrest the preceding day. Sumner Cunningham could still hear the echoes of the derisive laughter that trailed him and could yet smell the pungent odor of his dung-stained garb as he escaped at double-quick time into the distance beyond Forrest's gaze. But separation from the general failed to bring blessed anonymity. Too many Tennesseans had recognized him, snickering at him like Forrest and his coterie of officers. The other sergeants chuckled and gigged him with comments that Forrest had requested his transfer to the mounted troops.

As he tromped through the sludge toward Columbia with the men of the Forty-first Tennessee, he fought the daunting shame of a simple misstep and the malingering terror of the unknown ahead. As sergeant major, he had read the army handbook for the rank and file, understanding he should be a model soldier in dress and military deportment for the other troops, but Cunningham grasped his deficiencies as a fighting man and hoped only to disguise his shortcomings from the soldiers he accompanied. Though infantry marched ahead of him, beside him and to his rear, he felt alone, even among so many others, each lost in his own thoughts. Cunningham shivered as he advanced toward his fate, but he could no longer tell if his trembles came from the rains saturated with cold, from the fear that quivered through every fiber of his body, or from the malaria that occasionally recurred. Why had he survived when multitudes had died, beginning with the surrender at Fort Donelson and continuing through all the setbacks outside Atlanta? Had his cowardice saved him or merely prolonged his torment?

As he slogged through the muck, he glanced around at his brigade, soldiers from eight Tennessee regiments marching with him. At the start of the war, a brigade consisted of just four regiments, but due to heavy losses, it now required twice as many units to reach full strength. Even with eight regiments, Brigadier General Otho F. Strahl's brigade fell short on roll call. Cunningham knew because he tabulated the totals as other sergeants reported roll tallies. Only Tennesseans comprised Strahl's brigade, save for the general himself. Strahl was a Yankee, born in Morgan County in southeastern Ohio. After attending Ohio Wesleyan, he moved to Dyersburg in western Tennessee, just sixteen miles from the Mississippi River and the Missouri border. Though he arrived in Dyersburg just three years before the firing on Fort Sumter, Strahl sided with his new neighbors and their cause, raising Dyer County's first company of volunteers, who became Company K of the Fourth Tennessee Volunteer Infantry with Strahl as captain. He had acquitted himself well at Shiloh and had fought for the Confederacy from there to Corinth to Perryville to Murfreesboro. Next, he had led troops from Chickamauga to Chattanooga and then through skirmishes when his brigade took fire for sixty continuous days until a Minié ball knocked him from the saddle of his prized mare he called "The Lady Polk" and sent him to a Southern hospital. That wound confirmed to his troops that he was one of them, even if he could never shake his southeastern Ohio dialect nor his affection for The Lady Polk, which tickled his men because they believed a man who cared so for his mount would worry as much for them.

Strahl recovered in time to reunite with The Lady Polk and rejoin his brigade, or at least what remained of it after John Bell Hood's ill-considered and bloody encounters around Atlanta. Now Strahl's Tennesseans, their enthusiasm as gray as the clouds that spat rain, sleet and misery on them, followed Hood north into their home state. Whatever spark the Tennesseans felt entering their homeland a week earlier had been doused by the precipitation and the growing doubts they shared over their rash commander. Hood's ill-conceived tactics of attack at all costs terrified them. Those costs were paid in soldiers' blood and explained why regiments had to double up to even approach the size of a standard brigade. The Fourth, Fifth, Nineteenth, Twenty-fourth, Thirty-first, Thirty-third and Thirty-eighth Infantry regiments now accompanied Cunningham's own Forty-first Tennessee toward Columbia and what awaited ahead.

As the day advanced along with Strahl's brigade, the sleet and rain turned to drizzle and by late afternoon the drizzle turned to mist.

With each muddy step, Cunningham's muscles ached from his ankles to his shoulders. His stomach growled for food, and he longed to sleep on a feather mattress back in Bedford County, where he had grown up. There he had been infected with a mild case of war fever after listening to the rhetoric of old men who would never pick up a weapon for the cause when it was so much safer to fire words from a podium than bullets from a rifle at the enemy. With the approach of dusk, the sun setting around five o'clock on late November days in Tennessee, Cunningham heard the sound of horses behind him and twisted to see Colonel James D. Tillman, commander of the Forty-first, riding up with General Strahl himself. Cunningham stepped out of line, faced the approaching officers, dropped his Enfield to his side with the butt resting on the mushy ground and saluted.

"As you were, Sergeant," Tillman said, drawing up his mount in front of him.

Strahl reined up The Lady Polk, glanced at the soldiers marching past, then stared at the sergeant major.

Cunningham swallowed hard as he took in the general's long, unkempt beard and his steely, dark eyes that had never blinked before the enemy. Cunningham prayed for such courage in the days ahead.

A sliver of a smile cracked the general's beard. "Are you the sergeant that tumbled in front of General Forrest yesterday?"

Sighing as he felt the hot flush of embarrassment in his checks, he waited for the insult to come. "Yes, sir, that was me!"

Strahl grinned and wiped raindrops from his beard. "Better to fall before friend than foe, Sergeant. I'm a lawyer by profession. My first case in a courtroom, I tripped and stumbled into the judge's bench. I was never so embarrassed in my entire life as at that moment. Now I look back upon it with humor as time has a way of *warshing* away the humiliation."

Cunningham smiled as much at Strahl's odd way of pronouncing "washing" as at the relief that the general never intended to mock him. "Thank you, sir," he answered.

"Colonel Tillman tells me you are as fine a sergeant major as he's ever seen, always tabulating accurate rolls and keeping regimental records in order. Paperwork abounds in any army, but no army succeeds if the records are poorly maintained."

"Your words honor me, General Strahl," Cunningham said, wishing the war could be settled by pushing paper rather than by firing bullets, as he knew he might become the perfect warrior. "I try my best."

Strahl nodded, then studied his soldiers still marching by, their heads and shoulders drooping, their cheeks and hopes sunken. "They are exhausted, but yet they march on."

"It's home," Tillman answered. "They just want to drive the invaders out and get on with their lives."

"But how much more can they endure, Colonel?"

"As much as they must, General."

Strahl grimaced, shaking his head. "I hope you are right, Colonel." The general touched the heel of his boot to the flank of his mare, then moved on.

Tillman lingered a moment. "Sergeant," he said, "we'll make camp outside Columbia this evening. As it will be after dark when we get there, be prepared to assign guard duties quickly so the others can rest as much as possible."

"Yes, sir," Cunningham answered.

"Though I know not what we'll face in the coming days, I am certain we will need all of our strength if we are to prevail and rid this country of the Yankee locusts. That is our destiny, that or the grave."

The colonel spoke so matter-of-factly that chills raced down Cunningham's spine. "Yes, sir," he managed, as Tillman shook the reins and sent his gelding to catch up with Strahl in the encroaching darkness.

Cunningham lifted his Enfield to his shoulder and scurried to regain to his place in the line, stepping away from the well-trampled ruts of the road and trotting along the edge until his foot caught in an exposed root and tripped him. He stumbled ahead, then collapsed upon the mushy earth, his rifle flying from his hand. Even in the dimness, Cunningham knew others had seen him spill, yet none of them laughed. They were too exhausted.

Sam Watkins
Outside Columbia

It's an odd thing about death, Corporal Sam Watkins thought as he tried to doze after a weary and wet day of marching. Every passing second of every living day escorts a man that much closer to his own demise, whether by a Yankee bullet, a fall from a horse, a disease from an unpronounceable malady or merely old age. In war, a soldier couldn't escape death, as it was the only constant in his life. Battles might be won or lost, rations might be handy or scarce, weather might be pleasant or horrible, but death always lurked nearby, ever ready to claim another victim.

Now as he craved sleep beneath the leaking canvas of his tiny shelter just two miles from where his forty-two-month combat odyssey had begun and where his beloved Jennie still lived, Watkins realized how naïve he had been when he enlisted with the Maury County Grays before they became Company H of the First Tennessee Infantry. The only folks more guileless were the old women and young ladies who remained innocent about the cost of battle in the spring of 1861. Watkins now understood the glory of war came at home among the ladies, who stood with encouraging smiles and tearful eyes as their beaus and sons marched off to protect their homes and their virtues. The glory came in dress parades while the bands played "Dixie" or "The Bonnie Blue Flag," and while enlistees in their new uniforms impressed their girls before trudging away, sometimes forever.

Watkins now understood battle offered no glory, just death for the private or "webfoot" as infantrymen called themselves. After walking so many miles, the soldiers swore their feet were webbed like those of a duck. Maybe the generals shared glory among themselves, but what Watkins had observed was the soldiers did the fighting and the generals did the infighting, positioning themselves for the adulation of the public and the admiration of the future historians who might shower them with praise in their history books and biographies. Until then, the generals would squabble over personal glories they could recount in their memoirs. War had taught him the battlefield spawned more gore than glory for the webfoot.

His initial excitement of enlisting in the First Tennessee continued through two months of training and drilling outside of Nashville. Once the regiment voted to go east to help stem the Yankee invasion of Virginia, the grandeur of war endured with joyful demonstrations by citizens at parades through Chattanooga and Knoxville, Tennessee, then Bristol, Farmville, Lynchburg, Staunton, and other Virginia towns with names long forgotten. Then the First Tennessee crossed the Allegheny Mountains and reached Big Springs, Virginia, where the weather was cold and drizzly for August. The next morning Watkins stood as videt, a forward sentry watching for enemy, when he spotted a detachment of thirty Yankees approaching. Lifting his loaded rifle, he pulled back the hammer, slipped a cap over the nipple, aimed at the leading officer and pulled the trigger, certain that he alone would win the war with this shot. The cap merely popped as his powder was wet. A half dozen Yankees aimed and fired at him, but their damp powder only popped as well. As Watkins frantically tried to reload his rifle, his captain ran up with a seven-shot, repeating rifle and fired, driving the trespassers away, killing two. Lucky to be unscathed by Yankee projectiles, Watkins understood how fortunate he was that his captain was nearby. When he inspected the bodies his commander's rifle had produced, he saw the gore, not the glory, even for the Yankee dead.

A few evenings later, a fine-looking officer in a sharp general's uniform rode into camp to visit with the officers of the First Tennessee. The visitor carried no weapon and brought no staff with him. All Watkins saw was a pair of field glasses hanging around his neck by a leather strap. Tying his horse, the general had walked among the campfires, greeting the men, then sat on a camp stool as the regiment's officers gathered around him. Watkins slipped close enough to the officers' circle that he could hear the general's tender voice and see in the flickering firelight the officer's eyes that were as gentle as a dove's. The name meant nothing to Watkins when he was told the fellow was Robert E. Lee. Three years later, the name would mean everything to the South. When he realized General Lee was preparing to leave, Watkins strode over and untied his horse, leading him to the officer. Lee smiled. "Thank you, my son," he said. Watkins saluted and wanted to follow Lee wherever he went, like a grandson desires to trail his grandfather.

Days later at Cheat Mountain, Company H led the regiment on a march when a troop of Yankees ambushed them through the trees. Webfoot Pat Hanley died there on the trail miles from his Tennessee home, the company's first fatality. Four other boys sustained wounds. There was no glory in battle, just death and gore. Before the boys of the First Tennessee were ordered back to their home state, they served briefly under Stonewall Jackson, who was by Watkins' observation a disheveled and awkward-looking man in the saddle. Jackson, though, was developing a reputation as a wizard of battlefield tactics. Though he did not foresee it then, Watkins now knew that no such commander like Lee or Jackson would rise to the top of his Army of Tennessee. The soldiers deserved better.

When the regiment's webfeet left Virginia, they had barely been bloodied by Yankee iron and lead. Once they returned to their home state, the bloodletting began, proving once and for all there was no glory in combat, just fatalities and blood. First came Shiloh, then Corinth, Perryville, Murfreesboro, Shelbyville, and Chattanooga. If that was not enough, then followed Chickamauga, Missionary Ridge, the Hundred Days' Battle, Dead Angle, Atlanta, and Jonesborough. At Murfreesboro, both shrapnel and a bullet sliced through the flesh of his arm without striking bone. In Atlanta, he had taken a bullet wound to his writing hand and another to his thigh. Fortunately, nothing caused permanent damage. Watkins knew he was lucky. Dozens of boys he had enlisted with had been lost, both to the cause and to their loved ones forever. Dirponso Hooper, Gus Allen, and Joe Bynum perished in Virginia; Byron Richardson, John Allen, and Sam Campbell died at Perryville; Henry Webster, Fain King and Jim McEwin gave up the ghost at Chickamauga; Tom Webb met eternity at Missionary Ridge; Bill Wood, Jim Brandon, Walt Hood, and Bill Hughes died at the Dead Angle on Kennesaw Mountain; Conner Akin, Jim Galbreath, and Will Graham fell near Atlanta; and George Sanders departed forever in Alabama.

Even camp offered no refuge from death's icy hand. Fourteen-year-old Jimmy White died in winter bivouac in Dalton, Georgia, after a day-long snowball fight. During the winter merriment, a frightened team stampeded through the combatants, pulling a caisson that ran over Jimmy, breaking both his thighs. The doctor gave him no hope, and Sam stayed with the boy to comfort him, asking if he knew Jesus. When the youth admitted he'd never heard of him, Watkins explained how believers who acknowledged Jesus before other men would not die, but have everlasting life in the world beyond. Little Jimmy converted right then. Jimmy grew drowsy from the opiates the doctors provided for his pain and asked Sam to lift his hand until Jesus came. Watkins did until he tired, then propped Jimmy's hand up with a pillow and fell asleep himself. When he awoke, little Jimmy was dead, his hand frozen in place, aiming at the sky. When they wrapped Jimmy in his blanket and buried him in the cold wet earth, his hand was still upright, pointing to his eternal destination among the stars.

The most horrific death, one that lingered longest in his mind, occurred outside Jonesborough just three months earlier. On the eve of battle, Watkins sat at breakfast with Lieutenant John Whitaker, the commander of Company H, both eating out of the same tin plate when someone shouted Sam's name. Turning to see who had called, Sam felt the heat of a passing cannonball that singed the brim of his hat. Instantly, Watkins sat awash in blood. He turned to see the headless officer spewing blood. Glancing away, his gaze fell upon the plate he now held alone. In it lay smatterings of brains, but most horribly the lieutenant's face, as if it had been peeled from the officer's head and laid out on the tin implement. Sam dropped the tin dish and retched, then scrambled away from the dead officer to find water for a bath. He could wash the blood and the brains from his clothes and flesh, but not from his memory.

Gore, not glory, accompanied the First Tennessee. Immediate death seemed preferable to the long wait for it to arrive. Finally, Sam Watkins worried his tired body and restless mind to sleep, comforted only because he was so near his beloved Jennie in Columbia.

Hiram Granbury
Nearing Columbia

The previous day's conversation with Captain Samuel T. Foster had lifted Hiram Granbury's spirits, so he sought the Texan as the Texas brigade approached Columbia. It lessened the misery to converse with someone as they advanced through the interminable rains, which had let up little since the start of November. Granbury found Foster riding among the men of his dismounted cavalry regiment and assuring them he would do what he could to find more provisions for their shrunken stomachs.

His subordinates grinning at the approach of Granbury, Foster turned in his saddle to see who neared. He offered a salute when he spotted the general. The marching soldiers started to salute as well, but Granbury waved the gesture away. "Save your strength, men," Granbury said, doffing his hat at them as he turned in beside his subordinate.

"They're hungry, General. We've never had enough rations, but it's worse under General Hood. He don't care about their welfare, much less their morale. One of my men described our Tennessee campaign as 'rain, rain, mud, mud, march, march, starve, starve.' I've never felt more helpless."

"It's the same across all the brigades."

"Before Hood took command, General Johnston saw that we drew Irish potatoes, collard greens, and tomatoes besides our regular ration. He even made sure we got tobacco from time to time."

Granbury nodded. "All Hood thinks about is fighting, never giving a thought to what it takes to fight, whether it's food and shoes or powder and shot. Remember when we left Gadsden, Alabama, for Tennessee? We waited days to cross the Tennessee River because he neglected to order the pontoon bridges to accompany us."

"Under General Johnston, we fought hard and marched hard, but he made sure we always had something to eat. In bad weather or after a hard march, General Johnston would issue us a little whiskey for our extra effort. All Hood issues is criticism, that and blame." Foster paused, gauging his superior's reaction, then continued. "That's not just how I feel, but how my men feel as well ever since the day Hood took command. He's done nothing to change our minds. If Jefferson Davis had come to camp to announce the promotion, he would not have lived an hour before some of us would've shot him. He as much as murdered our boys by promoting Hood over better officers like General Cleburne."

"It galls me and makes me wonder if God truly *is* on our side," Granbury replied. "I fear time is running out for the Confederacy."

"And for us, General."

"The Army of Tennessee has never had a Joshua to bring down the walls of Jericho."

"But we had a Joe Johnston. He may not have been a Joshua, but neither was he a Judas, nor did he ever deceive us. Men respected that about him, whatever his other shortcomings may have been. We fight now for you, for Patrick Cleburne, and even for Frank Cheatham, but not for John Bell Hood. I'm surprised someone in this army hasn't shot him."

Granbury reined up his horse and stared at Foster, who stopped beside him. "I hope you're not writing these things down in your diary."

"I am."

"Some might consider that treason."

"It's reason, not treason. I'm a lawyer; you're a lawyer. Hood would be convicted in any court as the petty and vindictive man that he is."

Granbury agreed, but chastised his subordinate instead. "If you are injudicious in what you write or say, you could be hanged."

Foster's face revealed a wicked grin. "Let me shoot him first, then hang me. My life will be a fair exchange for the hundreds of lives I would save."

While Granbury knew the truth lay buried in Foster's comment, he issued a final order. "Talk no more of this to me or ever speak such words in front of your soldiers again."

Foster's grin disappeared behind a serious military demeanor as he saluted sharply. "Yes, sir. Am I dismissed?"

Granbury snickered. "Not at all. I said what I had to say as your commanding officer. Now I'm speaking as a friend. Your company keeps my mind off the rain, the cold and—"

"Fannie?"

The general nodded as they advanced toward Columbia, talking not about command leadership but about their plans after the war. By evening, they separated to handle their individual responsibilities as the brigade camped outside Columbia with their skirmishers trading desultory gunfire with Yankee pickets. The baggage train arrived, providing some comfort and shelter for the soldiers and the officers. Granbury rode among the soldiers, encouraging them as they ate the ears of corn they had been provisioned.

As the sun dipped behind the horizon, Foster found the general and asked if he might have a word in private. Granbury escorted him away from eavesdroppers.

"General, might I have permission to slip into Columbia tonight?"

"What for? There's Yankees in Columbia."

The captain hesitated, then answered, "To visit kin."

"Didn't know you had kin in Tennessee. Who is it?"

"I'd rather not say," he said with tight lips.

Granbury doubted Foster's excuse, then realized the probable reason. "You plan on foraging, scrounging up what food you can for your men."

"Again, sir, I'd rather not say, but you know how those Yankees take everything they can from Southern larders. I'd like to take something from their supply wagons before we attack."

"They'll take you as prisoner if you aren't careful. I won't say no to your request, Captain, though I can't give you permission, as we will likely drive them from Columbia soon. If you go, alert our pickets and know the sign and countersign. I don't want you shot by your own men."

"Thank you, sir. If I should go without your authorization, is there something I could bring you?"

The general smiled. "An apple pie would taste good. Fannie made the best apple crumb pie. It would remind me of her."

Rev. Charles T. Quintard
Beechlawn Plantation

Just after three o'clock in the afternoon, Cornelia Warfield welcomed Reverend Quintard to Beechlawn with the same weariness she had greeted General John Bell Hood and his entourage earlier. She was glad to be shed of General Schofield's Yankee officers, but not a Confederate officer approached her place without her hoping to see her husband, a major in the Quartermaster Department with the Army of Tennessee. A striking woman of thirty years, Cornelia showed the strain and the worry of operating their estate while mothering three boys, ages ten to four, plus a nine-month-old daughter. Her gaunt cheeks, drawn lips, downcast eyes, and slumped shoulders mirrored the exhaustion that all plantation folks felt after three long years of war and Union intrusion upon their land and their lives. When Quintard shook her rough hand, he understood the true effect of war because plantation mistresses before the conflict had soft palms and fingers unused to hard work. In her eyes, he had seen the fatigue of life without a husband, though she was luckier than most Southern women because her husband, as an officer, could periodically return home for a brief visit, thus their young daughter.

"Welcome, Reverend. We are honored by your presence and that of so many other distinguished men of the Confederacy."

"My dear Mrs. Warfield, it is we who are honored by your hospitality."

She smiled. "It's not as grand as it was before the war."

"But it is hospitality, nonetheless."

"Thank you, Reverend. We have planned supper, such as it is, for five o'clock before General Hood meets at six with his corps commanders. Would you care to join General Hood at our table for a modest meal?"

"I would again be honored if it is not too much of an imposition."

"Absolutely not, not like it was a few days ago when the Yankee command soiled our place."

"Let me tend to my boy and my horse, and I shall return to your manor to enjoy your hospitality."

Cornelia nodded. "I'll show you the slave quarters and the barn."

Quintard took her hand and squeezed it softly. "No, ma'am. We will manage, as I'm sure you have plenty to do."

"Thank you," she responded. "It's been hard, losing so many of our slaves and managing four children." She paused and sighed. "Nothing like what our boys have faced against the Yankees, I suppose, but trying and tiring nonetheless."

The reverend released her hand. "I will say a prayer for God to provide you strength for what lies ahead."

As Cornelia retreated to oversee the meal preparation, Quintard unpacked the bedroll and bag he would need for the evening and left them on the expansive front porch. He led Henry behind the big house to the barn, where he tied the horse with instructions for Henry to unsaddle and curry comb the animal once they found his lodging. Beyond the barn stood a line of slave quarters. They entered the nearest hovel, which seemed unused for weeks. Barely adequate, it was still shelter and would get Henry out of the weather. Quintard told him to find firewood, light a fire in the fireplace for warmth, and select one of the four beds for rest. The vacant beds of escaped slaves gave silent testament to the effects of the war on the people of middle Tennessee.

Quintard left Henry and returned to the big house, taking his belongings from the porch and placing them inside the parlor, where a half dozen officers studied a map they had laid across the back of a sofa. From the adjacent library, Quintard heard the voice of John Bell Hood as he discussed plans for the coming days. The reverend went to the dining room where he sat in a corner chair, saying his promised prayer for Cornelia Warfield and then reading his Bible as two overworked servants set the table for dinner.

When the meal was ready, Quintard joined Hood and six other officers at the table. Cornelia provided a modest dinner of chicken and dumplings—more flour and grease than meat. Quintard swallowed the food reluctantly, knowing it was taking nourishment from the mouths of her family. General Hood showed no such reflection, serving himself generous portions without regard for the other officers at the table, much less Cornelia's family.

Cornelia advised Quintard that he and the other officers would have to sleep on the floor in the library after Hood's meeting concluded. Quintard thanked her again for her hospitality and volunteered to help with clearing the table and doing the dishes, but she declined his offer.

He returned to his dining room chair and read his Bible by the light of a lamp.

Patrick Cleburne
Division Headquarters

By three o'clock, his three brigadier generals gathered to meet with their division commander. The wild-haired Hiram Granbury arrived first, as confident as his brigade of Texans, though Pat Cleburne detected a sadness in the widower's eyes. Cleburne knew the story of Fannie's loss to cancer at so young an age. Though he had yet to marry, Cleburne could not fathom losing Susan Tarleton, so he understood it must be a strain on Granbury's emotions. Perhaps the reason Hiram had become such a dependable general and exceptional leader of men was that he had devoted his life to the cause to help assuage the pain of her loss. Or, perhaps he no longer cared if he lived or died.

Entering Cleburne's tent, Granbury removed his hat and saluted his commander. "Will this rain ever end? We should send it to Texas where it's always needed. Tennessee seems to get more than its fair share."

Cleburne nodded. "Perhaps we should ask our preaching general for a special prayer."

"No offense, Pat, but why would the Almighty listen to Mark Lowrey? He rides a donkey half the time."

"Perhaps, but he's a fighter like you."

As the pair discussed Lowrey's idiosyncrasies, Lieutenant Mangum entered ahead of Brigadier General Daniel Govan, a resident like Mangum and Cleburne of Helena, Arkansas, where he had moved just four years earlier to settle on a plantation he purchased and shared with his wife, Mary Fogg Otey, who was the daughter of the late Tennessee Bishop James H. Otey. Cleburne had lost count of the number of children Govan had, but it was plenty, requiring two hands to count.

Govan's command held the remnants of ten Arkansas regiments. Though depleted by casualties and far from full force, his brigade remained a tough fighting force because of his no-nonsense leadership. He had raised a company of Arkansas men at the start of the war and had risen from captain to brigadier general the past December. He had performed bravely at Shiloh, Perryville, Murfreesboro, Missionary Ridge, and Ringgold Gap, where his decisive actions received commendation from Cleburne.

Three months earlier, Govan was captured after a fierce encounter at Jonesborough but was so valuable to the cause that he was exchanged a month later on October first for a Union general. Cleburne was glad to have him back in command, not only because of his steadfastness, but because he reminded him of Helena and their mutual friends.

"Welcome, Dan," Cleburne offered as Govan removed his coat. "Any news from Helena?"

"Nothing other than folks fear a hard winter ahead and not much relief for anyone. Mary's worried about feeding the kids in the coming months and not sure they'll be able to plant any crops come spring."

"Maybe this will be over by then, Dan."

"Not if we're depending on General Hood for our salvation," Govan answered, just as Brigadier General Mark Lowrey entered the tent.

"If you need salvation, General Govan, I'm here to help," announced Lowrey, a Tennessee native who moved south to Mississippi, which he now called home. Ordained a Baptist minister before the war, Lowrey had acquired the sobriquet of "the Preacher General" from his peers. He could preach hell and brimstone from the pulpit or deliver it on the battlefield. Like the others, he had fought at most of the battles with the Army of Tennessee, though he had taken a bullet to the arm at Perryville and spent six weeks recovering before rejoining the army, just in time for the horrific battle at Murfreesboro.

As Lowrey doffed his hat, Granbury stepped to the entrance and looked outside in the rain, shaking his head. "I see, General Lowrey, you're still riding that donkey."

"Indeed I am, Hiram. Way I see it, no self-respecting Yankee sniper will take a shot at a Confederate general on a donkey. They're bound to assume such an officer is touched in the head and a liability to the Confederacy. Besides that 'Flash'—as I call him—reminds me of General Hood. If you look closely at Flash, you'll see a facial resemblance between the two."

"I could've sworn," Granbury responded, "the resemblance was at the other end."

Everyone laughed, including Cleburne, who just shook his head at Lowrey. "Forgetting General Granbury's observation, Mark, do you think you could put in a good prayer with the Almighty asking for a change in the weather?"

"Indeed I will, Pat."

"And for General Hood. We need improving weather for sure, but we need greater wisdom in our leader."

Lowrey grimaced. "Changing the weather's one thing, but infusing wisdom in our commander is a tall order. I'm not sure I have that kind of pull with our Heavenly Father."

"Give it a try, Mark."

"Yes, sir, General Cleburne."

"Thank you," Cleburne responded. "Now, gentlemen, I asked you here to tell you what I know, which is little other than General Hood has called his corps commanders together for a meeting this evening to discuss strategy. I suspect he'll want to attack Columbia tomorrow and drive the Yankees out."

Lowrey grimaced. "If General Hood's planning strategy, I'll double—no quadruple—my prayers for wisdom in our commander."

"Didn't the general promise us in Alabama we wouldn't attack entrenched forces again?" Granbury asked.

Cleburne nodded. "That he did. Not only that, but we would determine a battlefield to our advantage, never letting the enemy force us into a fight of their choosing." The major general paused as he looked from face to face of his subordinates. Then he continued, "I should know something this evening about General Hood's plans, so be where I can find you and make your assignments for tomorrow and the coming days." He pointed his index finger at the preacher general. "And Mark, redouble your prayers for better weather, stronger leadership, and greater success."

Lt. Gen. John Bell Hood
Beechlawn Plantation

Like a king on his throne, John Bell Hood sat in the high-backed chair at the head of the ornate mahogany table in the center of the library that was the pride of Cornelia Warfield in her Beechlawn Manor. The heavy drapes were drawn on the windows to hold the warmth against the frigid temperatures outside and to prevent anyone from seeing or overhearing the dusk council of war. The candle flames from the crystal chandelier cast a jaundiced light across the library, where books stood in perpetual attention on the shelves of the two opposing walls. As Cornelia opened the double doors, Hood's four corps commanders—Benjamin Cheatham, Alexander P. Stewart and Stephen D. Lee of the infantry, and Nathan Bedford Forrest of the cavalry—entered the room, offering casual salutes in their bulky overcoats spotted with the moist shrapnel of melted sleet.

"Pardon me if I don't get up," Hood said, drawing smiles from the infantry commanders, but not from Forrest. "Please be seated."

Cheatham and Stewart took chairs to Hood's left, while Lee selected one on the right side. Forrest settled in the high-backed chair at the opposite end of the table from Hood.

Disappearing for a moment beyond the open doors, Cornelia returned carrying a silver tray with an elongated bottle of brandy and five snifters. Placing the tray at the table corner between Hood and Cheatham, she spoke softly. "We have been saving this fine brandy for a special occasion, so please accept it for your enjoyment with our prayers for success in your military endeavors."

"Thank you," the corps commanders said in unison as Cornelia backed out of the room. Forrest stood and acknowledged her as she closed the doors behind her. Forrest sat back down.

Cheatham grabbed the bottle, removed the stopper and poured a healthy glass, which he removed from the tray and sat in front of himself. He volunteered to fill a snifter for each, though Forrest declined the offer.

"My staff does all my drinking for me," Forrest said.

"I drink for all my staff," Cheatham replied.

"We know," Forrest said coldly as Cheatham passed snifters to the other generals.

Hood eyed the glass and took a tiny sip, choking and then clearing his throat as he sat the snifter aside. Then he coughed so hard that his limp arm jiggled. His generals looked at each other while he fought the paroxysm of hacking.

A native of Charleston, Stephen D. Lee had no familial connection to the more famous Lees of Virginia. A West Point graduate, he had resigned his army commission before the assault on Fort Sumter to return to his native South Carolina. An artillerist by training, Lee commanded the bulk of the Army of Tennessee's artillery. At thirty-one, he was the youngest lieutenant general in the Confederate Army, with boyish looks, a sly smile, thick black hair, and penetrating eyes.

Alexander P. Stewart took a courtesy sip of the brandy, then placed the glass back on the tray. Another West Point graduate, Stewart resigned his commission after three years to teach mathematics and philosophy at Tennessee's Cumberland University. Though a Whig strongly opposed to secession, Stewart could not turn against his native state and accepted an officer's commission when hostilities began, gradually rising to the rank of lieutenant general. He sported thick brown hair and tapered jaws accented by a well-trimmed goatee. He studied people and situations with the light gray eyes of a scholar.

Unlike his infantry corps peers, Cheatham had developed a reputation as one part fighter and another part buffoon because of his disdain for military protocol and his love for liquor. His disheveled look did little to counter his standing as a brawler.

No Confederate general was more feared than Nathan Bedford Forrest. Unlike Cheatham, he dressed as impeccably as possible for a fighting man. He regularly combed his wavy hair, kept his goatee trimmed over a slender, muscled torso. At forty-three, Forrest had a simple military philosophy: get there firstest with the mostest. His action at an encounter at Fort Pillow seven months earlier was rumored to be a massacre for his cavalry's slaughter of black Union soldiers after their surrender. Forrest cared not a whit what folks said or thought of him and his actions, for this was war.

Finally, Hood controlled his cough, but when he spoke, his voice came as a dull rasp over hard wood. Lee arose, marching to the door, slipping his head out and asking Mrs. Warfield for a glass of water. She returned with a pitcher and a glass, placing them before Hood, then retreating out of the room, Forrest again standing until she departed.

Lee filled the glass with water and slid it in front of his commander, who took large gulps, then let out a long breath. Finally, he spoke.

"We have trapped Schofield's army against the Duck River with General Lee's corps on the left, General Stewart's corps in the middle, and General Cheatham's corps on the right flank."

"Not for long," Forrest interrupted. "Schofield will not let us trap him in Columbia, but will evacuate while the two bridges still stand."

Hood seethed, his eyes narrowing. He despised being corrected, even when he was mistaken. "General Forrest, I am well aware of what Schofield might do, but I *know* what I *must* do. I am prepared to counter Schofield's moves. Now, if I may go on?"

Forrest nodded.

The commander hesitated a moment, still glaring at Forrest. "I plan to insert our army between Schofield and Nashville, forcing Schofield to make a fight against our fortified positions."

Lee looked across the table at Cheatham and Stewart, evident by his cocked head and raised eyebrows that he could not believe what he was hearing. The apostle of frontal assaults was considering a defensive battle? Unbelievable!

Hood turned to General Lee. "I want you to stay here with two of your divisions and the bulk of our artillery to demonstrate that we plan to attack. Your third division will go with the rest of the army."

"Yes, sir," Lee responded.

Forrest interrupted. "Our artillery should go with the fighting men, rather than wasting ammunition to decoy Schofield?"

"I'll send two or three batteries with the fighting force," Hood answered.

"That won't be enough," Forrest countered. "Leave three batteries outside Columbia and send the rest with the advancing troops."

Hood glared at the cavalryman. "I'll worry about the artillery, General Forrest. You worry about your cavalry and doing what I command." Hood took another sip of water, then continued. "I'm ordering you to lead your detachment east of Columbia to Davis's Ford. Drive any Union troops from the ford and screen the river so we can get our pontoons set for a crossing. Understood?"

Forrest responded with a curt nod.

Looking at Cheatham and Stewart, Hood finished his plan. "When we advance, General Cheatham, be prepared to cross the

Duck in the vanguard. General Stewart, you will follow with your corps and General Lee's detached division. We can get behind the Union army between here and Spring Hill. We'll dig in and force them to attack *our* entrenchments."

Forrest pounded his fist in his palm. "The route you suggest, General Hood, is more trail than road, certainly not a macadamized pike. It'll be sloppy, muddy, and slow going. I've been on that route. I must remind you, Schofield will not be caught flat-footed. He's likely already moving, and we haven't even begun."

Hood scowled. "Your job, General Forrest, is to get around General Schofield and screen our movements. That'll give us the time we need to get in position and prepare for their inevitable attack. When they come at us, we'll destroy them. Then Nashville will be ours."

Forrest shook his head and replied. "The roads are horrible."

"Then get out of here and start your cavalry moving. You're dismissed to carry out my orders."

His corps commanders escaped into the frigid outdoors where the sky still spat snow and sleet. John Bell Hood remained in the library, contemplating if his subordinates would fail him again.

Rev. Charles T. Quintard
Beechlawn Plantation

Reverend Quintard waited a half hour after Hood dismissed his corps commanders, then retreated to the parlor, where he grabbed his satchel and bedroll. He slipped past the dozen officers preoccupied with implementing their commander's plans for the next day and headed for the library to make his bed. He pushed the library door open, then stepped inside, surprised to see General Hood sitting in a plush easy chair with his good leg propped on a cushioned footstool. His crutch lay on the floor at the side of his chair. Seeing the commander, Quintard nodded and backed to the door to give the commander solitude.

"No, Reverend, please come in. I could use some spiritual guidance."

"Are you sure, General? I know you have much on your mind."

"I want you to pray for me and for victory. I feel the weight of the Confederacy upon my shoulders."

"Certainly, General." Quintard placed his carpetbag and bedding on the table, then seated himself opposite Hood.

The commander grimaced as he shifted in his chair. "My body's still pained from the loss of my leg. Sometimes I endure incredible itches in the foot and toes of my missing leg. I can't make sense of it. My eyes confirm the leg is gone, still I feel the tingling. Can you explain it, Reverend? I know you've had medical training besides your theological education."

"I can't explain it, though it's common among amputees. Phantom pain is what it's called."

"So, I'm not imagining things?"

"What you are experiencing is common."

"The itch and the pain, perhaps, but not the responsibility, Reverend. I firmly believe God has chosen me to save our cause, but I can't move without pain from my wounds. Some have encouraged me to take laudanum, but I have refused, so that my head remains clear and my judgments solid."

"As long as you believe in Jesus Christ as your Lord and Savior, God will see you and us through these trying times."

"I believe in God, and I believe in myself, Reverend. Though God and the Confederacy have placed many obstacles in my way, I feel certain of triumph once I forge the Army of Tennessee into the fighting force it can be."

"You have my prayers, of course."

Hood nodded and revealed to Quintard his strategy. The commander intended to get between Schofield's retreating Union army and Nashville, forcing the Yankee troops to attack Hood's fortified forces. After decimating Schofield's army and capturing their supply trains for needed food and ammunition, he would then turn troops invigorated by victory upon Nashville and General George Thomas's overall Union command. Hood estimated his casualties would be light, no more than seven hundred men, if his plans were properly executed. Those losses would be easily replaced by Tennesseans inspired by Hood's victories to join the Confederacy and see it to final victory on the march through Kentucky to the Ohio River and maybe even into Ohio.

Quintard believed Hood's faithfulness and sincerity, though Hood had never fought a major battle with as few as seven hundred casualties. "May God will it so, General."

Hood spoke of his faith in God, his hopes for success and his dreams for the Confederacy. Then Quintard saw the exhaustion in the general's eyes. "Let me pray with you, General." Without waiting for a response, the pastor bowed his head and offered thanks to God for placing this military man in command of the Army of Tennessee at this crucial time in the history of the Confederacy. He asked the Heavenly Father to provide an angel over Hood's shoulder to help him fulfill his destiny and save the Confederate States of America.

As he prayed, Quintard watched Hood through a slit in his eyes. The general's chin rested on his chest while Quintard continued his request to God, praying longer than he usually did because he thought Hood needed Providence's help more than any other man in the Confederacy. After he said "amen," Quintard raised his head, but Hood did not. He had fallen asleep during the prayer.

The general was exhausted, Quintard told himself as he arose, first thinking he would slip out of the library, but deciding instead to sit at the table and enter in his diary his daily observations of Advent Sunday and his meeting with Hood, careful not to record the general's plan for victory in the unlikely case his diary fell into the hands of the enemy. Quintard was still writing when the general's aides entered, woke him and helped him leave the room for his bed. When the reverend finished his diary entry, he took his satchel and bedroll to a corner and made his bed on the floor, offering a final prayer for all the soldiers who must spend another night without adequate shelter from the precipitation.

States Rights Gist
Camp outside Columbia

Hidden behind a shroud of clouds, the sun's muted daylight finally faded into evening, and States Rights Gist still fretted. He had started the day after a worrisome night, tossing with concerns that something had happened to Uncle Wiley and his favored horse. At least he had a canvas barrier between him and the rains, unlike most men who slept beneath gutta-percha, provided they were lucky enough to have the rubberized covering, or beneath trees or bushes that might give them a little shelter. With no sign of Uncle Wiley, Gist had spent his day among his soldiers, offering encouragement and praise until they set up camp. He wished he could provide them more than just words, things like food and even rest.

As the sun was setting behind the clouds, Gist asked his orderly to saddle Kitty, so he could ride to the evening meeting called by corps commander General Benjamin Franklin Cheatham, who had summoned his division and brigade commanders to the house appropriated from Mrs. Myrtle Francis for shelter from the cold and the rain. Cheatham and the fourteen generals of his three divisions and eleven brigades met on the covered front porch so not to track mud through the woman's house.

A native Tennessean with blood ties to two prominent state families, Cheatham lacked the refinement of a man of Gist's South Carolina upbringing. He drank hard and swore more. He cultivated a thick mustache, thick eyebrows, and a skull thick enough to withstand the periodic brawls he relished. His idiosyncrasies endeared him to his men, who called him "Old Frank" and savored the many tales of his bravado and his unmilitary ways.

The enlisted men's favorite story was of Cheatham berating an Irishman for some military infraction with more cusswords than a bookkeeper could tally. As the general caught his breath after his profanity parade, the insubordinate Irishman fired back, "If you wasn't a general, I'd whip you for talking to me that way." The commander ripped off his coat, flung it on the ground and pointed to the gray cloth with the gold stars on the collar. "There lies General Cheatham and here stands Old Frank. Have at him." The officer and the private battled with their fists, the general later recalling, "I didn't get the best of that fight." Though he lost the fisticuffs, he won the hearts of his men with such bravado and such lax military protocol. As long as his men fought well, he put up with more than any other major general in the Confederacy.

With his generals gathered around him, Cheatham explained General Hood's plan for feinting an attack at Columbia, then circling behind General Schofield's Union troops and whipping them on Confederate soil. Then Cheatham issued orders to division commanders Patrick Cleburne, John Brown, and William Bate for them to carry out with their brigades.

"Do you think this will work?" Gist asked.

"If it don't, I'm gonna challenge General Hood to an ass-kicking contest," Cheatham responded, drawing laughs.

"From what I hear, Frank, you better hope Hood's not an Irishman," Otho Strahl said, garnering even louder guffaws.

Cheatham chuckled too. "My sister still chides me for that fight in every letter she sends. Now be gone and do your duty so I don't have to kick our commander's scrawny butt."

John Brown motioned for his brigadier generals to meet him under an oak tree for their orders. Gist and Strahl joined John C. Carter and George W. Gordon beneath the branches as Brown detailed the plan for each brigade. As soon as he dismissed his subordinates, Strahl stepped beside Gist as they walked to their horses.

"Might I ride back with you, States?"

"I'd enjoy the company. Help me keep my mind off things."

"Your brow's furrowed."

"My manservant's been gone for more than a day, which is not like him, and he's riding my best horse in my only overcoat."

Strahl cocked his head at Gist. "Who do you miss more, your servant or your horse?"

As the two generals untied and mounted their horses, Gist grinned. "Right now, my overcoat, but all joking aside, Uncle Wiley, of course. He's been a fine servant and looked after me since I was a kid. You surprised?"

"I've never owned a slave, so I didn't know what to expect."

"Uncle Wiley's a decent and dependable man. That's why I'm worried."

They turned their horses toward their brigades.

"There's something I've been wanting to ask you, States, lawyer to lawyer. Do you mind?"

"About my name?"

Strahl nodded. "I suspect you get asked a lot about it."

"Yes, I do. I was born in 1831 when Senator John C. Calhoun was fighting tariffs that worked against South Carolina's best interests. Calhoun turned to nullification as an appropriate response under the Constitution. This nation was a compact between states, limiting the power of the federal government to specified duties and reserving all other powers to the states to use at their discretion."

"But how did that determine your name?"

"My father ardently supported nullification. He was an avid reader of the *Charleston Mercury*, which preached States' Rights and secession for years. When I was born, he wanted to make a statement about the overreach of an unfettered central government."

"Have you ever regretted the name?"

"I stand by my father and his beliefs, which I share. When the nullification crisis came to a head over tariffs, South Carolina voted to nullify the law and withdraw from the Union, though a compromise changing the tariff eventually evolved, and South Carolina withdrew the nullification threat. If South Carolina had stood by its guns, this might have been settled a generation ago with fewer casualties. Had it been resolved, we wouldn't be here riding in the rain to fight for our rights."

"Never considered it that way," Strahl replied.

"Now let me ask you something, Otho, lawyer to lawyer."

"You're a native of Ohio, right?"

Strahl nodded.

"Why are you fighting for the South?"

"I read law in Tennessee and took up a legal practice. I liked the people, so I made it my home and purchased land. When war came, I didn't see Tennesseans invading Ohio, but I did see Ohioans invading my adopted state. It offended my sense of justice."

"Did you buy any slaves?"

"Never did, never will. Slavery demeans labor and advances idleness and ignorance in society, distressing the powers of the mind and reducing the gainful activity of man."

"And yet, you fight with those who would preserve slavery."

"What they fight for is their call. What I fight for is my home and my wish to avoid the yoke of an oppressive government on my shoulders. You may fight for slavery, but I don't."

Gist nodded. "I can respect that."

The two generals rode silently until they reached their brigades, then said their goodbyes and started issuing orders for the move around Columbia. Gist wished Columbia, South Carolina, not Tennessee, was their destination. Though he had commands to obey, he worried still about Uncle Wiley. What had become of him? The anxiety over Uncle Wiley's absence plagued him more than what lay ahead for himself.

Monday Morning,

November 28, 1864

Sam Watkins

Chapter Five

Sam Watkins
Camp Outside Columbia

Sam Watkins felt a hand shaking his shoulder and heard a distant but familiar voice cutting through the fog of his sleep.

"Wake up, Sam, wake up!"

Slowly, he emerged from his sluggish trance and recognized the words of Billy Carr.

"Get up, Sam. You might should check on Jennie."

At the mention of Jennie's name, Watkins sat up on his blanket and rubbed his eyes. "What about Jennie?"

"She may need your help."

Watkins flung back the cover and reached for his dilapidated shoes, yanking them over his tattered socks. "What are you talking about, Billy?"

"I got up to take a leak and heard a commotion. A couple regiments of Tennessee boys—the Third and the Eighteenth—intend to hit Columbia. Some of the fellows think the blue-bellies have abandoned town. Our boys being as hungry as they are, no telling what kind of mischief they'll get into. I thought you'd want to know."

Watkins shoved himself up from his bedding and grabbed his coat. "Thanks, Billy. Cover for me while I'm gone. I'll be back once Jennie's safe." He yanked on his jacket, snatched his rifle, attached the bayonet, spun around, and dashed through the camp, guessing he had thirty minutes until sunrise. Though still early, this day seemed different. As he ran toward Columbia, Watkins realized the clouds had thinned, offering the promise of sunshine that might lift men's spirits and dry out their clothes and gear. He sprinted past a pair of pickets, shouting he'd been sent on a special assignment by the captain. The two guards, nearing the end of their watch, didn't care and waved him on. He sprinted as fast as he could, though he knew he was weak. He wished he had grabbed some walnuts from his haversack before rushing off to protect Jennie from the Third and Eighteenth boys in case they dropped their Tennessee upbringing and ransacked Columbia.

As he sprinted ahead, he thought of the last time he had seen her. That visit had come twenty months earlier, after the bloody encounter at Murfreesboro. He remembered his desertion coincided with Abraham Lincoln's announcement he had signed a proclamation freeing the slaves in the rebellious states. Watkins had never owned a living soul, though he wished he did, twenty slaves to be exact. With the Conscription Act, the Confederate Congress had exempted from military service any man who owned twenty or more slaves, reaffirming what many soldiers had said that this was a rich man's war and a poor man's fight.

After the battle at Murfreesboro, the First Tennessee had settled west of Shelbyville along the Duck River. Still angered that the Conscription Act had delayed his marriage, still aching from the Murfreesboro flesh wound to his arm, and still longing to see Miss Jennie, Sam found a canoe and paddle on the banks of the Duck River. Though he had seen other soldiers shot by a firing squad for leaving their posts, he still simmered over the indefinite extension of his enlistment duration, angry that an officer could just resign and go his merry way while a webfoot was bound for the remainder of the conflict. In his mind, he deserved a furlough, even if he alone authorized it. He loaded himself and his rifle in the boat and starting drifting with the current toward home some thirty miles away.

Once he had paddled into the river, Watkins realized the canoe had been abandoned because it leaked. He alternated between paddling the boat and bailing it out with his hat. Barely halfway home, he realized fighting the water was a losing battle, just the latest in the losses since he had joined the army. He beached the leaky craft on the southern shore before its rising waters saturated his clothes, then hiked through the brisk winter weather for Columbia, sticking to the trees by the river for cover because he could not be certain where Yankee cavalry lurked. Watkins reached Columbia an hour before dark, but hid in the woods until the only light was the yellow rectangles seeping from the windows of local houses. He crept toward town, aiming for his home, a modest structure that his father Fred had managed on a farmer's earnings. Watkins slipped around to the back porch and through the window saw his stepmother and father at the dinner table. He rapped on the doorframe and watched the woman arise from her chair.

"Who could that be at this hour?" his stepmother asked as she stepped to the door.

"Probably some straggler begging for grub. Send him on his way if it is, Marge."

"I can't do it, dear, not if he's one of our boys. I wouldn't want another mother to send Sam away if he asked for food."

"Maybe so, if it's one of ours," his father growled, "but we're not offering even a crumb to some Yankee boy that might shoot Sam."

Watkins rested the butt of his rifle on the porch's warped planks and straightened as Margaret cracked the door and peered out with a single eye.

"What can we do for you, son?" she asked, failing to recognize him in the dark.

"It's Sam. I'm home for a few hours."

His stepmother flung open the entry and stared. "You've lost so much weight, I didn't recognize you. Come in, Sam, come in."

She hugged him, then pulled him inside, closing the door so the heat from the stove wouldn't escape. Sam's father bolted up from the table, hugging him, then stepping back, placing a hand on each shoulder and studying his boy and his blood-stained uniform. "You look a little puny, son."

"You would too, Pa, if you marched halfway across the Confederacy on slim rations."

His stepmother broke Fred's hold on his son. "Take a seat, Sam. We'll share what we've got. It ain't much, not after your brother and sisters ate."

"I'll get them," said his father.

Sam grabbed his dad's arm. "I don't want a commotion. Nobody's to know I'm here."

Fred turned around, cocked his head, and studied his son. "Did you desert, Sam?"

"I intend to return, Pa," he said, as he stepped to the corner, leaned his rifle against the wall, and moved to the kitchen stove to warm himself, though his father's gaze remained hot.

"I've heard they shoot deserters. That true?"

Sam nodded slightly.

"You came to see Jennie, didn't you?"

"I plan on spending the day with her tomorrow, if you'll keep me tonight and the next."

"Of course we will, Sam," his stepmother answered, studying him, then shaking her head. "Your uniform is filthy and ripped on the sleeve. Is that stain blood?"

"It is."

"Bullet or saber?" inquired his father.

"Miníe ball."

Clucking her tongue, Margaret shook her head. "I'm not letting Sam visit Jennie tomorrow looking like that. Shuck that uniform, and I'll launder it tonight," she said. "Fred, you go tell the children their brother is home, but they aren't to tell a soul, even after he leaves. I don't want a Yankee sympathizer finding out and reporting us to the provost marshal. And, scrounge up some of his old clothes or some of yours while I heat water." She paused and studied her stepson. "Looks like you could use a bath and a shave, too."

"It's been months since I've had a hot bath."

Margaret turned to her husband. "Get moving, Fred. We've got work to do, but bring the children in here first, no shouting or screaming."

His father slipped out of the kitchen into the parlor, then moments later the door flung open as six-year-old Robert and nine-year-old Alice ran in all smiles, grabbing Sam's waist and hugging him. Sister Sarah, sixteen, followed and kissed his cheek. "Welcome home, Sam. It true you deserted?"

"I took a few days away."

"To see Jennie, I bet."

Robert tugged on Sam's arm. "How many Yankees have you killed, Sam?"

Stamping her foot on the wooden floor, Margaret scolded Robert for such a question.

The young boy hung his head and answered his own question with a whispered aside. "However many, it ain't enough."

"War is nothing but hardship and death, Robert. I've seen enough of it for the both of us, so let's not talk about it again."

Robert turned away from his stepbrother, disappointed until he saw the rifle propped in the corner. He scooted to it.

"Look but don't touch it, Robert," Margaret ordered as she dipped water from the storage barrel into a pot to heat on the stove.

Sam sat at the kitchen table, visiting about local happenings, seeking news about Jennie, and questioning how the family was handling the hardships of war as his father returned with clothes. When the water boiled, Fred brought in the washtub and retreated to his bedroom to retrieve his razor, strop, and mirror. Margaret dumped two buckets of cold water in the tub, then poured the boiling pot in after that. She flushed the children and her husband from the room, providing Sam with soap, a washcloth, and a towel, then she too abandoned him.

Sam removed his clothes, leaving them in a pile beside the washtub. He straddled the container and lowered his naked bottom into the warm water, his legs hanging out over the side as he lathered himself up and started scouring weeks of grime and lice. He soaped his hair and scrubbed his scalp. When he was done, he pushed himself up from the tub and dried off, then put on the first civilian britches since he had enlisted in the army. He wadded up his uniform, drawers, and socks and dropped them in the liquid to rinse away some of the filth and perhaps make his stepmother's laundering a little easier. After wetting his hands, he grabbed the soap and rubbed up a lather that he slathered across his face. As the soap softened his whiskers, he unfolded the razor and worked it back and forth on the strop before sitting down at the table, propping the mirror up against the lamp and attacking his whiskers. As he finished, he took the washcloth and wiped the sudsy residue away. After that, he completed dressing and poked his head out of the kitchen into the parlor to announce he was presentable.

The family flooded in to join him, taking seats around the table, but Margaret suggested they return to the anteroom, where it was more comfortable while she heated more water to give Sam's uniform the scrubbing it needed. Sam vetoed her suggestion, saying if she was going to launder his things, he would not abandon her to the chore alone. So, they sat in the kitchen and talked about what had happened at home and in Columbia, especially with the loss of so many sons, brothers, and fathers, most of them known to Sam and many of whom he saw die. He kept the grisly details of their demises to himself. There was no glory in war, only death.

Eventually, the conversation turned to Sam's planned visit with Jennie the next day. Fred suggested Sam remain hidden inside the Watkins home and that Sarah fetch Jennie to spend the time with Sam in their house. Sam rejected that option, saying he intended to go courting and nobody would keep him from it, not even an entire Yankee regiment. His father next suggested that Sarah escort Sam in civilian clothes to the Mayes' home, arm-in-arm as if they were courting, then leave him there for the day, returning at dusk to bring him home. Sam liked the plan.

His stepmother still worked on his uniform when Sam retired to a mattress for the first time since he had left Nashville for Virginia. He slept well and could've slumbered longer before his father rousted him from bed. He dressed in his civilian clothes, ate a breakfast of fried eggs, bacon, and biscuits with butter and apricot preserves, and paced the kitchen waiting for Sarah to dress and escort him to Jennie's home. While Sarah had favored her clandestine duty when proposed last night, she failed to realize she would have to do it so early in the morning, especially on a frigid, windy one. She was ready a half-hour after sunrise and escorted Sam the few blocks to his sweetheart's home. As they walked arm-in-arm down the street, they met two Yankee cavalrymen more interested in ogling Sarah than checking Sam out. The soldiers tipped their hats. Sarah responded with a flirtatious wink.

Sarah explained that Jennie's three younger brothers remained at home. Sam listened without looking up, wearing his father's hat low over his forehead to reduce the chances of being recognized. He breathed easier when they stepped on the Mayes's front porch. Sam lifted the door clapper and banged it. After a moment, the door opened and one of Jennie's little brothers answered. "What do you want?"

"Tell Miss Jennie a man's here to court her," Sam said, without lifting his head and making eye contact.

"Jen," yelled the boy, "there's a man here to court you."

Jennie emerged from an adjoining room. "Tell him I'm already spoken for." She froze when she recognized Sarah.

"She's already spoken for," her brother repeated.

Sam lifted his head and gazed beyond the lad to Jennie. Though her hair was mussed, she had never looked more beautiful.

"Oh, my stars," Jennie said, clutching at her neck with one hand and running the fingers of her other through her hair. "Sam, I didn't know. Please come in."

As Sam and Sarah stepped past the boy, Jennie rushed to hug him.

"I can't believe it's you, Sam. Is your enlistment finally over? Momma, Poppa, Sam has come home."

"Just for the day," he replied, as he embraced her and kissed her cheek.

Sarah answered before he could speak. "He deserted the Confederacy to see you, Jennie."

She broke from his grasp, grabbed his arms.

Sam grimaced and flinched at her touch on his injured arm.

"Is that true? Did I hurt you?"

Before he could answer, George and Elvira entered the parlor. "Welcome, Sam," Elvira said.

"Hope you've been giving them Yankees hell," George offered.

"Poppa, such language," Jennie scolded.

"Thank you, Mr. and Mrs. Mayes. I'm just here for a few hours, then must return to my regiment. I hope you don't mind that I didn't send word in advance, but it's difficult for an army private to do such things in these times."

Sarah elaborated, "He's hoping you'll put up with him for the day and feed him while he annoys Jennie."

"That's wonderful," Jennie answered. "Sam can stay as long as he likes."

"Bye, Sarah," Sam said, "I hear Father calling."

Sarah grinned. "I'll see you this evening, Sam. Behave yourself." She turned about and let herself out the door.

Once his sister left, Sam's time with Jennie seemed to pass by faster than a Yankee Minié ball. The only hiccup was Jennie fretting over his desertion and what it might mean, though she admitted she was flattered he would risk his life just to see her. Sam eased her worries, telling her he was unlikely to get shot and more likely to be court-martialed. Jennie's parents kept Jennie's brothers out of the parlor so the two could talk in private, though Sam suspected the boys were eavesdropping behind the door because he kept hearing little snickers and giggles. Her mother baked an apple pie, using scarce flour and sugar for the pastry, and at lunch served Sam a quarter of the pie while splitting the rest among the other family members. His sweetheart took a single bite of her small slice, then pushed her plate to Sam. He patted her hand, then gobbled down that slice as well after a filling meal of fried ham, hominy, and freshly baked bread. Sam hoped Jennie had learned to cook from her mother.

As supper approached, Jennie fretted over Sam's fate, not just over the desertion, but also what might happen for the duration of the war. "Can I ask a favor of you, Sam?"

"Anything, Jennie."

"Just come back to me, Sam. That's all I ask. I pray daily to God that you return to me so I can spend my life with you. I love you, Sam."

Sam took a deep breath. She had said those words previously, but never with such depth and longing. "And I love you as I have since I first saw you as a boy."

"Return to me, Sam, and I will darn your socks, launder your clothes, cook your meals, and raise your children. I suppose we could even find the preacher today, Sam."

"My heart says yes, Jennie, but my mind says no. I've seen too much on the battlefield that could destroy our plans. Let me return.

When I do, I promise—if I am whole—I'll provide a roof over your head, food for your stove, clothes for your back, and laughter for our children." Sam leaned over and kissed her.

Moments later, the clap on the doorknocker announced Sarah's arrival. Sam kissed his betrothed again and stood up, offering Jennie his hand as her parents and brothers emerged from the kitchen.

"I'll have supper ready in half an hour, Sam, if you care to stay."

"Thank you, Mrs. Mayes. Dinner was delicious, especially the apple pie, but I must leave early in the morning to get back to my regiment." He grabbed his coat.

Jennie's father opened the door and let Sarah in. "We better hurry, Sam. The streets are clear of Yankees, but I don't know how long that will last."

Sam turned to Jennie, whispering "I love you" in her ear and kissing her full on the lips, drawing the giggles of her little brothers. Then he strode outside, afraid her family might see the tears in his eyes, as he wondered if he would ever cast his gaze upon his beloved companion again. He slipped his arm in Sarah's, and they hurried home on a cloudless night as a cold breeze whipped through the town. They made it safely to their destination, and the next morning Sam arose well before dawn, changed into a clean uniform for the first time in weeks, grabbed his coat and rifle and started for the Duck River and his regiment, his spirits high from his moments with Jennie and her promise of a future together.

With the early start, he reached the camp on the outskirts of Shelbyville before sundown. Confederate sentries stopped and disarmed him since he lacked the countersign. They took him to the guardhouse when he failed to produce a pass. He was court-martialed three days later for desertion. Standing before the judge advocate, he entered a plea of not guilty. The only witness against him was the rollcall sergeant, who confirmed that Watkins had abandoned his post for three days without permission. In his defense, he claimed he had enlisted for a year in good faith, and the Confederacy had betrayed him by extending his enlistment for another two years, if not more. Further, he had not had a furlough in all that time, and he was eager to visit his betrothed so she would not be tempted by some other beau. On top of that, Watkins pointed out he returned with a clean and laundered uniform, a service the Confederate States of America had failed to provide since his enlistment. Further, he argued he had done the Confederacy a favor in his absence by not consuming scarce provisions and by foraging instead in the kitchens of family and friends. The board of officers stifled grins and shook their heads at the unorthodox defense, before writing their verdict on sheets of paper and passing them to the judge advocate, who tallied them, nodded, and ordered Watkins to stand.

"In the matter of the Confederate States of America against Samuel R. Watkins, private, Company H, First Tennessee Regiment, the board of officers has voted unanimously for a guilty verdict. Under article eight-ninety-five of Confederate Army Regulations, soldiers guilty of desertion may be punished by death, confinement, confinement on bread and water only, solitary confinement, hard labor, ball-and-chain, forfeiture of pay and allowances, discharge from service, formal reprimand or any combination of the aforementioned. Do you understand, Private Watkins?"

"Yes, sir," he nodded, thinking bread and water might be an improvement over the current diet provided by Jefferson Davis.

"Very well," said the judge advocate. "Considering your willing return to the regiment and your unusual defense, I am sentencing you to thirty days of fatigue duty and the forfeiture of four months' pay at eleven dollars a month for a total of forty-four dollars. Do you understand the seriousness of the charge and the terms of your sentence?"

"Yes, sir," Watkins said, saluting the judge. "It will not happen again, sir."

"See that it doesn't, Private Watkins, or the punishment might be even more severe," the stern judge advocate paused a moment, then smiled. "Private Watkins this very morning First Corps Commander Lieutenant General Leonidas Polk issued a directive pardoning all soldiers absent without leave who voluntarily return to their divisions. Once the recorder provides you with your copy of the paperwork, you will be escorted to General Polk's headquarters to rectify this matter. Until then, you will be remanded to the guardhouse. Dismissed."

Watkins turned about and marched out of the room where his guard awaited to shackle his hands and return him to the stockade. Late in the afternoon, the promised papers arrived in the hand of Reverend Charles T. Quintard, who escorted him to Polk's headquarters, where he explained his situation to the general's aides.

"Are you the private who claimed you had saved the Confederacy money for laundry and meals in your absence?" asked a ruddy-faced assistant with a cowlick of auburn hair.

"Yes, sir."

The aide turned about and entered the adjoining office, returning momentarily.

"General Polk will see you in his office," he announced. "You, too, chaplain."

Watkins gulped a breath of air, coughing for a moment, then stepped into the adjacent room with Quintard behind him.

Polk arose from his desk.

Watkins stood ramrod straight and saluted the general, who returned the acknowledgment.

"Are you a lawyer, Private Watkins?"

"No, sir, just a Tennessee farm boy with a little book-learning."

"You've got a shrewder take on matters than most lawyers I've met, plus a sense of humor. We need some laughter to get us through these grim times."

"Thank you, sir."

"I'll have my aides pardon your desertion charge and eliminate the thirty days of fatigue duty."

"Thank you, sir. What about the fine?"

Polk grinned. "It stays. It'll give you something to laugh about years from now."

"Yes, sir. So I saved the Confederacy three days of rations and forty-four dollars?"

"The Confederate Treasury thanks you, Private Watkins. Dismissed."

Watkins saluted, about-faced, and marched from the general's office, the chaplain snickering in his wake.

Those memories flooded back to Watkins as he raced to Columbia. Up ahead, he heard sporadic gunfire and the occasional shouts of soldiers, but not the sound of an impending engagement of significance. As he trotted toward Jennie's home, Watkins considered the vagaries of an unpredictable war and the horrible irony that he might survive and his beloved Jennie might die, if a major battle engulfed Columbia.

Patrick Cleburne
Near Columbia

Well before dawn, Patrick Cleburne awoke in his tent, dressed in the darkness, then parted the flap on the canvas and marched outside. The camp remained dark and still, except for the sentries making their rounds. It had been too wet last night to build fires, so the soldiers just constructed their meager shelters or collapsed on the ground. To the west, Cleburne heard the muffled sounds of troops on the move but no gunshots, so he figured the noise was insignificant.

Cleburne lifted his head skyward and smiled. Between the scattered clouds, he saw patches of stars and a sliver of the moon for the first time in weeks. The early chill seemed less biting, almost invigorating on this Monday morning. Perhaps the preacher general had more pull with the Almighty than Cleburne had credited him.

As it remained too dark to survey the Yankee fortifications around Columbia, Cleburne retreated to his tent to write a note to his beloved Susan. He lit a candle at his field desk and sat on his campstool, smiling at the thought of his betrothed and at the prospects of better weather for Hood's Columbia plans. Finishing his missive to his sweetheart, Cleburne blotted the ink, folded the paper, and slipped it in the envelope, which he sealed with candle wax. He wrote Susan Tarleton's name and Mobile, Alabama, on the outside and left the correspondence on his desk for Mangum to stamp and send off. Cleburne lingered on the campstool, wondering—hoping, really—that he might get a furlough for Christmas to marry Susan. Like all soldiers, he could only wish for such luck, as battle and commanders determined the fates of all, even major generals.

As he pondered the possibilities, the camp awakened, softly at first, then with the murmuring of men and even some cheers. Arising to investigate, Cleburne had taken but a step when he heard the squish of running feet in the saturated earth and saw the tent flap fling open. Lieutenant Mangum stuck his head inside.

"Good morning, General Cleburne. The enemy evacuated Columbia overnight."

Cleburne clapped his hands. "Excellent news indeed, Mangum! And the weather's improving. Our preacher general must have telegraphed his request upstairs."

"If General Lowrey unleashed his full hellfire and brimstone on the Yankees, we might be back home in Helena in time for supper."

The general pointed at Susan's envelope. "If the fighting stopped today, I'd go straight to Mobile, not Helena. I've got another letter to post."

"I'll take care of it." Mangum approached the desk and took it.

Cleburne scratched at the itch on his cheek. "I haven't received a letter from her in more than a week."

The lieutenant nodded. "The mails aren't dependable with Yankees muddying up things. Besides that, General Hood doesn't give a high priority on getting his men their mail—"

"Or food, or shoes, or clothing either, just powder and ammunition. That's all an army needs in his mind, certainly not provisions, though he feasts well each night as the guest of wealthy planters wanting to protect their slaves. Mark my words, if it's true the enemy has abandoned Columbia, looting will follow when our men enter town.

"Hunger'll do funny things to a man's judgment, General, so I can't say I blame them."

"Nor do I, Mangum. We both know who's to blame."

Rev. Charles T. Quintard
Beechlawn Plantation

The reverend reclined on the Beechlawn library floor, awaiting the dawn among sleeping members of John Bell Hood's staff, their loud snores stoked by fatigue and uncertainty of what lay ahead. The wooden floor was hard, but at least it was warm and dry, unlike the camps where the men these officers commanded made their beds. Carefully, Quintard arose to his knees, bowed his head and said a silent prayer, beseeching God first that Cornelia Warfield would find the strength to carry on for her family and for Tennessee. He prayed next for the soldiers that did the fighting that they might be spared; for the officers that led them so that they might show wisdom in all their strategies; and finally, for Tennessee that its people would soon live in peace, free of an oppressive Yankee occupation.

When he finished his prayer, he rolled up his bedding and tied it. Arising and grabbing his boots, he pulled them on, then stepped to the window. Through a crack in the drapes, Quintard saw a sliver of light as day was breaking. He offered thanks for the scattered clouds, for the encroaching sunlight, and for the warmth that would follow, as it would ease the burdens of the fighting men. The reverend felt ashamed that he had enjoyed such fine, warm, and dry comforts in recent nights. Around him, a few stirred, stretching and yawning as they arose to another challenging morning to address the vagaries of war and survival. As two staff officers murmured about the new day, others awoke with groans and aches, rising on their hands and knees, shaking their heads of slumber's cobwebs and pushing themselves to their feet, gathering up their bedding, uncertain where they would next throw their blankets this night.

One colonel straightened and wondered, "Has anyone heard General Hood fall out of bed yet?"

"Not yet," replied a lieutenant opening the drapes to let in the encroaching daylight. "Of course, we'll hear him tumble down the stairs."

Both men drew laughter. Humor, Quintard thought, was God's gift to help mankind navigate troubled times. He recalled Job 5:22: *At destruction and famine, thou shalt laugh; neither shalt thou be afraid of the beasts of the earth.* After all, as Ecclesiastes 3:4 proclaimed, there was *a time to weep, and a time to laugh; a time to mourn, and a time to dance.* When it came time to dance, Quintard wondered if it would be on the graves of Yankees or on the graves of his neighbors.

The chaplain grabbed his bedroll and carpetbag, then excused himself from the assembly, stepping out of the library into the entryway, exiting through the front door. Before him on the lawn camped a hundred Rebel soldiers guarding the general's quarters. In their ragged uniforms, they huddled around a dozen campfires, fixing their ersatz coffee and frying some salt pork for breakfast. When the guards saw it was a chaplain rather than a fighting officer, they ignored him, preferring the warmth of their fires to his company.

As Quintard walked to the side of the house, a courier galloped up, reined in his mount, and jumped from the saddle, making certain everyone knew he carried a significant communication. "This is from Richmond for General Hood. It's an important message."

The officer commanding the guard took the envelope. "All messages to General Hood are important. I'll see that he gets it."

"I was told to deliver it in person or get a receipt, so Richmond would know who to hang if it isn't properly delivered to General Hood."

The officer ripped open the envelope and removed its contents, handing the courier the empty cover.

"There's your receipt," the officer announced.

"Sign it," the courier demanded.

"I don't take orders from a private."

The messenger grinned, lifted the leather cover from his pistol scabbard and drew the weapon, aiming it at the officer's chest. "You'll take a ball of lead if you don't." He cocked the hammer on the revolver.

Instantly, the lieutenant lost his concern over rank, yanked a pencil stub from his uniform blouse, and signed his name to the envelope. "We're on the same side, fellow," said the officer.

"Just following orders, sir." The courier took the envelope, folded it in half and tucked it in his britches pocket. "You best get those orders to General Hood quick because Richmond's demanding action, as General Lee is bottled up around Petersburg, and General Sherman is raising havoc along the coast in Georgia and South

Carolina." The messenger released the hammer on the pistol and shoved it back in its holster. Jumping atop his horse, he grabbed the reins and bolted away from Beechlawn. Such were the fleeting fortunes of war as men interacted for a moment, then rode away, never to meet again.

Quintard strode to the stables, planning to saddle his gelding, then fetch Henry from the slave quarters and ride off in search of the First Tennessee. He felt like he had been pampered the last few days and needed to rejoin the fighting men to offer them what encouragement he could. Oh, if only General Hood were right, and he would limit the casualties to seven hundred or fewer. At the outbuilding, the reverend discovered the youth saddling his horse.

"Good morning, Henry. I'm surprised to find you here, already at work."

"Couldn't sleep, Massa Revrund. And, de roof leaks." Henry took the bedroll and secured it behind the saddle, then tied the carpetbag in place.

"Looks like we'll get sunshine today, Henry. You won't need to wear your gum blanket again."

"I's plans to keeps it handy, jus' de same."

"We'll figure out something for breakfast on the road, Henry. Too many folks have been eating off the Warfield family the last few days."

Quintard led the horse outside the barn, mounted, and helped Henry on behind him. They rode to the front of the big house, where Quintard spotted General Hood on his crutch, reading the telegram from Richmond. Looking up from the missive, Hood saw Quintard and motioned for him to ride over. The chaplain guided his horse toward the commander through the soldiers in front of the house.

"I enjoyed our visit last night, Reverend," Hood called. "I covet your prayers. It is my hope and trust that the enemy must give me a fight soon, or I will be in Nashville before tomorrow night."

"My prayers will beseech the Almighty likewise, General, and I will ask that an angel ride on your shoulder the entire route. May God ride with you and your men."

Quintard reined his horse toward the turnpike, mouthing a silent prayer for Hood and his troops. The reverend and his boy rode to the pike and headed north toward Columbia, passing stragglers and the pontoon wagons headed for the Duck River.

Both the reverend and his manservant enjoyed the increasing warmth of the sun. Then Henry spoke. "Massa Revrund, youse reads de Good Book. What says its abouts slaves?"

"That question has come up many times before and during this conflict, Henry. In first Timothy, chapter six, verse one, the Bible says, '*Let as many servants as are under the yoke count their own masters worthy of all honor, that the name of God and his doctrine be not blasphemed.*'"

"Dat word blas—"

"Blas-phemed. It means cursed, that you should never curse God, nor his Word, no matter your place in life."

"I's do knows me place in life, Massa. What's about yours?"

"To minister to the spiritual needs of my fellow man."

Henry pondered the chaplain's response, then spoke softly. "Massa Revrund, woulds youse rather bes a massa or a slave?"

"A master, of course."

"Why shouldn'ts I's be feeling de same way?"

Confound him again, Quintard thought, as he advanced toward Columbia. He would be glad to be among the soldiers again because they asked less perplexing questions.

Lt. Gen. John Bell Hood
Beechlawn

During breakfast in the Beechlawn dining room, General Hood pondered how to answer the message from Richmond while he received updates from his subordinates with his meal of fried eggs, bacon, biscuits, and cane syrup. His aide-de-camp reported that General Schofield and his Union troops had abandoned Columbia overnight, burning the railroad bridge and damaging the bridge on the pike. "Damn," Hood muttered, angered that Nathan Bedford Forrest had predicted the evacuation.

Hood despised Forrest more than he did his foe, John Schofield. Forrest remained a talented but insubordinate soldier of low learning, his formal education more accurately measured in months than in years. As for his enemy Schofield, Hood had known him at West Point, a Yankee who befriended him and encouraged him to stay in the U.S. Military Academy despite the challenging academics and his poor grades. Hood and Schofield often joked about their cadet standings, Schofield graduating first in infantry tactics and Hood graduating last in ethics. Despite the sectional tensions during their time at the West Point, never did the classmates imagine that one day they would face each other across the battlefield. Even so, Hood respected Schofield more than his own cavalry leader.

Hood's aide-de-camp also summoned an infantry captain who reported that two Tennessee regiments had entered Columbia at dawn, ransacking homes and businesses of wood for warmth and foodstuffs for nourishments. Between bites from his full plate, Hood dictated orders condemning the theft and destruction of civilian property, but refusing to dole out punishment.

"Shouldn't we punish some to set an example?" asked the aide-de-camp.

Hood shook his head as he wiped his mouth with a linen napkin. "We'll need all our men tomorrow when we ambush Schofield's army. He'll dig in facing south, but we'll slip behind him and force him to attack us behind our entrenchments. In the interim, instruct our officers to stop the looting by example and moral suasion with the threat of harsher means if discipline is not restored."

As he sent the captain away, he asked the aide to send in Cornelia Warfield. Moments later, the plantation mistress arrived.

"Yes, General Hood."

Pointing to his plate, he smiled. "Might I have more?"

Cornelia nodded with tight lips, then spoke. "Certainly, General Hood, but I ordered our remaining kitchen help to handle other chores, so it will take me a few minutes to prepare it myself. Every time the Yankees pass by, a few more of our slaves depart with them."

"Take what time you need, ma'am."

She collected his plate and exited the room, giving Hood a brief respite before other officers came in to report on how well his corps commanders were implementing his plan. The report on the cavalry was encouraging, as Hood could depend on Forrest's competence despite his Tennessee obstinacy. Forrest had divided his cavalry into four detachments and sent them across the Duck River at different locations, only one of which encountered significant resistance. The pontoon caravan was nearing Columbia and would be at the ford by late afternoon.

After the progress reports, Cornelia returned with Hood's second morning platter. As she exited, he requested she close the doors so he could eat in solitude.

"I won't require breakfast tomorrow, ma'am."

"That's good, sir, as we're short on food now, barely enough to feed ourselves."

"I'll be leaving in the wee hours of the morning to clear the Yankee vermin from Tennessee. So soon you will have all the food you need for yourself, your children, and your slaves."

After finishing his second helping of vittles, Hood pushed himself up from his chair and hopped to the wall where he grabbed his crutch and tucked it under his right arm, then crept across the room to the door leading into the parlor. He took a deep breath, nudged open the door with his shoulder and emerged into the room where a dozen aides awaited his new orders.

Mary Alice Carter McPhail
Carter Home

Mary Alice smiled from the back porch as the morning broke with scattered clouds and the promise of sunshine that would melt some of the snow and ice. The bogus coffee warmed her as the morning sun rose, casting long shadows from the house toward the barn, the toolshed, and the outbuildings, including the slave dwellings, empty save for Jack, Callie, and Oscar. Mary Alice caught the aroma of wood smoke from the cookhouse as Callie worked on breakfast for the family. She stepped to the south end of the porch, moving her gaze from the Columbia Pike to the wooden building her father used as an office, the stone smokehouse, and the other buildings toward the locust grove where she had so many fond memories of playing with her younger brother Tod when they were children.

As she studied the place, her dad came up the stairs from the basement, opening the door onto the porch and stepping to Mary Alice. Like her, he held a cup of the parched grain coffee from the pot Callie had left on the grate in the cellar fireplace.

"It'll warm up today," Fount said, as he placed his cup on the porch railing and stretched his arms. "These old bones need some heat and sunshine for a change. Winters are hard on an old man. If November is any indication of what's ahead, this'll be the worst winter in years. Cold weather saps my strength."

"You'll manage, Father, you always have."

"And you remind me of your mother, Mary Alice, always positive, and always spending a few moments early each morning reflecting on the day before us."

"You miss her, don't you?"

Fount nodded. "Hard to believe she's been gone twelve years. She always saw the good in things, just like you, Mary Alice."

"I don't know about that. I see the bad, but only speak of the good, especially around the children."

"Like your Sunday School lesson yesterday. I heard you talking about David and Goliath. We're David, but we're running out of stones against our Yankee Goliath. You never sowed a doubt among the grandchildren that we would do anything but prevail."

"We shall face what comes, Father. We must hope for the best."

"I hope to see Theodrick return home."

"Do you think Tod is with the Confederate army, wherever it is?"

"Wherever the Twentieth Tennessee is, that's where he'll be, but I worry about his luck. In life, a man has only so much luck. To be taken as a prisoner of war, and then to escape from a moving train in Pennsylvania was lucky enough. But to walk all the way south to rejoin his regiment without getting shot as a bushwhacker or hung as a spy requires even more good fortune." Fount picked up his cup and took a healthy swig of the steaming liquid. He swallowed, then sighed. "Like groceries, luck can only go so far."

Mary Alice grimaced because her father's instincts remained strong. "Tod's a survivor. Who would've thought he'd become a captain so young or quartermaster for his regiment or write newspaper reports from the field?"

Fount snickered. "Wasn't 'Mint Julep' the name he wrote under?"

"Yes, sir. I've kept under my bed all the copies of *The Chattanooga Daily Rebel* I could find with his stories in them. I remember Mint Julep describing a dress parade of the Army of Tennessee with trees and housetops filled with dirty-faced boys watching like pigeons in a roost. He always had a sense of humor and an eye for detail. The former made him so much fun, and the latter made him such a fine lawyer."

"I wish he was still practicing law, rather than war."

"Me, too, Father. What are you planning if the weather clears?"

He pointed to his muddy footwear by the porch steps. "After breakfast, I'll put on my boots and check on the gin, make sure nothing's been pilfered during the icy weather. In a regular year, we'd be ginning cotton by now. Not this year. So little cotton was planted this spring and with no slaves to harvest what there was this fall, there's no point in firing up the machinery. Even if we ginned a bale, the Yankees would steal it, and we'd be none the better for our work."

"I miss the days when we were kids playing in the locust grove," she answered, then finished her coffee. "Mind if I borrow your boots, Father?"

Fount gave her a puzzled look over the top of his cup as he took another sip.

Mary Alice smiled. "I want to walk among the locust trees for old time's sake."

Fount nodded. "Go ahead, but be back before I finish breakfast. I've chores to handle."

"Yes, sir," Mary Alice said, leaving her cup on the porch railing and hugging her father before sliding her feet with the slippers still on inside her father's footwear. Though the fit was loose, she managed to walk through the thin layer of snow and ice toward the grove. She strode by the cookhouse, stopping and slipping her head inside the door to greet Callie, who was busy preparing the family's breakfast.

"Morning, Callie. Thanks for the hot coffee."

"Yes, ma'am, buts ya didn't say it be good."

"Callie, you did the best you could with what you had."

Callie slapped her knee and giggled. "One of dese days I's gonna warms up some creek water and sees if ya knows de difference betweens it and de parched grain coffee."

Mary Alice laughed. "See you at breakfast."

"Be about thirty minutes," Callie replied, turning back to the wood stove.

Mary Alice closed the door and strolled to the locust trees, denuded of their colorful leaves by the cold spell. The rising sun lighted the tops of the trees like golden shards of glass as Mary Alice walked among them on a soft carpet of yellowed leaves intermixed with the thin layer of snow and ice. The trees had shed their feather-like leaves and their darkened seedpods, but not their thorns. Locusts were odd trees with thorns growing on their limbs and trunks. The danger was the allure to young Tod, who was seven years her junior. She had first gone with Tod when he was three or four to make sure he didn't harm himself, though it only took one prick by a tough thorn for him to learn not to get too close to the trees.

Despite the age difference, Mary Alice had found Tod to be a precocious delight, as much for his sense of humor as his intelligence, which surprised her even at a young age. Their other siblings were too scared—or too smart—to follow them to the copse of trees, so Mary Alice determined it was their special place. They had discussed the innocent topics of childhood like what they aspired to be when they grew up and who among their friends did they like most. Even when she outgrew the amusements, Mary Alice still played marbles with him or drew pictures in the dirt with sticks to amuse him because she enjoyed his company so. Though the boy had given way to the man inside him, Mary Alice always viewed him as an innocent youth. The memories moistened Mary Alice's eyes, so she ambled home where she found Moscow had joined her father on the back porch, discussing chores that needed attending.

"Should we fill in those trenches from last year, maybe discourage any soldiers from digging up our place again if they come here from Columbia?" her brother asked.

Fount shrugged. "What we do won't matter. They'll fight where they fight. Besides, I don't care to wear out our two remaining work horses. I must save them as much as I can for spring planting, especially since we don't have enough grain to feed them."

"Will we ever fill those trenches?"

"When the war's over, Moscow. The fighting will end one day, but our chores won't."

As Mary Alice climbed the porch steps, Moscow turned to her. "Where've you been?"

"To the locust grove."

Her brother laughed. "Did you find Tod or someone else to play with?"

"No, just uncovered a few memories. That's all."

Moscow grinned. "Why don't you let your kids play out there?"

"Too many thorns," she replied.

"It never stopped you," her father said.

"My children have more cautious parents than I had!" She smiled as she looked at her father.

Moscow laughed as Fount shook his head. "That's the last time I let you borrow my boots, Mary Alice."

She made amends by hugging her father as Callie came up the steps from the basement.

"Grub's on de table," she announced.

Hardin Figuers
Figuers Home

The clouds parted as dawn slipped across Franklin. The ground remained saturated as the snow and ice melted away under the gaze of the rising sun. Hardin Figuers rejoiced that he could finally escape the house, maybe go hunting with his slingshot. After a breakfast of two hot biscuits his mother had baked that morning, Hardin grabbed his coat, slipping his arms in the sleeves and starting for the back door before Bethenia grabbed his shoulders and turned him around to button his coat.

"You're missing two buttons," she said as she secured the two remaining orbs. "You should've told me."

Hardin shrugged. "What good would it've done? You don't have any, and no store in town has any to sell."

"We can improvise, Hardin, like we have since the war started. If you lose your other two buttons, the coat will be of little use to you when winter arrives in force."

"Do you want me to cut buttons from somebody else's coat?"

"Goodness no, Hardin. While you're out, see if you can find a peach pit or two. Some ladies at the church have been slicing them in half and using them for coat buttons."

"Peaches aren't in season, Momma."

"I know that, Hardin, but you and your friends have eaten peaches and thrown away the pits. Just see if you can find a place where you may have discarded them."

"I'd just as soon wear a coat without buttons than one with peach pits."

"You'll button your coat because I'll not have you get a chill and turn sick. I don't intend to lose another child, Hardin. Now, do as I say."

Hardin sighed. "Yes, ma'am." He grabbed his hat from the peg by the kitchen exit and stepped outside, delighted to be in the open air and away from his mother. He closed the door forcefully enough to let her know of his objections, but not so hard as to draw a tongue-lashing. The brisk morning air reddened his cheeks, drawing an admission he was glad for the two buttons that still secured his coat around his torso.

He strode to their modest barn and opened the door, then walked past their mule to the back corner where his hound Adele reclined on a carpet of hay beneath a saddle blanket. "Hey, ol' gal. You ready to go for a walk? Are you any good at sniffing out peach pits? Momma thinks we need some so she can make buttons for my coat. I brought my slingshot to do some hunting."

Hardin kneeled beside the blue hound and stroked her neck, then tweaked her floppy ears. The lethargic Adele remained still, enjoying the warmth of the saddle blanket. Hardin, though, was eager to go exploring and see what another day might bring, so he yanked the cover off his dog. "Come on, Adele, let's go for a walk."

Slowly, the hound arose, leaning forward on her forelegs and stretching, her big ears flopping as she shook her head.

"That's a girl." He rubbed behind Adele's ears, then stood up and started for the barn door. Glancing back, Hardin saw his hound trailing. Passing their mule, he patted the gray animal's rump, thankful the mule had not been taken by the Confederates to support the cause or stolen by the Yankees to further their mischief. After Adele followed him outside, Hardin secured the barn door and stepped past the empty chicken coop, whose occupants had not been so lucky, two dozen setting hens stolen by the same troops that would've shot Santa Claus if they ever had the chance. It had been weeks since Hardin had eaten an egg, thanks to Abraham Lincoln's minions.

Hardin led Adele south of the house beyond the six oak trees he had climbed many a boring day growing up and occasionally still did when rumors reached his ears of approaching soldiers from either army. The sight of armed men and the sound of their rattling and clanking armaments always thrilled him. As he walked through the thin ice, the ground crackled beneath him. The whack of an ax from his neighbor's house told him someone had beaten him outside. Hardin figured it was Jesse, the middle-aged slave his neighbors kept to handle chores. Jesse remained one of the loyal darkies who had stayed with his owner while so many others had simply disappeared or headed north to Nashville where the Union Army controlled the city. He walked around his house to the road and crossed Carter's Creek Pike aiming for the back of the neighboring place. There he spotted Jesse, swinging an ax and splitting firewood.

"Morning, Uncle Jesse," he called, startling the hand, who looked up and grinned when he recognized Hardin.

"Good day, Marse Hardin. I's sho glad de weather's broken." The white of Jesse's teeth glistened against his coal black face, as he responded with a sincere smile. He lifted the ax and rested the handle over his shoulder as he studied Hardin. "I's seeing yo'r slingshot in yo'r pocket. You mus' be huntin' for game. You be huntin' deer or you be goin' after bear?"

Hardin hung his head. "Peach pits, Jesse. Can you believe it, peach pits?"

Jesse snickered. "I be hearin' peach pits mighty dangerous game, Marse Hardin, but dere ain't much meat on de bones of a peach pit."

"Momma wants them for buttons for my coat." Hardin pointed to the two vacant button holes on his wrap.

"Yo'r ma be a smart woman, makin' do with what she's got. Dat's what us slaves does to survives. Yes, it is." As Adele sauntered up to him, Jesse bent over and rubbed her head. "A fine hound like Adele should pick up de scent of de peach pits in no time, Marse Hardin."

"Peaches aren't in season, Jesse."

"Reminds me when I's a little boy up in de big house where my ma dids house chores. Apples weren't in season, but dere in de dinin' room on dis fine mahogany table sats a silver bowl with a bunch of fruit and de pretties', de reddes' apple I's ever did sees. I's jus' had to have dat apple." Jesse straightened up and shook his head. "When no one be looking, I's takes dat apple and slips outside to eats it. It be so good lookin', I's a plannin' to eat it all from de peel to de stem to de core. When I's takes a bite, it taste like pizen. I's hacked and spits it up. I's didn't knows dey made apples out of wax to decorate de fancy tables of de rich white folks. I's returns it to the table, but Ma's mistress sure be angered when she find de bite mark in de apple. She banned me from de house for a year and threatened to makes ma a field hand. Ma sure be mad and give me a fine whippin', yes, she did."

"You think they make wax peach pits, Uncle Jesse?"

He laughed. "Who knews dey made apples outta wax, Marse Hardin? If I's be you, I's be looking behin' de outhouses. Dat's where de slaves eats tings deir massas don't wants dem to eat."

"I'll do that, Uncle Jesse." Hardin snapped his fingers for Adele to come to his side. "You heard anything through the grapevine about what's going on with the armies?"

"With de cold and wet days, news be scarce. What my kind be saying is dat de 'federates and de Yankees be tryin' to box de other in. I's bets even de generals don't be knowin' what be happenin'. Why else would dis war be lastin' dis long? I's jus' like to know if I's be slave or be free, dat's all, no offense to you and yo'r kind, Marse Hardin."

Hardin nodded. "None taken. You're a good man, Uncle Jesse, but I best find some peach pits."

"Good huntin', young'un. Remembers to checks behin' de outhouses. Don't lets one of dem peach pits ambush you." Jesse snickered as he slid the ax from his shoulder and resumed splitting firewood. Hardin led Adele behind Uncle Jesse's outhouse.

With the ground veiled in white from the snow and ice, Hardin decided to return later in the afternoon once the morning sun had melted the covering so he could look for peach pits. Crossing Carter's Creek Pike and passing the six oak trees by his house, Hardin headed for the locust grove a half mile away. He couldn't approach the grove without laughing about the day he sent Union infantry running from their bivouac by the trees after he knocked down the hornet's nest with his slingshot. The Yankees darted from their camp, yelling and cursing the stinging insects and whatever had disturbed them. They didn't return to their bedding until dark.

As he neared the locust grove, he saw one of the Carter women strolling among the trees. He wondered what she was doing up so early, but circled around the grove so not to disturb her in case she wanted the solitude. He looked south toward Breezy and Winstead hills, which were split by the Columbia Pike as it approached Franklin, passing between the Carter home on the west and the family cotton gin on the east. South of those structures, he could still see the remnants of trenches hastily dug by Union soldiers in April of 1863 to fend off an attack by Confederate cavalry. It had been a minor skirmish, each side suffering slightly over a hundred casualties each, nothing like Shiloh, Murfreesboro, or Chickamauga in significance or in numbers. For Hardin, though, the aftermath was exciting as he scoured the fields and meadows around the encounter for days, picking up spent shells, a sword, shrapnel, and personal effects left after the battle. They remained treasured souvenirs he kept in the room he shared with Tom.

Hardin crossed the Columbia Pike and marched all the way to the railroad a half mile east of the turnpike. He strode along the rail for a hundred yards, then turned back west toward home, hoping to flush a cottontail that he could provide for lunch or supper, but the animals remained in their dens, still reluctant to come out after so much cold weather. By midmorning, the sun had risen high enough to begin melting the snow cover. As he walked, Hardin unbuttoned his coat, enjoying the increasing warmth. As he headed back to his house, he meandered among the homes on the outskirts of Franklin, checking behind the outhouses but coming up empty. He circled north of the cotton gin, then ambled toward the Carter home where he saw Fountain Carter checking his rain gauge by his office. Hardin aimed between the house and office.

"Good morning, Mr. Carter," he called.

Carter dumped the gauge and placed it back in its holder. He held his arm up to let Hardin know he had heard him, but intended to first complete the task on his mind. He pulled a pad and pencil from his shirt pocket and wrote down the precipitation amount. After he shoved the pencil and paper back in his pocket, he looked at his visitor.

"Hello, Hardin. Three and a quarter inches of rain over the last two days in my gauge. Good to see a young fellow like you up and about."

"I'm looking for peach pits."

"Planning on starting an orchard?"

"No, buttoning my coat."

Fountain Carter scratched his head.

"Momma can't find or buy any buttons, but thinks she can split a peach pit and make replacements out of them."

"Good for her. I'll check with my girls if they have any to spare."

"Do you mind if I look behind your outhouses? Uncle Jesse says slaves sometimes'll throw them there."

"Sure, Hardin, go ahead. You shot any more hornet's nests down on Yankee soldiers?"

"No, sir. Momma put an end to that, telling me the Yankees might shoot me or hang me by my toes if they caught me."

"Bethenia's probably right, Hardin. You be careful and don't get in any mischief that'll get you hurt." Carter opened the door to his office and entered.

With Adele by his side, Hardin continued toward the outhouses, but had little luck finding any peach pits. His failure surprised him because he thought the Carter family had everything. They weren't prosperous enough to be considered plantation owners, but they had a sizeable plot of Franklin land, a fine house, farm office, a cookhouse, cotton gin, and outbuildings for animals and slaves.

By the time he returned home, his mother had a lunch of yams and buttered biscuits on the table. Hardin explained to her that he had searched for peach pits, but had not found any, noting the snow cover had made a thorough search impossible. He promised to resume his chore after lunch, following Uncle Jesse's recommendation to look behind his outhouse.

States Rights Gist
Outside Columbia

Arising early, General Gist moved among his men as they roused from their positions outside Columbia and groused about their growling stomachs. Yesterday's entire ration had amounted to a biscuit apiece. Gist strode among them, offering encouragement and sympathy, but his Georgians and South Carolinians could not eat his words. Periodically, he inquired if anyone had seen Wiley Howard. If the men even answered, they simply said no, but most of them just shrugged, wishing they had had a manservant to handle their chores or search for food to quell the rumbling in their guts.

Gist fretted that something had happened to Uncle Wiley. Perhaps Union scouts had captured him or worse killed him for his horse. As Howard carried a pass to get him through Confederate lines, perhaps the Yankees discovered he served a Rebel general and then tortured him for any intelligence he might divulge. Gist thought of a hundred possibilities, all with an unhappy outcome, but Uncle Wiley was a crafty slave, one who thought on his feet and could talk his way out of a bind. Maybe Yankees had stolen Joe Johnston, leaving Wiley afoot to get back to the army. Gist hoped that was the case. He could find another horse, and he could buy another overcoat, but he could not replace Wiley Howard. Sure Uncle Wiley was a slave, but he had remained a loyal confidant for years, the one man Gist could always count on for whatever he needed.

Disappointed that he had uncovered no clue to Uncle Wiley's disappearance, Gist returned to his tent, preparing to head to the morning meeting with corps commander John Brown when a courier rode up, calling his name. A chill raced through his body, not from the early cold, but from the fear that he was about to learn something had happened to Uncle Wiley.

"Over here," Gist waved, and the courier jerked his reins and aimed his bay mare toward the general.

The messenger sped over, saluted Gist and issued a report. "The enemy abandoned Columbia during the night. Forrest has taken his cavalry to harass and slow the Yankee march. Assemble your men and prepare for whatever General Hood orders. He may want us to head off General Schofield before he can get to Nashville."

Gist nodded. "Advise General Brown we'll be ready to move in less than an hour."

After saluting, the courier dashed off to deliver similar orders to other brigades, and Gist sprinted to alert his colonels. Shortly, the entire brigade sprang to life, readying for whatever they might be asked to do. Gist saddled Kitty himself and climbed atop his mount, riding among his men to confirm his orders were being obeyed. Beyond the hills to the east, the sky tinted pink and the heavens appeared through the scattered clouds for the first time in days. Though the morning chill brought shivers to him without his overcoat, Gist hoped the day would warm up enough to make it easier on the men to advance, whatever their orders were. Sunshine and warmth would dry the muddy ground and give men better footing when they marched.

Minutes later, another courier arrived from General Brown, ordering each brigade to start fires and fix their breakfast, slim as it might be. Reports indicated Schofield had established earthworks north of Columbia to await Hood's expected assault, once Hood repaired the two Columbia bridges Union troops had destroyed. As Gist understood the plan, Hood would send a small detachment of engineers to town to repair the crossings as a decoy. The bulk of the engineers, though, would create a pontoon bridge crossing east of town, so Hood's army could slip behind Schofield's troops. While Forrest's cavalry harassed Schofield's rear, Hood's army the next day would race to Spring Hill where Schofield's supply train might be captured to offer provisions and ammunition for an army short on both. Gist thought the plan solid and workable, but Hood was big on visions, though blind on details and logistics, aggravating the distribution of the South's precarious supplies.

As he moved among his men, he heard their grumbling complaints they would neither capture nor pass through Columbia, where food waited behind the locked doors of the residents. Even if they would be taking nourishment from the mouths of their Confederate kin, the soldiers felt certain their civilian allies would give up some of their provisions for the cause.

Every mention of this Tennessee town reminded Gist of another Columbia, his Columbia in South Carolina where his beloved Janie waited. He wished he were back home, defending the soil of the Palmetto State and his wife's plantation. Gist feared Sherman's devouring horde might raid her land, steal food from her mouth, or defile her. He regretted not being back in South Carolina to protect her and their future. As he rode Kitty among his men, he thought a lot of Janie. And of Uncle Wiley!

He wondered if he would ever see both again.

Hiram Granbury
Encampment outside Columbia

When he reached the camp of the Twenty-fourth Texas Calvary, Hiram Granbury saw Captain Samuel T. Foster approaching and smiling, as if he'd won a hundred dollars on a horse race.

The two exchanged perfunctory salutes. "Where's my apple pie, Captain?"

"I'm bringing you news that is better than any pie. I drove the Yankees out of Columbia overnight. When they heard I was coming, they skedaddled. They burned the bridges over the river, but no other major damage."

"Then we shall live to fight another day, Captain," Granbury said. "Your victory will certainly go down in the annals of Confederate military history as one of the grandest ever, except you failed your strategic mission to bring me an apple pie."

"You know how combat is, General. You don't always attain your goal. Now I'd like permission to take my regiment into town and find what food we can to put some breakfast in their bellies."

Granbury grimaced. "I have no orders to advance on Columbia, though I've heard the Third and Eighteenth Tennessee entered earlier this morning and pillaged the place. I can't let you take your troops, but I can authorize a foraging party to see what you can scrounge up. Be respectful but firm with the citizens as they are our people, and they face a hard winter ahead."

"Do I tell them the army will reimburse them?"

Shrugging, Granbury answered, "With what? Our dollars aren't worth a tenth of their face value."

"I'll do the best I can, General." Foster turned away and scurried among his soldiers, designating two dozen to accompany him into Columbia immediately. Shortly, they moved from camp toward town, as Granbury continued to check his regiments, telling them the good news that the Yankees had abandoned Columbia, and his Texans would live another day.

As the morning lengthened, his men enjoyed the bright sunshine, which warmed their bodies and provided a break from the dreary conditions they had plodded through almost daily since the beginning of November. Granbury prayed the Army of Tennessee's luck was changing like the weather—for the better!

Sumner Cunningham
Outside Columbia

While the skies had cleared to a vibrant blue, save for the white clouds that drifted by like the ghosts of Confederate dead, the sergeant major still shivered from his perpetual fear. Some men managed their battle anxiety through drink, mischief, or plain ignorance of the possibilities, but not Cunningham. He tried to bury his fears in paperwork. Each second delivered him closer to his demise, he thought, as he busied himself this morning filling out requisitions for supplies and totaling the morning's rollcall tallies to determine how many soldiers from the Forty-first Tennessee would be available for General Hood to squander.

Though Cunningham feared death at all waking times, on occasion the dread subsided with the thought that God watched over him for a special purpose when the terrible war ended and men returned to their families and jobs. A younger and wiser Cunningham had avoided the first call to arms in the spring of 1861 as Governor Isham Harris had issued the order at the beginning of hostilities. After the second call for volunteers that fall, Cunningham enlisted, swayed by words and women's wear. The words shot like an artillery canister from the mouth of Meredith Poindexter Gentry, the greatest man Cunningham had ever met. A former Tennessee statehouse representative and a four-term U.S. Congressman, Gentry had since served in the Confederate Congress and in the summer of 1861 had implored the sons of Bedford County, Tennessee, to enlist and shuck the oppressive yoke that Northern aggressors thrust upon the broad shoulders of Tennessee and the South. Gentry had spoken for an hour, his voice rising to make points, his cadence coming like the beat of army drums, and his passion inflaming the pugilistic urges of young men full of piss and vinegar.

While Cunningham knew who spewed the patriotic words of secession, he knew not who provided the women's wear. Delivered anonymously, the item arrived in a package addressed to him and left on his front porch. Opening the package, Cunningham had found a tattered petticoat, a symbol of cowardice sent to young men who had avoided the governor's first call to join the burgeoning Confederate army. Cunningham never mentioned the gift to anyone, but soon learned from young men less reticent to speak of the embarrassing present that several such garments had been sent to local boys hesitant to fight for the cause. Some recipients laughed it off, but most, including Cunningham that October had enlisted in the local guard—the "Richmond Gentrys" they called themselves—and marched off to war. Most of those boys were dead or crippled now. Except for the malaria and other infirmities, Cunningham had made it through more than three years of infantry service unscathed by enemy projectiles and blades.

He wondered whether his earthly presence would end within days or if God truly watched over him. Never would he have thought that the Almighty would give preference to him over so many others smote by violence and hardship since hostilities began. The South's initial optimism had soured after the fall of Vicksburg on July 4, 1863. In the following weeks, despair had hit the Army of Tennessee and many turned to religion, though not Cunningham, not initially. Nine months later in Dalton Georgia, however, dear Bedford County friend Henry Newsom of the Fourth Tennessee, invited Cunningham to attend a sermon in a makeshift chapel in a clearing among woods scarred and charred from recent battles and the ensuing fires. Cunningham at first refused the invitation, but decided a sermon, even a bad one, would be a change from the monotony of camp life. He attended and found himself conflicted by the chaplain's words, partly touched and partly terrified. Cunningham ignored his friend's entreaty to stay and discuss the sermon and instead retired into the trees to pray in solitude. He remembered it as an agony of prayer until his heavenly petition ended with a crashing crescendo, followed by the screams and cries Cunningham had heard so often on the battlefields after the shooting had ended and the misery lingered. He sprinted to the clearing with other soldiers to discover that a giant pine, weakened by the fires of war, had snapped and fallen upon the makeshift place of worship.

Henry Newsom, his friend, was crushed to death with nine others, all of whom had lingered where Cunningham had sat and worshipped. Was God protecting him or was that just another coincidence of war like a Bible stopping a bullet or a Confederate finding all the food he could eat? During the ensuing memorial service for the ten dead, the chaplain stared at Cunningham as if he had caused the deaths and must beseech the Cross for redemption. When his friend was buried, Cunningham confessed his sins and stood before others professing his faith and belief in Jesus Christ. Where many had found comfort in conversion, Cunningham had only found more confusion. Was he doomed or saved on this earth, regardless of his destination after death?

While Cunningham remembered his conversion, visages of combat's aftermath were burned into his brain—the horrible sights, the agonizing sounds, and the putrid smells of battle. Returning to his regiment after the battle of Chickamauga, he retched at corpses in death's infinite postures and at body parts scattered across the bloodied ground. He heard feral hogs squealing as they fought each other while rummaging through stacks of amputated limbs as high as a man's waist. The odors were the worst, the sickly sweet fragrance of deteriorating flesh or the pungent stench of men fried to a crisp in battle-spawned brushfires. He could close his eyes, put his fingers in his ears and even hold his breath to escape those encounters, but he could never erase them from his memory. These horrors lingered in his mind, tormenting him when his thoughts wandered.

Would he ever escape the terrors that marched with him each day? Or, was death—the thing he feared most—the only relief?

Worst yet, would he have to die just to find out? Even the paperwork couldn't take his mind off that question.

Monday Afternoon,

November 28, 1864

Hiram B. Granbury

Chapter Six

Sam Watkins
Jennie's House

He stood tired and exhausted in front of Jennie's home, guarding it against looters as he had since advancing into Columbia that morning beside men of the Third and Eighteenth Tennessee. At first, the Tennesseans had inched toward town, wary of a possible ambush, but the Yankees had left no rear guard to fend off any advance. With every forward step lacking any Union response, the soldiers grew confident, picked up their pace, and strode boldly to the outskirts of the community, then raced into the streets themselves, shouting their glee at having taken Columbia without losing a man. Then the skirmishers went wild, crashing into stores, smokehouses, and even homes in search of food and plunder.

"No," cried Sam Watkins, "these are Tennesseans like us." Not a man listened. They scavenged for anything they could eat. He raced toward Jennie's house, hoping to outrun any soldier that had targeted the Mayes's place. For a moment, guilt plagued him for not stopping at his parents' home, but he must protect Jennie above everyone else. He darted past the houses of neighbors he had known for years and past dwellings that had lost loved ones to this war. The sight of Confederate soldiers attacking Southern homes outraged him, especially when he saw a webfoot beating the butt of his rifle against the door to Jennie's house.

"Scat from there," he screamed, but the soldier ignored him until Watkins lowered his rifle and positioned the bayonet an inch from his jugular vein. "You'll be bleeding like a stuck pig if you don't get moving, soldier."

"You're one of us," he argued.

"Not if you break into decent folks' home, I'm not. Get going or start bleeding."

The fellow backed away, turned about, and scurried to the next house.

Sam saw eyes staring between parted curtains. "It's me. Sam Watkins. Stay inside. Our troops have gone wild."

The door cracked open, and Sam saw Jennie's brown eyes. "Thank you, Sam."

"There's only one of me, Jennie. Put your father and brothers at the back door and side windows. If someone tries to break in there, come and tell me. I can't keep an eye on the entire house." She closed the door to attend to her assignment. A dozen soldiers ran down the street, a couple veering toward Sam. He loaded his rifle, lifted the flap on his cartridge box and grabbed a percussion cap, which he fitted onto the nipple after cocking the hammer. The two soldiers ignored his movement until he aimed the gun, firing at their feet. They fled to another dwelling, and Sam reloaded his rifle.

When he finished and slid the ramrod in its sheath, he heard Jennie calling through the window. "Out back, Sam, out back."

He ran around the structure and shooed a couple of men away with his bayonet. After that, he spent the ensuing hours guarding the place. He marched around the dwelling, making sure no wide-eyed soldier approached it. Twice more, he fired his rifle to prove he was deadly serious. He even refused the two biscuits Jennie offered him through a crack in the door so not to give other men the idea food was inside for the taking. He stayed at his sweetheart's house through the early afternoon, chiding the Confederates for ransacking the homes of Southern folks.

"You should be ashamed of yourselves," he cried at a half dozen webfeet marching past with a ham taken from someone's smokehouse.

"The army should feed us," a soldier responded.

Barely had those troops ambled down the street than a captain rode up in front of the Mayes's home and glared at Watkins. "What's your regiment, soldier?"

"First Tennessee."

"Then get back to it."

Sam hesitated, wanting to say goodbye to Jennie.

"Now!" screamed the captain.

"Yes, sir," Sam said, turning away from the house and trotting through town toward his regiment's bivouac, worried what might happen to Jennie in his absence.

Arriving back at camp, a few of his men inquired what had happened. He told them the Tennessee boys had turned to looters, and he was ashamed to have been among them.

"Did you get anything to eat?" Billy Carr asked.

"I protected my Jennie's home."

Carr smiled. "Did you get a kiss?"

"Didn't have time, but I'll get plenty when this cruel war is over."

"If General Hood lets you survive," stated his friend.

"I'm depending on God, not General Hood," Sam replied. "Did I miss any services this morning?"

"Services?"

"Worship services? Has Reverend Quintard returned?"

Carr laughed. "Sam, you're losing it. Today's Monday, not Sunday."

Sam shrugged. "Maybe so." He missed Reverend Charles T. Quintard and his calming reassurances. Quintard had been with the regiment from the beginning, a solid man of the cloth, who looked after his flock, often sharing his horse with a fatigued webfoot so he could ride and conserve his strength while Quintard plodded along with the other soldiers. Besides his Bible, Watkins carried in his knapsack *The Confederate Soldier's Pocket Manual of Devotions*, compiled and distributed for free by Quintard to help the men through such difficult times.

Quintard stood as a compassionate and brave man of the cloth, one who placed his faith in God so strongly that the men placed their faith in him for spiritual guidance, unlike the brigade chaplain that had accompanied Company H—at least part of the way—as they advanced toward Chickamauga and battle. The reverend exhorted the webfeet to remain true to their cause, their sweethearts, and their God. "Aim low, shoot straight, and kill the invaders like wild hogs," he cried. "If only I had a rifle," he added, "I would advance with you." He ignored the offers of several to take their weapons. "Remember, boys, he who is killed will sup tonight in paradise."

No sooner had he spoken those words than the zip and whiz of Minié balls rent the air, followed by a bursting artillery shell. At the explosion, the sanctimonious parson yanked the reins around on his horse and burst for the rear, faster than any cannonball could catch. "The parson must not be hungry or doesn't care to eat at God's heavenly table tonight," shouted a webfoot. Other infantrymen heard him and laughed for the final times of their lives as they marched into the lead and iron wall that the Yankees threw at them at Chickamauga.

Unlike the cowardly preacher, Quintard was a man of honor and courage.

Hardin Figuers
Figuers Home

Following lunch, Hardin Figuers grabbed his slingshot, called Adele, and returned to Uncle Jesse's place to talk with the slave, but the man was nowhere to be found. So, Hardin wandered around the south side of town, checking behind the outhouses for peach pits. In two hours, he found three and tucked them in his britches pocket. Figuring that was plenty, he ambled over to the locust grove, hoping Adele could flush a cottontail or some other small animal that might offer a little meat for their table, but hares were scarcer than peach pits on this sunny afternoon.

He enjoyed the sunshine as he explored the trenches south of the Carter home to see if the rains or melting snow had uncovered any more artifacts from the earlier encounter between Union and Confederate troops, but the precipitation had revealed no new souvenirs.

Giving up his search, he pointed Adele toward home, eventually encountering Mary Alice Carter McPhail as she walked behind the locust grove toward her place.

"Afternoon, Hardin. Are you enjoying the sunshine?"

He nodded. "It's nice to get out and hunt for a spell."

"What've you been hunting?"

Hardin felt his face redden. "I'm ashamed to say, ma'am."

"There's nothing to be ashamed of in these hard times."

"But you don't know what I've been stalking."

"It wouldn't be peach pits, would it?"

Hardin stopped in his tracks and stared at Mary Alice. "How'd you know?"

Mary Alice just smiled. "Us mothers know and see everything, Hardin. Just ask Bethenia."

Grimacing, Hardin shrugged. "Okay, if you say so."

"I do," she answered and continued striding to the Carter home.

Perplexed by Mary Alice's knowledge of his exploits, Hardin walked to his place. Maybe mothers did know everything.

After he secured Adele in the barn, Hardin approached the back door, uncertain whether he should go in. As soon as he entered the kitchen door, his mom spun around from the pot of soup she was tending on the stove and handed her wooden spoon to Mary Louisa to keep stirring the broth. Stepping to Hardin, his mother threw her arms around him and hugged him.

"Thank you, Hardin?"

He shrugged. "I only found three peach pits."

"Maybe so, but you mentioned our need for buttons to Fountain Carter, and he told Mary Alice, who brought one over."

Finally, it made sense. His mother had told Mary Alice of his quest.

Bethenia pointed to the corner of the table where a solitary button lay. "See the button?"

Hardin shrugged. "It's not much."

"Maybe not to you, but it's like an early Christmas gift to me," his mother gushed.

"So, the Yankees still haven't shot Santa Claus," Mary Louisa said, scowling in Hardin's direction.

Patrick Cleburne
Encampment Outside Columbia

With Lieutenant Leonard Mangum mounted at his side, Major General Patrick Cleburne reined up and studied his division aligned before him. He sighed as he turned to Mangum and spoke softly. "I fear the challenge before us is greater than our leadership can manage." He lowered his head and, after a long pause, continued. "I must not let my doubts show when I talk to the boys."

"You'll do fine, sir. If you have no more need for me, I will take my proper place before your remarks."

Cleburne nodded, drawing a salute from Mangum, who reined his gelding toward the fighting men. Sitting proudly atop Red Pepper, Cleburne studied the soldiers arrayed before him in tattered clothes. His eyes moistened, both at the sight and at his frustration of being unable to ease their misery by providing them rations they could enjoy, uniforms they could be proud of, shoes they could march in, and ammunition sufficient to smite their enemies. All he could offer was hope. Though he had many doubts about the ongoing campaign and the leadership of the Army of Tennessee, he could never let those misgivings taint his remarks to the men who did his bidding in battle. At least the afternoon sun shone brightly, bringing them some warmth and a break from the precipitation.

When his brigadier generals—Govan and Granbury atop their steeds and Lowrey riding his infernal donkey—stopped in front of their brigades and turned to their commander, Cleburne saluted them.

He studied his troops, barely three thousand strong, less than half the size of his division on the day that Hood took command. Since he could not supply them with grub, clothing, or cover, all he had to offer was words, which seemed so worthless against what these men would face in the coming days. He wondered if his remarks would make any difference as he stared into their hopeful eyes. Taking a deep breath, he began.

"Soldiers of the South, men of my division, I salute you, as do the skies, which have blessed us all with sunshine on this day. I view that as a harbinger of the good days to come when our cause will triumph over our enemies. Before me, I see not just soldiers, but brothers bound by blood, by honor, and by a cause greater than ourselves. You have stood beside me on countless battlefields, faced trials unimaginable, and braved storms of lead and iron. You have fought with a courage and resolve that makes me proud, not just as your general, but as your comrade in this noble struggle. Today, I speak to you not as a superior, but as one of you—a man who has cast his fate with yours and embraced this cause with the entirety of his being.

"We stand here today on the cusp of what may be our greatest test. The winds of winter will soon blow, and the weight of war rests heavily upon our hearts and our shoulders as we dream of our homes and our sweethearts. I see in your eyes the desire to return to your places, to your families, and to the warm embrace of loved ones. You long for peace, as do I. Even so, we must not forget why we are here and why we must continue to fight.

"We fight for our land, our liberty, and our way of life. We fight because we believe that the soil beneath our feet—the soil that bore us, raised us, and will one day cradle our bones—deserves to remain free from tyranny and oppression. We are not just soldiers in an army. We are defenders of a dream and protectors of the virtues that make our homeland sacred. Why, you may ask, would an Irishman take up this cause? In Ireland, I lived under the oppressive boot of the British crown. I came to America to escape that subjugation and persecution. That is why I have served with you in the past and will do so tomorrow and the next day until we are shed of our persecutors.

"When we first donned these uniforms and when we first took up these rifles many months ago, it was not for the glory of conquest or the spoils of war. No, it was for something much deeper, something much more profound. It was for the right to determine our own destiny, for the right to live as free men upon our *own* land, to speak our *own* words, to sing our *own* songs, and to build a future for our *own* children, ever unburdened by the chains of distant masters.

"We did not seek this war. A heavy-handed oppressor thrust it upon us. And in its battles, we have been tested, tempered, and proven. We have seen friends fall beside us, brave souls who now lie in honored graves. We have witnessed the cost of conflict and the sorrow of loss. And yet, through it all, we have remained steadfast, for we know that our cause is just."

Cleburne paused and studied his men in tattered uniforms. They stared back with hope in their eyes. Many of them were no more than boys, though prematurely aged by the carnage and horrors they had seen on previous battlefields. He wondered how many would survive the coming battle under General Hood's leadership. He took a deep breath and continued.

"But make no mistake—the path ahead is difficult. Our enemies are many, well-equipped, and well-fed. Their ranks swell with fresh recruits, and their wagons overflow with provisions. But do they have what we possess? Do they have the same fire in their hearts, the same devotion to a cause that is worth every drop of blood and tears? I say to you today, they do not!

"We are outnumbered, yes, but we have never been outfought. Perhaps we are outgunned, but we are not outmanned. For every man standing here today, there beats the heart of a lion. You have proven it time and again at Shiloh, at Murfreesboro, at Chickamauga, at Atlanta. You have faced the worst that the enemy could throw at you, and yet you still stand, unbroken, unyielding. That is the spirit of the South, the spirit of our people, and the spirit that will carry us through these darkest of days.

"Remember why we fight. Remember the farms, the towns, the valleys, and the hills of our beloved South. Remember the children who look up to you as their fathers, their protectors. Remember the women who wait with prayers on their lips and hope in their hearts for your safe return. Remember the freedom for which we have taken up this fight. Remember our right to be free men, under God, with none to dictate how we live, how we labor, or how we love. That is the freedom we will defend today and every day, until victory is ours.

"We do not fight because we hate what is in front of us; rather, we fight because we love what is behind us. We fight for our hearths and homes, our fields and forests, our mountains and streams that define our land and our futures. We fight for the traditions that have shaped us, the values that sustain us, and the future that awaits us."

Cleburne hesitated, then stood in his stirrups to study his men, who stared silently back.

"But know this, my brothers, the time for wavering is past. The moment for decision has come. If victory is to be ours, it will be won not just with the strength of our arms, but with the strength of our hearts. We must dig deep within ourselves and find the courage to stand firm, to face every challenge with the same unyielding spirit that has brought us this far.

"There will be no surrender, no retreat for me. I would rather die on the battlefield than surrender to a life of submission. And, I know you share that feeling. I know you would rather stand and fight against overwhelming odds than to surrender to a fate that would strip us of our dignity, our pride, and our freedom.

"Let our enemies see our resolve. Let them know that we fight not because we must, but because we choose to. We choose to defend our homes, our rights, and our way of life. Let them hear the roar of our defiance in every cannon blast and let them feel the sting of our determination in every rifle volley. We are not a rabble to be scattered by the wind, but rather a force united by a cause that is righteous and true."

Cleburne settled in his saddle and removed his kepi from his head, holding it over his heart.

"I do not promise an easy road ahead, nor do I offer any assurances of safety for you or even myself. What I do offer is a chance to be remembered, to be counted among those who stood when others faltered, who fought when others fled, who believed when others doubted. What I offer you is the honor that accrues to free men fighting for a just cause against all odds.

"And so, I now invite you to stand with me, to fight beside me, and to see this through to the end, no matter the cost. Together, we will honor the legacy of those who fought and died before us, and we will forge a path for those who will come after us. If you believe as I do, let us march forward with faith, with courage, and with the spirit of the South burning brightly in our hearts. Let us prove to all the world that the men of this division, the sons of this soil, will never be broken, will never surrender, and will never forget that we are fighting for the South, for our homes, for our families and for our freedom!

"May God be with us all in the coming days!"

After replacing his kepi atop his head, Cleburne nodded to his brigadiers, who turned to their men and dismissed them. Instantly, the soldiers broke from their ranks and rushed toward Cleburne, surrounding him and Red Pepper like a wave breaking around a boulder. The troops grabbed at Cleburne's legs and raised their hands to shake his. Surprised by the affection, Cleburne leaned over and shook as many outthrust hands as he could reach.

"We're with you, General," shouted several.

"God bless you all," Cleburne answered. "We will get through this together."

The soldiers cheered.

In that moment, Cleburne thought of Susan Tarleton and wished she were here to see his men's affection for him.

Hiram Granbury
Camp Outside Columbia

An hour after General Cleburne addressed his troops, orders reached Hiram Granbury to lead his brigade closer to Columbia and set up camp on the perimeter of the town, so Union observers across the river might think preparations were underway for an attack the next day. Granbury issued directives to his staff to break camp and be ready to move. After a soldier brought him his saddled horse, he mounted and rode to the head of his brigade, where he saw Captain Sam Foster and his foraging party returning, each man carrying a burlap bag. Granbury nudged his mount in the flank and trotted out to meet the captain, who saluted at his approach.

"We're moving on Columbia. You and your men should wait here for our advance. Did you find much?"

"Folks were glad to see us after putting up with Yankees the past few days, though the blue-bellies were well enough supplied that they didn't loot the town, not like the Tennessee boys who preceded us earlier this morning. Some locals shared what they could spare, but most turned angry that our boys looted more than the Yankees did. Some of the Tennesseans broke into the schoolhouse and stole the desks for firewood. We didn't make many friends in Columbia. Only thing we had going for us was we weren't blue-bellies."

"It rankles me," Granbury said, "that our men'll steal at the expense of women, children, and old men. Distribute your provisions as evenly as you can among the Twenty-fourth. Maybe that'll keep them from slipping into town and stealing more from the folks."

"When we suffer under General Hood, the misery spreads. I fear the suffering's about to turn worse for us all."

Granbury grimaced. "I appreciate your optimism, Captain. I hope it shows through in your diary."

"Believe me, sir, it does."

The men saluted and parted with Granbury, overseeing the preparations for the move. When the brigade was packed and ready, Granbury led the advance, that covered two miles to the edge of Columbia. On the perimeter of town, he saw soldiers still looting and officers trying to get them under control. Granbury realized this would stand as a shameful day in the annals of the Confederacy and the Army of Tennessee.

Patrick Cleburne
Camp near Columbia

Minutes before sundown, Patrick Cleburne joined fellow division commanders John C. Brown and William B. Bate to complete their plans for the next day with their corps commander General Frank Cheatham. Before departing for the conclave, Cleburne instructed Leonard Mangum to summon his brigadiers to his camp to receive their orders for the impending move once he returned. Cheatham awaited his division commanders in a rocking chair on the porch of an abandoned home on the outskirts of Columbia. He welcomed the trio by offering them a drink from a bottle of whiskey he had conscripted to serve the Army of Tennessee. After his three subordinates declined the offer, Cheatham took a healthy swig, sat the bottle on the plank flooring at his side and took a deep breath.

As Cheatham outlined the maneuvers for the next day, Cleburne realized little had changed, other than the pontoons were arriving and would be in place overnight for the flanking move to begin well before sunrise. The corps commander repeated to his division leaders how Hood schemed to insert himself between Schofield's army and Nashville. To accomplish that, he would split his three corps, leaving Stephen D. Lee's corps and one hundred cannons around Columbia to feint an attack across the Duck River. General Forrest's cavalry would harass the Yankees to convince them a major offensive was coming from their front.

Meanwhile, Cheatham's corps would lead the flanking move, followed by A.P. Stewart and his corps. Those units would swing southeast of Columbia to Davis's Ford, where the pontoon bridge was being secured across the flooding Duck River. Once across the river, the troops would advance with all due haste to Spring Hill. There they would plunder the Yankee supply wagons rumored to be starting the trek toward Nashville, then await Schofield's army, which would have to go through them to get to Nashville. Once his force defeated

Schofield's, General Hood would then turn his fury on Nashville to save the Confederacy.

General Brown shook his head at his commander. "What do you think of the plan, Ben?"

"General Hood thinks it's brilliant, shades of Robert E. Lee and Stonewall Jackson and even the Almighty Himself in its pure genius," Cheatham answered, then picked up the bottle and took another swig of whiskey.

"I asked what do you think of the move."

"Old Frankie's job is to follow orders, not to question them. I suggest you three keep that in mind. General Hood's not one to cross."

Cleburne nodded. "I've got two problems—the artillery and the roads. Has General Hood considered our vulnerability without artillery?"

Cheatham swelled out his chest. "I asked the same question of our exalted commander, but he said the artillery would only slow us down on the back roads we'll have to follow to get to Spring Hill first."

"That leads to my second concern," Cleburne continued. "To accomplish his objective, we must move with all due speed to Spring Hill. Has he even checked the roads and their condition? These will not be macadamized routes like the turnpikes."

Cheatham leaned back in his rocker and lifted his arms and the whiskey bottle above his head. "General Forrest raised the same concern about the roads, but our esteemed commander ignored his uneasiness. General Hood thinks he's smarter than a tree full of owls, but we all know he's dumber than a barn full of jackasses."

The three generals nodded.

"I challenged him to that butt-kicking contest I've been talking about," Cheatham continued as he lowered his arms. "He accepted the challenge as long as he could use another man's ass. That's the way it is with Hood. He starts a fight, but someone else's ass gets kicked."

"I just pray it's not ours that are kicked in the coming days," Brown said.

"Fellows, I've done the best I can," Cheatham responded. "Now, if you'll get your divisions ready for tomorrow, I'll meet you all at the river. General Cleburne, I want your division in the lead. Be at the pontoon bridges by four o'clock so we can get your men across before dawn. Now, boys, if you will attend to your business, I've got some affairs to settle with this bottle." Cheatham took another healthy swig as his subordinates turned to do Hood's bidding.

Rev. Charles T. Quintard
On the Road to Columbia

Columbia remained in chaos as Reverend Quintard, with Henry B. Free riding behind him, entered the town mid-afternoon. The reverend felt shame for what he had heard of the Confederate occupation and for what he was seeing as he rode around. The first infantry to enter the settlement had gone wild. Driven by hunger, they had ransacked the place in their search for food. Quintard scowled as he advanced among the milling soldiers still scattered around the community. An army that took food from the mouths of the people whose homes and honor they defended would not attract volunteers on the march northward. Officers screamed and yelled at men, ordering them to get back to their regiments and companies and to remember they were better men than the Yankee hordes, which may have been true, but they were also hungrier than their enemies. He guided his horse away from the main street, saying a silent prayer for God to protect the civilians and their provender and to provide provisions for the soldiers so such events would never happen again.

Quintard directed his horse through town. "Get back to your regiments, men. These folks aren't your enemy."

Most ignored him, a few scowled, and others gorged on the food they had taken from the civilians. It was a shameful demonstration, a discouraging display of undisciplined soldiers with empty bellies. Quintard scolded several more, but they disregarded him. "You risk getting shot," he warned one soldier.

The gaunt fellow turned to the chaplain. "I'd rather die by a Secesh bullet than a Yankee one."

Quintard rode on, perplexed at what he saw and the question Henry posed.

"Massa Revrund, dos Secesh be stealin' food. Do dey stand to gets a whippin' like darkies do if dey be stealin' from white folks?"

"Likely not, Henry. There's too many of them, and they're too hungry."

"Hungry don't keeps us slaves from a beatin'. My last massa be feedin' de hogs better slop dan he be feedin' de slaves."

The reverend had no answer. "I've tried to treat you better, Henry, and share what I eat, maybe teach you a few things that will help you in life."

"I's can't complains about youse, but what goods duz learnin' me things do, if I can't be free?"

Quintard pondered his servant's query. "Henry, you ask difficult questions to resolve."

"I's s'pose I's knows de answer, Massa Revrund. Youse be's de top rail, and I's be de bottom rail, de one folks steps on first when dey climb de fence."

Shaking his head, Quintard sat stumped as he meandered through the commotion of Columbia. The passage from First Timothy did not ring as true now as when he had first recited it to Henry. The slave youth had a knack for lancing his conscience. Quintard wondered how an unlearned darkie could stump a lettered man such as himself, but then David had beaten Goliath. The clergyman questioned if God was trying to speak to him and was startled when a deep voice called his name.

"Reverend Quintard, Reverend Quintard," came the cry over the street tumult.

Twisting in his saddle, he saw General Otho F. Strahl, who commanded a brigade of Tennesseans in Brown's Division, eight under-manned Tennessee regiments in all. The bearded Strahl trotted up atop The Lady Polk, as fine a mare as ever carried a leader in the Army of Tennessee. Beside Strahl rode Lieutenant John H. Marsh, barely twenty-five years old. The preacher smiled at his friends, as he had baptized both since the war began.

The clergyman felt a special kinship to Strahl. Born a Yankee like himself, Ohio native Strahl had sided with Tennessee and the South once hostilities had begun. Marsh now served Strahl as an aide, and Quintard loved Marsh as a son, a young officer with a dignified demeanor who had resigned his West Point appointment to serve with his home state when war broke out. The young lieutenant began his service in the artillery, but a Minié ball had shattered his left arm at Chickamauga, leaving it useless and providing him an exemption from further service to the Confederacy.

Marsh earned Quintard's undying admiration and devotion when he baptized him in the Marietta, Georgia, hospital where he spent months recovering. Though bedridden and wracked by pain, Marsh insisted he would kneel before Quintard and God for the sacrament. "Let me kneel," he begged, then changed his request to a command. "I *will* kneel!" And, so he did, and so did Quintard baptize him, placing the sign of the cross upon his brow and sprinkling him with holy water. After that, Quintard visited the lieutenant in the hospital whenever he could and sent him home to western Tennessee to see his family and recuperate from his shrunken and useless left arm.

Despite his family's pleas he not rejoin the army, Marsh responded, "My country needs me more than ever, so I must go." He offered to assist General Strahl, who knew of his strong character. Though he then served the infantry, he insisted on wearing his artillery blouse with the red piping.

Quintard greeted both men cheerfully when they reined up before him. The reverend was glad to run into them, but even more relieved that they would give him an excuse for not answering Henry's imponderable questions. "Otho and John, so good to see you both, even amid this shameful display of human locusts."

"Our men's appetites are for anything but more war. They're tired of war, Reverend," responded Strahl. "Still, there's no excuse for this outrage. If we punish any of the perpetrators, we risk greater desertions. The best we can do is order the men back to their regiments and hope we can keep our army together for one more shot at victory."

The reverend nodded and turned to Marsh. "You're looking well, John."

"I'm doing okay for a one-armed man, though it pains me that other men have to saddle my horse." Marsh lifted his right hand and showed the unbuttoned cuff of his gray shell jacket. "I can button my left sleeve on my useless arm, but not the right one on my good arm. Little things like that you take for granted until you lose an arm."

"Lieutenant Marsh does just fine with a single arm," Strahl interjected. "Even with one arm, he's got smarts like this army needs from bottom to top."

"Thank you, General," Marsh said.

Strahl nodded, then cocked his head at Quintard as Henry peeked around the reverend's side. "What do you think of The Lady Polk, Reverend?"

"A superb mare, she is indeed!"

A broad smile cracked the general's face. "I'm so glad you said that, Reverend, and I'm pleased I found you today, even under these circumstances, because I'd like you to have her."

Quintard caught his breath as his jaw opened. He stammered for an instant, then responded. "I could never take such a fine animal, but why?"

"To honor our friendship."

"Our friendship needs no such embellishment."

Strahl coughed into his gloved fist, then eyed Quintard sternly. "I have a bad feeling about the coming days. I don't expect to survive. When I die, I want The Lady Polk cared for."

"You've been in tough fights before, Otho. Why now?"

"It's intuition, almost like how I felt before you baptized me. I felt the time had come. I feel the same way now."

Quintard bit his lip as he studied Strahl, detecting resolution rather than fear in his eyes. The general would not be denied. "If you insist, Otho." He twisted in the saddle and looked over his shoulder at Henry. "Think you could tend another horse, Henry?"

"I's can do dat, most 'specially if dat means I's be ridin' my own hoss."

The chaplain nodded. "Okay, Otho. I'll keep The Lady Polk for now."

"Thank you, Reverend," Strahl said. "Once I get back to headquarters, I'll change horses and send Lieutenant Marsh back with her if I know where to find you."

"On the edge of town near the river is the house of Reverend David Pease," Quintard replied. "I don't know if he's in town, but I will stay there until I hear from Lieutenant Marsh."

"Thank you, Reverend," Strahl replied.

"I expect to return The Lady Polk to you once this war ends."

"I doubt that will be possible," Strahl said. He eased his horse away from the clergyman. "Come along, Lieutenant. We've work to do."

Quintard watched them ride away, their shoulders slumped as they directed soldiers back to their regiments.

Gradually, order returned to the streets of Columbia. Quintard weaved among the chastised soldiers as he rode toward the river. He found Reverend Pease sitting in a rocking chair on his porch and holding a shotgun in his lap as he watched the retreating throng. Recognizing Quintard, Pease stood and waved him over.

"We've had a little excitement here today, Reverend. I hate to say it, but the Yankees didn't behave this poorly during their stay."

"Our boys are hungry and tired."

"Sin is sin, whether you're tired or hungry."

Quintard nudged Henry to dismount. The servant slid off the horse and took the reverend's reins.

"We are all sinners, and we are all tired," Quintard replied as he eased out of the saddle. "I hope you don't mind that I instructed a soldier to deliver a horse to your place for me."

"Certainly not. You're doing better than this poor soul, you being able to buy a horse in such times."

"It's a gift from General Strahl. I fear he's had a premonition that he will die in the next fight."

Pease arose from his seat and leaned the shotgun against the wall. "It's not loaded," he said, "but it kept looters from taking my eats. Have your boy tie your mount to the corner porch post. Keeping an eye on him will be easier in case someone is tempted to steal him."

The two clergymen met at the steps and hugged one another. "We must discuss what we will do as messengers of God once this conflict is over," Quintard said.

The men spent three hours sitting on the porch and discussing their responsibilities as men of God in returning Tennessee to normal. The conversation boosted Quintard's spirits that indeed the war would end, even if it meant picking up the pieces of a failed dream. He remained eager for that day to arrive. Until he visited with Pease, he had not realized how depleted he had become of hope and maybe even faith. For weeks, he had been the one who had encouraged others and offered them optimism, yet no one served that role for him. Reverend Pease would fulfill that need. He decided to spend this night and the next with his fellow pastor so they could minister to each other.

Later in the evening, Lieutenant John Marsh approached on his gray gelding leading The Lady Polk. Quintard envied this youth, even with his withered arm. Young Marsh would make a fine man to rebuild Tennessee for the future. As he reached the modest house, the lieutenant nodded at the two preachers.

Young Henry jogged out to take The Lady Polk's halter. With a wide grin on his face, the servant proudly led the mare beside Quintard's gelding. "I'll be riding Lady Polk," Quintard told him. "You'll ride my mount."

"A hoss is a hoss to me, Massa Revrund."

Marsh dismounted, and Quintard stepped from the porch to greet him.

As Quintard approached, he saw the same resolve in his eyes that he had seen in General Strahl's. "Thank you, John."

The lieutenant pursed his lips and sighed. "Otho knows you will care for The Lady Polk as you cared for us." Reaching the minister, Marsh threw his good arm around him, hugging him and kissing him on the cheek. "Goodbye," he said.

Before the clergyman could respond, Marsh turned about, awkwardly mounted his horse and galloped off.

"So long, good friend, and keep your faith," Quintard cried as his young convert disappeared into the twilight. He then said a silent prayer for the lieutenant and his general.

Patrick Cleburne
Division Headquarters

Once again, General Mark Lowrey arrived last and on his donkey for the evening meeting of Cleburne's brigade commanders with their major general and his aide-de-camp.

"Pray tell, Mark, why do you persist in riding that donkey?" General Daniel Govan of Arkansas asked.

"If it was good enough for Christ to enter Jerusalem before his crucifixion, it's good enough for me to ride into Columbia."

"Seriously, Mark, why do you ride your little pet? You're certainly no god," Govan continued.

"The only one that thinks he's a god in these parts is General Hood," Lowrey said, drawing several nods.

"No, Mark, why?"

Lowrey slid off the donkey and dropped the reins, joining his fellow officers afoot. "You want to know why, Govan? Two reasons. It saves my horse for when I truly need him. More importantly, it amuses my men, gives them something to laugh about and to take their mind off their mortality."

Hiram Granbury chuckled. "Who wouldn't laugh, seeing an ass riding an ass?"

Lowrey grinned at the lanky Texan with the wild hair. "Some of those boys'll die in the coming days. If they get a laugh at my expense, I'm fine with that. They've had so little joy since Atlanta, and nowhere to place their faith in man since Hood assumed command. They need faith in God for eternity, but for the here and the now, they need a little humor since they can't place their faith in someone tangible. Hood is not that man, nor is Jefferson Davis. Right now, our division commander has their respect, few others do."

Cleburne felt his face redden. "Enough with the chatter, and thank you, General Lowrey, for your prayer of yesterday as God has blessed us with clear skies, warming weather, and a retreating enemy. We will dispense with a prayer this afternoon, as we have much to cover. After meeting with General Hood, General Cheatham outlined the strategy to me and Generals Brown and Bate an hour ago. We've plenty to do to prepare for tomorrow."

The officers tightened the circle around Cleburne as he explained the situation and the next day's ground plan. Though Schofield's army had abandoned Columbia, crossed the river, and burned the bridges behind them, the Yankees were building breastworks, expecting an attack. His officers groaned.

Cleburne lifted his hand. "No, General Hood's not planning a frontal assault, but a flanking maneuver. It may save lives if the Yankees have to attack us behind our entrenchments." He explained that Forrest's cavalry had crossed the river to harass the enemy into thinking an attack was imminent. That move would screen from Schofield's infantry and cavalry the next day's encirclement.

Hours before dawn tomorrow, Cleburne explained, his division would lead Cheatham's Corps east to Davis's Ford and cross the pontoon bridges Confederate engineers promised would be finished. General A.P. Stewart's Corps would follow Cheatham's contingent while General Stephen Lee's Corps would remain outside Columbia with the bulk of the Southern artillery as a feint to keep Schofield's men tied down long enough for the rest of the Army of Tennessee to slip behind them.

"So, have your men up and ready to march so we can meet that schedule. Since General Lowrey has such pull with God, I want him to lead the advance. With luck, we can get behind Schofield's army and force them to attack us behind breastworks of our design for a change."

The officers nodded. "That would be a switch," Govan said.

"Can your men be ready, General Lowrey?"

"Yes, sir," the preacher general responded.

"General Hood will probably accompany you, Mark. Do you think you might find another mount for tomorrow?"

"I will."

Granbury cleared his throat. "General Cleburne, might I suggest Lowrey advance on his donkey as a bold strategic move?"

"How's that, Hiram?"

"If the Yankees saw him coming, they just might all die laughing," Granbury said, then snickered.

"Better yet," added Govan, "maybe General Hood would die laughing."

All the officers chuckled, save for Cleburne. "I've never once seen Hood laugh since I've known him."

The merriment among his subordinates stopped.

"As soon as you are dismissed, I'll write specific orders for each brigade. Please remain until Lieutenant Mangum distributes yours.

Tomorrow will be a critical day for the Army of Tennessee and for our division. See that you do your duty. Good day, gentlemen."

His brigadiers offered crisp salutes, which Cleburne mirrored. His subordinates turned to await their assignments.

Lt. Gen. John Bell Hood
Beechlawn Plantation

General John Bell Hood spent his afternoon at Beechlawn, receiving updates on the progress of his plan. He was pleased with the developments, having assigned General Lee's Corps to occupy Columbia with two missions. First, Lee's men cleared out the looters and sent them back to their units. Second, they positioned artillery for the bombardment as if they were preparing for a frontal attack once the engineers repaired the damaged bridges over the Duck River. That demonstration would freeze the Union Army overnight and give Hood's other corps the chance to outflank them tomorrow.

The afternoon reports sounded encouraging with Forrest's four detachments screening the army's planned movements. The army's engineering specialists were already grading the approach to the Duck to expedite installing the pontoon bridges that would allow the army to traverse the overflowing river before dawn. From down the Columbia Pike, Confederate teamsters rushed the pontoons toward the impromptu crossing. The engineers, sappers, and teamsters would work all night, but the chief engineer had already sent word to Hood, confirming the work would be completed well before dawn.

"Everything's taking shape," Hood told governor-in-exile Isham Harris, as he explained his moves and his plan. "Once I destroy Schofield's army, I'll turn on Nashville and take it. Then you'll be able to reclaim your place as the rightful governor of Tennessee."

Harris smiled. "It's been a long time coming. I've heard Patrick Cleburne called 'the Stonewall of the West,' General Hood, but I believe that appellation will belong to you after this campaign draws to a conclusion."

Hood nodded. "I learned the chess moves of war serving with Robert E. Lee and Stonewall Jackson. I'd be honored to have my name inscribed alongside theirs in the glorious history of the Confederate States of America."

The governor reached into his coat pocket and pulled out a cigar. "This calls for a celebration, General."

Hood took the cigar and bit the end off, spitting the residue on the library rug as Harris struck a match and helped the general light up.

Soon, a cloud of cigar smoke encircled Hood's head as he leaned back in his chair, exultant in his military genius. "Nothing's more satisfying than knowing you've outwitted your opponent, especially when he was a West Point classmate."

Harris retrieved a cigar for himself and the two men spent the rest of the afternoon receiving reports on the army's progress in implementing Hood's plans until a modest supper provided by Cornelia Warfield at the expense of her children. Though the impending battle remained to be fought, Hood ate as a victor would.

The commander retired right after supper, leaving word for his subordinates to awaken him by three o'clock so he could get an early start on what would be the greatest victory of his life and perhaps in the annals of the Confederacy. Though he had to share his bed with the governor-in-exile because so many of his staff had crowded into Beechlawn, he slept well on a soft mattress, confident that the events of the next day would restore the Confederacy's battlefield prowess and elevate him to the highest reaches in the pantheon of Confederate heroes.

Tuesday Morning,

November 29, 1864

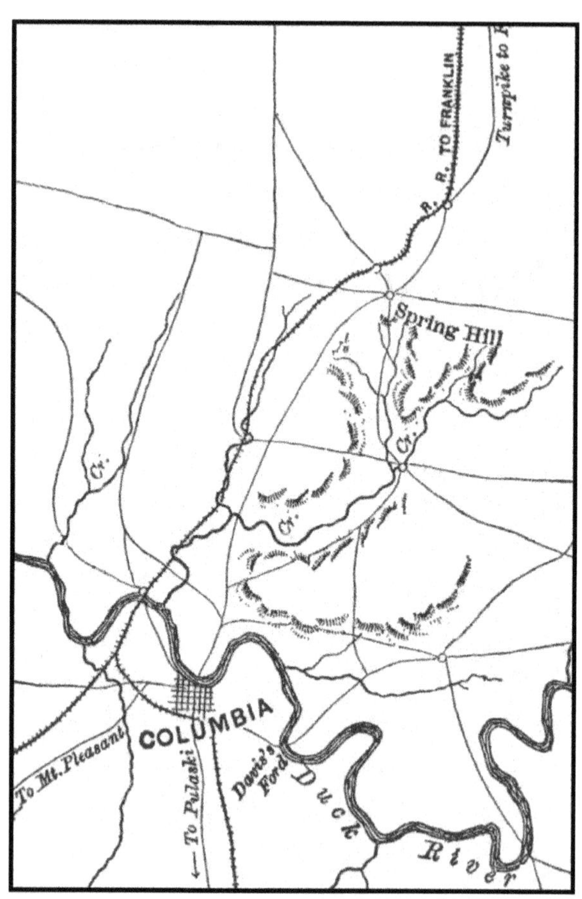

Columbia to Spring Hill Roads

Chapter Seven

Lt. Gen. John Bell Hood
Beechlawn Plantation

At three o'clock in the morning, two aides and Isham Harris awoke John Bell Hood and sat him up on the side of his bed. First, they assisted him in slipping his arms in his uniform blouse. Next they fitted the wooden prosthesis to the stump of his right thigh, strapping the artificial leg to his pale flesh. Then they pulled his uniform pants over his legs. When he stood up, they tucked his shirttail in his trousers, buttoned his fly and tightened the belt around his waist. Next, he sat back on the mattress while they guided his good left foot into his boot and attached the army spur. Then came the hardest job, fitting the artificial limb with boot and spur. The two lieutenants struggled to slide the device into the stiff boot leather. A less vain person might have dispensed with a boot for a missing foot, but Hood wanted his troops to see him as a whole man, fully in charge, though all his soldiers knew his right leg was false and his left arm useless.

Once booted, Hood grabbed the bedpost with his good hand and pulled himself up from the mattress so his assistants could put on and button his uniform coat. He hated this daily ritual necessary to accomplish such mundane tasks, but the inconvenience remained a small sacrifice for the greater good of the Confederacy. The next two days, Hood sensed, would bring victory and move the Southern states closer to independence, provided his men implemented his strategy and fought as he demanded. Once he destroyed Schofield's army, he would advance on Nashville and free the city from Yankee control. Then he would install Isham Harris in his rightful place as the elected governor of Tennessee. When he was dressed, an aide gave him his overcoat. After he slid his right arm in the sleeve, he wrestled the coat over his shoulders as an aide inserted his left arm in place. Finally, he took the crutch from his second helper, scooting out the upstairs bedroom and laboriously descending the stairs, a junior officer on either side in case he should lose his balance.

Cornelia Warfield waited at the foot of the steps with a porcelain cup of coffee on a silver tray. "Good morning, General. I thought this might warm you before you depart. It has been an honor to host you under our roof."

"Your hospitality has been delightful, Mrs. Warfield, and your mattress most comfortable," he said, sliding his crutch under his useless left arm to balance himself, then taking the vessel and drinking the hot liquid. He smiled. "Tastes like genuine coffee, not a substitute."

"It is," the plantation mistress replied. "I stashed some away for important visitors. Even my servants, or the few of them remaining, don't know where I hid it."

"I suspect you did not serve any of this to General Schofield when he stayed here," Hood said, then gulped down the rest of his drink.

"Gracious no, General. I said important visitors, not invaders."

Hood and his staff chuckled as the general leaned forward to return the cup to the tray, but lost his balance for a moment, dropping the cup as he grabbed his crutch, and the two lieutenants clutched his coat. The cup shattered on the floor at Hood's boots.

The general steadied himself, then moved his prop under his right arm. "My apologies, ma'am, for the broken cup."

Cornelia tucked the empty tray beneath her left arm and waved away the apology with her right. "It is a small matter, General. You have more important things to worry about today and in the days ahead. Go with our thanks and the blessings of Tennessee."

Nodding, Hood eased toward the door as staff members opened the entry for him. He stepped out on the portico, where the stiff breeze pricked his gaunt cheeks beneath his unkempt beard.

Hood moved across the porch to the steps where two orderlies awaited to assist him to his horse, while another soldier held the reins. At the mount's side, he offered his crutch to the soldier holding the leather lines. One orderly grasped Hood around the waist as he lifted his left foot to the stirrup and slid his boot in. As that assistant boosted the commander up, a second orderly lifted the artificial leg over his horse's back. After handing Hood the reins, the third soldier slipped the crutch into a modified rifle scabbard, while others strapped the commander into the saddle.

"All set, sir," said the one buckling the final straps.

Hood ignored him, shaking the reins, his artificial limb looking in the darkness like a stiff cancer protruding from the side of the horse. John Bell Hood rode slowly toward Davis's Ford to inspire his men for the immortality that awaited them—and him!

Patrick Cleburne
Approaching Davis's Ford

The men of Mark Lowrey's brigade led the division away from their camp toward the pontoon crossing. Division commander Patrick Cleburne left a dozen soldiers behind to start early morning fires that might deceive Yankee observers that his men were arising for another day. With Lieutenant Leonard Mangum at his side, Cleburne rode among his men, apologizing for their disrupted sleep and telling them this could turn into a memorable day for the Confederacy. He no longer knew if he believed his own words, but his job was to encourage and inspire his men, especially since John Bell Hood did not.

As he advanced among the Alabamians and Mississippians of Lowrey's brigade, he looked for their general, curious about the preacher's mount. Finally, he made out in the darkness the silhouette of the lanky officer, sitting high in the saddle. Lowrey had indeed exchanged his donkey for a horse. Cleburne reined Red Pepper toward the new mount.

Riding up behind his subordinate, Cleburne greeted him. "Morning, General Lowrey. You've worked another miracle."

Lowrey scratched his chin. "How's that?"

"You've resurrected your donkey into a fine looking mare."

"Gelding."

"At least now no one will die laughing."

"They've died every other way since Atlanta. I had a bad feeling when Hood first took over. Today I've got that same feeling. I fear things are about to worsen."

Cleburne looked up at the stars through the trees. "Skies are clear. Sunshine will lift everyone's morale."

"I'd trade higher spirits for better leadership."

Cleburne nodded. "Being in the lead, you realize General Hood may accompany you this morning, do you not?"

"That thought disrupted my sleep last night, and I prayed for compassion for the cripple."

"Few men would ride a horse missing a leg and the use of an arm. I'll give him that."

"I'm not talking about his physical injuries. General Hood's a mental cripple, stunted by his own pride. *'When pride cometh, then cometh shame; but with the lowly is wisdom,'* so says Proverbs eleven-two. The lowliest soldier in my brigade marching to do Hood's bidding possesses more wisdom than our leader. Others may view it differently, but that's how this Baptist—a *Southern* Baptist—sees it, General. If that's treason, so be it."

"Not as long as it is talk among officers."

"If you decide otherwise, I shall accept the consequences." Lowrey straightened in his saddle and saluted his division commander. "I must see to my men, General." He reined his horse about and trotted away into the flurry of soldiers marching toward battle and wondering if they would live to see the sunset on this still young day.

"A lot of men feel that way," Mangum said to Cleburne.

"I know lieutenant, but never acknowledge that in front of our soldiers."

"Yes, sir."

The major general wandered among the men to boost their spirits, Mangum remaining at his side, occasionally jotting notes on a square of paper of the details to handle to keep the division functioning at the level Cleburne demanded. Around them, the men moved quietly forward and whispered so their voices might not carry in the early morning stillness and alert the enemy of their movement. When the men advanced by brigade and regiment, Cleburne rode to the head of the line and nodded to Lowrey. "Pick up the pace, Mark. I don't want any delay that might draw blame from General Hood."

"Advance at a quick pace and pass it on," Lowrey commanded barely above a whisper. His order trickled down the column. Still almost two hours until dawn, the Alabamians and Mississippians trod forward with as fast and steady a gait as the darkness allowed. Their drowsy eyes strained to focus on the man in front of them, and their shoulders slumped beneath the burden of their rifles, knapsacks, haversacks, and bedrolls. Cleburne waited until Lowrey's brigade had passed, then checked that Govan's and Granbury's units were advancing as quickly as possible. Once he confirmed that, he slipped in the queue behind the preacher's men.

In the murky darkness, the soldiers advanced as best as they could with dilapidated footwear and dwindling faith in the Confederacy and its leaders. As dawn slipped over them, Cleburne saw how their feet dragged in the saturated earth and how some coughed and wheezed as they marched. When the sky lightened enough that he could put Red Pepper in a trot without running over a soldier, he caught up with Lowrey and ordered him to have his men leave their knapsacks and bedrolls on the banks of the Duck for the division's baggage train to pick up and deliver in the evening. Then Cleburne ordered Mangum to convey the command to Govan's and Granbury's brigades before sending a messenger to the teamsters to gather the belongings and deliver them to the men later. Cleburne made sure Mangum understood the teamsters were to attend to the men's gear before unloading and setting up his own tent and belongings.

The major general rejoined Lowrey as the serpentine column neared the ford, where a ground fog hung over the watercourse. The engineers had widened the approach to the landing and set up two pontoon bridges for the soldiers to cross the modest, though now overflowing river. As the soldiers approached the crossing, they unloaded their belongings, dumping them by company so they would be easier to distribute in the evening. Then the soldiers crossed the Duck River.

On the opposite bank, Cleburne spotted General Hood, whose distinctive profile with his artificial leg splaying wide of the stirrup was recognizable, even in the foggy gloom. Cleburne in the haze could not be certain what officers accompanied Hood. He thought he saw General Lowrey and corps commander Benjamin F. Cheatham. Cleburne had no stomach for joining them, so he rode back down the line of his unit, encouraging the men and checking with Generals Govan and Granbury on their progress.

By seven o'clock when the fog thinned out, Cleburne's Division had crossed the Duck River with the remainder of the army following. After his last troops traversed the pontoons, Cheatham and his staff rode up. The corps commander motioned for his aides to rest their horses while he conversed with his Irish general.

"Cavalry reports plenty of supply wagons in Spring Hill, General Cleburne. If we get there before the rest of Schofield's army, we'll have food in our bellies for lunch and plenty of bullets for our guns. It's a shame, it is, that the Army of Tennessee has to rely on them damn Yankees to supply our army."

"We're not there yet, General."

"Old Pegleg expects us to arrive by noon, just in time to eat their vittles for lunch."

Cleburne twisted his head from side to side. "This is only our second day without rain in what, two weeks? The ground's saturated.

This isn't a turnpike, but a trail the best I could determine from examining what maps I had last night and talking with my scout."

Cheatham shrugged. "Beats me. General Hood don't take too well to suggestions. He's so cocky he believes he could beat me in a footrace."

Cleburne chuckled. "That would be a sight. I'd put my money on you."

"He's so arrogant, he'd bet on himself."

"No, Ben, he'd order you to trip and fall, so he could win."

Cheatham scoffed. "No, sir, he'd have his artillery fire all their Napoleons at me and blow my ass to kingdom come." The burly general fell silent, his face clouding. "You know he's only bringing twelve Napoleons with us, don't you?"

Cleburne nodded.

"He's got a hundred pieces of artillery back at Columbia to put on a fireworks show for the Yankees, wasting a lot of our scarce ordnance. We're sure to need those cannon and shells before this week is over."

For a couple minutes, both generals sat watching their men march by, then Cheatham pointed toward Columbia. "I must check on Brown's Division. Why don't you catch up with Hood and ride with him for a spell. He frustrates me so I want to clobber him. You've got a cooler head on your shoulders."

Frowning Cleburne, asked a question, though he already knew the answer. "Is that an order?"

"I'm afraid it is. Look at it as a service to the Confederacy, you keeping me from a court-martial for kicking his ass."

Cleburne gave his commander a flippant salute. "Anything for the Confederacy, right?"

"That's the spirit, Pat. I'll see you in Spring Hill for a lunch on the Yankees' tab." Cheatham snickered, spurred the flank of his gelding and rode to find General Brown, his staff officers following behind him, like ducklings trailing their momma to a pond.

Cleburne sighed and turned his horse toward the head of the column, which had stopped moving. Cleburne eased Red Pepper forward over the spongy ground, which turned to mush beneath his mount's hooves. This route was not used enough to be hard-packed. A mile beyond the crossing, Cleburne found Hood in a conclave of officers with maps in their hands and perplexed looks on their faces.

*****

Lt. Gen. John Bell Hood
On the Trail to Spring Hill

Dawn broke gently across the forested route, the sky but a narrow strip between the tall trees along either side of the primitive road. John Bell Hood felt invincible as he accompanied Cleburne's Division across and beyond the river. Behind him, the approach to the watercourse was stacked with knapsacks, bedrolls, skillets, and personal items left for the baggage train, so nothing but the essentials for fighting would impede the march north. Speed was important to beat the Yankees to Spring Hill, just twelve miles from Columbia. By seven o'clock, Cleburne's men had completed the crossing, slogging along the muddy road toward their destination. Hood led the butternut caravan. Though the heavens said the precipitation was over, the soldier's feet and ankles answered it didn't matter because the muck tugged at every step.

From the direction of Columbia came the sound of General Stephen D. Lee's hundred-gun barrage. Hood grinned that the bombardment would demand Schofield's attention and worry his troops that they would hear the Rebel Yell by day's end. While the Yankees entrenched for the expected onslaught, Hood would steal a march on Schofield and get behind him. Then they would hear the Confederate cry for real from their rear.

When that occurred, he would have the Yankees where he wanted them, once his troops reached Spring Hill. Just over a mile from the river, Hood realized that not only was the road muddy, it was also crooked, heading away from his destination as often as toward it. He halted the column of troops and called for an orderly to find General Cleburne, but the Irishman arrived before Hood finished issuing his command. Cleburne saluted as his commander pulled a folded map from his pocket and examined it, then handed it to Cleburne.

"Is this map wrong?" Hood demanded.

"It's a simplified representation of the road, I fear. I'll call my local scout." Cleburne turned to Lieutenant Mangum and sent him darting off. Soon, his aide-de-camp returned with another rider. Cleburne handed Hood's map to the guide. "Is this accurate?"

The fellow studied the diagram for a moment, then laughed. "No, sir." He jumped from his horse, his boots splattering mud as he landed. He smoothed a plot of mud with his boot, then bent and grabbed a stick. Quickly, he scratched a couple circles for Columbia and Spring Hill and next connected them with a straight mark in the spongy soil.

"That's the turnpike. It's just over twelve miles between towns along the pike," the guide explained. Next, he etched a zigzagging route to the side of the two circles in the mud. "This is the route we are following. It's a backwoods road, little used except by the folks that farm here. It's the worst road in Maury County, much of it abandoned four or more years ago."

"Why so crooked, son?" Hood asked, scratching his beard.

"It skirts property lines."

Hood grimaced.

"How many miles on this road to Spring Hill?" Cleburne inquired.

The guide tossed the stick aside, scrunched his face, and pinched the bridge of his nose. "I'd say between seventeen and eighteen miles, five or six more than on the pike."

Hood studied the scout, then looked up at the sky. "At least we won't have rain to contend with today."

Cleburne lowered his head and stared at his saddle while a handful of eavesdropping soldiers snickered at the remark.

The guide mounted his horse. "Anything else, General?"

"You're dismissed," Hood answered, then sat sullenly silent.

Cleburne pulled a pencil from his pocket and drew a more accurate representation of the road on Hood's map before handing it back to him.

Hood seethed in his saddle, his frustration as evident on his face as the fake leg jutting from the saddle. "Why didn't Forrest advise me of the road's condition?" He grumbled and shook his head at the incompetence of his subordinates.

"He did," Cleburne reminded him. "What do you want us to do?"

"Advance, General, advance."

Cleburne touched spurs to the flanks of his horse and bolted to the head of the column. Moments later, the troops resumed their march, their destination half again as far away as their commander thought. Along the route, the muddy roads, the soggy fields, and the towering trees seemed to mock the soldiers as they pressed ahead.

Hiram Granbury
On the Trail to Spring Hill

Ninety minutes beyond the pontoon bridge over the flooding Duck River, Hiram Granbury and Samuel T. Foster watched John Bell Hood approach ahead of his retinue of officers. He sat strapped in his saddle, his wooden right leg sticking out like a lost wagon tongue.

His doe-eyes and his long, bearded face failed to inspire the plodding Texans as they fought the mud beneath their feet and the morning chill piercing their filthy uniforms, their tattered coats, and the thin blankets they bundled in to fight the breeze.

"Looks like he's coming our way, General," Foster said. "I shall make a tactical withdrawal so he doesn't hang me for insubordination. As a lowly captain, I'm barely better than the soldiers he calls cowards." Foster saluted, then trotted to the rear of the brigade where his regiment marched.

After the captain departed, Granbury edged his horse off the road to await Hood's arrival. He saluted as the commander reined up beside him. Hood never acknowledged the salutation.

"Keep your men moving. I know Texans can fight, and I'll need them to destroy Schofield's army."

"I push them as fast as I can, General, but they're weak from too little food, too little sleep, too much rain, and too much cold."

"We'll have sunshine today," Hood scowled. "With my Texas brigade at Gaines' Mill, I broke the Yankee line and turned the tide of battle for General Lee. I expect the same from you and your Texans, General Granbury."

"We will do our best, but Gaines' Mill was fought in the summer—June as I recall—and Lee's army was better provisioned than we have been, sir."

"It's not provisions the Army of Tennessee lacks, it's courage, the willingness to attack the enemy and prevail. I have grown to expect such abrogation of duty from soldiers of other states, but not from Texans. We are lost if this army's cowardice has seeped into the ranks of the Texans."

"This army has fought above the level of its leadership."

"By god, General, are you questioning my competence?"

"No, sir, just acknowledging it."

"That's insubordination, by god!"

Granbury glared at Hood. "Do you want my resignation, General Hood?"

"What I want is your loyalty. With that and God's help, we will triumph."

"Are you even worshiping the right God?"

Hood tugged at his beard, bewildered at the question. "What?"

"You were baptized Episcopalian, were you not?"

The commander nodded.

"Have you ever considered becoming a Baptist?"

"Absolutely not, General."

"If you ever change your mind, General, I can find plenty who would be honored to baptize you." Granbury offered a sharp salute to the commander of the Army of Tennessee. "If you will pardon me, General, I'll speed my men along."

Granbury yanked his reins and aimed for his marching Texans tramping ahead toward Spring Hill. He realized it would be a long day because the road narrowed and meandered through the woods and landforms, passing barren fields and the cabins of yeoman farmers. The dwellings they passed stood far humbler than the plantations they had marched by on the main roads. Despite their modest appearance, the cabins spewed out generous inhabitants—women, children, old men, and an occasional young fellow missing a foot or a leg or an arm in previous service to the Confederacy. The spectators offered the men encouragement and what food they could spare from the morning's breakfast.

Hood's dirt route took twice the time a main road would have taken because the troops had to fight the sticky mud that sucked at their feet, pulling off their worn shoes, men having to stop and retrieve their footwear from the muck. Some men gave up and carried their muddy shoes and walked barefooted. In places, the road narrowed between trees or outcroppings and the soldiers clumped together before funneling through the constrictions. Never once in the precession did Granbury raise his voice or tell his men to speed up. He merely offered encouragement. The soldiers took no break for lunch, doing without as they had so often since Hood took command, or finishing what food they may have saved in their pockets from the previous day.

Shortly before noon, Granbury heard the cry of riders from the rear, "Make way for the general, make way for the general." He turned to see Hood's staff officers calling for soldiers to get out of the path of General Hood, who was heading to the front of the army. The soldiers grumbled and moved aside. Granbury rode into the trees to avoid another encounter with Hood, who passed moments later, sitting like a cadaver in the saddle, his protruding wooden leg bouncing with each stride of his horse. As his retinue tramped by, their horses splattered mud and grime on the soldiers Hood would call on that afternoon to defend the South. Granbury spat in disgust as the entourage passed. When they trotted out of sight down the twisting, tree-lined road, Granbury rejoined his grumbling men.

One hatless Texan called to him. "Fine strategy, hiding in the trees so General Hood wouldn't dirty your uniform, General

Granbury." Then the soldier paused. "No offense, General, but your uniform's about as dirty as ours."

"I sleep on the field with my men, not in a plantation home with whoever will have me."

Another soldier cried, "We know. You're one of us."

"Thank you, boys. We're all Texans, and there's no fellows I'd rather lead into battle than you boys." Granbury rode to the head of his brigade as they trudged onward to Spring Hill.

Sumner Cunningham
On the Trail to Spring Hill

Following their commander's orders, Sumner Cunningham marched with his Forty-first Tennessee comrades in the mid-morning light toward the Duck River crossing outside Columbia. As Cunningham approached the pontoon bridge that would provide passage to the north bank, the chatter around him stopped as soldiers straightened at the arrival of Colonel James D. Tillman on the mare he called "Sergeant."

So deep in his thoughts was he about his own mortality that Cunningham kept marching without looking up at his commanding officer.

"Sergeant Major Cunningham," Tillman shouted.

When Cunningham felt the adjacent soldier elbowing him in the ribs, he looked up and grimaced, "Sorry, Colonel. I must've been dozing."

Tillman nodded. "After you cross the bridge, step out of the ranks so we can talk."

"Yes, sir."

The officer nudged his mare in the flank and trotted to the head of his regiment, leaving Cunningham to worry that he had failed to attend some important matter.

As the land sloped toward the river, Cunningham saw a ragged line of soldiers in tattered butternut and gray uniforms crossing the Duck on the pontoon bridges. The recent rains had swollen the watercourse, and Cunningham guessed it was a hundred or more feet from bank to bank. Eight wooden longboats or pontoons were linked to timbers that were covered with planks to provide the flooring. The temporary crossing provided a twelve-foot-wide passage for man, animal, and conveyance.

Cunningham had crossed pontoon bridges many times before, but never trusted them, in large part because he was a poor swimmer.

The closer he came to the bridge, the louder came the tromp-tromp-tromp of men on the march. As he stepped on the planks angling to the floating structure, he saw on the wooden slats the smudges of mud and blood from the men marching without shoes. Ahead of him strode his comrades, some with the seat out of their pants and a few with no drawers, their bottoms shining in the morning sunlight finally dissipating the fog. After tromping hundreds of miles in this war, Cunningham agreed with most soldiers that socks carried a greater value than underwear. To have the Union commissary and a full issue of clothing would be a dream come true for most Confederates. The reality was they marched on, whether they had shoes, drawers, socks, or coats, thankful for small blessings like the day's growing sunshine.

As he stepped on the bridge, the breeze along the river sent shivers up his back. Cunningham wondered how low the bridge would have dipped into the water had the troops had full provisions and full bellies throughout the war. These soldiers carried no extra weight on their bodies, nor in their haversacks, just a resolution to see this war to an end and return home. Cunningham, like many of them, no longer cared about the war's outcome as long as he made it home whole. The Bedford County men rejoiced at being back in Tennessee and closer to home than they had been during months spent in Georgia and Alabama. By distance, they marched nearer to their homes than they had been in months, but no one knew how far in time they remained from their families and their futures.

Halfway across the bridge, Cunningham spotted Tillman waiting atop his horse beside the road some twenty yards from the crossing. He took slow, deep breaths, calming himself as he trudged ahead, uncertain what his commander needed. As sure as he was crossing the Duck River, Cunningham knew he was destined for a major battle. He wondered if he could miss it, as he had so many others. Stepping off the pontoon planks, he angled for Tillman.

Drawing up in front of the officer, he saluted. "Yes, Colonel. What do you need?"

"It's what our men need. In a day or two, we'll fight the Yankees, I'm certain of it. The Forty-first has fought poorly in the past. I intend to see that is different this time. We *will* give our all for the South this time, Sergeant."

"Yes, sir," Cunningham replied, trying to hide his wobbly knees. "What can I do to assist?"

"Lead the charge," Tillman answered.

Cunningham gasped, fearing he might collapse on those weak knees in front of his superior. Just as he was about to protest, the colonel grinned.

"I'm pulling your leg, Sergeant. You're too valuable handling all the reports and paperwork, but I'll want you on the flank to see that we have no shirkers and that everyone does his duty. General Strahl is depending on us, as is the rest of the Confederacy."

Cunningham nodded. "I will do my duty."

"Until we draw battle lines, I want you to see if you can scrounge up extra food and ammunition from some of the other regiments, if they have anything to spare. I'd like my men to go into a fight with full cartridge boxes and full bellies."

"May I speak frankly, sir?"

"Certainly, Sergeant."

Taking a deep breath, Cunningham shook his head. "From the lowly perspective of a sergeant major, sir, General Hood itches more to fight than he does to provision his men. I doubt anyone has bullets or hardtack to share."

Tillman cocked his jaw and licked his lips, then spoke softly. "Many officers feel the same way, Sergeant. We can only pray to a merciful God that General Hood will live up to his promise before we left Alabama for Tennessee."

"Remind me, Colonel."

"That we will not fight unless we have the choice of ground and equal numbers. That was his promise. We all hope he keeps it. As for you, Sergeant, do the best you can. Even if you can't find extra supplies, I want the men to know we searched for provisions to feed them. You have never failed me or the Forty-first Tennessee."

"I'll do what I can." Cunningham saluted and trotted away with a troubled conscience to catch up with his unit. Deep in his heart, he knew he had failed his regiment many times before. He feared he would do it again.

Mary Alice Carter McPhail
Carter Home

Perhaps the cold, wet spell had broken for a time, Mary Alice thought as she walked to the locust grove for the second consecutive morning. While the air remained brisk, the dawning sky held no clouds to block the sun or spit rain, sleet, or snow. Yesterday's sunshine had dried the ground enough that Mary Alice wore her own shoes rather than her father's boots for the sentimental stroll. She could not explain this sudden surge of emotion over the locust trees from her lost childhood, and most especially over her younger brother, Theodrick Carter. She sensed he was calling her to meet him at the grove, even though the thought remained illogical. Still, she went to this rendezvous with a past that had disappeared like the Tennessee she had grown up with. At her destination, she stood among the locusts, bowed her head, and spoke a prayer.

"Our gracious and merciful God, please hear my request so Your loving mercy and compassion will flow over the heads of the Carter family and protect us one and all from the evils of this war and the outrages it has brought against the Southern people. Be especially with brother Theodrick by ministering to his needs and by blessing him night and day with Your divine protection so that we will be reunited as a family not only in this life, but also in the eternal life You have promised to all who have accepted Your benevolent grace. For this, I beseech You in the name of the Father, the Son, and the Holy Ghost. Amen."

With her spirits lifted, Mary Alice returned to the house and joined the adults at the breakfast table.

"We waited on you like pigs at the trough," Moscow observed as she took her seat on the long bench where she had sat as a little girl. "You've got a wide smile for someone who'll have the dregs of our meal."

"Our bodies and our souls need nourishment, the former may be lacking, but the latter is full," Mary Alice answered. "I am prepared for anything."

"Even teaching the children's lessons today?" asked her sister-in-law Sallie.

Mary Alice nodded. "Even that. I've got a special reading lesson for them."

"Will they ever return to school?" inquired her childless, widowed sister Annie, a year younger than Mary Alice.

"Not as long as a war's raging," Moscow interrupted. "I want our children within these walls should the gods of war ever return to Franklin. Battle is terrifying enough for them, even more so when separated from their parents."

Fount, the patriarch, nodded. "Family first," he said, before taking a bite from a biscuit.

"Do you want me to let the Lotz family know you'll be teaching?" Sallie asked.

"No, thank you," Mary Alice replied, "I'll walk down the road and inform them after I complete my preparations." She finished her small portions at the same time as the others, then lingered a few minutes, sipping coffee and complimenting Callie on another fine meal with the biscuits cooked to a golden perfection. Mostly, the family speculated about what moves the competing armies would make in the coming days. Yankees to the north of them in Nashville and Yankees to the south of them in Columbia remained a threat. Below Columbia sat the Confederate Army of Tennessee, the wild card in the hand middle Tennessee had been dealt. They gave up trying to foresee the vagaries of an unpredictable war to begin their day's work, the men starting chores, the mothers rousing their children and the other women helping Callie prepare the table for the breakfast they had set aside for the little ones.

Mary Alice retreated to her room, waking Adelaide and Marcus and seeing they got dressed before sending them to the basement for breakfast as they wiped their still sleepy eyes. Then she awoke one-year-old Lannie and changed his diaper, dressed him, and toted him to the breakfast table where Sallie took over and fed him a bowl of applesauce. Returning to her room, Mary Alice pulled from beneath her bed the box of *Chattanooga Daily Rebel* news clippings written by her brother under his Mint Julep pseudonym. Rather than an article Tod had penned, Mary Alice chose a letter authored by the Twentieth Tennessee's regimental surgeon and published in the paper. The missive spoke kindly of her brother, and it was short enough to keep the children's attention.

She gathered her pencil and tablet and carried them with the clipping into the parlor where she taught the seven oldest children. After advising her sisters she was stepping to their neighbor's house, she slipped outside and trod to the wood-frame home of Albert and Margaretha Lotz. Mary Alice knocked on the door and Margaretha answered, *"Guden morgen,"* in the thick tongue of her native Germany.

"A pleasant day to you, Margaretha. We will have school in an hour. Will Paul and Matilda be attending?"

"Ja, dey will be dere."

Mary Alice smiled. "Wonderful! They're always so well behaved, unlike the Carter clan, and so studious. They are a joy to teach."

"Danke, mein freund," Margaretha said, as she stepped on the porch and hugged Mary Alice. "Dey will be dere."

Mary Alice nodded. "I'll look forward to seeing them." She walked back home, thankful to have the Lotz family as neighbors. The couple had immigrated to the states more than a decade ago, becoming naturalized citizens as soon as they could. He was a master carpenter, and she an excellent cook, regularly providing the Carter family with apple strudel when the fruits were in season. During the war, Fount had helped keep food on their table by sharing some of the Carter provisions. Alfred, in turn, assisted Fount with his carpentry needs.

An hour later Margaretha arrived on time and left Paul and Matilda while the Carter and McPhail children were still dragging into the parlor. Mary Alice seated them all in a circle on the floor as she grabbed her tablet, pencil, and news clipping. She sat in a cushioned parlor chair to begin the lesson.

"Today I want to practice our reading from an article in the *Chattanooga Daily Rebel*. It's a newspaper article that mentions my brother Tod." She handed the clipping to Lena. "This letter was written from Fairfield, Tennessee, on May twenty-ninth of last year. Since you're the oldest, Lena, you read the first sentence."

Lena shook the clip, cleared her throat and started. "Dear editor, please send the *Daily Rebel* to the following officers and men of this regiment, placing each man's name on his paper, and send all in one bundle directed to Twentieth Tennessee, B.R. Johnson's brigade, Cleee—"

"Cleburne," Mary Alice assisted.

"—Cleee-burne's Division, War Trace, Tennessee."

"Very good, Lena. Now, let McKinley read."

Lena passed the clipping to her cousin, who took a moment to find the second sentence, then continued the letter. "We regard the *Rebel* as being the true champion of Tennessee pat—"

"Pay-tree-oh-tism."

"—pa-tri-o-tism. It has certainly proved to be a bi-edged and well directed weapon in defense of all the en-dear-ments of our home and country." McKinley finished with a smile.

"Excellent, McKinley. You are getting so good at sounding out words and reading."

"What's bi-edged mean?" asked Moscow's ten-year-old boy Walter. "Like goodbye?"

Mary Alice smiled. "This bi is spelled B-I, not B-Y-E. In this case bi means two, so the word bi-edged means having two edges like a sword. The writer gives you a clue by using that term with the word 'weapon' nearby. Always look for clues in other words to help you figure out their meaning."

"Now, Walter, your turn."

McKinley handed the clipping to him. Walter straightened, threw his chest out and continued the letter. "It's dig-ni-fied and cour-te-ous tone, and a display of good taste, wit, and humor and happy dis-po-si-tion has won for it the ad-mir-a-tion of num-er-ous readers."

"I'm proud of you, Walter, for sounding out the words so well." Mary Alice took the clip from Walter and handed it to Paul Lotz. "Your turn, Paul." She pointed where to begin.

Paul gritted his teeth, let out a deep sigh, and started to slowly mouth the words. "I met with our mutual friend 'Mint Ju-lep,' a few days ago."

"Your English, Paul, is wonderful. You and Matilda will know both English and German by the time you grow up."

Both Lotz youngsters smiled and nudged each other with their elbows.

"Now, children, do you know who Mint Julep is?"

"A drink," said Walter.

"Yes," Mary Alice answered, "but this is what is called a penname for an author who writes stories for the paper, but not under his own name. Mint Julep is my brother Theodrick or Tod, and the uncle to you Carters and McPhails as well as the neighbor of Paul and Matilda. What the letter writer is saying is that he knows Tod and wants newspaper subscriptions so the soldiers can read Tod's reports on the war."

"Wow," said the kids in unison.

"Let me finish the letter for you," Mary Alice said. "Mint Julep looks as fresh as a new rosebud, and might remind you of a 'Turnip Salad' in full bloom, since he has donned a new uniform tipped with gold trim. Enclosed you will find one hundred and ten dollars, for which please send said papers."

"A hundred and ten dollars," Walter gasped.

"Are soldiers rich?" McKinley wanted to know.

"No, far from it. The letter is signed by James F. Fryar, surgeon of the Twentieth Tennessee regiment. A surgeon is a doctor."

The children nodded.

"See a doctor needs a good education as does a writer like your uncle Tod. If you children mind your lessons, one day you can be a doctor or an author or anything you want to be."

Her students smiled at each other.

Mary Alice then passed out booklets to the children to read silently as she helped each individually from youngest to oldest.

*****

Hardin Figuers
Figuers Home

After breakfast, Bethenia sent Hardin to deliver a thank you note to the Carter family for the button they had provided the day before and to handle some errands downtown. Hardin thought it silly to spend the time, ink, and paper to write an acknowledgement for a single button, but his mother had informed him that the times when people have the greatest needs are the instances when such courtesies are the most appreciated. So, Hardin began his tasks wearing a coat with two original buttons, the mismatched Carter button and a halved peach pit that his mother had fashioned into a button. She fastened his coat for him and sent him on his way with a kiss, but no sooner had Hardin exited the house than he unbuttoned his covering and enjoyed the sun's increasing warmth. He loosed Adele from the barn so the hound could accompany him on his rounds.

On the way to the Carter house, he swung wide of the direct route and headed for the locust grove, still snickering at the spot where he had downed the hornet's nest and sent the Yankees to running. Then he and Adele ambled toward the Carter cookhouse where he cracked the door and saw the slave Calfurnia washing the dishes from breakfast while singing a spiritual. As his mother had left him no instructions on who to deliver the thank you note to, he thought about leaving it with Callie, but then he saw Moscow Carter standing on the back porch with a tin of coffee. Softly, he shut the door to the cook shack and aimed for Moscow, who had served with the Twentieth Tennessee army until his capture, imprisonment, and parole. Now he was of no more use to the Confederacy than Hardin or his duty-shucking brother Tom.

Moscow nodded at Hardin. "Morning, neighbor. What brings you to the Carter place?"

Hardin lifted the envelope with the thank you note. "I'm delivering an important message."

"From Jefferson Davis, I assume."

Hardin snickered. "No, from my momma."

"Bethenia outranks Jeff Davis in your world, doesn't she?"

The youth nodded. "She thinks a thank you is in order for the button Mary Alice delivered yesterday." He stepped onto the porch and handed the missive to Moscow.

"I'll see that the message is delivered. What else can I do for you?"

"You were a colonel, right?"

"Lieutenant colonel, Twentieth Tennessee."

"So you know soldiering?"

"Better than most, not as good as some."

"What's gonna happen?"

Moscow shrugged. "I doubt the generals even know. I fear the Yankees will retreat through Franklin, but with the bridges out, they'll be trapped here unless they can repair the crossings."

"So we could see a battle?"

"I don't care to witness a fight anywhere near Franklin, much less in town."

"I do."

"No, you don't, son. It's devilry, death, and destruction. If shooting starts, you take cover in your cellar and stay hid until the gunfire ends. Keep your hound hidden, too."

Hardin nodded. "Yes, sir. I best be going."

"Remember what I told you, for your mother's sake, if not your own."

"Thank you, sir. Come on, Adele." Hardin walked between the house and the farm office to Columbia Pike and turned toward town. At Main Street, he angled for the courthouse square and spotted five Yankee wagons lined up at the blackened bridges like hungry orphans. As much as the Yankees had stolen from the folks of Franklin, Hardin wondered what it would be like to steal a wagon of provisions and replenish his mother's cellar, which was almost depleted save for a bin of potatoes and a sack of flour that she used to make bread and biscuits. They were lucky to have those few provisions, as it was more than many local folk possessed.

Hardin Figuers sensed the tension in the Franklin air as he strode around the town square, finishing his mother's morning errands. The day reminded him of spring days when threatening thunderheads built to the west, towering over the horizon and by late afternoon blocking the sun before winds, hail, and torrential rains pelted the landscape. But on this November Tuesday, the day broke cloudless with a bright sun that would warm the land enough to melt even the snow lingering in the shady spots behind structures and trees.

Occasionally, a blue-clad courier astride his horse rode through town, passing the wagons bottlenecked at the blackened bridges too unsound to support the weight of a wagon and team. The Nashville Pike bridge burned by previous Yankees mocked the current retreat. The railroad bridge, too, had been weakened by fire, but could still support a horseman.

Rumors flew like autumn leaves in a strong wind, and Hardin tingled at the excitement of the uncertainty about what this and the following days might bring. He hoped to see an honest-to-God battle, not a minor skirmish like the year before. Besides desiring to add more military artifacts to his collection, he wanted to know what to expect when he enlisted in the army to fight the invaders.

As he walked around the courthouse, Hardin listened to the talk among the men and women attending their daily duties. Some considered leaving town, but had no destinations in mind that would be any safer until the armies committed themselves to a battle somewhere. After he completed his loop around the square, he stopped at three grocers, tying Adele outside while he went in, hoping to find a tin of baking soda for his mother, but the shelves everywhere were largely empty. Baking soda, like other necessities, was scarce. When he exited the last store, he untied Adele as a solitary Union wagon rumbled down the street to join the others at the river. The hound barked.

"Why you running, Yankee?" yelled a man too old to fight. "You afraid our boys'll whip your tail?"

"Leave our homes and our men alone," hissed a woman, herding two sons under ten along the walk.

The Union teamster ignored the taunts, directing his rig down the street to join the others lining up at the river.

He started down Main Street toward home, passing the office of Dr. Sylvanus O'Brian, who had tended the Figuers family but could not save Agnes. In fact, O'Brian never answered with certainty what had killed Hardin's sister. Hardin glanced up Fourth Avenue toward Rest Haven Cemetery where Agnes would spend eternity, then continued down Main, passing the First Presbyterian and St. Paul's Episcopal churches. Hardin wondered if the Yankees had churches or if they were as godless as they seemed. Adele growled at a feral tomcat that hissed and arched his back before scampering under the porch of the nearest house. He crossed Sixth, Seventh, Eighth, and Ninth streets, the last city street before his home and before Main Street became the Carter's Creek Pike.

Opposite his home, he saw Uncle Jesse out chopping wood for his neighbors. He walked over and greeted the slave.

"Is that all you do, Uncle Jesse, chop kindling?"

"Good day, Marse Hardin. Dat's about it. Wishes I's diggin' a hole, though."

"Why's that, Uncle Jesse?"

"I's gots a bad feelin' 'bout de comin' days. My kind's been slippin' from Columbia and Spring Hill, sayin' a bad storm be a comin'.'"

"It's a cloudless day, Uncle Jesse."

"Not de weather. Dey means a grim battle. Plenty scared, dey is. I's needin' to digs me a hole to hides in when de fightin' starts."

"If there's any shooting, Moscow Carter told me to hide in our cellar until the gunfire ends."

"We don't gots no cellar, Marse Hardin."

"No matter, Uncle Jesse. Stay in ours. There'll be room."

"Ya sure yo'r momma won't be mindin'?"

"If any shooting starts, she'll be covering her eyes and ears. Probably won't see or hear you anyway, Uncle Jesse."

"I's obliged, Marse Hardin. I's got plenty of bad feelin's about tomorrow, feels it in my bones, I do, lad."

Tuesday Afternoon,

November 29, 1864

Sumner A. Cunningham

Chapter Eight

Sumner Cunningham
Approaching Spring Hill

The sky above remained so clear the soldiers of the Forty-first Tennessee could almost see God through the treetops as they trudged along the sloppy back roads east of Columbia, angling northwest to Spring Hill and the macadamized turnpike to Franklin. Their stomachs empty, their clothes tattered, their faces gaunt and determined, the infantrymen marched northward toward the ultimate victory John Bell Hood had proclaimed in advance for the Army of Tennessee, the Confederacy and, most of all, for himself. Though the sky had cleared of clouds, the sunshine brought scant relief to men exhausted from days on the march with too little nourishment.

Sumner Cunningham trod behind his unit, worried that he would find no extra food or ammunition to supply his troops, as Colonel Tillman had requested. He would make his rounds to other units, once they bivouacked for the evening. Along the road, women, children, and old men welcomed the Confederates back to Tennessee, some civilians even sharing their sparse grub with the soldiers, providing apples, or biscuits, or fritters to men who ate them ravenously. But as always, more men appeared than apples, biscuits, and fritters to sate them. Most continued their march, hungry and tired. Cunningham asked several families if they had additional food to barter or sell, but they just shrugged, saying they had little to spare and still feed themselves as they were already sharing what they could. Finally, Cunningham gave up, knowing he had failed his regiment again.

Onward marched the men of the Forty-first Tennessee. Well after high sun, Colonel Tillman reined up beside Cunningham, accompanying him through the slush, the hooves of his gelding flinging small splotches of mud against his trouser legs. "We're depending on you, Sergeant, to find what provisions you can. General Strahl has asked me to keep him apprised of how we are armed and provisioned."

Cunningham saluted. "I know all the sergeant majors and commissary sergeants in our division are in the same shape as us. Nobody has anything to spare, no extra ammunition or rations. That's something General Brown needs to know."

Tillman grimaced. "I'll forward your report to General Strahl for General Brown. I don't envy the decisions he must make—," the colonel paused, "—or the orders he must follow."

"I wish I had better news to report, sir."

"Me, too, Sergeant, but do one more thing for me."

"Yes, sir."

"Cleburne's Division is leading the way to Spring Hill. We will camp the night close to his regiments. Check as many commissary sergeants as you can in his division."

"Sir, might I ask a frank question?"

"Certainly, Sergeant."

"Wouldn't it be simpler to ask the other officers what they could spare?"

Tillman cocked his head at Cunningham. "Perceptive inquiry, Sergeant. Fact is, the farther you climb the ladder of command, the more distorted the politics become, especially with Hood in charge. I trust our division commanders John Brown and Pat Cleburne and William Bate, but I'm uncertain about General Cheatham. I trust the fighting men more than our high command."

"You sound discouraged, Colonel."

"We all want it to end, but I fear it will end poorly under this commander." Tillman stared at Cunningham for a moment, then resumed. "Sergeant, forget this conversation ever happened."

"What conversation, sir?"

Tillman grinned. "I can always depend upon you, Sergeant."

Cunningham saluted as the colonel rode to the front of his regiment.

Though Tillman left, the misery remained with sucking mud, ankle-deep creek crossings, and occasional breezes that, in spite of the sunshine, pierced clothing and flesh like artic daggers reaching all the way to the bone. Even the trees shivered in the breeze, no birds providing any accompanying music, the only sounds coming from the slosh of muddied shoes and feet and the groans of men as empty of hope as they were of food.

At first, the midafternoon sound came as a slight rumble, like a distant runaway wagon, then more starkly. The soldiers lifted their heads and turned their gaze to the northwest, where gunfire announced a skirmish, or worse, at Spring Hill. Cunningham's grip tightened around his nine-and-a-half pound Enfield, fearing this was the battle he could not avoid. He stroked the stock of the rifled musket, his fingers running over the S-A-C initials he had carved with his pocketknife to prove his rifle's ownership. Carving his brand on the weapon had been a silly gesture since he had never once fired the weapon at an enemy, but at least he—and others—knew the Enfield belonged to him. It provided proof he was a soldier.

Lt. Gen. John Bell Hood
Nearing Spring Hill

Throughout the long day, they had plunged ahead through mud, mush, and muck. Those that were shoeless now wore brogans of sticky Tennessee soil. Despite his subordinates' missteps in following this route, John Bell Hood never doubted he would outwit Schofield and beat him to Spring Hill. But at three o'clock, the distant crackle of gunfire suggested otherwise. Hood looked at his staff officers and nodded for two of them to ride forward to assess the problem. By his estimate, his leading troops were still two miles from Spring Hill, with barely two hours before darkness enveloped the Tennessee hills. Hood prayed it was just Forrest's cavalry skirmishing with Union horse soldiers, but he feared the worst, that Yankee infantry had reached Spring Hill first.

Realizing he lacked the time to wait for his scouts to return with an explanation, he hurried orderlies to find General Cheatham. Were he a whole man, he would have chased down the general himself, but he could no longer stay astride a galloping horse. He feared that exploding powder might spook his mount and tip him from his saddle. Being strapped to the animal, he worried that should he slide off the saddle, the horse might kick him to death before he could extricate himself from the bindings.

Cheatham finally galloped up.

Hood pointed to the northwest. "It sounds as if General Forrest has encountered a significant force, not just cavalry."

"My men are ready, sir. What do you want me to do?"

He nodded toward a hill a quarter mile distant. "Follow me."

Accompanied by his staff and Cheatham, Hood directed his horse at a trot for the knoll, hoping its elevation would give him a view of the situation. Reaching the peak of the bald knob that overlooked the meadow skirting the pike, Hood frowned at what he saw: an unending line of supply wagons scurrying for Spring Hill. "It's just the supply train," Hood announced. "I see a handful of fighting men and artillery, but not many. Those teamsters are frightened like rabbits. Soon they'll boil in our pot, Cheatham. Send your three divisions forward at double quick to support General Forrest. Report back to me when your task is complete."

"Yes, sir," the corps commander responded.

Cheatham nodded and dashed away, screaming orders as he departed. Shortly, the infantry on the road behind Hood jogged toward their cavalry comrades.

Schofield was retreating, Hood thought, first sending his supply train to safety while the bulk of his army remained outside Columbia. Hood smiled. Perhaps the Almighty had blessed him with the opportunity to whip a small guard of cavalry, then capture the wagons teeming with the needed supplies of food and ammunition.

As they watched the procession snaking down the road, Hood realized his party had been spotted when a Yankee officer raced to a retreating cannon and gestured toward the hill. The artillerymen directed their gun, limber, and caisson off the pike, unhitched the weapon and swung it around toward the hill. Scurrying around the Napoleon twelve-pounder like ants, the men flew into their tasks, a pair elevating the barrel, another sighting the fieldpiece, and others toting powder and projectile to the mouth of the weapon. As the enemy pushed in the charge and then the shell, Hood turned his horse about.

"I've seen enough, gentlemen," Hood said. "Time to withdraw!" He nudged the flank of his mount with his good leg and the animal retreated down the knoll, followed by his staff. Barely had they descended the backside of the rise, than he heard the discharge of the Yankee artillery piece, his horse flinching, but not changing his pace. An instant later, the shell exploded on the hilltop behind them, shrapnel whistling in the air overhead. Hood's horse lunged ahead, but an aide riding beside the commander leaned over and grabbed the reins before the skittish animal bolted away and dumped Hood.

The dozen officers with Hood returned to the line of gray soldiers jogging toward Forrest's men and the small arms skirmish outside Spring Hill.

*****

Patrick Cleburne
Advancing toward Spring Hill

After multiple delays to sort out the route to Spring Hill over a road seldom used for years, Major General Patrick Cleburne knew Hood's grand strategy would fail. The extra five or more miles the meandering route took to Spring Hill doomed his plan. Instead of a noon lunch with Cheatham on Yankee provisions, Cleburne realized the sloppy road and the extra distance would put them in Spring Hill late afternoon at the earliest. They would be lucky to have supper on Union rations, if at all. Hood would blame everybody but himself for the miscalculation. Cleburne wished Cheatham would live up to his boasts and whip the commander. A dose of good old Tennessee common sense would benefit Hood, assuming it didn't kill him. And if it did prove fatal for their commander, more Army of Tennessee soldiers would survive the war.

While the weary soldiers mushed along this remote road, the families in their isolated cabins came out to greet the soldiers. Most of these country folks had heard of the army, but never seen so many troops at once. One family rolled out three hogsheads of tobacco, yanked the lid off the kegs and invited passing men to take a handful. On hearing the army's approach, one wrinkled woman kept her lunch fire going, frying fatback, and saltpork, which she handed out to marching troops. Cleburne himself drew the attention of another wrinkled matriarch who couldn't believe he was *the* Patrick R. Cleburne, the most famous infantry commander in the Army of Tennessee. "You're our savior, General Cleburne," she called.

Embarrassed by her comment, Cleburne mentioned his crippled commander to deflect the attention away from himself. "General Hood commands the Army of Tennessee."

The woman spat a stream of tobacco juice on the ground. "He lost Atlanta. You done good for the cause, not him." She reached up to shake his hand.

Leaning over in the saddle, Cleburne took her callused fingers. "Thank you for your kind words."

"General Cleburne," she said, "if you'll return this evening for supper, I'll fix you the finest turkey dinner you've ever had."

Releasing her grip, he smiled. "I must pass on your gracious offer tonight, ma'am, as I expect we'll be too busy teaching Yankees some table manners. If the invitation stands for tomorrow night, perhaps I'll be back for your supper with many thanks."

"Give them Yankees a hot dose of hell, General Cleburne," she said. "You and General Forrest are our only remaining hopes."

As she backed away, Cleburne saw tears moistening her eyes and tobacco juice seeping from the corners of her mouth. He rode on, feeling helpless to do anything more than offer her optimism he might return the next night for supper, an offer he knew he would never fulfill.

Later up the trail, Cleburne heard the muffled sound of distant gunfire. Spring Hill must be near, he thought, and Forrest's cavalry must be engaged. He looked at the sun and estimated it was well past three o'clock. Only an hour and a half or at most two hours of daylight remained. Time was running out on the day and on the Confederacy, Cleburne feared.

Soon a courier galloped toward him from the head of the column, yelling, "General Cleburne, General Cleburne!"

Lifting his kepi and waving it at the courier, Cleburne slapped the reins against Red Pepper's neck and started for the messenger. "Come on, Mangum," he called to his aide-de-camp. "Things are heating up."

When they met, the courier handed Cleburne written orders scribbled in the hand of Benjamin Cheatham. The breathless messenger gasped and delivered verbal orders. "General Cheatham says you are to rush to General Forrest's aid on our right flank and advance on Spring Hill, if the opportunity presents itself."

Cleburne unfolded the paper and confirmed the written order matched the commands relayed by the courier. He handed the paper to Mangum. "Hang onto this, Lieutenant." He nodded to the dispatch rider. "Tell General Cheatham we'll be there shortly."

The messenger saluted and galloped away. Cleburne turned to Mangum. "Issue the orders to our brigades, Leonard."

"Yes, sir," he cried and slapped his mount into a run.

Lt. Gen. John Bell Hood
Nearing Spring Hill

Spotting General Patrick Cleburne urging his division forward, John Bell Hood aimed his mount toward him. When he saw Hood turn his way, Cleburne trotted over to meet him.

"General Cleburne," shouted Hood. "Send your division en echelon toward the pike and engage the enemy."

The Irishman removed his kepi and waved it toward Spring Hill. "Sir, General Cheatham ordered my division to Spring Hill to support General Forrest and his cavalry."

"I'm countermanding those orders, General Cleburne. I'll send General Brown's Division to support Forrest and protect our right flank. Be prepared to attack with you entire division once you hear the sound of Brown's guns. Then take and hold the road."

"So be it, General," Cleburne answered, tugging his kepi back on his head and galloping off to change the destination of his three thousand men.

As Cleburne departed, Hood's scouts returned from the cavalry skirmish, reporting that Forrest's men were running low on ammunition. At most, they reported, the Union force was a couple of regiments, possibly a brigade, but not Schofield's entire army.

Hood nodded. Despite the labored march, he realized victory remained within his grasp. He stood on the brink of changing the destiny of the Confederacy. Though exhausted from rising so early to accompany his command, he would await a report from General Cheatham on his progress supporting Forrest and taking Spring Hill, then retire for the evening to his headquarters arranged by his staff at the home of Colonel Absalom Thompson, two miles south of town. Today was the chance for Cheatham to repay Hood's faith in his leadership as he had promoted the Tennessean to corps commander over Patrick Cleburne, the officer most felt fittest and most deserving of the promotion.

But Cleburne had been a close friend of General William J. Hardee, who had criticized Hood's appointment and generalship around Atlanta, undercutting the effectiveness of the Army of Tennessee. The two generals loathed each other, but now Hardee was somewhere in Georgia harassing, but not stopping General Sherman's march across the state. Hood still resented Cleburne for his ill-founded proposal that slaves who volunteered to fight for the Confederacy be freed along with their families. The South would never be so desperate as to require the service of Negroes fighting side by side with white boys. Cleburne may have been a true warrior, but he was not a true Southerner, reason enough for Hood to deny Cleburne's promotion and his request for a fall leave to marry his betrothed.

*****

Sumner Cunningham
Nearing Spring Hill

As the Forty-first Tennessee moved closer to Spring Hill, the sound of rifle fire joined the roar of occasional artillery explosions, and Cunningham tensed, then quivered. A skilled marksman could load and fire an Enfield possibly four times a minute. Cunningham's fingers trembled so much, he doubted he could manage more than one shot every sixty seconds.

A soldier at his side placed his hand on Cunningham's shoulder. "The sun hasn't warmed us up much, has it, Sergeant?"

"It's my malaria," he replied.

"Sounds like things are hotter up ahead."

Cunningham gritted his teeth and nodded, trudging onward. For half an hour, the noise of the skirmish continued, then faded away with the day. When the road they traveled topped a rise between two modest hills, Cunningham saw through the haze of spent gunpowder the small Tennessee community in the distance. As he breathed the pungent aroma lingering from the recent engagement, he observed a line of supply wagons numbering in the hundreds, all inching north through Spring Hill. Yankee ammunition and provisions were there for the taking, with only a thin blue line of soldiers between the Confederate Army and their desperate needs. On this side of the Yankee positions, Cunningham spotted Cleburne's Division turning toward the enemy. Officers on horseback galloped among Cleburne's brigades, issuing orders.

Colonel Tillman bolted toward the Forty-first Tennessee, shouting commands, "Double quick to the right flank of Cleburne's Division. Prepare to attack." Tillman yanked his sword from his scabbard and waved it over his head, encouraging his men to hurry. "Daylight is short," he cried. "Drive them from the field."

Cunningham readied to die as his regiment lined up for battle. He took his place on the left flank of the Forty-first Tennessee. Then he waited, along with all the other Tennesseans, as daylight and time trickled away. Suddenly, the colonel dashed off, heading for a trio of other officers. In the distance, Cunningham recognized General Strahl among the three officers. After exchanging brief words, Tillman spun about and rode back toward his men, sliding his sword back in his scabbard. Reaching his troops, Tillman pulled off his hat and waved it at his men. "General Strahl informs me our attack has been canceled on the orders of General John Carter." A spontaneous cheer arose from all. "Make camp here tonight and be ready to fight tomorrow as we have outflanked General Schofield's army. We'll put them to the sword in the morning." Around Cunningham, men cheered again as Tillman directed his horse to their left flank.

When Cunningham realized the colonel was headed for him, he took a deep breath, trying to tighten his mushy knees and stop the shivering. Tillman stopped in front of Cunningham, studying his tremoring body.

"Sergeant," he said, "is it malaria or the chill?"

"The malaria, sir," Cunningham lied.

"I can't send you to the hospital because I'll need you in the coming hours. We'll bivouac here tonight. Once the men build their fires and you warm yourself up, go ahead and complete my earlier assignment, and see if you can scrounge up any extra food and spare ammunition from Cleburne's Division. Report back to me when you return. Tomorrow will be a treacherous day because Schofield must either pass us or die."

"Yes, sir, Colonel. I'll be on my way as soon as I can." Cunningham, for once, felt blessed by the brisk breeze because it had disguised his cowardice. Around him, men broke ranks and scurried for firewood and anything else that would burn. They found tree limbs and fence rails as the thump of axes and hatchets echoed across the encampment.

As dusk turned to night, dozens of fires appeared across the grounds. Cunningham stood around a couple of fires to cut the growing chill, rubbing his hands together to improve the circulation. When he was done, he started walking east toward Cleburne's Division, following the fishhook line of campfires that extended from Strahl's brigade all the way to the Columbia-to-Franklin pike two miles distant. Marching tomorrow would be easier along the macadamized turnpike, once Hood's army destroyed Schofield's.

Patrick Cleburne
Nearing the Columbia Pike

Lieutenant Leonard Mangum galloped over to Patrick Cleburne, who shook his head and yelled the new instructions. "General Hood's changed our orders. We're to form en echelon along the pike and prepare to attack."

"What about supporting Forrest's cavalry?" Mangum asked, as he leaned over the saddle and pulled out a map.

"Hood said he's sending Brown's Division to cover the right flank. Once his division is set, he will attack. At the sound of his guns, we are to take the turnpike."

"Does General Cheatham know of the change?" Mangum unfolded the map.

Cleburne shrugged, then both men studied the chart, noting the creek between them and the Yankee caravan on the road. The Irishman decided to send General Lowrey's Brigade across the creek toward Spring Hill, where he could pivot either to the town or the turnpike, whichever seemed most beneficial once the fighting began. Cleburne wanted General Govan's Brigade to protect Lowrey's right flank. General Granbury, the fighting Texan, would move straight for the turnpike on the left flank. Cleburne repeated his plan to Mangum to confirm the lieutenant understood his orders.

"They are to take actions they deem prudent until they hear the sounds of Brown's guns, then they are to attack in force and take the pike," Cleburne repeated.

Mangum nodded, and both headed toward their brigade commanders. Together they reached General Lowrey, Cleburne commanding him to cross the creek and move toward the pike south of Spring Hill as fast as he could. Cleburne then sent Mangum racing back down the line to tell Granbury of his assignment while he headed north to inform General Govan. Clearing the creek bank where some soldiers paused long enough to remove their shoes and socks and roll up their pants legs, Cleburne put Red Pepper into a gallop toward the sound and smoke of battle. He found Govan and conveyed his orders.

Beyond Govan, he saw Forrest atop his gelding, staring through field glasses at his fighting cavalrymen. Cleburne lifted his kepi and waved it over his head, drawing the attention of one of the cavalry general's staff, who shouted at Forrest and pointed toward Cleburne. Forrest turned his field glasses toward the Irishman, dropped them to his chest, and slapped his mount into a gallop. Moments later, the two generals met.

"I'm relieved it's you, Pat. Our ammunition's almost depleted. The enemy's behind solid cover. We don't have enough ammunition to drive them out and whip them."

"Hood changed our orders. We've been instructed to prepare to attack the turnpike," Cleburne informed the cavalryman. "Now, Brown's Division is supposed to reinforce you."

"Does Hood even know what he's doing?"

"Hard to say. First, he ordered Ben Cheatham to have me support you. I was headed your way until Hood caught me and said to move to the turnpike and the wagons."

Forrest shook his head. "It's not just wagons, Pat," Forrest said. "A few fighting regiments are mixed in with their train, and some may be hidden behind the hills. Be careful, but be quick, or I'll have to withdraw. Then your flank'll be vulnerable."

"I'll be fast as I can. We don't have much daylight."

The two generals saluted each other and reined their horses about to return to their troops. Reaching Lowrey, Cleburne pointed to the position he wanted him to occupy south of Govan's men and east of the turnpike. As he issued initial orders, General Hood rode up with his staff.

"General Cleburne," called Hood, "position your three regiments en echelon facing west so we can swing south and block the road should General Schofield send reinforcements."

Cleburne scratched the scar on his cheek. "I prefer to position Govan's Brigade on my right flank facing north to support General Forrest? The cavalry's running low on ammunition."

"Face west," Hood shouted, "and attack the enemy line at the sound of Brown's guns."

"I'll stagger my regiments so they can swing toward the road to attack the wagons or move north to help Forrest."

"Forget Forrest," Hood shouted, his face reddening. "Follow my command! Now," he screamed, angrily slapping his reins against his mount's neck. The animal tossed its head to bolt away until an aide grabbed the bridle and held the horse.

Cleburne spun his horse around and dashed off to change orders to his regiments. As he delivered the instructions, the rattle of musketry and the clank of sabers announced a fight was looming for the division. From the enemy pike, though, emerged one regiment of Yankee soldiers rushing to counter any impending charge. As the enemy took their positions, Cleburne saw that Granbury's men were the closest to the new threat. The wild-haired Texan realized it, too, and without direct orders, initiated an attack, his line loading their muskets, fixing bayonets and then moving forward until the advance faltered in an explosion of rifle fire.

*****

Hiram Granbury
Approaching the Columbia Pike

By the middle of the afternoon, Hiram Granbury heard the sounds of the distant skirmish and suspected the havoc came from Nathan Bedford Forrest's troopers creating mischief ahead.

About three o'clock, Lieutenant Leonard Mangum rushed along the line, issuing orders for an impending attack on the road. Lowrey's Brigade, which had just crossed the creek, two and a half miles south of Spring Hill, would hold the center of Cleburne's line. Govan's Brigade would hold the right and Granbury, when he arrived with his Texans, would position his men on the left flank for the charge against the position held by the Yankees south of town. Once they aligned, they would, at the sounds of the guns from Brown's Division on the far right flank, strike the detached Yankee positions and drive them into town, then swing around and block the Columbia-to-Franklin pike.

By the set of the sun through the trees, Granbury estimated they had less than an hour before darkness enveloped the land. He felt a knot of anxiety in his gut, as he doubted enough daylight remained for him to accomplish his assignment as Brown's Division trailed well behind him. Nearing the creek, Granbury saw Hood and his staff clumped together astride their mounts on the far side of the stream. They peered through binoculars and gestured to each other. Having had plenty of Hood for one day, Granbury crossed to the opposite side of the road, so he would be as far from Hood as reasonable when he and his men traversed the stream.

Once his soldiers waded through the water, he issued orders for them to move double quick and take up their positions on the left flank of Lowrey's Brigade. Granbury sat in his saddle, directing each company to its position for the westward attack. To the north, he could see the small burg of Spring Hill with supply wagons creeping toward Franklin. Shallow, rolling hills with yellowed grass stood between Granbury's unit and the enemy. Detached Yankee troops lined the top of a wide knoll ahead. He ordered his men to load their rifles, fix their bayonets, and prepare to advance.

With his troops lined up for battle, Granbury glanced behind him to see the vanguard of Brown's Division just crossing the creek. Brown's troops would have to hurry if his division initiated the broader attack before darkness set in. Granbury then drew his sword and waved his command forward. As his men advanced, Granbury saw Hood's party turn and retreat into the trees. Just like Hood to send his troops into battle, then desert them, likely to decide which plantation he would select for his evening meal and bed. Granbury rode to the front of his Texans as they unfurled their regimental flags and tromped ahead. Enemy gunfire picked up as Granbury's troops angled toward the road, holding their fire until he gave the order.

Sensing the moment was right, his men increased their pace to a jog and then a run as they headed for the small Union detachment. The enemy fired, then received reinforcements as two caissons rolled up, pulling twelve-pound Napoleons. The artillerymen bounded from their caissons, unhooked the cannons and rolled them into place. As they did, Granbury heard the retort of other cannons. Through a swale between distant hills, Granbury saw a battery of eight Napoleons belching smoke. The skilled artillerists were firing over the heads of their own men and into his Confederate line.

Ahead of him, Granbury watched as the Yankees loaded their artillery, then stepped back and pulled the lanyards. Both cannons belched fire, lead, and smoke, the shells landing in front of his men. Once his Texans moved closer, grape and canister would decimate them. Granbury hesitated. Without support on his left flank, the Union troops on the hill might enfilade his brigade.

"Withdraw, men, withdraw," Granbury cried as two more shells fell among them. He heard a scream as other men took up the cry, "Retreat, retreat," they shouted, and the line fell back before the artillery could do more damage. But the retreat turned out as well as the attack because the detachment with the two Napoleons limbered up and raced for Spring Hill. So, too, did the Yankees atop the low hill, turning and jogging toward town. When Granbury's men realized their change in fortune, they turned around and took refuge on the slopes of the hill that moments earlier teemed with their enemies, but stopped shy of the turnpike to await the sound of Brown's guns.

A hundred yards from the Columbia-Franklin pike, Granbury waited and waited and waited yet longer to swing west and block the road. After darkness engulfed the land and the roar of Brown's guns never came, Granbury ordered his men to bivouac for the night.

Patrick Cleburne
Outside Spring Hill

With his field glasses, Patrick Cleburne studied the Texan battle line, pleased with Granbury's initiative, especially as the Yankees artillery withdrew after a few volleys and the Texans positioned themselves so they could take and block the road at the sound of Brown's guns.

"We'll re-form Granbury's regiment and reinforce him with Lowrey's and Govan's regiments when we next attack," Cleburne informed Mangum. "Ride to Govan and Lowrey and instruct them to prepare to support General Granbury when he takes the pike at the sound of Brown's assault. I'll ride to General Cheatham to clarify our orders and plan."

The riders dashed off in opposite directions, Mangum toward the turnpike and Cleburne toward the creek, where he found Cheatham, riding back and forth among his headquarters staff.

"We encountered artillery on the road and were driven back briefly before Granbury's Brigade reclaimed positions to take the turnpike."

"The turnpike?" Cheatham shouted. "Your orders were to support Forrest and attack the town."

"General Hood found me and ordered me to attack west instead of supporting Forrest."

Cheatham cut loose a line of profanity that would've made the devil blush. "Hood didn't inform me of any change with either verbal or written orders."

"When Forrest withdraws—"

"He can't withdraw," Cheatham shouted.

"His men are running out of ammunition. When they withdraw, I'll have no support on my right flank, until Brown's Division arrives."

The stocky corps commander cursed again. "Brown's Division? I've had no orders to post Brown on the right flank."

"Hood himself told me he was ordering Brown to support Forrest and cover our right flank. We were to attack the pike and block the road to town at the sound of Brown's guns."

Cheatham shrugged and cursed. "I have no idea what's going on. Hood never sent me orders of any kind on this."

"Then what should I do, Ben?"

"Do the best you can, Pat. The best you can."

Cleburne retreated to his division, lining up his regiments, some within a hundred yards of the turnpike where wary Yankees watched them as the army's superfluous supply wagons kept rolling toward Spring Hill.

Sunset came and tugged a blanket of darkness over the countryside. Cleburne kept his men ready, as he hoped to strike and capture needed supplies from the Union's baggage train.

Six o'clock came, then seven o'clock passed. Cleburne sent Mangum to clarify the orders, but the lieutenant returned with no answers. Then eight, nine and ten o'clock marched past.

The sound of Brown's guns never came, though the sounds of muffled movement along the turnpike remained audible for hours.

Without explicit instructions from his commanders, Cleburne ordered his men to sleep at their posts, most lacking their knapsacks and bedrolls because the baggage train never caught up with them to return the bedding they had discarded beside the Duck River.

Disgusted with Hood's countervailing commands, Cleburne walked among his sleeping troops until well after midnight. Then exhaustion overwhelmed him, and he retired, like his men, on the ground with nothing between him and the stars.

Mary Alice Carter McPhail
Carter Place

After watching the children eat lunch, Mary Alice spent the afternoon helping them with their ciphering and arithmetic. She ended the lesson at three-thirty, letting the Carter and McPhail children play while she escorted Paul and Matilda Lotz to their parents. As she walked back home, she saw a line of wagons emerge between Breezy and Winstead hills on the Columbia Pike.

She ran to the house, shouting for her brother as she burst through the front door. "Moscow, trouble's coming. Moscow, where are you?"

"What is it, Mary Alice?" Annie asked.

"Wagons! Yankee wagons! Dozens of them! Where's Moscow?"

"He's with father at the gin," Annie answered.

"Take the children to the basement while I find Moscow."

Mary Alice dashed back out the front door, leaving it for her sister to close. She sprinted to the massive building across the pike. "Moscow, Moscow," she screamed as she ran. "Trouble's coming."

As she neared the gin, Moscow emerged to meet her. She pointed south at the road. The line of wagons was a half mile closer, a quarter of the way to their farm. Mary Alice discerned the Stars and Stripes rippling from a pole over the lead wagon. "It's Yankees," she yelled, panting as she approached her brother, who grabbed her arms to keep her from collapsing.

"Lock up the gin, Father," Moscow yelled to Fount at the door, "while I get Mary Alice home." He steered his sister toward their brick dwelling.

Catching her breath, Mary Alice asked, "What—is—it?"

"It's Yankee supply wagons."

"Don't they," she gasped, "follow the army?"

"Not when they're retreating, Mary Alice."

"Does that mean we've won?"

"Likely not."

"Are we in danger this evening?"

"It's just a couple hours until sunset and dark. Only a fool would attack this late in the afternoon. And only a fool would send a supply train to a river crossing with no reliable bridge. It's a war of fools, Mary Alice."

Moscow helped his sister across the pike as the family patriarch caught up with them.

"What do you think, Moscow?" he asked.

"It may be a long night, Father."

Lt. Gen. John Bell Hood
Approaching Oaklawn Plantation

Impatiently waiting for Cheatham to update him on his corps' progress but exhausted from the long day, Hood turned toward Absalom Thompson's Oaklawn Plantation as couriers scurried back and forth, issuing new orders. Cheatham reached Hood's party about six-thirty, reporting that his far flank remained vulnerable and that Cleburne aligned poorly for the planned assault on Spring Hill, delaying his orders to attack the town.

"I told Cleburne to engage the enemy along the pike," Hood replied.

"No such word reached me, his commander," Cheatham noted.

"Those orders came direct from me," Hood huffed. "What's Cleburne accomplished?"

"Granbury's Texas Brigade drove Union artillery from the pike, and now Cleburne's Division is positioned to attack, when you give the order."

Hood glared at Cheatham. "I ordered the pike be taken once General Brown initiates his advance on the right flank."

"I received no such orders. Last you instructed me was to position ourselves to attack Spring Hill and support General Forrest."

"I promoted you to corps commander for just such a moment. See that you take the road at the sound of Brown's guns. Come tomorrow, we'll destroy Schofield's army."

Cheatham rode off at a lope, and Hood continued to Oaklawn, as darkness enveloped the land. He stopped by a pond near the mansion and commanded his orderlies to unstrap him and assist him from his horse. Taking his crutch, he limped to a stump by the water's edge, sat down, and tossed pebbles into the pool. Any moment he expected to hear the sounds of Brown's guns, but gunfire remained sporadic, not the sustained roar of a significant attack. Hood instructed orderlies to build a fire near the pond so officers and couriers could more easily spot him in the darkness.

Still, no sound came of a large encounter.

As Hood awaited Cheatham to report back to him, General Alexander Stewart rode up to indicate his corps had arrived and was awaiting Hood's orders. "Wait in reserve. Tomorrow victory will be ours."

Stewart returned to his command. A quarter hour later, Cheatham found Hood again.

Seeing him approach on his mare, Hood grabbed his crutch and pushed himself up from his stump seat. "Why in God's name have you not attacked the enemy and taken possession of the turnpike, General Cheatham?"

"I'm awaiting General Brown to protect our right flank, per your orders. He was to support our right and take Spring Hill, last I heard."

"The pike runs through Spring Hill, General. It's the same thing. Why haven't you attacked?"

"If I advance, the Yanks will roll up my corps from a flank attack."

Hood spat toward the pond in frustration. "I will send Stewart's corps to cover your flank."

Cheatham shrugged. "Night makes it more difficult."

"You're a corps commander now, General. Show some leadership."

His shoulders sagging, Cheatham nodded and yanked the reins on his horse. "Yes, sir," he cried, galloping back to his troops.

As the corps commander disappeared in the darkness, Hood turned to two orderlies. "Write out commands for General Stewart to divert his troops to the far flank of Cheatham's corps so I can sign them."

Moments later the orderlies brought two copies and a pencil for Hood to initial his instructions. Once he signed them, the aides gave the orders to couriers and sent them to deliver new instructions to General Stewart.

Hood sat satisfied that he had straightened out his confused subordinates. Soon Spring Hill and the pike would be in Confederate hands, along with a substantial portion of the Union supply train.

After dispatching those orders, Hood and his senior officers retired to Oaklawn, where Mrs. Thompson provided a sumptuous dinner for her guests, including adjacent plantation owner Nathan Cheairs, a Spring Hill native. During the meal, Cheairs offered his Rippavilla mansion for breakfast the next morning. When Hood accepted the gracious offer at dinner's end, Cheairs dismissed himself to inform his wife so the servants would have breakfast ready. After the Oaklawn meal, the officers drank brandy and smoked cigars, complimenting Hood on a military genius that rivaled that of Robert E. Lee and Stonewall Jackson, both noted for their famous flanking maneuvers.

"I'd be honored that my name accompanied theirs in the history books," he replied. Though he feigned humility, Hood knew in his heart they were correct. Had he not been so tired, he would have listened to more of their flattery, but he retired to bed at nine o'clock to a room he would share with governor-in-exile Harris, Hood's chief of staff, and another staff officer for needed rest. But multiple visits from confused generals interrupted his sleep. First General Stewart sought to confirm if his orders were to stand in reserve or cover Cheatham's right flank. Hood said it would be settled after sunrise. Then General Forrest arrived, reporting that a sizeable Union force was moving north on the pike. Hood ordered him to confirm the account and take action, although Forrest reported his limited ammunition reduced his options.

"Wherever Schofield's infantry are," Hood grumbled, "I'll find the Yankees in the morning." He dismissed his cavalry commander.

Sam Watkins
Marching toward Spring Hill

"Corporal Watkins," cried the captain, "tighten your ranks and keep them moving. We may have a fight ahead of us."

"Yes, sir," answered Sam as the captain galloped down the road. He turned to the men marching at his side and counted nineteen, all that remained of Company H. When they had paraded gloriously away from Maury County three years earlier, they were a hundred and twenty strong. Of those at his side, only he and eleven others survived from the original group. "You heard the captain. Squeeze your ranks and keep moving."

"Why, Corporal? So General Hood can get us slaughtered?"

"So I don't kill you, webfoot," Sam responded. "Do I hear a 'yes sir,' men?"

"Yes, sir, Corporal," answered the remnants of Company H.

Sam cringed every time he was identified by his rank. On occasions, like at the Dead Angle on Kennesaw Mountain, when he deserved a promotion for battlefield bravery, those actions went unnoticed or the witnesses all died before they could report his valor for commendation. That was the conundrum of war with its total randomness and its blatant unpredictability, like Hood's appointment as commander. Two days after his appointment, General Hood attacked General Sherman's Union forces at Peachtree Creek. Twenty-five hundred men who awoke that morning hungry but alive were dead or wounded by sundown. Hood's bloodletting had begun. Watkins remembered it for the hard fight and the withdrawal as Hood called it, though everyone else knew it was a retreat. After the departure, a former sheriff of Maury County had found the troops and delivered letters from home for the survivors of Company H. Sam received a missive from his father and one from Jennie, who had enclosed rose petals and two apple blossoms with a note and a poem. Her delicate hand had written, "Receive me, such as I am; would that I were of more use for your sake, Jennie." Then she penned a poem:

"I love you, O, how dearly,
  Words too faintly but express;
This heart beats too sincerely,
  E'er in life to love you less;
No, my fancy never ranges,
  Hope like mine, can never soar;
If the love I cherish changes,
  'Twill only be to love you more."

That missive lifted Sam's spirits on an otherwise depressing day of battlefield defeat and humiliation. Two days later, to disrupt General Sherman's supply lines, Hood ordered his army to attack a fishhook of a Union line east of Atlanta. The men of the First Tennessee with their Confederate comrades ran up steep hillsides that spit fire from ten thousand rifles and pistols. Forty cannons hurled missiles at the attackers, spewing the fiery flames of hell in their faces. Sam remembered the roar of battle sounding like unbottled thunder, as the Rebels broke the Yankee ranks and chased them away. As the others raced after the enemy, Sam fell from the ranks, winded and frightened. He sat down and drew deep breaths, tainted with the odor of spent powder and spilled blood. As he pondered what to do next, he spotted within reach an orphan battle flag, an enemy standard abandoned on the field. It seemed in decent shape without the rips and tears of an older banner that had seen more battle. The cloth was broad enough that he thought Jennie might one day make him a shirt out of it, if he got it back to Columbia, so he picked it up and sat there fondling it in his muddled haze of war. While Sam had seen dozens of discarded battle flags in the past, he had never before retrieved one.

He was still deliberating his next move when his captain rode up. Expecting a scolding for his cowardice, Watkins got up for the expected tongue-lashing. Sam stood at attention as best he could, but his foot suddenly burned with a scorching pain. Looking at his shoe, he saw blood and realized he had been wounded, though in the charge's chaos he had never realized it.

"Watkins," called the officer, "I'm proud of you for taking an enemy flag."

"I sort of picked it up, Captain. Nothing more."

The captain smiled. "I like your humility. I'm promoting you to corporal, Watkins. Now get to a field hospital so someone can examine your foot. I'd hate to lose to amputation a man as brave as you."

Before Watkins could clarify that his death-defying bravery was not nearly as grand as the captain perceived it, the officer turned his horse around and raced to the roar of the battle, that would ultimately cost the South another five thousand dead and wounded. The paradox of war made no sense to Sam. As long as he had fought courageously in battle, he never received a pat on the shoulder, much less a promotion. Then the first time he drops from the ranks, sits on his buttocks, and picks up an abandoned battle flag, he receives an instant advancement in rank. If he had known that earlier, he could've picked up enough battle flags over the years to head the Army of Tennessee or even replace Jefferson Davis as president.

Somehow word of his honor reached Jennie, and Sam still smiled at her next letter when her delicate hand wrote, "I heard you captured a flag outside Atlanta and earned a promotion to corporal. Is that some high rank? I know you will be a general yet, because I hear you are always the foremost man in every attack, but do be careful for my sake and don't let the Yankees kill you."

Sam lacked the heart to tell her a corporal was just a single step above being the army slave that a webfoot was. Though he was proud his promotion had thrilled his betrothed, the yellow stripes on his uniform blouse burned his conscience as Watkins marched toward Spring Hill. Sam wasn't as brave nor as deserving of the corporal's stripes as Bill Hughes. In fact, if it wasn't for Bill Hughes, Watkins would be moldering in a mass grave on Kennesaw Mountain.

Back in the good days of this past June when Joe Johnston still commanded the Army of Tennessee, the Confederate commander had judiciously retreated before the onslaught of General Sherman's superior numbers, vying for a slipup by the Union commander so he could pick off one of Sherman's three armies—Army of the Cumberland, Army of the Ohio, and Army of the Tennessee—to even the odds. Sherman never slipped up, though he came close at Kennesaw Mountain when he attacked entrenched Confederate positions on the peak. The First Tennessee and the Twenty-seventh Tennessee held a strong salient near the middle of the Rebel line.

Sam and other members of Company H manned the apex of the line, looking over the slope westward toward an open plain where Union troops gathered to advance. Sam, with Bill Hughes and others at their sides, waited for the onslaught. They saw the enemy organize into battle lines a mile distant and then watched them advance eastward across the wide clearing. And then, two-thirds of the way across the meadow, the Yankee soldiers just disappeared from sight. Vanished completely. The steep incline of the mountain screened the approaching Yankees from the salient. Sam and his allies could still hear the enemy's advance, but they could not see them until they reappeared at the top of the incline, just fifty feet from the Rebel trench. And, when they emerged from the mountainside, they boiled over the ledge like hornets pouring from a hive. The Confederate entrenchments erupted with a sheet of flame and lead, the explosions ripping through the blue wave of flesh and bone and drowning out the screams of the dying men. Still, they rushed forward, gaining ground with every Confederate pause to reload. Sam fired as many as thirty times with Hughes and the others matching him, before the enemy reached the line. Unable to load, some men swung their rifles as clubs or stabbed with bayonets or slashed with sabers. Some around Sam picked up rocks and flung them into Yankee faces. The attackers fell back for a moment, but more Yankees kept streaming over the slope and charging into the jaws of death.

Sam loaded and fired, loaded and fired, repelling wave after wave of Yankees. His gun became so hot that the powder would flash before he could ram a ball home. Still he fought on, grabbing weapons from the dead and wounded, loading and shooting into the unending tide of blue uniforms that all seemed to converge at him.

Two Yankees leaped atop the trench, one behind the other, and Sam fired, killing them both with a single shot. As he hurried to reload his rifle, a third Yankee jumped up.

"You murdered my brothers," he screamed, "and now I'll kill you, you Secesh bastard!"

Sam fumbled to set the next round with his ramrod when the Union soldier pointed his musket at him. With his life at its end, Sam saw everything he had ever done flash through his mind as Bill Hughes lunged over dead bodies and grabbed the muzzle of the Yankee gun just as it exploded. Sam felt the flash of fire, but not the hot lead it expelled. Without yanking the ramrod from the barrel, he fired his rifle, the rod and the bullet striking the assailant, who flailed over backward. Sam turned to Hughes, whose right arm spurted blood from wrist to shoulder. Bill Hughes lay dying at his side, but Sam could not attend him or others. So, he threw his own gun aside and picked up Bill's, firing away as quickly as he could reload.

Time evaporated in the haze of smoke and in the minds of men standing on the precipice of immortality. Finally, it ended, the attackers and the defenders spent, though some still threw curses or rocks at the other. By then the dying Bill Hughes was weak, but Sam dug among the dead and pulled him free so he could breathe. He yelled for a litter bearer to take Hughes for treatment, and two eventually came. The infirmary corps carried him away. Hughes cried out that Sam Watkins should get his rifle, his blanket, and his clothing. Watkins wept, knowing he would never see his friend again.

All around him were the dead and dying. Those that weren't dead or wounded were doubled over from heatstroke or exhaustion, some vomiting, some soaked in sweat and the mingled blood of their comrades and their enemies. With parched lips and swollen tongues, every soldier craved water. The deceased lay stacked four and five deep in the trench. On the Yankee side of the entrenchment, the motionless and writhing casualties looked like a field of wheat stalks blown over by a vicious wind. That very evening the men of Company H dubbed that bloody spot "Dead Angle." Afterward, the very mention of the name produced shivers and tears in the survivors. Those that weren't dead or wounded counted the bullet holes in their clothes and hats, some having as many as a dozen.

The next day when Sam withdrew from that hell hole, he trod away, stopping at a stream to bathe away the filth of Dead Angle. When he stripped, he saw that his right arm and shoulder were bruised and blistered from the rifle recoil of what he estimated were a hundred and twenty shots. In most engagements, riflemen could never be certain if they hit an enemy or not, but at Dead Angle, Sam knew—as did his comrades—they could not miss attackers bunched so tightly together. The ones who lived to talk about it estimated they had hit between twenty and a hundred attackers each.

As Sam neared Spring Hill after the difficult march from Columbia, he grimaced at the thought of Dead Angle, knowing he was lucky to be alive and undeserving of the corporal's stripes for merely picking up a discarded flag.

When he arrived on the outskirts of Spring Hill, everything seemed as confusing as Dead Angle was bloody. Officers scurried everywhere as the sun slipped behind the western horizon. Nobody knew what to make of the conflicting orders, wait or attack, dig in or retreat, live or die.

As he had approached Spring Hill, Sam had actually seen General Hood retreating in the opposite direction from which Company H marched. Never had he seen a commander so derelict in his duty to his country or in his responsibility to his men. Competent commanders stood with their men, near the point of conflict rather than retreating from it. Sam directed Company H where he was ordered and awaited further instructions. None came, so the men set up their meager camp. Sam fixed his blanket and retired with a queasiness in his stomach, just as he had experienced the night before the carnage at Chickamauga. Sam sensed trouble and death would follow the next day, the last day of November 1864.

Uncle Wiley Howard
Confederate Camp near Spring Hill

Uncle Wiley Howard rode Joe Johnston to the outskirts of the Confederate line south of Spring Hill. Earlier in the afternoon, he had heard skirmishing from that direction and had ridden toward the noise, but the firing had stopped as the brigades established their night camps. Never had he intended to be gone for three days, but he had evaded Yankee scouts a whole day, fearful they would take his horse or shoot him in his gray overcoat. On Sunday he had ridden upon a forbidden slave church service in the woods, and had attended, praying mightily for Marse Gist and himself that they both might return to South Carolina alive and whole. Howard found the worshipping slaves optimistic, but frightened. They believed freedom came closer with each passing day, and yet they feared what emancipation meant. None owned land or livestock, few could read, write or count beyond ten, and only a handful had a trade beyond fieldwork. They worried they could not support themselves and their children.

Like them, Howard had seen the decline of the Secesh army, though from a closer vantage point as Marse Gist's manservant. The Confederacy was doomed, and its defenders exhausted. As he approached the military encampment in the gloom of early night, not a single picket challenged Howard. Before Hood assumed command and bled the army's youth, Howard would never have ridden so close without being contested a dozen times. Perhaps some pickets recognized Joe Johnston or his overcoat as that of a general, but not all the soldiers would have.

As for Marse Gist, he had treated Howard well over the years, in part because they both loved horses, and Howard treated the equines gently. Otherwise, the general would never have let him leave camp astride Joe Johnston, Marse Gist's favorite horse. Howard felt sorry for his master. True, Howard was a slave, but so was Marse Gist and the thousands of dead and crippled boys in butternut and gray. They were a slave to the idea of slavery as a way of life.

Nearing another brigade's encampment and the horses picketed behind it, Howard heard a familiar nicker from one animal.

"Kitty must've smelt you, Joe," he said, leaning over and patting the gelding on the neck. "We're near de general and camp now." Though they both loved horses, Howard and Gist disagreed on Kitty and Joe Johnston. Uncle Wiley knew Kitty to be the better animal, while Marse Gist preferred Joe Johnston, largely for his untamed spirit. Both were fine animals, but Howard considered Kitty superior, a calmer mount in the tumult of battle. That was why Howard had taken Joe Johnston on his search for food. Should battle break out in his absence, Uncle Wiley didn't want Gist riding into combat on a skittish horse that could get him killed.

Finally, from the light of a hundred campfires, Howard saw the general beyond the picketed horses. He lay on the ground asleep, his head resting on his saddle. Drawing the gelding up at Gist's feet, Howard dismounted and called to him. "How's you getting on, Marse Gist?"

The general shook his head, squinted up at Uncle Wiley, then bounded to his feet. Gist grabbed his manservant and hugged him, spooking Joe Johnston.

Howard tugged on the gelding's reins to steady him and to keep his balance.

"I'm delighted to see you, Uncle Wiley. I worried over you."

"Hads to dodge de weather and de Yankees. You ain't where I lefts you last."

"We're chasing Yankees. What did you expect?"

The manservant shrugged. "Mostly nothing. How abouts you?"

"Food. You got any?"

"Just some cold chicken and biscuits, but it be a day old and cold, less what I ates."

"I'll build a fire, and warm it, if you'll do me a favor?"

Howard nodded.

"General Strahl's Brigade is just down the line for us. Find him and invite him to share supper with me."

"I'll do dat."

Gist released his manservant. "It warms my heart you're back and safe, Uncle Wiley."

Sumner Cunningham
Among Cleburne's Division

Sumner Cunningham left his Enfield in camp and pulled his tin cup from his haversack, as most men would share their coffee with a fellow soldier. The sergeant major walked beyond Brown's division, passing the South Carolinians of States Rights Gist's Brigade and the Tennesseans of John Carter's Brigade before he reached the first of Cleburne's Division, starting with Daniel C. Govan's Brigade of Arkansans, followed by Lowery's Brigade of Alabamans and Mississippians and then Granbury's Brigade of Texans, whose camp ran parallel to the pike. Whenever he met his equals in rank, they shared their coffee and information, but nothing else, for they had too little to meet even their own needs.

Like the regiments in Brown's Division, those in Cleburne's had prepared for a late afternoon attack on the Union line. Their orders were to charge at the sound of Brown's guns and swing north into the Yankee position, driving the invaders back to Nashville and blocking the road from further enemy traffic. At each stop, Cleburne's men thanked Cunningham that General Brown had never attacked, giving them a chance to start their own fires and live another day.

By the time he reached Granbury's Brigade, it was well after nine o'clock. At that point, he had consumed a dozen cups of coffee, more than his bladder could hold. So, he stepped west of the camp in the darkness, moving forty yards from the campfires so he could pee in the darkness. As he unbuttoned his britches, he heard the soft tread of footsteps, the whispers of soldiers and what sounded like the muffled creak of artillery and caisson wheels. He wondered what Confederate units were blithely marching toward the Union line, when two men exited the stream of passing soldiers and approached with the same intent to relieve themselves.

As the fellows unbuttoned their britches, one spoke to Cunningham. "We could march all the way to *Warshington* tonight, as dumb as those Rebs are over there. What unit are you from, soldier?"

"Forty-first," Cunningham started, then stopped. The only other person he'd ever heard say "warsh" for "wash" was General Otho French Strahl, his brigade commander. Strahl was from Ohio. Cunningham gulped. These fellows were Yankees. The quiet, moving line of soldiers was surely Schofield's army.

"Forty-first Ohio is it?" said the second soldier.

"Yeah," Cunningham grunted.

"You boys've had it easy since the fall of Atlanta, from what I hear."

Cunningham had to confirm these were Yankee troops. "From where do you boys hail?"

"Ohio," said the first.

"Illinois," answered the second. "Even if we're advancing in the dark, at least we're heading north toward home."

The Ohioan whispered. "I can't believe we're marching past Hood's sleeping army. They didn't even put out sentries."

The soldier from Illinois agreed. "Thank you, General Hood. We greatly value your incompetence."

Ohio answered, "I say it's stupidity."

"Yeah," Cunningham agreed, hoping his new friends would finish and leave.

"Why aren't you with your regiment? Wasn't the forty-first Ohio way up the line?" asked Illinois.

"I got detached," he said, scrambling to come up with something to send on their way.

"How'd that happen?" Ohio wanted to know.

Cunningham took a deep breath. "The colonel didn't want me marching with the others for fear they'd catch the smallpox, too."

The two Yankees stumbled forward, buttoning their pants and racing back to the others.

"Hope you get better," Ohio cried as they evaporated in the darkness.

His knees buckling, Cunningham collapsed on the ground. He remained there a minute, collecting his wits. When he heard a trio of

Yankees step from the passing parade, he got to his hands and knees and crawled through the still damp earth to Granbury's camp. He reached the encampment without being challenged by a sentry. He arose and trotted toward his own men and away from the Union army, slipping past Hood's command along the Franklin Pike.

When he arrived an hour later at his camp, he reported to Colonel Tillman's tent and saluted the officer, who worked at a field desk by candlelight. "Sir, nobody has food or ammunition to spare. Folks would share coffee and information, but little else."

"It's as I feared," Tillman responded.

"There's something else, Colonel."

"What's that, Sergeant?"

"The Yankee army's marching up the pike right now."

Tillman arose from his campstool and marched to Cunningham. "It's been a long day, Sergeant. When we're exhausted, we don't always think straight. You've done all I've asked of you. Get a good night's sleep because I think we will have a hot time in the morning when Schofield's army arrives. I'll need you thinking straight come morning."

Lt. Gen. John Bell Hood
Oaklawn Plantation

Around midnight, an aide roused John Bell Hood from his bed and slumber, saying a barefoot infantryman had asked to see the general, reporting the *whole* Union army was slipping past slumbering Confederate units on the Columbia-to-Franklin Pike. Groggy from exhaustion and interruptions, a drowsy Hood instructed his chief of staff to order General Cheatham to investigate the report and to attack the enemy if it was true.

Hood then ordered the aide to dismiss the straggler. An axiom of war, Hood lectured him, was never to trust information from a straggler or a wounded soldier. They lacked the broad vision of a commander, he informed his aide. Hood then turned over on his feather mattress and went back to sleep.

Wednesday Morning,

November 30, 1864

Southeast Corner and Front
Fountain Carter Home

Chapter Nine

Mary Alice Carter McPhail
Carter Home

The rattle, creak, and groan of Union wagons and ambulances as they passed forty-five feet from the Carter house kept Mary Alice awake well past midnight. In the dwindling hours of Tuesday afternoon sunlight, the children had slipped to the front windows, parting the curtains enough to watch the passing parade to see if they could spot the horns on the Yankee teamsters. They stood in silent awe and fear of the retreating horde, one child occasionally thinking he had seen points or spikes, but without confirmation from the others. Though the adults shooed the young ones away from the panes multiple times, the kids always slipped back, their childhood curiosity pulling them to the glass and the spectacle of an army on the move. The lads remained fascinated with the display, but the lasses eventually moved away, Lena playing with her doll and toy trunk. Finally, their worried parents sent them to the two upstairs rooms where the girls changed the clothes of Lena's doll repeatedly, and the boys spoke in awe of the soldiers and their wagons they had seen. That night, the children slept together on pallets and blankets on the wooden floor upstairs, Mary Alice sleeping on the bed in the same room with all the little ones. As the mother of the toddler Lannie, Mary Alice dozed on the mattress with her one-year-old son at her side. She hardly rested, thrashing about in the bed so much that she woke Lannie multiple times, then comforted him back to sleep. From pure exhaustion and worry, she finally fell into a deep doze in the early morning hours.

Then sixty minutes before sunrise, someone banged on the front door, the noise reverberating upstairs and throughout the house. Startled from her sleep, Mary Alice bolted up from her mattress as the pounding continued, muffling the shouts from the front steps. Bouncing up from the bedding, Mary Alice threw on her robe, slid into her slippers, and stepped around the sleeping children to the door, which she closed behind her. As she inched down the staircase, a match flared in the entryway, and a lamp came to life. At the foot of the stairs, Mary Alice saw her father with the lamp. Behind him stood Moscow, holding a revolver behind his back.

Over the beating on the entrance, Mary Alice heard the cry of a Union officer. "Open the door!" he shouted. "We mean you no harm, but we need your house."

Fount looked at his son, who nodded. Moscow kept the pistol behind his back as his father unlatched the door and eased it open, the lamp's ball of light illuminating a Union general in a soiled blue uniform.

"I'm Jacob Cox, commander of the U.S. Twenty-third Army Corps. We intend to use your house as headquarters until we evacuate Franklin." Cox stepped inside.

"Doesn't the Bill of Rights say no citizen must quarter soldiers, General Cox?" Fount asked.

Cox lifted his chin and grinned. "It does indeed, sir! However, since Tennessee seceded from the Union, you no longer have that constitutional protection."

Fount nodded. "It was worth a try, General Cox, but before I give you permission. I must tell you that my son behind me is a Confederate officer taken as a prisoner of war and paroled by your government. I shall allow you to use my home, provided my son is accorded the rights promised him upon his release."

The Union general looked behind Fountain Carter. "Your name and rank, sir?"

"Moscow Branch Carter, lieutenant colonel paroled, Twentieth Tennessee."

"Very well, Colonel Carter. For your own safety, I want you confined to your property. We'll respect your parole, provided you do not carry a weapon in violation of the terms."

Mary Alice spotted Moscow wiggling his gun hand behind his back at her. She eased to him and took the revolver from his hands, sliding it up her robe sleeve.

"That's acceptable, General Cox," Moscow replied, lifting his arms. "Would you care to search me now?"

"I'll accept your word that you're unarmed."

Mary Alice stepped around Moscow beside her father. "General, we have children upstairs sleeping. Would you confine your men to the first floor so as not to frighten them?"

Cox nodded and turned to the officers behind him. "That's reasonable. Men, did you hear that request?" The subordinates acknowledged the restriction as Cox turned to Fount. "May my men enter?"

"Please, sir. I am Fount Carter and this is my daughter, Mary Alice McPhail. You've met my son." He moved from the doorway, allowing the others to file in.

In the yellow glow of the lamplight, Mary Alice noted the weariness in their eyes and in the slump of their shoulders. They nodded or tipped their hats at her as they tromped inside. The officers removed their sword belts and their holsters, lowering them to the floor and easing down beside them. Instantly, some were snoring.

Cox turned to Mary Alice. "Forgive them for their manners, ma'am, but they've been up fighting or marching for forty-eight hours now. They're exhausted."

"Thank you for considering our children, General Cox. They fear Yankee soldiers."

"We'll be leaving, ma'am, as soon as our engineers bridge the Harpeth."

Fount closed the front door, but left it unlocked.

"General, sir," said Mary Alice. "When the weather's acceptable, I take a morning walk. Can I still do so without being shot or molested?"

"You certainly may, ma'am. Just stay away from the pike as thousands of troops follow us, and I can't always guarantee their proper behavior."

"Thank you, sir."

Cox removed his hat and stepped to a corner, where he sat on the floor, leaned back against the wall and dozed off.

Fount blew out the lamp and placed it on its table, then tiptoed past the snoring Yankees toward his room in the ell. Mary Alice tugged Moscow toward the stairs, whispering for him to follow her to the children's room. "You stay with the little ones because you'll be safer in the house. I intend to go for my walk when it lightens up. Those walks have done my spirit good the last two mornings, giving me time to reminisce and pray. We need prayer now."

"You be careful, Mary Alice. Keep my revolver. You remember how to use it, don't you?"

"I lived in Texas for years, Moscow. What do you think?"

He grinned and hugged her.

Mary Alice slipped out the door, closing it behind her and stepped softly down the steps and around the snoring soldiers and out onto the veranda, where she entered her regular room next to her father's and retrieved her coat, pulling it over her robe. She slipped the pistol from her robe and slid it into her jacket pocket. She replaced her slippers with her shoes for chores and retreated outside to visit the grove. As she reached the cookhouse, she encountered Callie coming in to prepare breakfast.

"Morning, Callie," Mary Alice said.

"Ya be out earlier dan normal dis mornin'. Sunrise be a half hour away."

"We've got Yankees in the house."

"Lordy, I hopes I ain't havin' to cooks for dem, too. I hears deir wagons all night."

"No, just cook for the family, as usual."

"Be careful headin' to de locust trees. Dey be mean trees, dose thorns like dey crowned Christ's head."

"I'll be fine."

Mary Alice walked beyond the cookhouse and around the barn and corn crib. Nearing the grove, she turned and in the dimness could just make out a line of Union soldiers marching down the pike past her house. When she reached the grove, she appreciated the locust trees as they screened her from the blue horde. She prayed for the family's safety now that Yankees had invaded their home, and she beseeched God for extra protection for Tod, wherever he was.

Completing her prayers, she stepped to the far edge of the trees, looking to the south, but ignoring the pike where the soldiers marched north like a never-ending line of Yankee piss ants. She watched as dawn's glow sprayed the treetops with a sheen of gold, but her gaze fell upon a solitary rider she could just make out across the undulating fields to the south. He advanced alone through the countryside, far from the turnpike. A hundred yards from the trees, the man dismounted and led his horse by the reins toward her. Something about the man struck her as familiar, the long neck, the angle of his shoulders, the tilt of his hat. She stepped beyond the copse and squinted her eyes to study him. As he came within fifty paces, she gasped.

The man was her brother!

Theodrick Carter had returned to the locust grove to reclaim his youth and play games just as he had as a child. She rushed toward him, then stopped. No! Absolutely not! Yankees occupied the house and were flooding their farm and Franklin. Much as she wanted to welcome and hug him, the dangers were too many, especially if he were seen or they were observed together. He saw her, removing his hat and waving it at her. Mary Alice lifted both hands above her head and waved him away. "Yankees," she called as loudly as she dared. "They're in our house. Leave while you can."

He replaced his hat, blew her a kiss, mounted his horse, and rode back toward the hills and away from the enemy. She watched until he disappeared in the distance. Turning toward the house, she ran home, ignoring the Yankee soldiers that had drifted into the yard and around the office, smokehouse, and cookhouse.

"Who goes there?" shouted a Yankee sentry as she ran past.

"I live here," she cried, racing by him and bounding up the veranda steps and into the house. Mary Alice bolted up the stairs, flinging the door open and startling Moscow, who sat in the rocking chair with Lannie in his arms.

"I saw him, Moscow!" she gasped. "I saw him! Yes, I did!"

Her brother startled and leaned forward in his seat, waking Lannie, who started bawling. "Who? You saw who?"

"Our brother. I saw Tod in the field. He was returning home, but I sent him away for fear the Yankees would shoot him."

Moscow grimaced as he tried to calm Lannie and keep him from waking the other children. "Your imagination is playing tricks on you. You're tired like all of us. Lie down and rest."

"But I saw him, Moscow, I really did," she pleaded as she took her toddler in her arms.

Her brother nodded. "I'm sure you did, Mary Alice. Now get a little rest while you can."

Hardin Figuers
Figuers Home

Adele's howling awoke Hardin Figuers just before dawn. Though his hound's dirge had wakened him, it was the low, distant rumble that intrigued him. Whatever had disturbed Adele was more than just a stray skunk, raccoon, or other varmint in the barn. Hardin, dressed, pulled on his shoes and coat, grabbed his slingshot, and slipped out the backdoor before his mother arose to fix breakfast. As he stepped outside, he heard the shouts of officers to subordinates and realized the varmints were soldiers of the Union army.

Standing mouth-agape in the soft glow of the emerging dawn, Hardin glimpsed through the trees and structures to the southeast a stream of wagons intermixed with soldiers inching up the Columbia Pike toward town. Craving a better view, he dashed to the barn, opened the door and ran to Adele, petting and calming her, then tying her up so she wouldn't escape in the excitement. Next, he grabbed their ladder, dashing back outside and leaning it against the side of the structure. He scurried up the rungs like a squirrel climbing a tree and fell on his belly at the roof's wood-shingled crown. From there, he stared at the unending line of soldiers, thousands of Yankees, plodding along with slumped shoulders and heavy feet. Occasionally, a battery of artillery advanced between regiments. Never had Hardin seen so many soldiers or cannons. He only wished the troops and big guns were Confederate, though he lay transfixed at the enemy army in motion. As the brigades neared the Carter house and gin, they angled from the road, establishing a line along the breastworks left from the 1863 skirmish.   At first, he thought they were lengthening and strengthening the entrenchments, but mostly the exhausted soldiers collapsed on the ground like men craving sleep.

Gradually, the blue line of Yankee troops inched toward his home, digging their positions south of the Carter place between it and the locust grove. Hardin doubted enough hornet's nests or rocks for his slingshot existed in all of Tennessee to drive these Yankees away. He watched with the tangled emotions of fear and awe as Yankee soldiers covered ground from the Columbia Pike past the Carter's Creek Pike fronting his home. The gloom gave way to the early dawn light.   As the sun rose around six-thirty, a half-dozen mounted officers broke from the line and angled their horses toward his home. Hardin saw the lamp glow from the kitchen window where his mother worked on breakfast, unaware he had escaped the house to watch the Yankee spectacle.

Hardin inched down the barn roof to the ladder, scrambled down the rungs and darted around the house as the soldiers drew up in front of the structure.

The leading rider studied Hardin. "Is this your place, son?"

He nodded. "Yes, sir."

The officer leaned over, extending his arm to Hardin. As he shook the Yankee's hand, Hardin noticed a gold star on the shoulder of the officer's uniform. He was shaking hands with a general, something he had never done before. He wished it were a Confederate general instead.

"Is your pa home?"

"Pa's dead!"

"I'm sorry to hear that, son. I hope he wasn't a battlefield casualty."

"He died before the war, so my momma runs things now."

"Might I have a word with your mother? I'd like her permission to establish my brigade headquarters in her yard."

"She's fixing breakfast. I'll fetch her." He bolted around the side of the house to the back, flung open the door and burst into the kitchen.

"Hardin Perkins Figuers, where have you been?" a startled Bethenia cried as she put biscuit dough on a baking pan.

"Watching the Yankees, Momma. There's millions of them. A general outside wants to talk to you about making his headquarters here."

"Goodness, Hardin, I look a mess this early in the morning."

"He's a Yankee, Momma. Just tell him no and be done with it."

"No, sir. You go tell him I'll meet him on the front porch in a moment. And don't tell him anything else."

"Yes, ma'am," he answered, starting out the kitchen door.

"And, Hardin," she said, extending her palm to her son, "give me your slingshot. I don't want any mischief."

"Momma," he cried, "what if I need to defend myself?"

She shook her hand. "The slingshot."

Hardin yanked it from his back pocket, slapped it on the table and burst out the door, racing to the general and stopping at his side. "She'll meet you at the front door, if you will give her a moment."

"Thank you, son," the general said, dismounting and handing the reins to his orderly. He walked to the porch and climbed the three steps to the entry.

Hardin followed him, hoping his momma would never come to the front, but the brightening glow of a lamp illuminating the parlor told him his wish was futile. The door opened, and his mother stood with the ball of yellow light behind her.

The officer removed his hat. "Good morning, ma'am. I'm General William Grose of New Castle, Indiana, and I'm sorry to bother you so early in the morning."

"I understand, General Grose, times being what they are. I'm Bethenia Figuers. You've met my son Hardin, though he likely didn't introduce himself."

Grose patted her son on the shoulder. "No, he forgot, but he was a mannerly young man, unlike many we meet. Now, Mrs. Figuers, let me get right to the point as time is critical. I would like your permission to establish my headquarters here in front of your place, set up a couple tents until we move on. We will be digging entrenchments just south of here, and I intend to stay near my men as the day develops."

"Thank you, General, but I would prefer you not put anything in my yard that will draw gunfire."

Hardin burst with pride, watching his mother stand up to a Yankee general.

The officer sighed. "You know we can use your place without your permission, don't you?"

"I do, but I didn't say you couldn't use my place. Rather than my yard, I would like to offer my parlor for your use."

"*Momma!*" Hardin blurted out, shocked that Bethenia had stabbed the entire Confederacy in the back. Stunned though he was, he said nothing more when he saw his mother's glaring eyes.

"I am also fixing breakfast. It's only biscuits, but I can provide some for you and a few of your officers."

Grose returned his hat to his head. "We would be obliged, ma'am, if it's not too much trouble. We haven't eaten in twenty-four hours."

"There's me and my three children. We'll have one rather than our usual two biscuits, and I'll make another pan as well."

"Thank you, ma'am. That is most hospitable. I don't mean to throw a fright in you, but I worry a fearsome battle faces us today."

Hardin's heart raced with excitement. He might see war after all!

His mother clutched her throat in fear. "Dear God, no!"

"I wish it were otherwise, ma'am, but General Hood's an aggressive opponent. Little will deter him, if he's of a mind to attack. As the day develops, you might take your children closer to town and farther from our earthworks. This is where the greatest danger will likely be, should an assault occur."

"Thank you, General Grose. Once it is full daylight, I'll decide what to do. For now, give me ten minutes to get my family fed, then you can use the parlor and eat in our kitchen." She turned to her son. "Come along, Hardin. We've work to do."

"You are most generous, Mrs. Figuers. We value your courtesy."

"Ten minutes," she replied, "then come on in."

Hardin passed the general, who put on his hat and retreated from the porch to his officers.

As soon as his mother closed the door, Hardin turned to her. "I can't believe you invited Yankees into our house and offered them our food, not after they've stolen so much from so many families around here. What would General Hood say about this?"

"General Hood can look out for the Army of Tennessee. I intend to look out for my family and my property, young man. If the general's in our house, it's less likely to be looted by other Yankees.

I intend to survive this war and protect my family, whatever it takes. If I hear another complaint from you, I'll twist your ear. Now go rouse Tom and Mary Louisa. Tell them to dress quickly and get to the kitchen for a biscuit."

Soon Hardin, Tom, and Mary Louisa moved to the kitchen table and gobbled down their meager breakfast as the Yankees knocked on the front door and entered the parlor. Bethenia worked feverishly on another pan of biscuits, scowling at her two sons and her daughter. "You treat our guests with the same courtesy you would any of our other visitors, regardless of their politics, or I'll tan your hides unlike any whipping you've ever received."

The threat took with Mary Louisa, but Tom and Hardin had grown past the age when a spanking was a concern. Swats no longer intimidated them. As he ate his biscuit, Hardin listened to the officers in the next room, wondering if he could discern useful information he could convey to General Hood. The more he listened, the more confused he got about what the regiments were to do beyond dig in and wait. As best Hardin could determine, Grose commanded three regiments from Indiana, four from Illinois and one from Pennsylvania.

When the siblings finished their biscuits, Bethenia dismissed them, asking Mary Louisa to invite the officers into the kitchen as she removed her second pan from the woodstove oven. Hardin picked up his slingshot, but Bethenia grabbed his wrist. "You don't shoot at any Yankee, whether man, horse, or mule, young man. Promise me, or leave your slingshot here."

"I'll do as you say," he replied as Mary Louisa extended her momma's invitation for breakfast.

"Momma says for you Yankees to come to the kitchen so you can eat all our biscuits," she offered, then spun around and retreated to her mother.

Scowling at her daughter, Bethenia rushed into the parlor door. "Gentlemen, please come in and eat, despite my daughter's ungracious invitation."

General Grose led his seven compatriots into the kitchen. "We've heard worse, Mrs. Figuers, but never from one as cute as your daughter."

"Thank you, General Grose. Now help yourselves. I'm sorry there's not enough chairs to go around."

"Don't worry, ma'am, it's the biscuits we're interested in. They smell delicious." Grose picked up a hot one from the pan and bit into it. "They're as good as they smell, men. Dig in."

"Could I ask one thing of you, General?"

"Certainly, Mrs. Figuers."

"If it looks like an attack, please let me know so I can evacuate the children."

"Indeed I will, ma'am."

Hardin grabbed his coat and marched past his mother to the back door. "I'm gonna watch the soldiers."

"Hardin," said a stern General Grose, "you stay near your home here. If shooting starts, head to your cellar. You've got a cellar, don't you?"

"Yes, sir. On the west side of the house."

"Then get in it and pray for deliverance. Don't come out until the shooting is over."

If Grose had been a Confederate general, Hardin would've saluted him, but instead slipped on his coat, opened the door and headed outside to watch the Union circus. The youth returned to the barn, thinking about releasing Adele, but feared so many strangers nearby would frighten her, so he left the hound tied up. Throughout the morning, he watched the soldiers prepare for an attack, periodically changing his vantage point from the barn roof to the woodshed to the oak trees south of the house. Up and down a line that stretched from the Harpeth on both sides of town, the men in blue worked like beavers building earthen dams. To fortify the entrenchments, they ripped apart fences and to the east removed timbers from the Carter gin to make headboards above the mounded dirt. When they placed their rifles between the entrenchment top and the bottom of the salvaged timber to fire, the headboard and the dirt protected them except for the six-inch opening through which they could shoot attackers.

As the sun climbed higher, the morning chill gave way to a gentle warmth. Hardin felt shivers of excitement pulse through his veins until noon. He grumbled when he heard his mother call him for lunch because he didn't want to miss anything.

Patrick Cleburne
Camp outside Spring Hill

Like his blanket-less men, Major General Patrick Cleburne awoke chilled on the frost-strewn ground. Without his tent, writing desk, paper, and ink, he would not write Susan Tarleton, though he thought of her and hoped this conflict would soon end so they could entwine their lives in marriage. He pulled her handkerchief from his uniform pocket and sniffed at the sweet perfume, then kissed the cloth. Around him in the early morning gloom, his men slept, only a few stirring as all had learned over the course of the war to get what sleep you could, whenever you could, wherever you could, even in the cold.

Cleburne mulled over the events of the previous day, uncertain where the command had failed. General Hood had delivered conflicting orders to General Cheatham first and later to him. Not only that, but Hood had disappeared from the field after issuing those orders, retreating to the Oaklawn mansion, where he most certainly had a peaceful night in a soft bed in a warm room. Why hadn't General John Brown attacked and initiated the assault on the enemy? Maybe it didn't matter with so little daylight left by the time Brown got his division in place to relieve Forrest's cavalry, but many questions remained unanswered about the unconsummated attack. Cleburne believed he had followed his orders as best he could with the conflicting instructions issued by Cheatham and Hood. Perhaps it would not matter, and things would be sorted out on this day, the last one of November. Tomorrow would be December first, and Cleburne would request a Christmas furlough to go to Mobile and wed Susan Tarleton. He smiled at the thought.

"General Cleburne?" came a call just above a whisper. "General Cleburne, where are you?"

He recognized Lieutenant Mangum's voice. He sat up from the ground and waved his kepi over his head. "Here, Lieutenant, over here." Slowly, he arose, the cold earthen bed kinking his legs and arms. He shook them to remove the stiffness.

Mangum threaded his way among the soldiers, getting to Cleburne as quickly as he could without tripping over the exhausted and snoring men. Almost breathless when he arrived at Cleburne's side, he wheezed, "They've escaped, General. They're gone?"

"Who, Lieutenant?"

"The whole Yankee army, that's who. The fish slipped the hook, and they're on the turnpike to Franklin. They passed not a hundred yards from General Granbury's regiment during the night."

Cleburne shook his head in disbelief. "Schofield's entire army?"

Mangum nodded vigorously. "There'll be hell to pay, General. We were the closest division to the pike."

The major general released a long, slow breath. As spiteful as John Bell Hood was, Cleburne realized he would receive no Christmas furlough this year. "The sound of Brown's guns never came. We followed our orders, Lieutenant."

"That won't matter, General, not with Hood. He's yet to make a mistake that he didn't blame on somebody else."

Cleburne nodded. "That's for another day. For now, rouse the men so our division is ready to march when the orders come."

Mangum saluted, turned, and went to find his bugler. Shortly, reveille rang through the camp. The soldiers grumbled as they arose and stretched, retrieving whatever they could find in their pockets for breakfast.

Mangum returned with word he had sent couriers to Generals Govan, Granbury, and Lowrey to get their troops ready to march." Then he apologized. "I couldn't find you last night. The wagon with your baggage arrived. I could've set up your tent and bed."

"Things were too confused. It's no matter, now. Besides, it's good for the men to see their general sleeping on the ground, rather than in a plantation every evening like some." Cleburne hesitated, scratching the infernal itch on his left cheek. "There is one thing, Mangum."

"What, sir?"

"I have a new uniform in my trunk. This will be a tough day, so I should look my best. Please fetch it for me so I don't look like I slept on the ground all night."

"Yes, sir."

Lt. Gen. John Bell Hood
Oaklawn Plantation

John Bell Hood exploded at the report. How could Schofield's army have escaped from the trap he had so brilliantly set? Hood fumed as his aides fumbled to affix his leg and dress him for the mile-long ride to Rippavilla, Nathan Cheairs' plantation two miles south of Spring Hill, for breakfast. His first orders of the day went to his senior generals to meet him at the redbrick mansion with white shutters and Corinthian columns. The commander of the Army of Tennessee wanted answers for the failures of his subordinates, especially from Benjamin Cheatham.

When dressed, Hood took his crutch and hobbled out of the mansion to his horse where his attendants waited to boost him onto his mount, strap him in the saddle and point him toward Cheair's place through the light ground fog that gave a ghostly start to the fateful day. Hood cursed his foul luck to be stuck with incompetent generals and officers who could not implement his orders. And, with tentative soldiers who feared attacking an entrenched enemy, how would he ever fulfill his destiny? And, that of the Confederacy? As he advanced, he asked his command staff what went wrong. How could his entire quarry pass his Army of Tennessee? The ineptitude of his officers verged on treason. He wondered how many additional Southern lives this failure would cost, especially if Schofield should get his men to Nashville and unite with General George H. Thomas's forces. If that happened, everything Hood had envisioned and worked toward would be for naught. Yesterday, his brilliant flanking move had been comparable to the maneuvers of Generals Lee and Jackson. This morning, the effort was wasted.

Reaching Rippavilla, Hood sat sullen and silent in his saddle as his aides unstrapped him and eased him to the ground. One pulled his crutch from the scabbard and gave it to Hood, who limped toward the portico where Nathan Cheairs saluted him out of military protocol, then greeted him with the personal hospitality of an honored guest.

"Good morning, General Hood."

"Far from it," Hood scowled. "General Schofield has stolen a march on us and is now between here and Nashville. Have my generals arrived?"

Cheairs grimaced. "Generals Cheatham and Stewart are here."

"What about Forrest?"

"I have not seen him, nor General Lee."

Hood scowled. "Lee is bringing his division up from Columbia. He had no part in this failure. I can't say such for the others."

Cheairs moved up the steps to the door, opening the entry for the commander, who hobbled through, then paused inside as he stared at the magnificent staircase leading to the second floor.

"Breakfast will be to your right, General," Cheairs directed.

Hood grumbled and passed through the parlor into a smaller room with a drop-leaf table ready and awaiting diners.

Cheatham and Stewart stood in the corner, looking out the window toward the Columbia Pike, until they heard the clump of Hood's footfall and crutch. They offered their commander perfunctory salutes as Hood's chief of staff and three others of his command retinue stood against the wall.

Hood ignored the two generals, scooting to a chair at the end of the table, hopping on his good leg until he could slide his wooden leg under the table and slip awkwardly into his seat. He thrust his crutch toward Cheairs. After taking the prop, the plantation owner leaned it against the wall by the kitchen door and stepped inside to check on breakfast.

"You have both disappointed me, and you have cost the Confederacy immeasurably by your failure to implement my orders."

Without waiting for an invitation to sit at the table, Cheatham grabbed a chair and plopped in it. "That ain't so, General," Cheatham shot back. "General Brown was to start the attack, but his right flank was unprotected, so he delayed until General Stewart was in position to cover."

"Hold on," cried Stewart, lifting his right hand as he towered over both sitting men.

Cheatham ignored him. "General Cleburne was to begin his attack at the sound of Brown's guns and swing across the road and envelop the enemy. Brown couldn't attack until Stewart's men were in place. Once they were in position, it was too dark and too late to attack."

Stewart yanked a chair from the table and splatted into it. "I'll not take the blame, no sir," Stewart answered. "I was ordered to block the Columbia Pike with my division. On the verge of fulfilling that order, I received another order from headquarters directing me to support General Cheatham's right flank. That necessitated I circle around his division to get in place. By then it was dark, but I didn't bivouac my men until ten or eleven last night, after I had visited you at Oaklawn to explain my predicament. You told me to stand fast."

Cheairs tiptoed into the room, carrying a silver tray with three cups and a pot of coffee. After placing the tray on the table, he filled the three cups, sitting one in front of each officer, then retreated into the service area, closing the door behind him.

"Perhaps I should've appointed Cleburne as corps commander rather than you, Ben."

Cheatham seethed. "I did what I was told, and I'll whip any man that says otherwise, including you. In fact, I'll bind up an arm and a leg to make it a fair fight, General Hood."

"That's insubordination," Hood screamed.

"Then so be it." Cheatham thrust his hands toward Hood, his wrists together, like he expected to be manacled.

Cheairs entered with a platter of fried ham and a pan of hot biscuits and placed them on the table. He exited and returned with a bowl of redeye gravy. "I'm serving because I didn't care for any of our servants to overhear army business that they might pass on to the enemy. Do you need anything else, General Hood?"

Hood shrugged as Cheatham forked two slices of ham and slapped them on his plate, then took three biscuits, which he broke apart and drenched in gravy. He started eating as Stewart and Hood served themselves.

After a long sip of coffee, Hood picked up his fork and aimed it at Cheatham's nose. "It's incompetence bordering on outright cowardice," he announced as he lowered his fork and struggled to cut his slice of ham.

A seething Cheatham pointed his fork at Hood's plate. "Want me to cut your meat for you, General?"

Hood felt his cheeks heat with anger. As he and his subordinates ate, they exchanged accusations and offered defenses until Hood ended the meeting with orders to return to their corps and resume stalking the enemy. Hood ordered Stewart's Corps, less the division temporarily assigned him from Lee's Corps, to lead the advance past Spring Hill toward Franklin and Nashville. Cheatham's Corps would follow. The detached division would rejoin Lee's Corps when it reached Spring Hill.

"Whatever comes today," Hood admonished them, "obey my orders. Otherwise, I will prefer charges against one or both of you for dereliction of duty."

"At least I can still cut my meat," Cheatham grumbled as pushed himself from the table and stormed out of the room.

Hiram Granbury
On the Franklin Pike

A pall hung over the Army of Tennessee, especially Cheatham's Corps, as the men marched north toward Franklin along a macadamized road littered with burnt Union wagons, dead mules with US branded on their flanks, and equipment discarded by the fleeing Yankees. To take his mind off the accusations, Hiram Granbury counted the abandoned wagons, thirty-four in all, most with their mules shot in their harnesses. Word of Hood's breakfast with his corps commanders had spread through the ranks. The soldiers chafed at their commander's accusation of cowardice against Cheatham and his indictment of everyone but himself.

Granbury and his men had remained on the field throughout the night while the commanding general had retreated to Absalom Thompson's plantation. Rumors spread that Hood sat on a log by Thompson's fishing pond and threw pebbles in the water awaiting the implementation of his murky orders. When he tired of pestering the pond fish, according to the gossip, Hood moved indoors where he enjoyed a sumptuous feast provided by his host. The word was Hood relished the toasts to his military genius before heading to a feather bed that night. Before retiring, so the story went, Hood had told some officers, he expected Schofield to surrender his army rather than sustain the casualties that would surely follow. Schofield was, after all, a cautious man on the battlefield, unlike Hood.

Granbury rode in silence toward Franklin, knowing Hood had likely blamed him for not blocking the road instead of division commander Brown for not beginning his attack on the right flank as ordered. Major General Patrick Cleburne had never blamed Granbury and, instead, took more than his share of the responsibility for what Hood called the "Spring Hill fiasco," but Granbury also knew those above Cleburne in the high command accused him of the blunder. Granbury decided Hood's mind was as wooden as his replacement leg. Twice Captain Sam Foster offered to ride with him, but Granbury waved him away. Granbury did not know what his reputation was among the Army of Tennessee, but he realized forevermore that he would be linked to the failed Spring Hill trap. He was no coward, nor were his men. Neither was he a fool like Hood, who overvalued his capabilities and underestimated the abilities and courage of others. If he excelled at anything, it was in destroying his own army, both in morale and in number. Granbury was confident in nothing now except one thing: A lot of men would die before sunset because of Hood. If he were among them, he would join his beloved Fannie in eternity.

Lt. Gen. John Bell Hood
On the Franklin Pike

By midmorning the ground fog had dissipated and a clear sky appeared on a warm Indian summer day. John Bell Hood might have to deal with the incompetence of his own officers and men, but at least on this day he wouldn't have to fight the weather as well. Up from Columbia ahead of his corps, General Stephen D. Lee caught up with Hood on the northern outskirts of Spring Hill as Hood headed north, intent on leading Stewart's Corps to avoid any additional foul-ups. From north of the little village came the distant sounds of small arms fire, telling Hood that Forrest's cavalrymen were harassing the trailing dregs of Schofield's army.

Lee reined up beside Hood and saluted smartly. "I can't believe the enemy escaped, General."

Hood grumbled. "They marched right past Cleburne's Division and Granbury's Brigade in the darkness, despite my numerous commands to block the road. At times, I fear they don't want to fight, and the Confederacy is doomed."

"Should I take the lead with my corps? We've had a fast march this morning, but it was over good roads, not like what the other corps faced yesterday."

Hood shook his head. "Your corps is not responsible for this predicament. It'll be up to Cheatham's and Stewart's corps to correct the problem, if we even get the chance to attack. There's a possibility we could catch them at Franklin, trap them with their backs to the Harpeth River."

"Should I send up our artillery? We have a hundred pieces."

"Keep them with you, General Lee. Cheatham and Stewart likely wouldn't know how to deploy them. Maintain a steady advance with your corps until your detached division rejoins you, then come to Franklin at a pace that doesn't exhaust your men in case we need them later."

"If that's how you want it, sir."

Hood shrugged. "It's not how I want it, but it's how it is after the failures of Generals Cheatham, Cleburne, and Granbury last night." The commander turned his horse toward Franklin, still simmering over the incompetence of others.

Patrick Cleburne
On the Franklin Pike

Rumors traveled through the Army of Tennessee faster than the army itself moved. Cleburne felt the stares of soldiers and officers—all wondering who was at fault—as he rode ahead of his division, looking for fellow division commander John C. Brown. The Army of Tennessee had been on the move since dawn, trailing the fleeing Yankees. The pike was littered with the Union's discarded equipment and abandoned wagons, either burned or the spokes of their wheels axed so they would be of no use to the South. General A.P. Stewart's Corps led the procession with Hood and his headquarters staff riding with them. Cheatham's Corps followed on Stewart's heels. General Stephen D. Lee's Corps was moving up from Columbia with the bulk of the Army of Tennessee's artillery, but would not catch up with the main body for hours.

After two hours on the march, Cleburne spotted Brown and angled Red Pepper toward him. When Brown saw Cleburne, he motioned toward a line of pines along the road. The two division commanders met among the trees.

"Not a good day," Brown said as he reined up facing Cleburne. "General Hood's wrathy as a rattlesnake and striking at anything that moves. He blames you, me, Granbury, and Cheatham for Schofield slipping away in the night."

"He issued conflicting orders to us all."

Nodding, Brown responded. "General Hood will admit to no such blunder."

"My orders were to attack at the sound of your guns on the right flank, John. I never heard such."

Brown nodded. "We never attacked. When I got in position, Forrest withdrew. When he retreated, I had no protection on my flank and no knowledge of what was beyond the hills. Without daylight to reconnoiter, I couldn't attack without risking an enfilade that would've rolled up our flank. I couldn't take that chance and be blamed for losing our whole army."

"He'll blame you, me and the rest of our corps."

"Likely so, but I'll not have the unnecessary deaths of my men on my conscience. Hood'll blame you and Hiram for not blocking the turnpike."

Cleburne nodded. "I'll demand a court of inquiry to address such accusations. War is challenging enough with a competent leader. It's impossible without one. Hood's a fighter, not a leader, but he fights his generals as much as he fights the enemy."

"Hood has friends in Richmond," Brown noted.

"But very few around here."

"As angry as he was earlier this morning," Brown started, then paused, "he'll have even fewer when this day is over."

Lt. Gen. John Bell Hood
Farther Along the Franklin Pike

As he advanced beyond Spring Hill near the head of Stewart's Corps, John Bell Hood saw signs of hope. He counted almost forty abandoned or burned wagons, some with their teams shot in their harnesses. The roadsides were littered with heavy gear Yankee infantry had discarded in their flight toward safety. The Yankees were running scared.

Tennessee civilians along the road clapped and cheered their Southern troops, shouting "Push on, boys, push on! They are on the run." A terrified army on retreat remained vulnerable. Hood would make the enemy pay despite Cheatham's, Cleburne's, Granbury's, Brown's and Stewart's blunders. Hope bubbled in Hood for himself and for the Confederacy. He would overcome the mistakes of his subordinates and save the Confederate States of America yet. It was his destiny, if only his troops didn't fail him again.

-233-

Wednesday Afternoon,

November 30, 1864

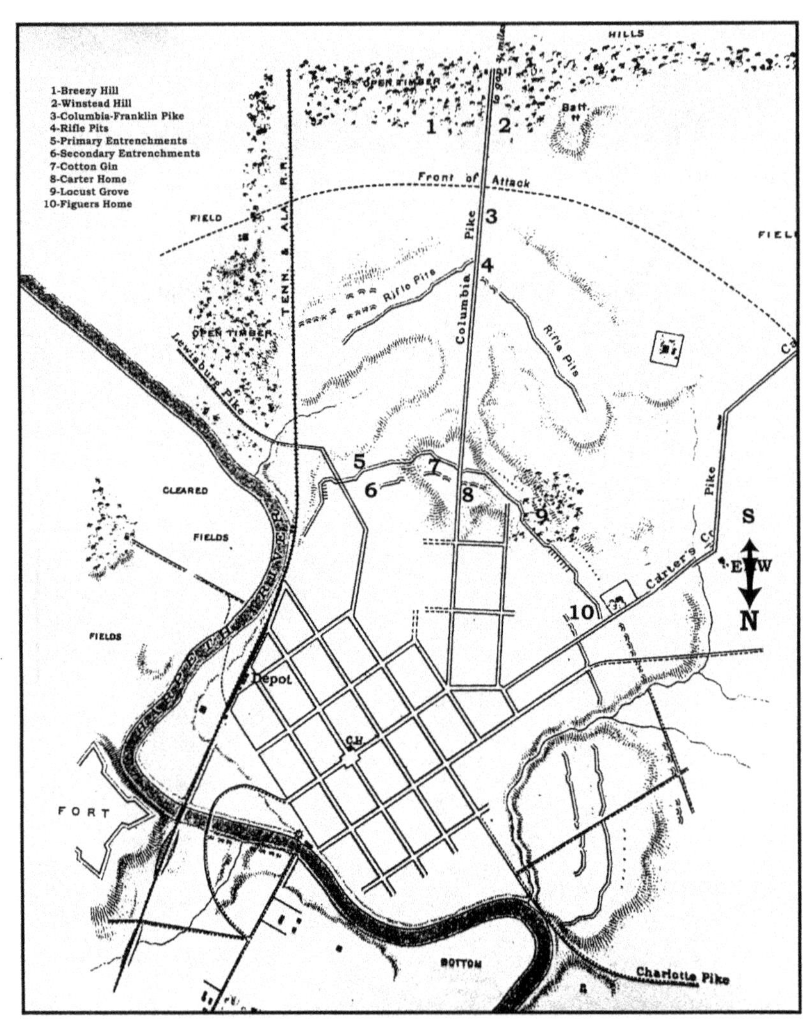

Franklin Battlefield with Union Entrenchments

Chapter Ten

Lt. Gen. John Bell Hood
Franklin Pike near Harrison House

Just past noon, the advance slowed near a modest plantation home identified by the locals as Harrison House. Farther up the road, the army's lead infantry units approached two companies of Forrest's cavalry harassing the rear guard of Schofield's army. John Bell Hood nodded. He would indeed have a second chance to destroy the Yankee army before it reached Nashville. If he did, even George H. Thomas with whatever detachments he had cobbled together to defend Tennessee's capital would not stop Hood's advance through the state and on into Kentucky, all the way to the Ohio River and victory for the Confederacy.

Hood lifted his hand for his staff officers to halt, then handed his reins to an aide. "Field glasses," he said, and another officer slid a pair in his fingers. The commander held them to his eyes, awkwardly focusing the eyepiece. A mile beyond the Harrison House, he spotted a handful of nervous Yankee infantry staring back, a cannon on either side of the road pointed toward the Confederate advance, but it appeared the artillerymen were hooking up the fieldpieces and preparing to retreat. As he lowered the field glasses, General Nathan Bedford Forrest approached on horseback.

"Why haven't you attacked, General Forrest?"

"We're out of ammunition, and they're preparing to retreat anyway."

"What's the lay of the land?"

Forrest raised his gloved hand and pointed at the enemy. "The road passes between Winstead Hill on the west and Breezy Hill on the east. They provide the high ground before the Harpeth Valley opens up to Franklin, two miles distant. We're about a mile from Winstead Hill, so three miles to the edge of town."

"Are they retreating beyond Franklin?"

"Slowly. The two bridges are so damaged they can't carry much weight. Yankee engineers are repairing them, but I suspect it'll be several hours before they can handle much traffic, especially supply wagons."

"So, they're trapped, right?"

Forrest shook his head. "No, they're entrenched."

"That doesn't matter. Drive their rearguard from Winstead, General Forrest, so I can look for myself."

"I need ammunition," Forrest replied.

"Do it," Hood scowled.

Forrest yanked his horse around and galloped to his men. As he shouted instructions, his subordinates ordered the cavalrymen to advance, bullets or not. As the horsemen prepared to attack, the enemy scurried from the hill and down the road with their artillery. Forrest and his officers advanced in the enemy's wake, quickly taking the strategic point without firing a shot.

Hood handed the field glasses to his assistant, took his horse's reins and sent the steed trotting to the knoll where Forrest awaited. After he gave his reins to an aide, another put field glasses in his hand again. The commander studied the enemy two miles away. Franklin's streets teemed with wagons bottlenecked at the rickety river bridges. Between the supply train and the near edge of Franklin, the Yankees dug entrenchments that stretched from one side of town to the other. The Columbia-Franklin Pike passed between a redbrick farmhouse on the west and the massive skeleton of a cotton gin scavenged for fortifying lumber on the east. A mile in front of the main line of defense at the town's edge, other Yankee troops furiously dug rifle pits a hundred yards long on both sides of the turnpike as the rearguard raced between them for the safety of Franklin. The impromptu rifle pits and mounds provided cover where Yankee skirmishers could pester any Rebel advance before retreating to the main defensive line.

"I've seen enough," Hood announced. "They're trapped, and they're ours." He handed his field glasses to one assistant and took his mount's reins from another. "Tell my corps commanders to meet me at that plantation house back down the road. I want Cheatham's Division commanders there as well, especially Generals Cleburne and Brown." General Cheatham had created this predicament and now he would solve it, Hood thought as he retreated to the meeting place, and his couriers scurried to deliver his orders.

Hood looked over his shoulder for a last glimpse at the Union lines. He saw Forrest lagging behind and studying the Yankee positions, then shaking his head as he turned toward Harrison House. Hood scowled that once again he would have to fight Forrest and the cavalryman's doubts about his plan. Why had God placed so many impediments before him in leading the Army of Tennessee to victory?

Patrick Cleburne
On the Franklin Pike

Furious with the accusations of John Bell Hood, Major General Patrick Ronayne Cleburne advanced toward Franklin as angry as he had ever been, so much so that he had ridden ahead of his division on the turnpike, accompanied only by Lieutenant Leonard Mangum, who read his mood and trailed two horse lengths behind his superior. Sunshine from a cloudless blue sky cut the chill of the fall air, as did the crisp new uniform Cleburne now wore. Occasionally, he pulled Susan's handkerchief from his pocket and inhaled the faint aroma of her perfume. Once he rubbed the silk cloth against his left cheek and the infernal scar that never stopped itching, wishing her lips comforted him with kisses. The fleeting memories of his sweetheart lifted his spirits, but only briefly before the specter of John Bell Hood trampled his thoughts and muddied his mind with unending animosities.

By early afternoon, Cleburne neared the head of the advancing column led by A.P. Stewart's Corps. By the stares, pointed fingers, and whispered gossip of Stewart's soldiers, Cleburne understood word had spread that his division was blamed for the Spring Hill debacle by not blocking the Columbia Turnpike as Hood said he had ordered. To counter their malicious suppositions, Cleburne straightened in the saddle and trod forward with his chin held high, despite the itching cheek. As soon as this campaign ended, Cleburne intended to clear his name as he preferred honor over glory, unlike Hood, who sought adulation at the expense of integrity.

Passing the striking William Harrison house on the west side of the turnpike, Cleburne knew Franklin sat in the valley just three miles ahead. The road snaked between Winstead and Breezy hills. Either knoll would offer a solid vantage point to examine what awaited the Army of Tennessee. He aimed his mount toward Winstead Hill until he saw the deformed profile of General Hood on horseback, his wooden right leg jutting from his saddle like a malignant growth. Cleburne yanked Red Pepper's reins and crossed the pike through a gap between the infantry and trotted into the trees behind Breezy Hill. He had no stomach for the company of John Bell Hood.

A brigade of Louisiana troops blocked Mangum from immediately joining his superior. When the Louisianans passed, the lieutenant galloped across the turnpike to Cleburne. "I'll wait until General Hood departs before inspecting the enemy works."

Mangum nodded. "I've never cared for Hood, either."

"I fear you'll care for him less once this day is over."

"You sound pessimistic."

The Irish general hesitated, then answered in a voice barely above a whisper. "I am. His anger will strangle what little tactical judgment he has." Cleburne said nothing for a quarter hour until he saw Hood pass from Winstead Hill with General A.P. Stewart at his side. Hood pointed to the east and appeared to be giving Stewart instructions. Cleburne kicked his horse in the flank and started back across the pike, where the march had halted, and the soldiers awaited new orders. Again, Cleburne moved into the trees to screen himself from Hood. Mangum followed.

Only when Hood departed south down the road toward the Harrison House with General Forrest trailing did Cleburne ascend the slope of Winstead Hill to study the enemy positions. Staff officers from Stewart's Corps scurried between the hill and the road, screaming orders for Stewart's divisions to abandon the pike and take up positions on the east side of the road toward the Harpeth River.

Cleburne dismounted and handed his reins to Mangum, then angled down the slope to a tree stump where he could study the field of impending battle. He lifted his field glasses and examined the Union line. The strength of the Yankee fortifications extended from Carter's Creek Pike on the west past the cotton gin and the railroad to the river on the east.

"Their entrenchments are formidable, Leonard." He swung the field glasses to the east, seeing Stewart's men marching that direction to take up positions between the cotton gin and the Harpeth River. "You know what Stewart's Corps moving east means for our men?"

"No, sir."

"General Hood's saving the strongest point in the Union line for Cheatham's Corps. It's retribution for Spring Hill."

"Surely, Hood's not that petty, not with men's lives and his army's future at stake."

"A man's vanity can cloud his judgment, even when the lives of others are at risk," Cleburne said as he focused the field glasses on the entrenchments at Carter's Creek Pike on the west. As he moved down the enemy line, he called out what he saw. "There's a single entrenchment running south southeast from the western pike to a grove of locust trees. Then there's two trenches from the grove past a farmhouse and outer buildings to the Columbia pike. The double trench extends eastward away from the pike to the cotton gin, which has been stripped of wood for the breastworks. From the gin to the river, there's a single trench. There's more cannons around both the farmhouse and the cotton gin than we have with us."

Cleburne then studied the town beyond the trenches, its streets filled with stalled wagons waiting for engineers to strengthen the damaged bridges so the supply train could cross. On the northeast side of the river sat an earthen fortress with a half dozen long-range cannons.

"There's earthworks across the river with long guns," Cleburne said.

"That's Fort Granger," Mangum replied.

Cleburne lowered his field glasses and offered them to the lieutenant, who dismounted and tied their horses to a sapling.

Mangum examined the fortifications and whistled. "Either side of the Columbia Pike is strong, but the east side in front of the cotton gin looks the toughest."

"That's my assessment," Cleburne answered.

The lieutenant studied the Yankee positions. "What about those rifle pits in front of their primary line of defense?"

"That's for their skirmish line, though it's not a wise placement. When we overrun it, our soldiers will overlap theirs. The enemy can't shoot us without hitting their own men."

Mangum lowered the field glasses. "Surely, we won't attack so strong a position this late in the day."

Cleburne sighed. "Vanity will determine our fate, Mangum."

"Should we return to our division in case Hood summons us?"

Cleburne shook his head. "Let him find us. How about a game of checkers?"

"Huh?" replied Mangum, offering the field glasses back to Cleburne.

The major general refused them, so Mangum hung them over his own neck. Cleburne picked up a broken stick and moved to a clear spot of earth, scratching checker squares in the damp soil. "Grab some yellow leaves, and I'll find some red ones for checkers."

Cleburne played three games with his aide-de-camp, losing them all until a courier from headquarters found him, ordering him to report to General Hood at the Harrison House. In parting, Cleburne instructed Mangum to get his brigade commanders Govan, Granbury, and Lowrey to meet him across the road at the base of Breezy Hill as soon as he returned from the commander's conclave.

Rev. Charles T. Quintard
Pease Home, Columbia

The extra day of rest in David Pease's home, plus the prayers and discussions over Tennessee's future, had invigorated Reverend Charles T. Quintard. Henry B. Free remained delighted with the gift of The Lady Polk because now he had a horse of his own to ride. The clergyman had never seen such a broad smile across such a black face as that morning when he told his servant to saddle the mare and put a halter on the gelding because they would be riding toward Nashville following lunch. Henry hummed "Dixie" as he readied the mounts for the ride to catch up with Hood's army.

After a modest meal and a promise to repay Reverend Pease for his hospitality when the dove of peace flew over Tennessee once again, Quintard and Henry mounted their horses and turned toward the pike to Franklin at two o'clock. With a little over three hours until darkness set in, Quintard doubted he would reach General Hood before sunset. After all, the crippled commander had vowed to exterminate Schofield's men and enter Nashville by nightfall. Perhaps the guardian angel Quintard had prayed for had indeed perched on Hood's shoulder, guiding him toward victory. He beseeched God for success, so the Army of Tennessee would share the joy of triumph, much as Henry delighted in having a mount.

The slave sat tall on the gelding's bareback, smiling as if he had been born free. Best of all, thought Quintard, the horse kept his manservant occupied, so he asked no questions and created no theological conundrums to torment him. The reverend's exuberance lessened after they crossed the Duck River, his grin fading as they rode past the camps deserted by the Yankee army and marked by cold fire pits, abandoned tents the enemy left behind in their haste, and the accoutrements tossed aside by infantrymen on a quick march. As they neared Spring Hill, Quintard spotted dozens of broken wagons, some torched so as not to fall into Confederate hands and others with the wooden spokes broken from the wheels. On some shattered rigs, the Yankees had not even taken time to unharness the teams, shooting the animals instead and slashing the harnesses, so neither the mules nor the leathers could be turned against the Union.

Such a waste, war was!

*****

Patrick Cleburne
Harrison House

Among the last to arrive at the Harrison House, Patrick Cleburne entered the redbrick, white-columned home with General John C. Brown. An orderly escorted the pair to the library where the others had gathered around John Bell Hood seated behind a table in front of a fireplace with an ornate mirror hanging above the mantle. His crutch leaned against the table covered with a rolled map held open by three books, including a massive family Bible. Hood glared at Cleburne and Brown as they entered.

"Late to this meeting and late at Spring Hill," he scowled. "I'm glad you two generals could finally join us, so there's no misinterpreting my orders and my intent on this day. We will prevail, or die trying."

Cleburne seethed as he slipped beside Ben Cheatham. Across the table from Cleburne stood an enraged Nathan Bedford Forrest.

Cheatham challenged Hood. "You, General Hood, share as much blame as anyone else. You issued conflicting orders, then left the field."

Hood glared at his stocky corps commander, then grabbed his wooden crutch and slammed it against a table leg. "There'll be no more insubordination, General Cheatham. Today you and your corps will have the chance to redeem yourselves."

Forrest leaned over the table and pounded the map. "A frontal assault is madness," he shouted, "especially without artillery support. We can outflank the enemy and whip them without the casualties of a frontal assault."

"Wars are won with casualties," Hood growled.

"Enemy casualties, not our own," Forrest shot back.

Hood drew back the crutch to slam the table again, but dropped it on the floor with a clatter. "Hear my plan and prepare to follow it, all of you," Hood grumbled.

Most watched him with narrowed eyes and tight lips, realizing his vindictiveness would cost many lives, whatever his scheme might be.

The commander reiterated his order for Stewart to lead his corps to the east side of the pike, then told Cheatham to position his troops astride the road so that the full force of his corps would fall upon the middle of the entrenched Union line. He instructed Forrest to protect the flanks of each corps with his cavalry.

"A direct attack against the enemy's strongest position, that's suicide," Forrest shouted, banging his fist on the table by Hood. "I've studied the entrenchments. Only a fool would attack them." His flashing eyes glared at Hood. "Supply me with ammunition and give me one strong division of infantry, Cleburne's Division, and with my cavalry we'll flank them, drive them from their works, and destroy them at only a fraction of the cost in blood and powder of your plan."

Hood slapped his palm against the table twice. "No, General Forrest! You'll do as I command. Those that created this mess will solve it." Hood glared from Cheatham to Brown to Cleburne.

Infuriated by his commander's response, Forrest shook his fist at Hood's nose. "If you were a man of full body and mind, I'd teach you a lesson with my fists."

"That's insubordination, General Forrest, and grounds for execution," Hood shot back.

"Hanging me will be far less costly to our cause than the losses your plan will spawn."

The two men glared at each other, their gazes dripping with venom.

Cheatham broke the standoff. "Can't we wait until General Lee brings up the artillery to pound the enemy entrenchments? We only have twelve artillery pieces with us, Stewart's corps and mine."

Hood refused the suggestion. "It will be night before they arrive. We'll use what artillery we have. I can't have the enemy escape in the dark again, can I, General Cheatham?"

His subordinate eyed him, but said nothing in response.

"Now, carry out your orders and drive the fiends from the field at all costs. You are all dismissed." Hood paused, then added a last instruction. "General Cheatham, when all is ready, you will give the command to advance. Don't fail me this time."

Cleburne looked at Brown, who gritted his teeth and shook his head. Both men knew the orders represented retribution for Hood's own failures. Cleburne balled his fists and planted them on the table, leaning toward his commander. "When this day is done, I will demand a court of inquiry to review my actions and clear my good name, General Hood."

The crippled general ignored him, instead addressing the group. "Men, you will attack and drive the enemy from the field, even if it takes all night."

Forrest exploded again. "Those entrenchments will be taken only with a great and useless loss of life when we can better accomplish our goal with a flanking maneuver."

His face reddening, Hood pointed his finger at Forrest. "The Yankees don't want a fight. They are only feigning until they can get across the river and skedaddle to Nashville. We've got them trapped, if you're men enough to whip them."

"General Hood, I repeat, give me ammunition and a strong infantry division, Cleburne's Division." Forrest pounded his left palm with his right fist. "With them and my cavalry, we'll flank the Federals and drive them from their works in two hours."

Cleburne lifted his hands from the table. "General Forrest is right. I've studied the terrain and the enemy's position, General Hood."

"So, have I," Hood shot back.

"A frontal attack," Cleburne continued in the face of obstinacy, "must cross two miles of rolling fields and overwhelm an entrenched force supported by extensive artillery."

"You had your chance at Spring Hill, Cleburne, and you failed," Hood grumbled.

The Irishman lifted his chin and stroked his goatee. "As I stated before, when this campaign ends, I will request a court of inquiry to clear my name and reputation of your malicious accusations."

Cheatham placed his hand on Cleburne's shoulder and pulled him back as he stepped toward Hood. "Both generals Forrest and Cleburne are right. Your plan's foolhardy, with more risk than potential gain. We can't support your proposal when other options carry less risk and more benefit."

"You will support my tactics or suffer the consequences of insubordination," Hood shouted. With a sweep of his arm, he shoved the map and Bible on the floor at the Cheatham's feet.

As Cleburne bent to pick up the Bible, Forrest exploded. "If you weren't a cripple, I'd beat you to a pulp, John Bell Hood."

"That's insubordination," Hood shouted.

"Make of it what you will," Forrest answered, yanking his hat over his head and storming out of the room.

Cleburne placed the Bible back on the table.

Hood glared at him for his simple courtesy, then issued specific commands to Cleburne. "Attack the cotton gin. Order your men not to fire until you run the Yankee skirmishers from the rifle pits up front, then shoot them in the backs and charge the main entrenchments with bullet and blade. Take their position at all costs, as Franklin is the key to Nashville, and Nashville is the key to our independence." Then Hood turned to the others. "Tend to your duties and don't fail me again."

The men piled out of the room and past the double doors of the Harrison House, mounting their horses and turning to deliver orders to their subordinates. As Cleburne climbed atop Red Pepper, Nathan Bedford Forrest rode up.

"You've got a tough nut to crack, General Cleburne. God be with you." Forrest hesitated a moment, then continued. "It's been an honor to serve with you."

"Likewise, General Forrest."

Forrest shook his head. "I fear this will be the second worst blunder of the war."

Cleburne studied Forrest, wondering if he would bring up the failure at Spring Hill. "The worst?"

The cavalry commander winked. "Me not shooting that son of a bitch Hood yesterday when he left me on my own without supporting my men or seeing I got more ammunition."

Both men laughed, then parted, never to meet again.

Mary Alice Carter McPhail
Carter Home

By noon thousands of men in blue uniforms scurried about the Carter farm digging trenches and fortifying the place for an expected attack, although no men in gray had yet appeared around Winstead and Breezy hills. For Mary Alice it seemed she was walking in a dream—or a nightmare—but she no longer knew which. Doubt crept into her mind whether she had actually seen Tod approaching the locust grove earlier that morning. Had the enduring deprivation and the threat of battle so warped her mind she could no longer separate reality from fantasy? The day's possibilities, all bad, overwhelmed her as she watched the children finish the meager lunch Callie had prepared and delivered to the basement, ignoring the offers by Yankees to escape north with them to freedom. Mary Alice just wanted the young ones safe and the soldiers gone.

When the youngsters finished their meals, Mary Alice picked up Lannie, lined the others up behind her and led them up the basement steps onto the wooden porch. She zigzagged among a half dozen soldiers resting in the veranda's shade. As Mary Alice turned to make sure the kids still followed, she saw six-year-old Ruth Carter stop by one soldier and tug his uniform blouse.

"Mr. Yankee," she said, "can you show me your horns?"

Mortified, Mary Alice stepped to Ruth, grabbing her hand to pull her away and get her inside the parlor, but the Yankee smiled.

"Honey," he answered, "the bands won't be playing today, but if I see a musician around, maybe I can get him to show you his saxhorn or trumpet."

Relief surged through Mary Alice, until Lena spoke.

"She means your devil's horns, you dumb Yankee." Lena lifted her defiant chin until Mary Alice grabbed her arm and yanked her toward the door. "Come along, children."

"Secesh scum," responded the insulted Yankee. "Vermin all of you, even the little ones. You all deserve what this war brings you."

Mary Alice pushed Lena ahead of the others, then pulled Ruth along the porch, accompanied by the sound of Yankee profanities.

As she opened the door to escape the tongue-lashing, Mary Alice counted each passing child, relieved that nine had entered. Stepping beyond the four officers hunkered over the parlor table looking at a map, she herded the little ones upstairs to the bedroom where they had spent the night. "You children stay here and don't you leave. If you do, I'll find a tree switch and give you a thrashing you won't forget. She put Lannie on the bed, but he squealed to stay with her. "Take care of your little brother, Adelaide," she ordered as she walked out and firmly shut the door. She stepped in the room across the hall where her sisters and sister-in-law sat on the bed, fretting and whispering so the Yankees would not overhear. Closing the door behind her, she told of the women about Ruth's and Lena's exchange with the Yankees. The women stifled their giggles.

"Can y'all watch the children?" Mary Alice asked. "I'm exhausted. I don't know if I'm going crazy or what, but I could've sworn I saw Tod this morning approaching the grove."

Sara nodded. "Moscow told me you thought you had seen him."

Mary Alice shrugged. "I'm sure I did, or I was sure then. I'm no longer certain about anything. I just want some time away from the children to collect my thoughts."

"We'll mind them, go rest," Sallie offered.

"I'm too nervous to nap. I want to get out of the house for a spell and walk off my frets."

"You do that, Mary Alice," Annie said. "Just don't ask any Yankee to see his saxhorn."

The women tittered again as Mary Alice left the room, Annie and Sallie moving behind her into the children's chamber.

Mary Alice stepped down the stairs, past the four Yankees still studying the map and exited by the front door, not caring to leave by the veranda and chance an encounter with the offended Yankee. She hesitated on the steps, taking in the three tents now standing in their yard and the two wagons parked at the north end of the Carter home. The noise overwhelmed her. Officers shouted orders; soldiers grunted at their chores; axes chopped into wood; horses neighed; and military rigs rumbled down the pike. When she looked to the south and east, she sighed at the destruction. A new trench and embankment extended westward from the pike some three hundred feet toward the locust grove. The new ditch separated the house, office, smokehouse, cookhouse, and outbuildings from their fallow garden. As she looked to the southeast across the pike, Mary Alice watched the Union vultures stripping lumber from the side of the cotton gin and using it to fortify the previous entrenchments that now extended eastward as far as she could see.

Next Mary Alice walked between her home and the cookhouse and realized the previous entrenchment had been fortified and extended east through the middle of the locust grove and beyond. The Yankees had despoiled hers and Tod's special place. She heard a crash and saw a locust tree fall as soldiers downed timber south of the new ditch to provide a thorny barrier between them and potential attackers. Mary Alice wanted to cry, more so when she heard the grumble and rattle of artillery and caissons pulled by wild-eyed horses around the side of the house. The Yankees unhitched their Napoleons west of the cookhouse at the near edge of the secondary entrenchment and spun them about to cover the pike or, after a turn of thirty degrees, the locust grove. Mary Alice had seen soldiers preparing for battle before, but never this many this close with such determined faces. They seemed as scared as she was.

Mary Alice stood amidst the chaos, terrified by the preparation for a fight that might follow. She looked at the house, wondering if it would still be standing the next day, and saw her father talking with General Cox. She scurried over to listen.

"I don't know what to tell you, Mr. Carter," the officer said.

"I've got daughters and grandchildren, nine of them to protect."

"If you leave your home, I wouldn't know where to tell you to go that would be any safer. And, if you leave, you won't be able to protect your property. It'll be looted, either by our men or yours."

"Tell me, General Cox," Fount continued, "if you were on the other side approaching Franklin, would you attack?"

Cox gave a sweep of his arm from the road to the artillery pieces lining up. "By the time my soldiers finish, this line will be unbreakable. The enemy must charge across two miles of open land with very little cover beyond the swales of the fields. If I were attacking, I'd order a flanking maneuver, try to roll the defenses up from the side rather than head on, but I am not John Bell Hood, who is a rash commander. If I did a flanking maneuver, I'd first pummel this line with an artillery barrage as a diversion. Even if there's no attack directed at your house, it could still be damaged from artillery. So, I can't tell you to stay or leave, and I can't tell you what Hood will do. Once the firing starts, though, hide in your basement as it will be too late to escape."

Fount nodded. "Thank you, General. I suppose we'll stay."

"Even so, Mr. Carter, I'd have your family bundle up some clothes and food you could take with you in case you had to escape in a hurry. Make sure your son takes his parole papers. Now, if you will excuse me, I must attend my men should Hood be foolish enough to attack." Cox turned to an orderly holding the reins to his horse. He mounted and rode toward the gin.

Fount looked to his daughter, who saw doubt in his mind, torn over what to do to protect three generations of his family.

"I'm an old man, Mary Alice. If I die today, I'll get to see your mother again. I can accept that, but I couldn't live with a decision that would harm my children or my grandchildren with their whole lives ahead of them."

"We will do what you think best, Father."

Fount removed his hat and wiped his brow. Though the day was pleasant, it was not hot, yet her father dabbed beads of perspiration from his forehead. "I'll tell Jack and Callie to bring Oscar and join us in the basement if things turn bad. Then I'll have our family bundle up some clothes in case we have to go somewhere. Would you mind going to the Lotz house and telling Albert and Margaretha that right now we plan to stay? Invite them to join us in the basement, if the worst comes. Their wooden house won't offer much protection."

"Neither will our house if they fire cannons at it."

Her father shrugged and turned toward the slave quarters while Mary Alice started for the Lotz house and squirmed through the unending tide of Union soldiers preparing for an attack she hoped never came.

Patrick Cleburne
Breezy Hill

The faithful Lieutenant Mangum awaited with brigadier generals Govan, Granbury, and Lowrey at the base of Breezy Hill as Cleburne approached. From the grimaces on their faces, Cleburne knew they had studied the enemy works and found them formidable.

Mangum stepped to Cleburne to take his reins as he dismounted Red Pepper.

"Afternoon, Gentlemen," Cleburne started. "It has been a trying day, and it's about to get worse."

"Can't it wait until tomorrow since we've only got an hour or so of sunlight left?" asked Lowrey.

Cleburne shook his head. "General Hood insists those entrenchments are to be taken today and taken at all costs. He says the enemy is only feigning and will retreat once we attack."

All three brigadiers scowled.

"I've studied the works and they're strong," Granbury said, especially between the pike and the cotton gin. They've stripped planks from the gin for headboards over their trenches. That means we only have six inches of target."

"Several of us—me, Cheatham, and Forrest—tried to talk General Hood out of an attack, but he would have none of it. We're to carry the day, no matter the cost in our blood."

Granbury stood stern. "This is punishment for Spring Hill, isn't it, General?"

Cleburne pursed his lips and stroked his goatee before answering. "It would appear that way, Hiram."

"That bastard thinks we're cowards."

"We've proven him wrong time after time, and we will do so again today," Cleburne responded. "After this is over, we'll clear it up with a board of inquiry."

"If we survive," Granbury replied.

"Should we survive," Cleburne echoed, then paused, scratching the scar on his cheek. "Whatever happens, I will be with you and give it my all as I know you and your men will, too. I will call for the advance when we get the signal from General Cheatham." Cleburne looked toward the formidable objective before issuing orders for the positions each brigade would take in the attack. "We've just an hour of daylight. Let's do our best."

His subordinates nodded.

Cleburne marched to his generals, stopping first at Lowrey and shaking his hand. "Preacher, we need a double dose of prayer for this one."

"I'll do what I can."

"Forrest told me after the meeting, this will be the second worst mistake of the war, the first being his failure to shoot the son of a bitch yesterday."

The three brigadiers laughed.

"You know," offered Granbury, "one of us could correct that before the fireworks start."

Cleburne grabbed the lanky Texan's hand and pumped it. "Know this is not my doing, but we're to advance east of the pike and take the line around the cotton gin. Hiram, cover the left flank with your Texans. Advance along the road, then sweep to the east and see if you can attack the gin from the flank, once you empty the entrenchments in front of it."

"Yes, sir," the wild-haired Texan responded.

"Preacher," Cleburne continued, "line your men up and aim for the east side of the gin."

"You can count on your Alabama and Mississippi boys," Lowrey responded.

"Now, Dan, your brigade'll take the center. Have our Arkansans aim for the gin straight on. This will likely be the hottest spot, so I'll accompany your brigade. To reduce possible artillery casualties, advance in a column until you get within a few hundred yards, then spread out in battle formation and go double quick to the enemy. With God's help and Preacher's prayers, we'll succeed."

"Amen," said Lowrey.

Cleburne wished them all luck and God's blessings. Granbury and Lowrey raced to their mounts and their brigades.

Govan lingered a moment. "General, not many of us will return to Arkansas after this day ends."

Cleburne sighed. "Well, Govan, if we are to die, let us die like men."

Hiram Granbury
At the Foot of Breezy Hill

General Granbury mounted his horse and galloped to his command, a hundred yards in front of Breezy Hill. Riding in front of his soldiers, he shouted for them to fix their bayonets and aim for the breastworks between the pike and the cotton gin.

He shouted encouragement above the rattle of equipment. "You have fought many hard battles, but this will be the fiercest of all. The enemy remains strongly entrenched and in plain view. Now if I have a man unwilling to make this charge, let him step to the rear. I shall hold no animosity to any such a soldier."

Granbury rode the entire length of his brigade and not a man retreated. Instead, each Texan took a step forward.

"I knew I could depend on you Texans."

"And we on you," shouted one soldier.

"Hooray for General Granbury," cried another and the Texans took up the chant.

He smiled at such cowards as his, then yanked his sword from its scabbard and touched the blade's side to his forehead in salute to the men he would soon lead into a cauldron of hell on earth.

As his men loaded their rifles and attached their blades to the barrels, Hiram Granbury dismounted and slapped his horse on the rump with the side of his blade. The horse galloped off toward Breezy Hill. His flag bearers unfurled the distinct blue flags with the white moon in the center, a mark of distinction for Cleburne's Division.

With his free left hand, he yanked his revolver from his scabbard, ready to advance with his men. He knew his Texans would fight like demons and prayed he would match their mettle. And if he should fall, he knew he would join his beloved Fannie before the next earthly dawn.

Hardin Figuers
Figuers Home

Disgusted that his mother shared their boiled potatoes with the Yankee officers during lunch, Hardin Figuers abandoned the house as soon as he finished eating, taking his slingshot but leaving his coat. Barely had he exited the kitchen than he saw a dozen Illinois infantry men from Grose's brigade approach the barn with axes and crosscut saws, intent on fortifying their entrenchments with lumber from the building.

"No," Hardin screamed, running to stop their vandalism, or at least save Adele.

General Grose, though, heard his cry and aimed his horse toward the commotion. The dozen soldiers stopped and awaited their commander's instructions.

"What are you planning on doing, men?" Grose asked.

"Take lumber for our trenches," one answered.

"Leave this place alone, the house, the barn, all of it," Grose ordered. "A widow lives here. We'll not make this war any harder on her."

The men saluted, but as soon as he rode away, they grumbled that the general was more concerned about a Rebel widow woman than his own men. Hardin thought about plugging one with his slingshot, but decided it best to honor his promise to his mother, who had likely saved their place by inviting the Union officers into their parlor and sharing their scarce biscuits and potatoes with them. His momma, he admitted, was shrewder than he realized.

Hardin spent the next three hours wandering around their place, watching the soldiers going about their preparations. Within two hours, the entrenchments were finished near his house and manned by Yankees who fidgeted while chattering whether or not General Hood would foolishly attack. Hardin eavesdropped on their gossip and speculation as he strolled among them or spied on the impromptu fortifications from the barn roof. An hour later, young Hardin saw the vanguard of Confederate troops appear on the Columbia Pike between Winstead and Breezy hills. Thrilled at the prospect of battle, Hardin moved from the barn to the oak tree nearest the Union entrenchments. He shimmied up the trunk and climbed to a high limb to watch a trickle, then a flood of Southern boys filing down the road, then fanning out on both sides of the pike across the undulating plain of fields and meadows. Unlike the arrival of the Yankees, the Confederates lacked a convoy of supply wagons or substantial artillery. Hardin spotted only a dozen cannons among the troops, half of the pieces being diverted to the east side of the pike and the remainder to the west.

Hardin stood on the tree branch and looked along the Union entrenchments where soldiers stood protected by embankments, loading or resting their rifles on the tops of the mounded dirt to await the onslaught. Behind the trenches, Hardin observed dozens of artillery pieces pointed toward the assembling Confederates. His knees trembling, Hardin feared he might fall from the tree, so he slid down and straddled a substantial limb closer to the ground. General Grose rode back and forth behind his brigade's trenches, issuing orders and reassuring his soldiers. Other Yankee officers shouted directions to their men up and down the line. Hardin studied the earthen fortifications from his front all the way to the Carter House and the Columbia Pike and reveled at the gathering armies preparing for combat. Whatever followed would be a great show, Hardin believed.

Lt. Gen. John Bell Hood
Winstead Hill

Sitting astride his horse atop Winstead Hill while an aide on the ground held the animal's reins, John Bell Hood stared through field glasses at the line of butternut and gray arrayed on the valley floor beneath him. He had missed witnessing Pickett's Charge at Gettysburg, having been carried off the field with his arm wound the day before, but it could not have looked any grander than this. Where the Pennsylvania attack had failed, this one would succeed because Hood knew he was destined to save the Confederacy. Franklin, not Spring Hill, was the key to Nashville, and Nashville was the key to Confederate independence.

He scrutinized the Union's makeshift battle line from the west to the east where Fort Granger loomed across the river ready to menace with its artillery any advance by Confederate soldiers. Beyond the Yankee entrenchments, Hood examined the village of Franklin, its streets flooded with wagons and teams waiting to cross the bridges Union engineers were strengthening. More dangerous than the heavy guns at Granger were the batteries of twelve-pound Napoleons the enemy had positioned behind their breastworks. The field glasses trembled in his hand, not from nerves, but from the excitement of what was to come. He wished he was whole once again so he could lead his men into battle—a brigade or even a company—and see the terror of an opponent about to be vanquished. He missed the acrid smell of spent powder with the sweet aroma of Yankee blood, and he longed for the sounds of gunshots, clanging steel and dying foes. He envied those about to advance for the Confederacy as they would have memories for a lifetime—if they survived.

From somewhere below Winstead Hill as the bands awaited, General Benjamin F. Cheatham waved the flag that signaled the advance. The bands started playing, the brigades unfurled their battle flags and the line of men started forward, a vast expanse of humanity advancing in rank and file, save for Cleburne's Division, as he proceeded in columns to minimize the exposure of his troops to fire until they were upon the enemy, then they would fan out and charge. As the battle flags rippled with the onslaught, the dying sunlight reflected blood red on the gleaming Confederate bayonets.

For the first third of the procession, the troops advanced with parade-like precision, the men maintaining their lines as straight as the rolling terrain would permit. Those of Cheatham's Corps aimed for the rifle pits in front of the main defensive lines. Hood recognized the earthworks as a foolish defensive position because the soldiers could not hold it. Once they retreated, Confederates could fall in behind them, and Yankees in the primary trenches could not shoot for fear of hitting their own men. Hood figured that mistake would allow Cheatham's troops to flood and break the center of the line, then roll up both wings of the Union army and quickly end the impending melee.

Three quarters of a mile into their advance, the gray line increased the pace to a trot as they approached the rifle pits and as artillery shells rained down from Fort Granger. The tumult grew as they neared the outlying rifle pits. The Rebel attackers held their fire as ordered, planning to overwhelm the skirmish line with bayonets. Cannon fire from Fort Granger knocked gaps in the advancing infantry with the screams of the wounded and dying adding to the noise. Gradually, the regimental bands stopped playing, their tunes replaced by a devil's mix of noise. Soon, the charge overwhelmed the skirmishers in the advanced pits. The Yankees turned to run, pursued by the boys in butternut, using their blades to dispatch the panicked skirmishers and to save their bullets for the main line of the enemy ahead.

Past the rifle pits, the Confederates dashed for their ultimate destination, the main a line of Union infantry. They halved the distance to their target, then halved it again when the whole Yankee line exploded in a deadly volley of rifles and cannons. Almost instantly, the line was enveloped in a cloud of smoke and haze. As the soldiers at the trailing edge of the attack neared the entrenchments, they, too, disappeared into the veil of war.

Patrick Cleburne
Attacking Franklin

Stewart's and Cheatham's corps lined up from the Harpeth River on the east to Carter's Creek Pike on the west. From his position east of the Columbia Pike, the best Patrick Cleburne could tell, his was the only division staged in columns rather than battle formation, giving enemy artillery a narrower line to shoot at and limiting casualties.

He sat proudly atop Red Pepper, riding in front of his regiments, pleased that his division alone among the Army of Tennessee had special battle flags, a blue background with a white moon in the center. The other divisions carried the red battle flag with the St. Andrew's Cross, but his men, by their hard fighting, had earned the honor extended to no other division in the army.

As he rode back and forth in front of his men awaiting battle, he felt that itchy twinge in his left cheek. He rubbed it with the back of his right hand. Behind him, he heard the bands strike up the music, but they played different songs that delivered a battlefield cacophony. Then the signal came from Winstead Hill and the advance began.

"Onward, men, onward," cried Cleburne.

Somewhere behind him, a pair of the twelve cannons Hood had brought with him exploded, sending their shells toward the town, shattering Franklin's peacefulness. The gray-and-butternut troops advanced at common time, seventy yards in a minute. From the Union line, a battery erupted, showering balls toward the Southern boys without effect. Then the long guns from Fort Granger fired, ineffective at first, but becoming more deadly as they determined the range and opened holes in the ranks of the advancing troops. As the Rebels marched inexorably closer to their objectives, the officers called out quick time, and the men moved at eighty-six yards a minute.

"Onward to victory," Cleburne screamed at his unbreakable line.

Sam Watkins
Advancing toward Franklin

In all his marches—and he had been on nearly all of them with the Army of Tennessee since 1861—Sam Watkins had never seen his men, at least those remaining, so somber. They realized they were on a death march, even if no muffled drums sounded with the foreboding cadence of ominous drumbeats. As the First Tennessee advanced north from Spring Hill along the macadamized pike to Franklin, rumors rippled through the ranks and knotted the guts of the webfeet, who understood they paid the price for their commander's faults. Gossip held that John Bell Hood was furious at the debacle at Spring Hill, blaming various generals—but never himself—for the failure. Webfeet did the fighting, Sam remembered, while the generals did the infighting. The infantry would suffer today, not the generals. Watkins wondered if the fighting rooster Fed had sensed such despair before he faced John Hell.

By midafternoon, the men of the First Tennessee rested off the pike in a gap between the hills overlooking Franklin. Watkins and his men could see the whole damn Yankee army awaiting them behind fresh entrenchments, their rippling battle flags taunting the Confederates in the light breeze that blew hints of death across the undulating meadow and fields separating the two armies. While awaiting orders among the trees on the slopes of the gentle hills, Watkins watched a courier dash up to General Cheatham and exchange salutes. The officers visited for a minute, then saluted again, and the courier galloped on down the line. Moments later, Cheatham sent his staff officers riding to the various regiments with their orders.

"Attention!" came the cry as his regiment's captain reined up in front of his depleted detachment.

"The First Tennessee will form a skirmish line ahead of our brigade," he cried, pulling his sword from his saddle scabbard. He waved the saber toward the farmhouse and its outbuildings, then swung it toward the setting sun. "West of the farm place, you will see an orchard. You will attack there, drive the enemy from the entrenchments, and through the orchard, then swing back north and east to capture the artillery pieces between the farmhouse and the orchard. Once you turn that artillery on our enemies, we will win the day. As Tennesseans, you know this is for your homes and your sweethearts. Good luck, men, and may God be with you every step of the way to victory."

"Shouldn't General Hood be with us every step of the way?" shouted a webfoot.

"It'd take him a month to walk that far," the captain answered, drawing a few snickers.

"We can wait, Captain," answered the webfoot, sparking louder laughs.

The captain nodded and snorted, then trotted off to give the assignment to the other companies in the regiment.

After he departed, some men removed their canteens to reduce the weight they would carry into the fight. Watkins kept his. The soldiers loaded their rifles, placed percussion caps on the firing nipple, and gently lowered the hammer back in place. When it came time to shoot, all the soldiers would need to do was cock the hammer and pull the trigger.

"This is like the Dead Angle," Billy Carr mumbled to Watkins.

"Only in reverse," Sam answered. "We won't have any mountain slope to screen us until we're fifty feet away."

"I fear this is my last battle, Sam."

"You've taken more than your share of Yankee lead. How many times has it been?"

"I've never counted, but I got shot at Perryville, Murfreesboro, Chickamauga, the octagon house, Dead Angle, and outside Atlanta. I guess that's six times, but I took more than one bullet on three occasions. How about you?"

"Multiple fragments at Murfreesboro and Atlanta, though nothing serious either time. I figure I'm due more than you are on this attack."

"The way I look at it, Sam, you're just luckier than me."

Watkins shook his head. "We may both run out of luck this afternoon."

Their guns loaded, the men turned silent as they awaited orders to form up. Finally, the word came for the skirmishers to move to their positions.

On both sides of his company, Watkins saw the regiments of the Army of Tennessee unfurl their battle flags and ease into place. Sam wished he were a bird so he could fly over the field and see the majesty of the battle line. Even if the men wore tattered uniforms and worn shoes, it would be a bird's-eye spectacle worth seeing, but if he were a bird, he knew he would fly away from the confrontation all the way to Jennie.

The First Tennessee advanced thirty yards in front of the brigade, the men spreading out ten to twenty paces apart. Behind them, the other regiments lined up in attack formation. Then the bands played as officers galloped back and forth between the skirmishers and the main battle line, encouraging the soldiers to give their all. With darkness less than an hour away, the signal came to advance.

The rumors were true. Hood was sending his men to assault well-entrenched forces without a cannon barrage to soften the lines. This was not what Hood had promised in Alabama before entering Tennessee. Near the pike, Watkins spotted two Confederate cannons preparing to fire toward the farmhouse, but saw no other Confederate artillery. This was insanity. The gossip was true. General Hood was furious. Good men would die because of Hood's orders. Watkins prayed he wasn't one fated for death on this day. He hoped he would live to see Jennie again. At that moment, he wished he could fly.

Sumner Cunningham
Outside Franklin

Sergeant Major Sumner A. Cunningham stood on the right flank of the Forty-first Tennessee staring two miles distant at Franklin, nestled in a bend of the Harpeth River. Somewhere before him was the place where he would certainly die on this pleasant afternoon. He waited some forty yards west of the Columbia pike, the dividing line between Brown's and Cleburne's divisions. In Brown's Division, they aimed for a brick home and outer buildings while Cleburne's

Division pointed to a larger wooden building identified as a cotton gin. Between those buildings and Cunningham awaited more Yankee soldiers than he had ever seen at once in his life. In front of the main line, a host of Union men served as skirmishers behind makeshift rifle pits they scrambled to reinforce with shovels and pickaxes. Several hundred yards to their rear stood the massive earthworks that zigzagged from beyond the cotton gin on the east to as far as Cunningham could see past the houses on the west. In places outside the parapet were lines of abatis, downed trees with pointed ends to hinder the movement of an attacking force. A thick locust grove abutted the abatis.

Beyond the embankments, Cunningham saw hundreds of Yankees scurrying about, looking like ants at this distance. He wondered which one of those ants would fire the shot that would kill him. Unlike so many previous days, this Wednesday was warm and pleasant, though that would change once the sun disappeared. If he was fortunate enough to have a tombstone, the inscribed date of his death would be November 30, 1864. He looked from side to side and saw a line of tattered butternut and gray extending from the Harpeth on the east to the Harpeth on the west. The sight inspired Cunningham, as had never seen so many soldiers, maybe twenty thousand of them, ready to attack and die.

Colonel James Tillman rode back and forth in front of his regiment, making certain the men aligned properly and loaded their rifles. Halting his gelding before them, he lifted his sword. "Fix bayonets," he cried.

The men groaned as they realized a close, vicious fight loomed. Above the groans came the cacophony of over five hundred metallic clicks of bayonets being attached to their Enfields.

"Give the skirmishers your blades, but save your fire for their main line and push the invaders into the river," Tillman cried. "Do this for the Confederacy, for Tennessee, for your sweethearts and for yourselves, so you can one day tell your grandchildren."

The soldiers cheered his words as Cunningham took a deep breath. He felt strangely calm. Perhaps fearing death carried a heavier burden than death itself. Cunningham knew he would soon learn the answer to that question. Looking behind him, he saw the regimental musicians with their trumpets, coronets, and saxhorns. He knew all the musicians by name and hoped he had done nothing to offend them because once the battle began and the injured fell, the musicians picked up litters and tended the wounded. As he looked behind him and past the band members, Cunningham saw a signal flag waving from Winstead Hill.

Colonel Tillman shouted to his men, "Shoulder arms! Forty-first Tennessee forward! Music! Quick Time! March!" The musicians struck up "Dixie" and the Forty-first Tennessee advanced. Cunningham looked around. It was a magnificent sight, the regimental flags waving as the soldiers advanced. As the onslaught of brave men in tattered uniforms moved ahead, terrified rabbits darted for cover ahead of the charging soldiers. Coveys of quail exploded from the grass and fluttered away to safety. Cunningham raced forward with exhilaration in his blood, proud to be a part of this spectacle of Confederate valor. Nothing could stop this Southern wave. Cunningham thought himself invincible.

Then the first artillery shell exploded in front of his regiment. After the shower of shrapnel, Cunningham suddenly felt vulnerable after all.

Mary Alice Carter McPhail
Carter Home

The afternoon had dragged by, the women, children, and Fount Carter waiting inside the house with their bundled clothes and belongings in case they had to run to safety. Moscow Carter had fetched his father's ladder from the barn and climbed on the house rooftop to watch the Confederate army as it approached. With each passing minute, the Carters felt the suspense lessening, as surely General Hood would not attack so close to dusk.

Then the outside noises went silent, no sound of moving wagons, no orders from officers, no curses from their subordinates, no noise of spades hitting dirt or axes thumping timber, just a haunting stillness, as if the entire world caught its breath.

From the distance, the Carters detected the slight strains of "Dixie," then a cacophony of music as multiple bands played that or "The Bonnie Blue Flag" without coordination. While that noise came from the south, a closer Yankee band to the north of the Carter home played the poignant melody of "Before the Battle Mother," sending its melancholy notes across the land. Everyone in the parlor looked at each other when they heard a clatter on the roof and realized Moscow was retreating from his perch.

Shortly, Moscow burst through the front door. "They're coming," he cried. "The fools are coming."

Everyone jumped up. "Where to?" Mary Alice screamed.

"The basement," Moscow shouted. "We don't have time to go anyplace else." The adults hurriedly herded the children toward the door and the back porch.

Hardin Figuers
In an Oak Tree

Still, the Confederates spilled down the turnpike like ants from a hole and spread out in a long line of soldiers that mirrored the defensive perimeter. For an hour or more, the Southern boys assembled beneath the eyes of their mounted officers parading in front of assembled troops. From the branch, Hardin sat thrilled, fascinated, and fearful. When he lifted his hand, he realized his arm and fingers trembled. He gritted his teeth, vowing to show no more fear, but he failed. His extremities quivered still. Hardin intended to watch, but his instincts said he should retreat to the cellar like General Grose had recommended. He decided the tree offered him safety at his height. He leaned down on the limb and wrapped his arms around it, planning to observe whatever followed from that vantage point.

As he hugged the tree branch, he saw the Southern regiments unfurl their battle flags as a thin line of skirmishers advanced about twenty yards ahead of the others. For a moment, all was silent around Hardin as the Yankees realized an attack was imminent. Hardin gulped, holding his breath, terrified about what would soon transpire, but too fascinated to leave his perch.

General Grose rode back and forth behind his regiments, shouting instructions. "Load your rifles, men, but hold your fire until they are within twenty yards. Aim low when you fire. Maintain your positions, no matter what."

Moments later, a Confederate regimental band broke the calm with the strains of "Dixie." Another band struck up "The Bonnie Blue Flag," then others joined in until the music was a festive dissonance like competing barkers at a county fair. Toward the Carter House, Hardin heard a Yankee band strike up "Just Before the Battle, Mother." Then signal flags waved from Winstead Hill and butternut-clad officers along the line waved their swords toward the Yankee entrenchments. At that signal, the attackers stepped forward toward the jaws of death. Hardin caught his breath at the magnificent sight, fighting men on the prowl in an unstoppable wave. For a while, it seemed like every approaching soldier was aiming straight for Hardin's tree. He trembled so much that his limb shook.

When Grose saw the Rebel advance, he turned his horse and raced to the Figuers house. "Bethenia Figuers," he screamed. "They're coming. Get your little girl and head for your cellar or town for safety."

Hardin saw the front door fly open as his mother ran out, pulling Mary Louisa to the street and toward town. Thomas followed, but he retreated to their cellar, holding the door open so Uncle Jesse could dash in from across the road.

"May God keep you and your girl safe, ma'am," Grose cried as the two fled. When Grose reversed his mount for the entrenchments, Hardin saw his brother slam the cellar door behind him and Uncle Jesse.

The jumbled racket of overlapping band tunes provided the only sound of the advance until cannon fire from Fort Granger across the Harpeth exploded in front of the oncoming line. Then the jaunty tunes subsided under the horrific screams from the throats of the charging Confederates. Artillery shells from Fort Granger peppered the field among the charging soldiers, who held their own fire as they drew closer.

Hardin saw two Confederate Napoleon's shoot over their advancing allies, but the Southern artillery was insubstantial compared to the Union's guns, which showered the Confederate soldiers with lead. Soon the field grew hazy from dust and smoke. As the Rebels neared the Union entrenchments, they fired their first volley and disappeared in a cloud of white smoke. Hardin heard the hiss and zip of projectiles, fearing at first that Union soldiers had loosened a nest of hornets upon him for a change. Then one projectile thudded into the limb where he clung, just inches from his fingers. He spotted the misshapen leaden Minié ball in the wood and reached out to pull it free, then yanking his index finger away from the burn of the still scorching slug.

The hiss and splat of bullets increased and Hardin realized the tree provided no safety from the Confederates' errant aim. He shimmied across the limb and down the tree trunk, leaping to earth and falling to his knees when he stepped to the ground. Bullets thudded into the oak's bark. Stumbling to his feet, he raced for the house, then angled for the barn when he heard Adele's terrified howls. He flung open the door and bolted inside, spotting the hound cowering in the back corner. Hurrying to the dog, he untied her, lifted her to his chest, then barreled out of the barn toward the cellar's safety. He dropped the hound at the cellar door, grabbed the handle, and yanked it open, Adele rushing down the steps. In the dying afternoon light, Hardin glanced across the street where a Yankee soldier ran toward the entrenchments before his head exploded in a bloody haze. Hardin gagged, then stepped inside the opening, closing the door over his head as he descended into the dark, damp basement, lit only by two head high cellar windows.

"Where've you been, Hardin?" Thomas asked from the corner farthest from the door.

"Watching."

"You always wanted to see a battle."

"I've seen enough of war."

"It's just started, Hardin. There's plenty to come."

Hardin stepped to the corner and sat down in the darkness, grabbing Adele and pulling her to him. The dog trembled and moaned as the sound of war and death roared outside, occasional bullets splatting against the house or the cellar door. One bullet shattered a thin place in the door, then pinged against the potato bin and sizzled as it lost its fire among the cool potatoes. Hardin laughed nervously.

"Marse Hardin," whispered Uncle Jesse, who trembled as much as Adele, "don'ts you be laughin' none or we's all bound to dies. Iffen we mocks death, we's will surely dies."

"You'll be a free man if you die, Uncle Jesse."

"No matter, Marse Hardin. I's rather lives to see if I's free, dan die to be free."

Uncle Wiley Howard
Near the Franklin Pike

Battle was imminent and Uncle Wiley Howard argued with his master.

"I told you to saddle Joe for me, Wiley."

Howard shook his head. "Marse States, you got no business riding dat horse. Joe ain't got no sense when he hears de bullets and smells de powder."

"Kitty's broke down, been stumbling around," the general growled. "Joe'll just have to get used to the bullets. Now saddle him, Wiley, and be quick about it."

Howard had heard that timbre in his voice when Gist was angry or impatient and knew he had lost the argument. He spun about and raced to the two horses, removing the bridle and saddle from Kitty and securing them to Joe Johnston. Like many South Carolinians of the planter class, Gist was a fine horseman in Howard's mind, but he hadn't ridden Joe as much as Kitty, so he didn't know him as well, especially in battle.

Completing his task, Howard led the saddled Joe Johnston back to Gist, who showed no remnant of his previous anger. He nodded as his manservant stepped beside him. "Thank you," he said, then lifted a pair of field glasses hanging from his neck and studied the entrenchments outside of Franklin. Lowering the instrument with his left hand, he shook his head and lifted the strap over his head. He handed Howard the field glasses. "I'll be close enough to the Yankees that I won't need these."

Howard accepted the gift and offered Gist the reins.

The general refused them, reaching instead in his coat and pulling out his watch and wallet. "Wiley, I might get tripped up this evening. You take care of my money and my watch. If anything happens to me, use what cash you need to get back home and give Miss Janie my watch."

"Yassir," Howard replied.

Gist hesitated still, his lip quivering for an instant as he reached for the gold band on his ring finger. He removed it slowly, reluctantly, then handed it to Howard. "You take care of my wedding ring, Wiley. If I don't return, give it to Miss Janie and tell her it was the greatest gift I ever received."

"Yassir, I wills."

Without another word, the general pulled the reins from Howard's hand and mounted Joe Johnston.

Hearing a commotion behind him, Howard turned to see General Hood riding stiff legged in his saddle, approaching with his staff. When Howard turned back, Marse Gist had ridden toward his brigade, shaping up a hundred yards west of the turnpike. The best Howard could tell, Gist never acknowledged Hood's arrival. Howard shoved the money and watch in his pants pocket, but feared losing the ring, so he slid it on his index finger. He tucked the binoculars inside his shirt so Hood's retinue would not see it and demand the field glasses from a slave.

He walked away from the turnpike about a hundred yards west and stood on an emptied ammunition crate so he could see Gist riding in front of his troops, waving his sword and encouraging his men for the task before them. Behind him near the road, he saw one of Hood's men swinging a flag overhead. At the signal, the bands played, the regimental flags unfurled and the gray line marched toward Franklin, half of the twenty thousand men on west side of the pike aimed for the farmhouse and the other half on the east side aimed for the cotton gin.

The sight and sounds of the music and the men sent chills up Howard's spine until enemy artillery fire turned the concert into a strident symphony of horror. Howard watched his master through the binoculars, seeing Joe Johnston turn skittish, even under Gist's firm rein, then the horse tumbled forward, throwing Gist free, but he was soon up and waving his sword over his head. Howard last saw his master as he approached an abatis near a sugar maple tree in front of the entrenchments about seventy-five yards from the farm's outer buildings. Then Gist disappeared in the cloud of smoke and fire that engulfed that section of the battlefield.

As Howard lowered the field glasses, tears streamed down his cheeks and the wedding ring seemed tight on his finger, like the knot in his throat. Wiley knew he would never see Marse Gist alive again.

Lt. Gen. John Bell Hood
Winstead Hill

The commander of the Army of Tennessee sat atop his gelding, watching the cloud of combat, making out nothing beyond the flashes of rifle and cannon fire. After thirty minutes of seeing little and understanding less of the clash before him, he handed his field glasses to his aide and pulled in his reins.

"Let's move down the hill, closer to the battle, so couriers may more easily find us," he instructed his command staff. They rode to the pike, turning north toward Franklin. His chief of staff found a modest home next to the road and told the widow who lived there that General John Bell Hood requested the use of her house until he drove the Yankees from Franklin. The widow gladly agreed. When he reached his new headquarters, Hood received help from his men to unstrap him from the saddle and lower him to the ground.

"I'll watch from here," he said as he pulled his crutch from its scabbard.

Around him, his minions scurried, one unfurling a blanket on the ground and another removing the saddle from his mount. That orderly dropped the saddle at the head of the blanket and helped his commander hobble to the spread. Hood watched the battle a mile and a half away. A staff officer gave him a cigar. Hood shoved it in his mouth, accepted a lit match from another officer and sucked on the rolled tobacco until the flame took hold, and he exhaled smoke. He then reclined on the blanket, remaining there as he received messages and issued orders. Hood consumed two cigars before the dropping temperatures forced him inside to the warmth of the widow's home and another featherbed for the night.

Wednesday Evening,

November 30, 1864

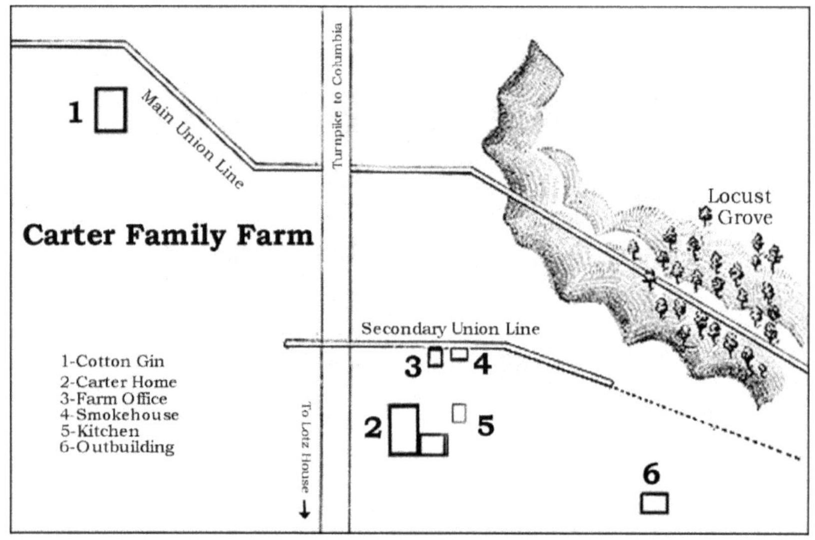

Union Entrenchments at Focal Point of the Battle of Franklin

Chapter Eleven

Mary Alice Carter McPhail
Carter Home

Mary Alice grabbed Lannie and her bundle of clothing, and the children put on their coats and hats, then clutched their packets and started for the back door. Cannon fire exploded from the backyard as the family scurried out onto the veranda. McKinley stumbled and fell down the steps into the yard. Confused, he scrambled to his feet and walked toward the battery when his hat flew in the air. Moscow leaped off the porch and grabbed McKinley and his hat, carrying him toward the basement where the others headed. Mary Alice herded the children toward the cellar steps, her sisters standing between them and the gunfire as they scurried down the stairs. At the landing, Jack and Callie pointed the little ones into the northernmost room, where they huddled with the little black slave Oscar in the far corner. Mary Alice rushed after them, offering Lannie to Adelaide.

In the dim light, Mary Alice counted, "One, two, three, four, five, six, seven, eight, nine, they're all—" she hesitated. "Wait! One of those is Oscar. Who's missing?"

"Lena's not here," little Walter cried.

"Oh, my God," shouted Mary Alice, bursting out of the back room into the main one where her father and brother were barring the door. "Wait, Moscow. Your Lena is missing."

Her brother flung the bar aside to race up the steps, but Albert Lotz blocked the stairway as he shepherded his family to safety. Once they passed, Moscow bolted up the stairs, stopping at the entry as Lena approached, her doll in her left hand while she dragged her toy trunk with her right. As he pulled her into the stairwell, a horrendous crash reverberated throughout the house. Moscow looked around, then slammed the outside basement door and started down the stairs. "Hurry, Lena," he cried.

Once he rushed Lena into the basement, Fount Carter shoved the inside door shut behind them and secured a bar across it.

"A cannonball just struck your room, Mary Alice," Moscow shouted.

Mary Alice's throat tightened. She remembered General Cox's warning about an artillery barrage and worried that she and her children might be buried in the rubble of her childhood home. Terror raced through her every fiber. She thought of her husband and realized what Daniel must endure in the heat of battle.

The ping, zip, and thud of bullets increased, one breaking a south-side hopper window and ricocheting around the first room.

"All you women in the back room. Protect the children," Fount shouted, then turned to his son, pointing to a large tool trunk. "Moscow, I've got six coils of rope in that chest. We need them for the windows."

The men darted to the chest, flung it open and lifted the coils out, toting them to the basement windows and shoving them on the sills to absorb or deflect bullets. The noise picked up and someone pounded on the barred door.

"Let us in," screamed a Yankee voice.

"Fight like a man, you coward," shouted Moscow. Then he and his father tried to move the heavy chest to block the door, but it barely budged. "Albert, Jack, come here," he cried.

The two men bolted into the room.

"Help us," Fount screamed. They slowly muscled the heavy chest to the door, blocking the entrance against soldiers trying to hide from the fight. "That'll have to do," Fount cried above the growing din of battle. The quartet then retreated to the back room, positioning themselves in front of their families to protect them from any errant bullet that might enter through a hopper window.

The martial music preceding the assault gave way to an opus of death as gunshots, cannon fire, screams, and shrieks melded into a hellish hymn.

"Momma," cried Adelaide, her voice just audible over the roar of battle, "I'm scared."

"Whenever you're scared, Adelaide, sing 'Jesus Loves Me'," Mary Alice responded, trying to soothe the fears of the little ones. "Children, let's sing it together." Mary Alice led the song, but their soft voices could not be heard over the rumble of battle, only their quivering lips showed the children were singing.

When the song ended, the fighting continued, seeming to grow even louder. The children held their ears and screamed, but their shrieks only added to the dissonance of death. The brawling went on for a quarter hour, a half hour and more, until time became meaningless. The only sign of its passing was the last light of day gave way to the darkness of night and the invisible horrors of death outside. The flashes of explosions from the yard lit the room, sending flickering shards of light into their hiding place before evaporating in the darkness. Mary Alice suggested lighting a lamp to soothe the children's fears, but Moscow and Fount responded a light might draw fire. They huddled in terror, clinging both to one another and to the hope that this horror might soon end.

It finally did. Five hours later. And even then, the men waited another hour before emerging into the hellish wreckage that was the Carter farm.

Sam Watkins
Attacking Franklin

As the troops advanced, excitement pulsed through their veins until a walk became a jog, a jog a dash, and then a dash a run. Within fifty yards of the orchard, which Sam Watkins recognized as a grove of locust trees, the Yankee line exploded in a ribbon of flame as bullets zipped past, searing the air. Watkins dropped to his knee, fired his bullet, then fell flat as the rest of the brigade passed by. Once they were beyond him, he rolled over on his back, loaded his rifle, jumped up and fell in behind the others, screaming as he ran and waiting for an opening to shoot again. When men collapsed in front of him, he discharged his rifle, fell to the ground, loaded his musket again, scrambled to his feet, and resumed his charge into a cloud of fire, smoke, screams, and death. The attack stalled as his company reached the downed trees, their thorny branches providing an effective abatis. Around him, Tennesseans hacked at the limbs with Bowie knives or bayonets or sabers, clearing a path toward the entrenchment despite the lead buzzing past like angry wasps. Still the troops advanced, Watkins trailing. He lost sight of Billy Carr, hoping his friend survived.

Time lost its meaning as Watkins fired and advanced, scrambling to kill and not be killed. The stench of gunpowder mingled with the odor of the viscera the powder had created. The sounds, the sights, the smells, even the tastes of battle overpowered his senses until Watkins reacted from instinct rather than reason. Somehow, against all odds, the men of his brigade drove the Yankees from their primary line back to their secondary entrenchments. Watkins ran with his allies, the gray tide advancing until the cannons his allies hoped to capture exploded in their faces, their chests, their guts, and their limbs. In that instant, the howls of the dying rose above the sound of detonating explosives.

Watkins fell back to the primary entrenchment, diving in and continuing the fight against the Yankees firing at him from the second line of earthworks. All around him, he heard the thud of bullets hitting the tree trunks and the squish of the lead striking flesh. Darkness enveloped the hellish landscape, lit by the explosion of gunpowder and littered with bodies torn asunder by the fiendish thunder of pistol, rifle, and cannon.

The brigade fought off successive charges of Yankee reinforcements to take back the primary entrenchment. Watkins lost track of how many times the Yankees charged or his allies counterattacked. Still, the cannons roared in favor of the Union, subverting every Confederate effort to capture them. The horrors seemed endless.

Toward midnight, the fury abated after Watkins and everyone else ran low on ammunition and hope. Exhausted and thirsty, he took a drink from his canteen, his hands shaking so violently he used both to hold the container to his mouth. Horrified at what he had seen and exhausted from all he had done, Sam Watkins collapsed into a deep slumber. Unlike most around him, he would awake from his sleep the next morning. The others would sleep forevermore.

Hiram Granbury
Attacking Franklin

Major General Patrick Cleburne rode in front of his division atop Red Pepper and signaled for his men to advance. As the bands played, Hiram Granbury led his troops toward the Union line. The grand spectacle sent chills up Granbury's spine. He wished he could watch the ensuing battle from a soaring eagle's vantage point. The Texans, whose bravery was questioned by General John Bell Hood, pressed forward toward the line of skirmishers behind shallow embankments from the rifle pits on both sides of the road.

Everything remained serene until the first artillery shell hit, then the music of the bands ceased, replaced by the yells of those attacking the fringes of hell. Some soldiers fired at the skirmishers, but most charged after them with bayonets leveled for the kill. Granbury raced ahead, waving his sword and firing his pistol at the head of a Yankee peering over the embankment. As he attacked, Granbury thought of

Fannie, wondering if he would soon join her as the thud of a bullet sent a soldier beside him tumbling across the ground. His troops reached the rifle pits, driving the advanced Yankees back. The enemy fled, screaming and tossing their rifles aside to run unencumbered by the extra weight in their dash for the primary Union entrenchments.

Granbury glanced at his Texans and saw Captain Foster shouting and laughing as he chased the terrified Unionists back to the main earthworks. The Confederate charge was exhilarating. The Yankee fire was subdued until the retreating skirmishers scurried past their Yankee comrades in the fortified entrenchments. Then hell exploded in front of Granbury's Texas Brigade. Their general waved his sword and cried, "Forward, men, forward! Never let it be said the Texans lag in a fight!"

Before he could say another word, a bullet silenced the lanky Texan forever, the projectile striking his jaw and angling through his brain. Granbury stumbled, dropping his weapons, and falling to his knees, his hands reflexively cradling his face as blood washed over his fingers.

Patrick Cleburne
Charging the Cotton Gin

As his division advanced, Patrick Ronayne Cleburne yanked his saber from its scabbard and waved it over his head, imploring his men to attack. Just as he was about to order them into battle formation, Red Pepper stumbled, then fell to his knees, tossing Cleburne to the ground. The animal thrashed around, then keeled over as Cleburne bounced up to continue his charge afoot. Cleburne shouted for a replacement horse, and an officer galloped up on one, jumping off and holding the reins so Cleburne could remount.

"Battle formation!" Cleburne screamed, swinging his sword over his head. "Attack formation!" Standing in the stirrups, he watched the men in Govan's regiment swing out of the column into rank-and-file formation like an unstoppable gray flood. When Lowrey's and Granbury's officers saw Govan's movements, they repeated the order and the entire division spread out before their enemies, but Cleburne missed the sight as his second mount took a bullet and fell, tossing Cleburne to earth again. The soft ground from the recent rains cushioned his fall, and he jumped to his feet as soldiers around him passed. Oddly, his itching cheek bothered him more than the ground's blow to his shoulder. "Double-quick time," he cried, and those nearby dashed for the main enemy line, as the Union skirmishers turned and scurried toward the cover of their allies in front of the cotton gin.

Cleburne yanked his kepi off with his left hand, waving it as his men passed him. He pointed his sword toward the blue line, racing within eighty yards of the enemy, yelling for his men to dash ahead. At sixty yards, his troops loosed the Rebel yell. Some Confederates fired at the enemy within forty yards. At twenty yards, a guttural roar of men and weapons echoed across Harpeth Valley. Then Cleburne's soldiers crashed into the main Yankee entrenchments like the ocean tide breaking against rocks. Even in the excitement, Cleburne's cheek still itched. He swatted at the scar with his kepi.

Suddenly, the infernal irritation stopped forever. There, just twenty yards from the entrenchments with his face to the enemy and a bullet in his heart, Patrick Ronayne Cleburne, the Stonewall of the West, died like a man.

Sumner Cunningham
Attacking Franklin

He stumbled and fell flat on his face, his Enfield flying from his grasp. His regiment and the Rebel line charged ahead without him. The sergeant major scrambled to his feet and grabbed his rifle as more cannon shells exploded in clouds of smoke, dust, and iron in front of the gray and butternut surge. The shrapnel cut swaths through the dwindling attackers, drawing agonizing screams and cries. Still, the men advanced. Sumner Cunningham raced on, trying to catch up and take his place on the flank. Ahead, he saw the Yankee skirmishers lower their rifles and fire in a fog of gray smoke that obscured his enemies for a moment. The whizz, zip, and thud of Minié balls filled the air around him as deadly trajectories flew past or struck flesh and bone, killing some, wounding others, angering the rest. From thousands of throats spewed the Rebel yell, a guttural chorus of rage, hatred, and determination audible even above the thunder of detonating gunpowder.

Despite the wall of deadly missiles, his screaming men charged forward, lowering their heads and their rifles so their bayonets reflected the blood-red glow of the day's dwindling sunlight. In front of the gray tide, the blue-clad skirmishers panicked, some scrambling to reload their rifles, others fumbling to attach their bayonets, several grabbing their weapons by the barrels to use as clubs, and others throwing down their rifles and sprinting toward the massive entrenchments of the main Union line, the only break in the rifle pits being the Columbia Pike.

And then, the Forty-first Tennessee ran headlong into the skirmishers standing against the tide, and soon the sunlit reflections on Confederate bayonets were dulled by the blood of Yankees brave enough to stand and fight. Opposing soldiers stabbed, clubbed, and shot each other, but the Forty-first Tennessee held their fire as ordered and drove their enemy from their position with their blades. Almost at once, the Yankee skirmishers realized they could never stem the overwhelming gray groundswell and bolted for the safety of the main earthworks to their rear. Though winded from the run, Cunningham cheered with his men as they chased the Yankees, who ran like terrified rabbits from the smoke and tumult. The sergeant major saw Colonel Tillman leading his men afoot after his horse had fallen beneath him. The officer waved his sword overhead, encouraging his men to hold their fire until they reached the primary enemy line.

"Stay fast on their heels," Tillman screamed. "Their own men won't shoot until they reach the entrenchments."

Onward charged the demons of the Forty-first Tennessee, drawing within three hundred, then two hundred and a hundred paces of the Yankee entrenchment, trailing twenty feet behind the cowardly skirmishers. Still, the Yankees held their fire for fear of hitting their own retreating men. When the charge came within seventy-five paces of the earthworks, the entrenched blue-bellies made Colonel Tillman a liar. The enemy fired over the trenches, as thousands of rifles exploded in a gray line of smoke, the leaden missiles striking friend and foe alike. Ahead of Cunningham, several Union infantrymen crumpled to the ground. Around him, friends and allies fell. Still, the Tennesseans raced toward their objective as the noise of men and weapons assaulted the ears like some hellish concerto.

Cunningham stopped to catch his breath, looking to his right and seeing Cleburne's Division charging the entrenchments before the cotton gin, which seemed but a ghostly apparition through the gray veil of battle. Then he resumed trotting toward his destination, the main breastworks in front of the two-story, crimson brick farmhouse with a stepped parapet wall and chimney on each end. As he resumed his charge, Cunningham realized he had yet to fire his rifle or thrust his bayonet at a single enemy. He lifted the weapon to shoot, but all he saw were the backs of his own advancing men, so he lowered his gun and charged onward. Soon his allies reached the entrenchment and scrambled over it, oblivious to the artillery and small arms fire thrown against them.

A flag-bearer even topped the mound, waving the banner of the Forty-first Tennessee for all to see until a cannonball severed his arm. He fell with the regiment's standard upon the blood-soaked earth that protected the Yankees. Inspired by the flag-bearer's bravery, his allies charged up and over the entrenchment, shooting and bayonetting the enemy, who fled to a smaller entrenchment just south of the farmhouse and two outer buildings. Over the entrenchment, Cunningham followed his men, who screamed like demons from Hades as the dying daylight gave the battlefield a hellish glow from the flames of cannons, rifles, and pistols. Cunningham dashed across the remnants of a broad garden where only the brown vines and stalks remained of summer crops long since harvested. When he reached the second entrenchment, he topped it with other stragglers in his regiment and fired at a Yankee over the heads of his fellow soldiers, his first shot of the war. Barely had he pulled a cartridge from the cartridge box on his belt than a horrific cry came from the north and a column of Union reserves appeared around the farmhouse and outbuildings, racing toward the leading edge of the Forty-first Tennessee.

Lit by the flames of their spitting rifles, the fresh Union soldiers came as a wave too great for the depleted Forty-first to withstand. Some lingered, slashing their attackers with their bayonets or clubbing them with their rifle butts, but the Yankee numbers increased and the gray line retreated. Cunningham leaped down the earthen breastworks and raced back across the depleted garden and over the main entrenchment where he jumped in the ditch. With his deep breaths, Cunningham inhaled the aroma of the trench's freshly turned dirt. As others leaped over the parapet into the ditch with him, Cunningham realized these men represented multiple regiments that had mingled with the Forty-first in the attack.

Instantly, his neighboring warriors started loading their weapons, prompting the sergeant major to do the same. Cunningham reached for his cartridge box, but realized he still carried a cartridge in his hand. He bit on the end of the paper wrapping and spit out the remnant as he poured the powder down his barrel. He pressed the ball in the barrel, then yanked the ramrod free and shoved it down the muzzle, setting the projectile. Removing the rod, he placed it by his side as his trembling fingers pulled the hammer to the half-cock position. He extracted a percussion cap from his belt box and pressed it over the nipple. As the men around him lifted their rifles above the mounded earth and fired at the enemy, Cunningham did as well, cautiously looking over the earthen protection, raising his rifle to his shoulder, aiming at a charging Yankee and firing. He thought he caught the soldier in the chest, but dirt, kicked up from enemy bullets hitting around him, clouded his vision.

What he saw in that instant before ducking behind the earthen cover terrified him. He had never seen so many snarling Yankees so close. The demons in blue all appeared to be charging straight at him as the last Confederates tumbled over the embankment and into the shallow ditch he occupied with the dead and dying. Yankees leaned over the crown of the embankment and shot at Cunningham and his allies in the creeping darkness, their grit-and-powder-stained faces briefly exposed by the flash of their rifle discharges. Cunningham froze until a soldier leaned over the embankment and pointed his long weapon at Cunningham's nose. In fear and desperation, Cunningham flung a handful of dirt at the assassin's eyes. His would-be killer screamed and flinched as he pulled the trigger, the bullet missing Cunningham but striking the infantryman at his side. The unfortunate target fell against Cunningham, grasping weakly at the sergeant major's uniform, before sliding among the bodies of so many others. The Confederate side of the trench held the fighting few, the writhing wounded, and the silent dead. Troops on both sides of the embankment lifted rifles over the top and fired blindly into their enemies.

As he reloaded his rifle, Cunningham knew this day would become the date etched on his tombstone, if he was lucky enough to even get a grave marker.

Hardin Figuers
Figuers Cellar

The roar of battle grew so loud that they could no longer understand one another's words. The perpetual roar tortured Hardin Figuer's ears. Hardin, his brother, Uncle Jesse, and the hound huddled in the corner until it darkened outside, the only light in the cellar being the flashes of gunfire through the cracks in the wooden door. Adele trembled. Uncle Jesse prayed for his life. Thomas wished for a candle and a book to read. Hardin fretted, longing to do something, anything, to help the cause. Then an expended cannonball crashed through the cellar entry, striking the earthen wall at Hardin's side.

He bolted up from the floor, shoving the cowering dog aside. "I've got to get out of here!"

"You'll be killed if you do," Thomas shouted.

"I'd rather take my chances up there than be trapped down here." Hardin felt his way across the darkened pit, then shoved his shoulder against the cellar door and emerged into Franklin's inferno. Dropping the cellar door, he scurried to the front porch, catching a flash of cannon fire and a glimpse of the mounted General Grose directing his troops. Where he had seen but one body upon entering the earthen sanctuary, he saw dozens of dead and wounded as he exited. He darted inside the house parlor, expecting to find it empty. Instead, Hardin saw four men dragging wounded inside to join twenty or more injured soldiers lying on the floor, staining his mother's carpet with their blood. Most were Union casualties, but two were Confederates. He had to help them, all of them.

Squatting among the wounded, Hardin asked what he could do. Some didn't answer, either dazed or dead, but others asked for drinks or a pillow or a blanket. Hardin scurried around the house, getting the water bucket and dipper from the kitchen to quench their thirsts; adding firewood to the embers in the fireplace to provide warmth; finding blankets to provide pallets or cover for the wounded. As the flames took hold in the hearth, the wounds that had been obscured by the room's dimness now appeared malicious and malignant as life drained away from soldiers. Hardin crawled among the injured, unable to make sense of it all, but certain he could not save any of these men with sips of water, pillows for their heads, or blankets for their cover.

Hardin dashed out the front door while shooting still raged south of the house and raced toward town and the office of Sylvanus O'Brian, the family doctor. Reaching the office out of breath, he pounded on the locked door. "Doctor, doctor," he cried, "our boys need your help." The physician took longer to answer than Hardin expected, so he battered the entry, screaming the doctor's name. Finally, the physician cracked open the door.

"We need your help, Dr. O'Brian."

"Who's we, Hardin?"

"The soldiers. There's dozens of them wounded in our parlor and on the street, terrible wounds. There's no doctor for them. Please come with me. I'll show you the way."

O'Brian shook his head. "Hear all that shooting?"

Hardin nodded.

"It's too dangerous to go outside."

"But doctor, I just came from there, and those boys are dying."

"If they're as badly wounded as you say, I can't help them."

"Then help the boys you can."

O'Brian shook his head and shoved the door shut.

Hardin dropped his head, bit his lip, and cried, vowing to never forget the shameful cowardice of his doctor. Catching his breath, Hardin raced back home, running against the trickle of wounded Union soldiers seeking safe harbor and treatment.

Reaching his house while the combat still raged just yards away, Hardin plunged inside and did what he could to care for the wounded, paying special attention to the Confederates. He tied rags around their arms to stop bleeding; washed their parched lips with wet cloths; placed pillows beneath their heads; prayed with them; removed their boots and loosened their clothing; pulled the corpses out on the porch so others could be brought in; and tended each as best he could, Confederate or Yankee, man or boy. Though the noise of combat died away as the battle gradually ended, Hardin had long since ignored the sounds so intent was he on saving as many as he could.

Around two o'clock in the morning, he felt a soft hand on his arm. He turned to check what wounded soldier needed help at that moment, but was surprised to see his mother with a drowsy Mary Louisa at her side. Hardin stood up and wrapped his arms around them both, sobbing on his mother's shoulder.

"I did what I could for them," he cried. "Even went to Dr. O'Brian for help, but he refused to come, saying it was too dangerous."

Bethenia snarled. "We're done with him. Now take your sister and find a place out of the way for her to sleep. I'll start helping the boys."

Sumner Cunningham
The Entrenchments

Had it been hours or mere minutes? In the confusion Sumner Cunningham had lost track of time as he battled men just inches away. He loaded rifles and passed them to braver men, who fired them over the mounded dirt at the unseen enemy. Other desperate Confederates, most separated from their units, clambered into the trench to fight the blue-bellied invaders. One officer crawled among them, encouraging the soldiers and loading guns to pass to those brave enough to shoot over the parapet. As the fellow inched over the dead toward him, Cunningham recognized General Otho Strahl, his brigade commander.

"Keep loading, Sergeant," Strahl cried as he picked up a discarded weapon and ripped a cartridge box from the belt of a dead man. He loaded proficiently, then exchanged weapons with a marksman, who quickly discharged the gun over the embankment. "Falling in the mud was a picnic compared to this, wasn't it, Sergeant?" the general noted as he reloaded another weapon.

Cunningham was stunned the general remembered him, much less the details of their previous encounter and his tumble before General Forrest.

"Yes, sir."

"In this ditch, we're all the same rank," Strahl yelled above the din of battle. He handed his loaded rifle to the brave soldier over his shoulder. When the man raised to return fire, a bullet struck him in the head, and he tumbled backward over Strahl and Cunningham.

The general shoved the body aside, grabbed the weapon, and thrust it at the sergeant major. "Show your mettle for the Confederacy, Sergeant."

Cunningham yanked the Enfield from the general's grasp, raised and pointed the rifle over the top, firing blindly, the kick of the discharge wrenching the rifle from his grasp. As he reached for the weapon, Strahl grabbed it and began reloading. Another loader offered him a charged rifle. Cunningham stepped on the bodies at his feet to rise enough to fire his weapon over the ramparts. A sudden exhilaration surged through his veins as fighting blood replaced the coward's bile he had endured for so many months. He raised and fired, raised and fired so many times that he lost track of the minutes.

Long after darkness enveloped the land, a wounded soldier in the ditch suggested retreat, but Strahl yelled, "Never."

Cunningham glanced around, but could only make out a dozen Confederates returning fire nearby. "What should we do?" he cried.

"Keep firing," Strahl shouted, then dropped his rifle, threw up his hands and fell forward on his face.

Cunningham reached for Strahl's shoulder to turn him over, but missed and grabbed the general's bloody neck. With the general dead, Cunningham felt terror overtake him, especially after the infantryman at his side rose to fire and received a bullet through his chest for his defense of the South.

"Where were you shot?" the sergeant major yelled at his unknown ally, who said nothing.

"In the neck," answered Strahl, slowly turning over.

Strahl wasn't dead after all. Cunningham shouted, "The general's been hit! General Strahl's been hit."

Three men crawled to Strahl, taking him by the arms and shoulders. Cunningham tossed his weapon aside and grabbed the general's legs to carry him to safety. He stumbled with the others toward the cover of trees. Before they reached their destination, two more bullets plowed into Strahl. He died before they could drop him on the ground and attend to their own safety.

Cunningham scurried to a tree and collapsed behind it, sobbing at what he had seen and the horrors burned in his mind. As the night lengthened, the gunfire gradually lessened, and the sergeant major succumbed to total physical and emotional exhaustion. He ended the most horrific day of his life asleep but alive.

Lt. Gen. John Bell Hood
Widow's Home

The fury of battle evaporated after five hours, but the furies of the commander had only strengthened. Disgusted that his troops had not demolished Schofield's army, Hood summoned his infantry corps commanders to his headquarters before midnight. They arrived one by one, Stephen D. Lee first as his newly arrived corps had not joined the combat; then Alexander P. Stewart; and finally Benjamin Cheatham, who showed up with shoulders slumped and eyes burning with hate.

"You have let me down again," Hood shouted. "The enemy still holds."

"My corps has been crippled," Stewart answered, his voice low and calm.

"Mine has been massacred," Cheatham wailed. "My men attacked entrenchments stronger than we ever faced around Atlanta. They charged into the furnace of hell, and you say we have failed you?" Cheatham spat at the commander's foot. "You, General Hood, failed every man, living and dead, in this army. You promised our men the battles in Tennessee would be on grounds of our choosing and not against entrenched forces. You lied, General Hood, and my men died because of it."

"You could've avoided this, General Cheatham, by following my orders at Spring Hill and blocking the Columbia Pike. The blood is on your epaulets, not mine."

The furious Hood turned to General Lee. "It'll be up to you to finish what these generals didn't."

"My corps will be ready to attack in the morning, if you so order."

"We will attack again after daylight, and we *will* drive the enemy from their works and into the river. Bring up your artillery, General Lee. Position them at the foot of Winstead and Breezy hills to bombard the enemy works before we attack again."

"All hundred pieces?" Lee asked.

"Yes, and they will fire a hundred rounds each."

"We may not have that much ammunition," Lee responded.

Cheatham cursed. "If you'd ordered a bombardment before today's attack, we wouldn't've been slaughtered."

"And if you'd followed orders at Spring Hill, we *would* have won, General Cheatham. Alert your officers to organize their regiments for tomorrow's attack."

Cheatham pounded his right fist into his left palm. "My officers are all dead or wounded."

"Do as I command, Cheatham. Same for you, Stewart."

Stewart clenched his jaw, then spoke softly again. "Bludgeoning the enemy is not the only way to secure victory."

"It is when your men fear battle, especially when facing entrenchments."

"General Hood," shouted Stewart, "I will not abide you slandering my troops. Many lying on that field today sacrificed more than you ever gave, even as a cripple."

"Enough insubordination, General. The attack will resume tomorrow, as I have commanded. The bombardment will begin at seven o'clock. Two hours later, the infantry will resume their assault and this time they will drive the enemy from the field."

The three generals stared at their commander, their lips tight, their eyes narrow, their mouths wordless.

"See that it is done," Hood growled.

Rev. Charles T. Quintard
Approaching Franklin

North of Spring Hill as darkness enveloped the countryside, Quintard and his servant caught up with the tail of Stephen D. Lee's decoy corps, steadily passing the weary soldiers and one hundred pieces of artillery. Nearing the head of the column, he spotted a pair of Tennessee officer acquaintances he knew and asked them what they had heard.

"Nothing good," one replied, barely visible in the night's gloom.

"Last we heard," said the other, "General Hood's dead set on attacking, even though we hold all but a dozen of the army's cannons. Schofield slipped around Hood last night while he slept."

"The boys in Cheatham's and Stewart's Corps are doomed," added the first officer. "I don't trust General Hood any farther than he can hop on his good leg."

"He'd rather hammer the enemy than outmaneuver them," interjected the second fellow, who trotted away to encourage his men to move faster to support their Confederate brothers up the road.

"I'll say a prayer—," Quintard started, before the remaining officer interrupted.

"Don't bother, Reverend. God hasn't answered our prayers since General Hood took over." With that, the man in gray slapped the reins against his mount's neck and sent him trotting into the darkness.

"—for our boys and the men who lead them." Quintard felt like he was spitting against the wind or writing a history that could never be. He longed to gallop ahead to find Hood and his army, but that could be dangerous in the night, especially with all the debris the Yankees had left in their wake. Too, he might outdistance and lose Henry or, heaven forbid, his manservant might just ride the gelding into the trees and race for freedom in Nashville.

So, Quintard paced The Lady Polk slower than he liked, for he did not care to injure the mare as he planned to return her to Otho Strahl after the battle. Between six and seven o'clock, Quintard detected the distant rumble of gun and cannon fire, which carried menacingly through the brisk air of the cloudless night.

About eight-thirty, Quintard and Henry topped Winstead Hill and halted their horses. The reverend stood in his stirrups to see a sight unlike any other he had witnessed in this war. Before him lay a mile-wide cloud of gun smoke that flashed with splotches of bloody and jaundiced light from cannons and small arms fire. Yellow pinpoints of light bounced about like vindictive fireflies. Distant shouts and screams came softly up the valley toward the hill like the whispers of malicious ghosts.

Once he descended the hill and moved closer to Franklin, Quintard spotted Lieutenant General John Bell Hood on the west side of the road. Hood reclined on a blanket and his saddle in a ball of lantern light on the ground outside a modest farm home. The commander seemed strangely calm like his subordinates. Quintard thought it odd that couriers were not scurrying from the melee with news of the battle or racing back to convey the latest orders. The contrast of the serenity around Hood and the violence at the edge of the attack he had unleashed sickened Quintard, who moved away from the road so Hood would not spot him and invite him over to visit while so many young men died a mile away.

Young Henry sat transfixed on the gelding as the acrid smell of expended gunpowder assaulted their noses. In the morning, the stench of death would supplant the odor of powder. The agonizing cries of the wounded and dying would replace the sound of rifle shots and cannon blasts. The reverend felt impotent, questioning the power of God and the value of prayer, then chastising himself for his doubts. He bowed his head and prayed for Strahl and Marsh and Watkins and every other man whose name he could recall. Except for General Hood! The crippled commander didn't need prayer now. The men he sent to their deaths did.

For a moment, Quintard resented Henry and his kind as they were responsible for this, unwilling to accept their station in life. Then the reverend chastised himself. Maybe Henry was right, and the bottom rail had been stepped on too many times by others climbing the fence to prosperity. Quintard couldn't believe an uneducated and youthful slave had raised so many unanswered questions in his mind. He wanted to turn away from the clouded violence he saw before him and reject his God for not answering his and so many other prayers of the South. Yet he could do neither, as the South's fate could depend on the outcome of the raging battle. After this battle, even more Southern souls would rest in the benevolent embrace of God's arms. Time both raced and crawled by to the point Quintard lost track of seconds, minutes, and hours, as if the past comprised all who were dead, and the future was nothing but a list of the others doomed to die.

Gradually, though, the gunfire slackened and the cloud of smoke dissolved into a misty veil of death that covered the battlefield like a shroud over a corpse. But as the shooting died away, the agonizing cries, moans, and screams of the mangled men fighting pain and death steadily arose like the discordant chorus of hell's choir. Around midnight, balls of light meandered beneath the haze as soldiers and Franklin's townspeople carried lamps, candles, and lanterns among the casualties to render what aid they could.

"Come on, Henry," Quintard said. "We must go help."

"I's scared, Massa Revrund."

"God'll protect you, Henry."

"God didn't protects dem Secesh boys."

Thursday Morning,

December 1, 1864

Lt. Gen. John Bell Hood

Chapter Twelve

Mary Alice Carter McPhail
Carter Home Carnage

After midnight when the calendar turned to December, the month in which both North and South celebrated the birth of the Prince of Peace, Moscow and Fount Carter with Johann Lotz and the slave Jack shoved aside the chest blocking the basement entrance, unbarred the door and climbed the stair steps that led to their back porch and the fiendish nightmare beyond. Their home and outbuildings still stood, though damaged, but the ground was littered with debris and bodies. Mary Alice waited for their return, thankful that the young ones had fallen asleep, but terrified at what they might see when they left their shelter. The men returned in thirty minutes.

"It's horrible," Fount told Mary Alice and the other women, "but we best get the children back into the house where they slept last night." The men and women picked up the sleeping kids and herded the bigger ones up the stairs. The adults covered the youngsters' eyes so they would not see the carnage, but the grownups could not plug their ears or their noses to avoid the sounds and smells of war and death. Though the roar of battle had ceased, its echoes still reverberated through the wails and moans of the injured and dying. All around the Carter farm came the groans of men pleading for help to the battlefield trinity of God, mother, and water. A veil of spent gunpowder lingered like a deadly fog above the ground, and the aroma of blood mingled with the tang of expended powder to create the sickening odor of death. Already Confederate soldiers and local families carried lanterns and lamps into the fields, searching for friends and family, each ball of yellow light revealing an unsettling horror of bloody and mangled bodies.

A couple of hours before dawn while Mary Alice dozed from exhaustion, young Adelaide slipped from her upstairs bed, stepped between the wounded being treated in her parlor, and headed for the back veranda to watch. Outside, she stood at the railing where her mother drank coffee each morning. Adelaide remained wide-eyed and scared, yet fascinated by the residue of slaughter from the previous day. As she lingered on the porch, an officer on horseback rode up to her and removed his hat.

"Missie," he said, "is this Squire Carter's house?"

"He's my grandfather."

"Would you tell him his son has been seriously wounded? I can lead him to the captain, if he is quick about it."

Adelaide darted into the house and back up the stairs where her mother slept with Lannie and the other children. She grabbed her mother's arm and shook it. Mary Alice woke with a start and turned to face her daughter.

"Momma, a soldier outside says Uncle Tod's been hurt."

Mary Alice gasped and sat up in bed. "You shouldn't've been outside, Adelaide," she scolded as she bolted up and yanked on her robe.

"The man says he will take us to find him if we hurry."

Mary Alice dashed past the children sleeping on the floor and down the stairs, shouting, "Father, Moscow, where are you?"

"Over here, in the parlor, tending the wounded," her brother answered.

She dashed to them, weaving among those lying on the floor in the pallid glow of a solitary coal-oil lamp.

"Tod's been hurt. A soldier outside knows where to find him. Go with him, and I'll watch the children."

"Rouse your sisters, Mary Alice, so they can help us bring him home," Moscow ordered.

Moments later, the two men and the four women stepped out on the back porch and announced they were Tod Carter's kin. The Carters followed the officer to Tod, who had taken a serious wound over his left eye and nine more bullets to his arms and legs. The family members loaded him on a discarded long coat they found nearby and struggled to carry him a hundred yards to his home, past all the bodies and debris that littered their path. Once home, they fixed a bed for him in the corner of the room where he had been born, even as two doctors on the opposite side of the chamber amputated limbs and tossed them outside the window. While the surgeons worked on their grisly task, the Carters gathered around Tod and prayed.

When dawn arrived, the sun revealed a butchery unlike any Franklin had ever seen. Civilians and soldiers scoured the field, some seeking to rescue the wounded and others trying to scavenge the dead, while physicians and town folks hurried to save or comfort as many soldiers as they could. By the time the surgeons finished their work that evening in the Carter House, the stack of discarded limbs outside the window stood six feet tall.

During that first day of December, Jack and Callie learned that many wounded Confederates would rather die than accept help from a black man or woman. So, they worked at cleaning the litter and debris from the back yard. They spent most of the day raking up spent lead and shrapnel that lay in clumps atop the ground. By the time they had finished the chore that evening, Jack and Callie had gathered enough lead and iron to fill a freight wagon.

Patrick Cleburne
Dead on the Battlefield

After daylight, Patrick Ronayne Cleburne's body was discovered, stripped of his boots and sword. His new uniform was stained by blood from the chest wound and his kepi had fallen over his face, hiding the surprised look of his eyes and the ragged scar on his left cheek. Soldiers carried him to the Carnton plantation, where they reverently laid him on the porch along with five other generals and officers. Lieutenant Mangum retrieved Sue Tarleton's perfumed handkerchief from his pocket and gently placed it over his face until his commander could be buried in a temporary grave. A day later Cleburne was disinterred and reburied in the churchyard he had admired on Polk family lands during the march to Columbia.

Susan Tarleton was walking the grounds of her garden in Mobile, Alabama, on December fifth when she heard a newsboy's cry of a horrible battle at Franklin, Tennessee, with General Cleburne heading the list of fatalities. She fainted. For twelve months, she wore black in mourning. Three years after Cleburne's death, she married a former Confederate captain, but died less than a year later in 1868, many said from a broken heart over her one true love.

Sumner Cunningham
Battlefield Survivor

Sergeant Major Sumner A. Cunningham awoke at daybreak to the shrieks, cries, and pleas of the wounded, some begging for water, others crying for momma, and most just moaning from the pain of their wounds. The aroma of decay mixed with the sulfuric odor of spent explosives hung over the ground like the devil's blanket. Cunningham awoke shivering from the morning frost, but had never realized the cold during the night, so deep was his slumber. He pushed himself up from behind the tree and in the early dawn light saw how Yankee bullets had stripped its bark in a waist-high band facing the Yankee entrenchment. Cunningham stumbled through the carnage, his breakfast appetite disappearing at the sight of the butchery before him—broken bodies, severed limbs, torsos without heads, blood and entrails smeared across the ground.

He marched to the trench where he had spent his combat blindly shooting at the unseen enemy just inches away. He searched for his rifle among the corpses piled three, four, and sometimes five deep. Blood pooled in places like puddles after a rain. Cunningham pulled three wounded soldiers and over twenty rifles from under the dead before he discovered the one with his initials carved into the stock. It was sticky to the touch from so much blood. As the sunlight crept over the hills, the sergeant major saw that his Enfield had changed. Rather than a rich brown, the stock and most of the wooden grip had turned crimson with the blood of Confederate men and boys.

Hardin Figuers
At Home

He awoke on the kitchen floor near the wood stove, where the fire helped cut the chill of the December morning. Mary Louisa still slept beside him. There had been no place else to sleep, the house being filled with the wounded. As he got up, he saw his mother sitting at the table, leaning over with her head in her palms. Hardin could not tell if she was asleep or crying. As he arose, she stirred and looked at him, her eyes reddened with tears. A slight smile cracked her melancholy demeanor.

"We're all alive, Hardin, but we'll have tough days ahead. There are so many wounded and so little food. I'll need your help to find food to save as many of the boys as we can."

"Yes, ma'am."

"And take your slingshot with you. We'll need any meat you can kill."

Hardin slapped at his pocket, but his slingshot was gone. He didn't tell his mother, as he didn't care to worry her because she had more important things on her mind.

"I hate to ask this of you, Hardin, but you might walk over the battlefield and search for food to help feed these wounded. You will see the horrors of war and the reason I would not sign for your enlistment before you came of age. Take an empty flour sack or something to carry your finds in and, yes, you can pick up a souvenir or two, but don't forget, we need food most."

"Yes, ma'am."

A raspy voice called out from the parlor. "Little Mother, Little Mother."

Bethenia smiled. "That's what they call me now, 'Little Mother'."

As she arose, Hardin saw the exhaustion in her drooping shoulders and her sagging eyelids, but she turned and entered the parlor to check on the wounded man who called her.

Hardin went to the back door, removed from the hook his coat with the peach-pit button and headed outside into the hellish landscape that was Franklin. The brisk air bit at his cheeks and a thin frost lay upon the earth, giving spots of spilled blood a pink hue. He opened the cellar door and marched into the dim enclosure. Thomas was gone, but Adele still trembled in the corner and Uncle Jess lay asleep beside the hound, resting his head on a pair of burlap bags he had folded for a pillow.

Leaning over, Hardin shook the slave's shoulder. "Get up, Uncle Jesse."

Jesse startled at Hardin's touch, then shook his head.

"We laughed at death and survived, Uncle Jesse. All of us."

"Praise be to Gawd, Marse Hardin!"

"Momma wants me to scavenge the battlefield, looking for food for the wounded. Do you want to go along?"

"I's not sure my massa be approvin'."

"We'll be looking for food."

"I's could use somethin' to eats."

"That and I got to find my slingshot. I lost it yesterday."

Hardin called his hound, but Adele still shuddered so he decided to leave the terrified dog enclosed in the cellar.

Uncle Jesse arose, stretched, grabbed the sacks, gave one to Hardin, then headed up the steps and out into the chill. Hardin checked the potato bin, which was still a third full, so there would be some food, but it wouldn't last long, not with so many wounded. He followed Uncle Jesse outside, closing the door on Adele and heading for the barn, checking around for his slingshot without success. The planks on the barn's south side were peppered with bullet holes, one errant projectile killing their mule. Not finding the slingshot, Hardin then moved to the oak trees and discovered his weapon at the base of the tree he had climbed to watch the battle. His slingshot must have slipped from his britches as he jumped from the tree before retreating to the cellar. Rather than climbing over the littered entrenchments, Hardin led Uncle Jesse back to the Carter's Creek Pike, where he discovered another body, a little Yankee boy about his own age and size. The young soldier lay in the middle of the street, his hands thrown back over his head, a look of surprise in his open eyes above the chest wound that had killed him. Hardin wished he could have saved the boy. As he looked at the youth's pale flesh, he understood now why his mother would not let him enlist early. He would see hundreds more bodies this day as he scavenged the battlefield, but only one other would be so etched in his memory as this boy of his age. He wondered if the boy's momma would ever know of his fate.

Together, Hardin and Uncle Jesse continued down the pike, turning east toward the locust grove and then to the Carter place. From the scattered gray-clad bodies lying outside the entrenchments General Grose and his men had defended, Hardin realized the combat had been less vicious near his home than it had been closer to the Carter place, especially from the locust grove to the cotton gin. There, thousands of the dead, dying, and wounded pimpled the pockmarked land, like an earthen plague of smallpox. The melancholy calls of the wounded for help, for God, for water, for mother, for relief, and even for death had replaced the jaunty music of the martial bands from the day before. It felt heartless to pass hundreds in need, but Hardin knew he must find more food for those in his house. He could not help all the boys.

Across the battlefield, citizens and relatives wandered among the wounded, some looking for kin, others looking for valuables and still others, like him, looking for food. As they neared the locust grove, Hardin and Jesse watched each stride to be certain they didn't step on a body or a wounded man. In front of positions where Yankee artillery had fired, they had to watch that they didn't trod on severed body parts or entrails eviscerated by grapeshot. All around them, the injured groaned and whined and sobbed and, if they had the strength, flailed at the ground with their frustrated fists. Hardin and Jesse found few haversacks to check for grub, and the ones they discovered contained little more than a piece of hardtack or a few kernels of parched corn or maybe a handful of walnuts. Hardin placed any edibles in his burlap bag, as did Uncle Jesse.

Reaching the locust grove, Hardin stood stunned at what he saw. Several trees had been chopped down to create a thorny abatis in front of the breastworks. A handful of trees with trunks six to eight inches in diameter had toppled by the thousands of bullets fired in the attack. Those trees still standing were denuded of bark and limbs as high as a man stood. Though Hardin saw several weapons and artifacts that would make fine souvenirs, he left them where they fell is if it were irreverent to collect them in the presence of so much death. There would be time in the days to come for souvenir hunting. The entrenchments bordering the Columbia Pike were stacked with the dead and dying, in places four or more bodies deep on the Confederate south side and only one or two thick on the Union's north side.

Hardin saw deceased men still standing against a tree or an entrenchment, other deceased men sitting on the ground forever oblivious to the living around them, and still others with body parts so scattered that Hardin wondered if even God could put them back together again. As they neared the Confederate side of the entrenchment by the cotton gin, Hardin spotted a butternut-clad soldier sitting with his back against a fencepost. Hardin grimaced when he saw the man lacked a jaw. It had been shot off, his exposed tongue resting on his neck. Uncle Jesse turned from the grotesque man, bent over, and battled dry heaves. Hardin eased away from the dead soldier until the man's eyes blinked at him. Shock and revulsion raced through Hardin's mind and body, and he felt sorriest for this man among all that he had seen on the battlefield, even the boy his own age. Hardin stepped to the man he knew was doomed and kneeled beside him.

"What can I do for you?" Hardin asked.

Unable to speak, the dying man shook his head, then lifted his arms to reveal an envelope in his left hand and a pencil in his right. Hardin assumed he was writing his last message to his family.

"Can I help?" Hardin asked.

Determined to respond, the soldier placed the paper in his palm and scribbled on it with the pencil, then handed the sheet to Hardin.

"No," he started, "General Hood will be in Ohio within three weeks."

Hardin admired the man's confidence in his leader. He nodded, patted the man on the hand, then stood up and looked around at the hundreds of gray-clad forms that would never fight again.

After the Franklin carnage, Hardin thought, if Hood ever reached Ohio he would command an army without a single soldier behind him.

States Rights Gist
Dead on the Battlefield

After States Rights Gist disappeared in the carnage, Wiley Howard retreated to the tent the general's orderlies had set up for their leader and waited. He comforted himself by finding the mare Kitty and stroking her neck. "Your pal Joe Johnston be gone, Kitty, maybe Marse States. It be a terrible day jus' endin'."

About two o'clock in the morning, a teamster Howard knew approached the tent where the manservant awaited his master's return.

"Wiley," he said, "I'm mighty fearful the Yankees killed General Gist."

"How does you knows?"

"I talked to some Georgians that was with him when he fell."

"I's intends to finds him."

Howard strode from the canvas shelter in the direction Gist's Brigade had attacked. The first half of the walk was easy across an open, debris-free landscape, but the second half taxed him as the farther he went, the more litter of man and matériel he encountered, stumbling over abandoned rifles, discarded equipment, and lifeless bodies. As he reached the entrenchments, the ground was piled with the silent dead and the moaning wounding. He thanked God that the darkness shielded him from many of the carnage's horrors. He asked if anyone had seen General Gist or where he was. Finally, a soldier led him to a makeshift hospital and pointed him to a Dr. Wright, who stood in lantern light over a workbench where he sawed on a man's leg.

"What do you want?" Wright asked without looking up.

"I's comes to see about General Gist."

"I did all I could for him, but he died at half-past eight." He paused and wiped his sweaty brow with his sleeve. "He suffered at first from the pain, but towards the end, there was little pain."

"Dids he say anythin', Doctor?"

"Very little. Once or twice before he passed, he cried out, 'Take me to Miss Janie.' Then he died."

*****

Hiram Granbury
Dead on the Battlefield

Even without their general's leadership, the Texans of Granbury's Brigade breeched the Union entrenchments only to be massacred between the primary breastworks and a secondary entrenchment. Of the eleven hundred men who charged Franklin's earthworks in Granbury's Texas Brigade, only four hundred and sixty answered the roll call the next morning. Captain Samuel T. Foster was one of the lucky ones. He survived unscathed. Among the dead was Brigadier General Hiram Granbury, who was found as he fell, upright on his knees, his face in his palms as if he still wept for his beloved wife Fannie.

Lt. Gen. John Bell Hood
In his Bed

For the second consecutive day, Hood awoke furious in his featherbed. It was past seven, and he had yet to hear the sound of the artillery barrage he had ordered. Why didn't they follow his commands? His generals would pay for this dereliction of duty. He called for help to get out of bed and to dress.

His chief of staff burst into the bedroom that the widow woman had given up so that Hood might sleep soundly on a soft mattress.

"Am I deaf? I don't hear the roar of our guns."

"And you won't," replied the officer. "The enemy repaired the bridges overnight and abandoned the works. They're gone."

Hood yelped and slapped the mattress with his good hand. "I knew we could drive them from the field if we impaled them with our steel and our lead."

As Hood arose and the covers slipped off, he realized the weather had turned colder during the night. He shivered as he kicked the cover with his only foot and twisted to the side of the bed for others to help him up. Once his aides strapped on his leg, he implored them to dress him quickly and provide writing paper and pen. Once dressed, he slipped into the modest parlor, sat at a small table, and wrote out a message: *The Army of Tennessee has driven the enemy from the field. Franklin is ours. Nashville is next.*

He handed it to his chief of staff. "See that this is wired to Richmond."

"Don't you think you should inspect the battlefield before you send this?"

"Absolutely not. This is what I have been waiting for, a clear victory that will be the first of many to come on our way to independence."

The officer saluted. "I'll see that it's done."

By the middle of the morning, Hood sat in his saddle again, riding amidst the carnage of Franklin as soldiers and civilians fought the cold to save their friends and sons. The cries of the broken and hopeless serenaded him as he meandered among them, tears at times moistening his eyes. Many of his soldiers ignored him. Others glared with hate at the architect of so much death.

Before noon, he dictated to his chief of staff a general order to be read over his name to each regiment that afternoon, stating: *The commanding general congratulates the army upon the success achieved yesterday over our enemy by your heroic and determined courage. The enemy have been sent in disorder and confusion to Nashville, and while we lament the fall of many gallant officers and brave men, we have shown to our countrymen that we can carry any position occupied by our enemy.*

The callousness of his message to his troops and the disingenuous nature of his victory telegram to Richmond demonstrated that West Point had been right in grading him the lowest in ethics among his graduating class.

Rev. Charles T. Quintard
Bewildered on the Battlefield

Dawn revealed the horrors the night had hidden. Reverend Charles T. Quintard had seen horrible battlefields before—from Perryville to Murfreesboro to Chickamauga to Atlanta—but never anything like this, not with so many bodies piled in such a cramped line of battle. Surely he could walk from one end of the battle line to the other and never touch soil for all the bodies and body parts scattered over the ground. He had witnessed nothing like it and hoped never again to observe such a sight. Henry had been brave, but he vomited three times at what he saw.

The casualties were so many, they were like a bloody gravel thrown across the landscape. They were so numerous, Quintard could not help them all, so he ignored the pleas of most, looking for officers and men he knew, especially those of the First Tennessee. As he meandered among the dead and dying, he heard others cry out names of the deceased in Benjamin Cheatham's depleted corps. Major General Patrick Cleburne of Ireland and Arkansas, dead. Brigadier General States Rights Gist of South Carolina, dead. Brigadier Hiram Granbury of Texas, dead. Brigadier General Otho F. Strahl of Ohio, dead. Brigadier General John C. Carter, mortally wounded. Major General John C. Brown, wounded. Dozens more officers had yet to be found.

Quintard wept at the news. His friend had been right. Otho Strahl would never again ride The Lady Polk, which now sat beneath the reverend's saddle. He prayed that his beloved friend, the one-armed John H. Marsh, had survived, but by mid-morning he learned that all of Strahl's command staff had perished. Quintard wept again, vowing to give Christian burials to as many of the officers as he could and regretting his Advent Sunday sermon. Yes, he had requested an angel to watch over the shoulder of General Hood, but never the Angel of Death.

By sunset, Quintard saw that Cleburne, Gist, Strahl, and Marsh were buried in temporary graves. It turned into the hardest day of his life, as he could not look at Henry during all those burials without blaming him for their deaths. When he returned to the battlefield after the burials, thousands more remained to be attended or interred.

Days later, Quintard would re-bury Cleburne, Gist, Strahl, and Marsh in the cemetery at St. John's church near the grave of his religious mentor James H. Otey. The service for those re-interments would be conducted in the home of Lucius J. Polk and in the same parlor where he had delivered his Advent Sunday sermon.

Sam Watkins
Battlefield Survivor

The screams and shouts around him woke Sam Watkins from his deep trance. He had dodged the clammy embrace of death, but around him lay the earthly remains of those who didn't and those who were still fighting to cling to life despite their savage wounds. Some men were blown apart. Others showed no sign of a wound, though their unblinking eyes were frozen in a perpetual stare of terror. As he climbed over bodies in the trench, he took his rifle and stumbled among the dead, looking for survivors of Company H. He found Billy Carr alive, wandering through the slaughter. The two men spotted each other in the early morning light. Dropping their rifles, they rushed to hug one another. At least Watkins had one friend to celebrate with, even if the others were all gone. After they embraced, they retrieved their rifles and stumbled among the mumbling, groaning, weeping, and shivering men.

As Watkins tried to make sense of the bloodshed, his flesh trembled, crept, and crawled with revulsion, sorrow, and anger. He profaned the name of General John Bell Hood. He cursed the unfairness of war, that the thousands of dead webfeet would be buried where they fell or in vast unmarked pits. By contrast, the generals would lie in graves with stone monuments atop them and with garlands of flowers placed around them by reverent women who never would know how many of their sons, brothers, husbands, and fathers they had sent to eternity by their vanity and stupidity.

There was no glory in war, just death, and Watkins would forever remember Franklin as "a grand holocaust of death."

Aftermath

**Final Resting Place
Patrick Ronayne Cleburne**

Chapter Thirteen

Mary Alice Carter McPhail

Mary Alice's beloved brother Tod died December second, never regaining consciousness, so she could ask if she had really seen him beyond the locust grove the day of the battle or if she had just imagined the encounter. Tod's tragic story became a staple of Battle of Franklin lore. Just as Mary Alice never confirmed if she had actually glimpsed her sibling the day of the battle, neither did she attend church at the First Presbyterian the following Sunday. On that morning, the house of worship served as a hospital for Union soldiers in the battle's aftermath. Of the forty-four makeshift hospitals established in Franklin after the conflict, only three held Northern wounded.

Her husband Daniel McPhail survived the war and returned to Franklin to reunite with Mary Alice and meet his son Orlando for the first time. Mary Alice outlived Tod by five years, dying in 1869 and being buried in the Tennessee soil like her brother. Daniel never remarried and eventually returned to Texas, where he died an indigent, living solely on his Confederate pension.

The Carter House was the focal point of perhaps the most savage fighting of the Civil War. A young boy who lived there after the turn of the twentieth century recalled decades later as an old man that as a child he could not play outside the house barefooted for fear of cutting his feet on human bone shards and broken teeth.

Patrick Ronayne Cleburne

In 1870, the citizens of Helena, Arkansas, sought to have Patrick Ronayne Cleburne, the major general they now considered a native son, returned home. By then, his peers revered him as the Stonewall Jackson of the Western Theater of war.

Cleburne's former aide, Leonard Magnum, supervised the logistics and accompanied the body from Columbia, Tennessee, to Memphis to Helena. The procession from the train station to the Memphis docks and the gathering along the route were the longest and the largest in the history of Memphis. The procession behind his hearse included ex-governor Isham G. Harris, Benjamin Cheatham, and multiple other former Confederate generals and officials. Even Jefferson Davis, who had refused to endorse Cleburne's proposal to enlist slaves in the Confederate Army, marched behind the hearse and praised the Irish general's valor.

John Bell Hood opted not to attend the solemn ceremonies.

Sumner A. Cunningham

Sergeant Major. Cunningham accompanied the remnants of the Army of Tennessee to Nashville for the showdown with the Union army under General George H. Thomas, but deserted at the first opportunity, hiding out in Bedford County until May 1865 when he returned to Nashville and took the general amnesty oath. As a civilian, he worked as a dry goods merchant and a bookseller before getting into journalism with the purchase of the *Shelbyville Commercial* and later the *Chattanooga Times*.

In 1893, Cunningham established *The Confederate Veteran* in Nashville to commemorate the South's failed rebellion, to tell the stories of the men who fought for its cause, and perhaps to atone for his own cowardice. Some historians have estimated Cunningham fought at Franklin for the only hour of sustained combat he faced in more than three years of service to the Confederacy. As editor of the publication, he became one of the leading proponents of the Lost Cause mythology. *The Confederate Veteran* survived until 1932, nineteen years after Cunningham's death.

Though his actual combat in defense of the Confederacy amounted to little more than an hour, by the time of his demise on December 20, 1913, Cunningham was eulogized in a front page *Nashville Banner* story as the "Hero of a 100 Battles."

States Rights Gist

With help from the doctor, Wiley Howard secured a cedar box in which to bury States Rights Gist in a small family cemetery near where he died. The matron of the family allowed Howard to display Gist's body on her parlor sofa so the men of his brigade could pass by and pay their final respects. The South Carolinians and Georgians who remained unscathed in his brigade attended the funeral, but it was a small gathering.

When the Army of the Tennessee moved toward Nashville less the dead and wounded of Franklin, Wiley Howard made the treacherous return to South Carolina, presenting to Janie Gist what remained of her husband's cash, his watch, and his wedding ring with the words States Rights had proclaimed when he removed it from his fingers. Janie Gist wept.

Though Yankees marching through South Carolina looted and vandalized Janie Gist's Live Oak Plantation, they did not burn her home, though they did impoverish her. Even so, she wanted to bring her husband home. Uncle Wiley Howard, who remained with the Gist family after emancipation, returned to Franklin, Tennessee, with their support and brought Marse States back to South Carolina.

On May 10, 1866, under the suspicious eyes of occupying federal troops, States Rights Gist was buried in Columbia's Trinity Episcopal Church graveyard, just across the street from the South Carolina State House. Janie Gist wept again. As did Wiley Howard.

Hardin Figuers

In the last days of November and the first weeks of December 1864, Hardin Figuers learned more about the glory of war from his mother than he did from all the soldiers he ever met. The glory came in patching up the wounds of combat rather than creating them. Bethenia Figuers to her dying day received letters of thanks from those who she had tended, both Union and Confederate. Two wounded soldiers Hardin had treated even named sons after him.

The Battle of Franklin killed Hardin's ambition of joining the army and fighting for the Confederate cause. The memories of what he saw that day changed him. He could not walk around his hometown without the recurring images of that horrific day and night flashing through his mind. As a young man, he studied law and began practice in Franklin, where he operated a weekly newspaper for four years. After courting and marrying Miss Lilly Dale of Columbia, he moved to that community to escape the daily reminders in Franklin of that terrible day and its aftermath. He spent the rest of his life practicing law in Columbia, where he and his wife raised a daughter.

Whatever doubts Hardin may have had about God and religion before the Battle of Franklin evaporated in the aftermath of the carnage and the Christian example of compassion displayed by his mother. He became a devout member and steward of the First Methodist Church of Columbia. For thirty-five years, he taught Sunday school, and by the time of his death, he had one of the largest classes in all of Tennessee, consistently drawing over a hundred attendees a week.

Figuers became one of the most successful and prominent lawyers in Tennessee. Though he never served in the Confederate army, he regularly graced conventions of Southern veterans and spoke of his civilian experiences around the Battle of Franklin. The Confederate veterans considered him one of their own. When he died in 1917, his death made statewide news throughout Tennessee.

Hiram B. Granbury

After a temporary grave in Franklin, Hiram B. Granbury was re-interred near Patrick Cleburne. Three decades after his demise, his remains returned to Texas for final burial. His casket stayed in a Fort Worth bank vault until November 30, 1893, twenty-nine years to the day after his death.

On that anniversary date, his coffin—draped in the First National Confederate Flag emblazoned with Granbury's Texas Brigade battle honors for Chickamauga, Ringgold Gap, Missionary Ridge, Dug Gap, Resaca, New Hope Church, Kennesaw Mountain, Peach Tree Creek, Atlanta, and Franklin—was loaded on a train and delivered thirty-five miles to the town named in his honor. The horse-drawn hearse weighted with flowers led a procession of five thousand mourners in a line three-quarters of a mile long from the station to the cemetery.

Granbury would have multiple gravestones over the year, unlike his wife. For a century, her Mobile, Alabama, grave remained lost and unmarked before being rediscovered in 2002. In his final resting spot, Hiram B. Granbury would forever be linked to the man who sent him to his death. The town of Granbury was the seat of the Texas county named for John Bell Hood.

*****

Samuel T. Foster

Captain Foster survived the war in the Army of Tennessee, surrendering and receiving his parole in North Carolina the following May. He returned to his Texas home in Oaksville, Live Oak County, where he practiced law. Ultimately, the county's lawlessness forced him to move his wife, two sons, and four daughters to Corpus Christi, where he worked for a merchandising and banking house and where he established the First Baptist Church, which met in his home before building a chapel.

He was elected to a term in the Eleventh Texas Legislature. In 1880, he moved to Laredo on the Rio Grande, where he resumed his practice and public service career and received a presidential appointment as commissioner for the U.S. District Court, Southern District of Texas. He held the position until his 1919 death.

In 1893, when his brigade commander was re-buried the final time in Granbury, Foster chose not to attend the ceremony because he did not care to set foot in a county named for John Bell Hood. A century after he finished his Civil War diary, a university press published his account of service in the Confederacy.

Foster wrote of the Battle of Franklin, "General Hood has betrayed us. This is not the kind of fighting he promised us at Tuscumbia and Florence, Alabama, when we started into Tennessee. This was not a 'fight with equal numbers and choice of the ground' by no means. And the wails and cries of widows and orphans made at Franklin, Tennessee, November 30, 1864, will heat up the fires of that bottomless pit to burn the soul of General J.B. Hood for murdering their husbands and fathers at that place that day. It can't be called anything else but cold-blooded MURDER. He sacrificed those men to make the name of Hood famous; when (and) if the history of it is ever written, it will make him *infamous*."

John Bell Hood

For the rest of his life, John Bell Hood zealously defended his decisions and actions relating to the slaughter at Franklin and the ensuing destruction of the Army of Tennessee at Nashville. In his memoirs *Advance and Retreat*, he blamed Cheatham for the failure at Spring Hill. "Had I dreamed one moment that Cheatham would have failed to give battle, or at least to take position across the pike and force the enemy to assault him, I would have ridden, myself, to the front, and led the troops into action."

Consequently, as Hood remembered it, "The best move in my career as a soldier, I was thus destined to behold came to naught" and caused him "to experience grave concern" about his troops being "unwilling to accept battle unless under the protection of breastworks." Even so, he contradicted himself later in his memoirs saying he noticed "improved morale of the army" between the debacle at Spring Hill that morning and the attack at Franklin that same afternoon. He attributed it to the belief that Hood's pressure had terrified the Yankees and sent them in panic toward Nashville.

Hood's greatest calumny slandered the martyred Patrick Cleburne, who—according to him—on the day of his death realized Hood "was not the reckless, indiscreet commander" his enemies claimed and further that Hood had been "feebly sustained by the officers and men." Hood continued, "It has been said he stated, upon the morning after the affair at Spring Hill, that he would never again allow one of my orders for battle to be disobeyed, if he could prevent it." Hood co-opted Cleburne's death into unverifiable support for his command decisions with the implication that Cheatham and his subordinate had intentionally disobeyed his murky orders.

While Hood's disingenuous message to Richmond said he had driven the enemy from the field, Hood, and his tattered Army of Tennessee would be driven from the state two weeks and two days after the failure at Franklin. The only reason it took that long was inclement weather delayed General George H. Thomas's decisive Union attack in the Battle of Nashville. Just over a month later as full and accurate details of the debacles at Franklin and Nashville reached Richmond, Hood would be replaced as commander of what was left of the Army of Tennessee, which returned to the command of Hood nemesis Joseph E. Johnston until the final surrender.

After the war, Hood settled in New Orleans, working as a cotton and insurance broker. He married in 1868 and fathered eleven children over a decade. Perhaps driven by his conscience, he raised funds to support orphans, widows, and disabled soldiers. He, along with his wife and oldest daughter, died in a yellow fever epidemic in 1879, leaving ten orphans behind. Ultimately, all his children were adopted and supported largely through the donations of the Texas Brigade veterans he had commanded in Lee's Army of Northern Virginia. Less support was forthcoming from survivors of the Army of Tennessee.

Throughout his career and even after his death in his posthumous autobiography, he always found reason to blame others for his shortcomings and failures. In a speech to the Louisiana Division of the Army of Tennessee Association shortly before his death, he claimed "they charge me with having made Franklin a slaughter-pen, but, as I understand it, *war* means *fight* and *fight* means *kill*," a comment similar to one previously attributed to Nathan Bedford Forrest. An uncontrollable rashness unsuited for army command countermanded Hood's unquestionable personal courage. His leadership was best described in a comment variously attributed to Robert E. Lee, Stephen Vincent Benet and others as "too much the lion, too little the fox."

Rev. Charles T. Quintard

The reverend remained in service of the Confederacy until the end of the war. His manservant Henry B. Free, though, did not stay with the clergyman, choosing instead the offer of freedom from three Yankee soldiers. The last Quintard saw of Henry, he was being cursed with a racial epithet the reverend had never used and being beaten with the side of a sword by a Yankee officer offended by Henry entering the soldier's tent. As Quintard wrote in his diary, "Such was his first taste of freedom."

Though he lost his manservant to the Yankees, he kept The Lady Polk after the fall of the Confederacy. In memory of his colleagues Otho Strahl and John Marsh, he sold the prized mare and used the funds to create a stained-glass window as a memorial to his beloved friends. He placed the finished glasswork in St. James Church in Bolivar, Tennessee, to memorialize the two honorable soldiers.

Confederate nurse Kate Cumming remembered Quintard in her memoir as "a man of great energy" and Sam Watkins, in his recollections of the war, called him "one of the purest and best men I have ever known." Quintard's *Confederate Soldier's Pocket Manual of Devotions* and his *Balm for the Weary and the Wounded*, published largely at his own expense during the conflict, were salve to the souls of many a soldier in the Army of Tennessee.

Barely four months after the Army of Tennessee disbanded, the national Episcopal Church selected Quintard as the second bishop of Tennessee, succeeding his theological mentor James H. Otey in the post, which had gone unfilled after Otey's 1863 death. Quintard helped the church and the state rebuild after the war and assisted with establishing the University of the South at Sewanee as a permanent institution of higher education in Tennessee. He also played a key role in founding Hoffman Hall, a seminary for Negroes, near Fisk University, a private black liberal arts college, in Nashville.

In 1898, in declining health, he traveled to Meridian, Georgia, where he died near where he had purchased Henry B. Free thirty-four years earlier.

Sam Watkins

Samuel R. Watkins survived the war, though his friend Billy Carr did not, dying in the Battle of Nashville. Sam and Billy had advanced as skirmishers through thick grass to find themselves surrounded by Yankees belly flat in the grass. Ordered to surrender, both men threw down their weapons. As soon as they did, a Yankee shot Billy in the eye. Enraged by the murder, Sam grabbed his weapon and killed the bastard that had shot Carr, then fled, taking a bullet in the thigh and a fragment in his writing hand.

Watkins survived his wounds and rejoined the Army of Tennessee in time to surrender in North Carolina with Joseph Johnston. Watkins returned to Maury County, Tennessee, that summer four years after he had left with visions of glory. Of the one hundred and twenty men who had first enlisted with Watkins in the Maury Grays in 1861, only Sam and six others returned unscathed to their homes around Columbia.

As he had always dreamed, Watkins married his fiancée, Virginia Jane "Jennie" Mayes, on September 5, 1865, supporting his wife and their ensuing family by farming and running a general store in Columbia. The couple produced eight children, described by him seventeen years after their marriage as "a house full of young 'rebels,' clustering around my knees and bumping against my elbow while I write these reminiscences." The referenced reminiscences were a series of articles on his Civil War experiences he penned for publication in the local *Columbia Herald*.

In introducing his series of articles, Watkins wrote, "The histories of the Lost Cause are all written out by 'big bugs,' generals and renowned historians...I propose to tell of the fellows who did the shooting and killing; the fortifying and ditching; the sweeping of the streets; the drilling; the standing guard, picket, and videt; and who drew (or were to draw) eleven dollars per month and rations; and also drew the ramrod and tore the cartridge."

At the time of his writings in 1882, he remained an unreconstructed Rebel. "Secession may have been wrong in the abstract, and has been tried and settled by the arbitrament (sic) of the sword and bayonet, but I am as firm in my convictions today of the right of secession as I was in 1861. The South is our country; the North is the country of those who live there. We are an agricultural people; they are a manufacturing people…We believe in the doctrine of State (sic) rights, and they in the doctrine of centralization."

His newspaper reminiscences would later be compiled and published under the title *Company Aytch: A Side Show of the Big Show*. The self-effacing memoir would become a classic of Civil War literature, unlike John Bell Hood's self-serving *Advance and Retreat*.

Epilogue

Finis

The fighting ended in 1865, but the infighting among surviving Civil War generals continued for decades as they sought to earn credit for victories and allay blame for losses. Among Confederate officers in the Eastern Theater, the Battle of Gettysburg generated the most speculation and accusations. In the Western Theater, the two days from the encounter at Spring Hill to the tragedy at Franklin spawned the most heated debates. The debacle at Spring Hill resulted in a command breakdown so egregious as to become a textbook example of how not to lead an army. The Battle of Franklin so decimated the Army of Tennessee's officer corps as to make the surviving force ineffective for the remainder of the war.

Besides the fault-finding, the common bonds between Gettysburg and Spring Hill-Franklin were the massive but unsuccessful infantry assaults eighteen months apart. Pickett's Charge remains the most famous, but the Tennessee attack was the largest, covering almost twice the distance with nearly twice as many men as the Pennsylvania assault. Both failed, with casualties exceeding six thousand dead and wounded. The disastrous charge at Franklin stands as the last major offensive attack of the dying Confederacy.

On the monument marking Patrick Ronayne Cleburne's final resting place are engraved these words:

> *Rest thee, Cleburne! Tears of sadness*
> *Flow from hearts thoust nobly won*
> *Mem'ry ne'er will cease to cherish*
> *Deeds of glory thou hast done.*

Though those words were engraved in stone, the memories of General Cleburne were not. Today Patrick Ronayne Cleburne, like the battle that took his life, remains largely forgotten in the annals of American and Civil War history.

Sources

Although this is a work of historical fiction, numerous books were used in the research. Those that were the most helpful in putting together this novel were the following:

About the battles—*Five Tragic Hours: The Battle of Franklin*, James Lee McDonough and Thomas L. Connelly, 1883; *For Cause & Country: A Study of the Affair at Spring Hill and the Battle of Franklin*, Eric A. Jacobson and Richard A. Rupp, 2006; *The March to the Sea-Franklin and Nashville*, Jacob D. Cox, 1882; *The Battle of Franklin*, James A. Crutchfield, 2009; *Kennesaw Mountain*, Earl J. Hess, 2013; *The Confederacy's Last Hurrah: Spring Hill, Franklin, and Nashville*, Wiley Sword, 1993; *Hood's Tennessee Campaign: The Desperate Venture of a Desperate Man*, James R. Knight, 2014; and *Shrouds of Glory: From Atlanta to Nashville: The Last Great Campaign of the Civil War*, Winston Groom, 2004.

On the individuals—*"Co. Aytch:" A Side Show of the Big Show*, Sam R. Watkins, 1882; *Co. "Aytch,"* Sam R. Watkins, edited by Ruth Hill Fulton McAllister, 2007; *S.A. Cunningham and the Confederate Heritage*, John A. Simpson, 1994; *Reminiscences of the 41st Tennessee*, John A. Simpson, ed, 2001; *Doctor Quintard, Chaplain C.S.A. and Second Bishop of Tennessee: The Memoir and Civil War Diary of Charles Todd Quintard*, Sam Davis Elliott, 2003; *Stonewall of the West: Patrick Cleburne and the Civil War*, Craig L. Symonds, 1997; *Invisible Hero: Patrick R. Cleburne*, Bruce H Stewart Jr., 2009; *A Meteor Shining Brightly: Essays on Maj. Gen. Patrick R. Cleburne*, Mauriel Phillips Joslyn, ed, 1998; *One of Cleburne's Command: The Civil War Reminiscences and Diary of Capt. Samuel T. Foster*, Norman D. Brown, ed, 1980; *Lone Star General: Hiram B. Granbury*, James Drake, 2008; *The Confederacy's Greatest Cavalryman: Nathan Bedford Forrest*, Brian Steel Wills, 1998; *General William J. Hardee*, Nathaniel Cheairs Hughes, Jr., 1965; *General Stephen D. Lee*, Herman Hattaway, 1976; *Advance & Retreat*, John Bell Hood, 1880; *John Bell Hood: The Rise, Fall, and Resurrection of a Confederate General*, Stephen Hood, 2016; and *The Lost Papers of Confederate General John Bell Hood*, Stephen M. Hood, 2015.

For reference—*Encyclopedia of the Battle of Franklin*, Lochlainn Seabrook, 2012; *Confederate Emancipation*, Bruce Levine, 2006; *Homespun Tales: The Battle of Franklin*, Sue Berry and Martha Fuqua, eds, 1989; *Franklin: Tennessee's Handsomest Town*, James A. Crutchfield and Robert Holladay, 1999; *Tennessee's War, 1861-1865*, Stanley F. Horn, ed, 1965; *Civil War Almanac*, John C. Fredriksen, 2007; *The 1865 Customs of Service for Non-commissioned Officers and Soldiers*, August V. Kautz, 1865; *The Military Handbook & Soldier's Manual*, Louis Le Grand, 1861; *Reluctant Witnesses: Children's Voices from the Civil War*, Emmy E. Werner, 1998; *Handbook for Active Service*, Egbert L. Viele, 1861; *While God Is Marching On: The Religious World of Civil War Soldiers*, Steven E. Woodworth, 2001; *Granbury's Texas Brigade*, John R. Lundberg, 2012; *This Band of Heroes*, James M. McCaffrey, 1985; *The Civil War Military Machine*, Ian Drury and Tony Gibbons, 1993; and *The Official Military Atlas of the Civil War*, U.S. War Dept., George B. Davis, et al, eds, 2003

About the Author

Preston Lewis is the award-winning author of some sixty western, historical, juvenile, and nonfiction works. In 2025 he was honored with the Will Rogers Medallion Awards' Lifetime Achievement Award for his contributions to the literature of the American West. The Texas Institute of Letters in 2021 elected him to membership for his literary achievements.

Western Writers of America (WWA) has honored Lewis with three Spur Awards, one for best article, the second for best western novel, and the third in 2025 for juvenile nonfiction. He has received ten Will Rogers Medallion Awards—six gold, two silver and two bronze—for written western humor, short stories, short nonfiction, and traditional Western novel.

Lewis is a past president of WWA and the West Texas Historical Association, which named him a fellow in 2016. He holds a bachelor's degree from Baylor University and a master's degree from Ohio State University, both in journalism. Additionally, he has a second master's degree in history from Angelo State University.

He lives in San Angelo, Texas, with wife Harriet Kocher Lewis.

Websites: prestonlewisauthor.com
    Barisopress.com
E-mail: prestonlewisauthor@gmail.com
Facebook: prestonlewisauthor